My Name Was Mary

Gayle Rogers

My Name Was Mary

Gayle Rogers

SOJOURNER
PUBLISHERS, INC.

Sojourner Publishers Inc.
23119 19th Drive N.E., Arlington, WA 98223
www.sojournerpub.com

ISBN: 0-9723078-1-8
Library of Congress Control Number: 2003110446

Cover art by Holly Smith

Sojourner Publishing hard cover edition.

Printed in the United States of America.

To Jack, my husband gone, but no further than my heart.
To my beloved sons, Kendall Brown and Kevin Brown.
To Rose White who carries the Lincoln genes from a first cousin
to Tom Lincoln and all the tenderness of Abraham Lincoln.

Chapter One

My name was Mary, and I was married to a very famous person who still shapes your own life today. I am going to tell you my story just as I lived it. You don't know me at all. I have been demonized - how does that little saying go?

They wreathed her head with thorns when living,
With nettles though dead.

This was mainly because of one odious, noxious little man I did not like, and his hatred for me was such an obsession, it became a mental illness of its own. He lied about me, and he lied about my husband, and people believed him because he had been my husband's last law partner. He became accepted as an authority on our marriage, when he was never once in our house, never close to our intimate life in any way, shape, or form.

You well know my husband's famous face, and, somehow, you revere him as an almost sacred part of the American experience, but without my story, you have an incomplete one of his. What kind of a lover was he? What kind of a husband and father? What part of his story did I play?

I had deep valleys of despair, but my life was so blessed, for I found a man to love who was my *all*, my own *completion*, and if this sounds as if I did not or do not value myself as myself, that is not true. Love expands far beyond individuality. Love is God's grace to bring light into the dark. Its miracle is as sacred as the rapture of finding God within you, as the rapture of knowing that love is eternal, and that love is what makes life itself eternal.

I was born on December 13, 1818, and I was born into what was called an aristocratic family. That is a wealthy family and an educated family, with a long line backwards of ancestors in about the same situation. My mother was named Elizabeth Ann Parker Todd; the family called her *Eliza,* and my father was Robert Smith Todd, and he was a prominent banker in Lexington, Kentucky, being president of the Lexington branch of the Bank of Kentucky. In fact, his family was one of the main founders of Lexington. Henry Clay, the leader of the Whig Party, was a frequent dinner guest. When on my thirteenth birthday I received a white pony, I rode it to Mr. Clay's house, *Ashland,* for his approval. It did not matter to me that the servants said he had guests - *six fine gentlemen* - and was entertaining *them*. I said, "Tell Mr. Clay that Miss Todd is here to show him her new pony," and Mr. Clay and all of his guests came to see my pony and invited me to eat dinner with them. I had a good time and loved to hear them talk about the dreadful Democrats.

My father was an ardent Whig, and political affairs at our home were constantly discussed. By the time I was fourteen, I thought Andrew Jackson to be a thoroughly dreadful man. In 1832, we moved from the smaller house on Short Street, next to my mother's family home, where my father had built his home right on an adjacent lot. My mother had had seven children in this house. I was the fourth named Mary Ann, and how my mother loved to dress me up and show me off in my pretty clothes, more so than with my older sisters, Elizabeth and Frances. When I was seven my mother died in July of 1825 from the birth of George Rogers Clark Todd, and it was the crashing down of my world, of praise for being pretty in dainty hand made muslins - of praise for *anything*. In the custom of the time her body lay in state in the front room and before we children went up to bed for the night we were to kiss those cold lips, that face frozen from animation - soul. *Why can't you wake up and tell me again that I am pretty, precious, loved, that your love for me reaches the stars so far up in the sky? If father does not know my tears - does God? Why are you like this - stiff - cold – uncaring? Do you want father to put you into the cold ground?*

I was seven, but I never really gave up my own mother. When I grew and became an adult, this became my fatal flaw. I never accepted the death of one dear to me, and its awful anguish was to drive me into a physical and mental breakdown.

My father married again and my grandmother Parker did not like this. We moved into a very spacious and more elegant house on West Main Street, about a block away from her - in another brick mansion with white porch columns, and she did not like this at all.

Our home had acres of woods and grounds that included the coach house, extended quarters for the slaves, always called "servants," in the South, and one of the most beautiful gardens in Kentucky. It had a stream running through the back part of it. My father loved the stream because it was filled with minnows. None of the boys were to ever wade in the stream, or even think of fishing one of the minnows out of it. They did both, of course, for little boys live to stretch beyond parental boundaries. We had a summer home called *Buena Vista* that was some miles outside of Lexington on the Leestown Pike. My family was even proud of being proud!

My father's new wife was another Elizabeth he called *Betsy,* and by her he had nine more children. My new stepmother was in delicate health and was always harried and rushed, and at first, I did not like her, and my nearby maternal Grandmother Parker did not like her *at all*. So often children find their parents grow smarter as they themselves get older, and as I grew older, my feelings toward my father's second wife grew more - amiable.

There were many family slave *servants*, but I guess even with help, being pregnant, which we then called "confined", for so long must have made my step mother seem in a constant ill temper. In those days women in advanced pregnancy stayed in their rooms, as if they had done something shameful in growing out the way they did. *Betsy* did not give me any leeway about anything, my way about *anything,* and I was very quick to temper, I freely admit.

When I was eight my stepmother's niece, Elizabeth Humphreys, came to live with us. We were close to the same age and became very good friends. Also when I was eight, after my tutor teaching at home, Elizabeth and I were sent away to private school. It was for the children of the best families in Lexington, coeducational, and we had our recitations beginning at dawn, when the brain was supposed to be most alive with the rising of the sun. There I was happy. It was a friendly and marvelous school run by a former Episcopal bishop, Dr. John Ward, and he found I had a quick mind and a very strong memory for learning.

Elizabeth and I walked several blocks to that school, so we had to be up early and dress by candlelight, and Elizabeth recalled in print, that I was always in high spirits and even loved the sleet and the snow on the way to the school I so adored. She recalled that I was an ardent tomboy, loving to ride my horse sidesaddle, *pell mell* through town. Then, apparently, I decided to be a girl and always wore a fresh rose in my hair. She remembered, as I did, the marvelous sleigh rides in farm wagons filled with straw, corn popped by the grate fire, roasted apples there, too - and how I loved to learn poetry and could recite it by the hour. Then there was dear Mammy Sally who ruled us with an iron hand aided by her tie in with the blue jay, with a pea green tail no less, that reported every Friday night to old man devil anything her "chillens" did wrong.

By the time I was ten I loved fashion, and wanted the most fashionable clothes, lovely clothes - hand made by French seamstresses in New Orleans. Fine clothes meant that my world was safe, and I could hear again my mother, *Eliza,* saying, "Now, doesn't Molly look just *exquisite?*" When my step mother would not let Elizabeth and me wear the fashionable hoops to church, we made our own from some willow branches off of a neighbor's tree, sewing them into our skirts all night long, by *very dim* light of one candle, but she still would not let us wear our new hoop skirts to church. I told *Betsy* I was gong to be kind to my children, and never would be a mean, cold, *hateful* stepmother. I had a tantrum because I could not wear what I wanted to wear. I became vain about looking nice, and if looking nice meant costly clothes, I wanted them until I did not care about my appearance any longer. Strangely, for one so vain, that did happen. For one who so loved bright color, I was to wear nothing but black, for the world had become colorless, cheerless, and my vibrancy was gone with its. For one who loved the theater all of her life, I never went into another one, or read a line about the famous players within them.

Still preserved, my family recorded how they saw my character. I was judged merry, high spirited, highly intelligent, *unladylike* in being consumed with politics, which only male brains were supposed to fathom, and very sarcastic, which I most certainly was. I loved to make a quick retort that made people laugh. I loved to imitate people I thought to be fools, but I usually liked people, and I always *adored* children. I made little gods and goddesses out of all my little brothers and sisters. In my heart, they were precious angels. That is how I felt about children all of my life.

When I was young - how did they *physically* describe me? I *am not* describing me, for if I was vain about my clothes, I was never vain about what wore them. I was small, never grew over five foot two inches, and they said I had a beautiful pink complexion, a dimpled smile, deep blue (or some said, *violet*) eyes with long, *long* lashes, and chestnut hair that "glistened with auburn highlights." My nose was upturned; I had a firm chin, a lovely *fashionable* figure, meaning then a small waist and hips and full breasts, breasts that were never written about or mentioned, along with the female leg. God forbid if in public an ankle was even *slightly* revealed - by only an errant breeze of course.

My goodness, even a piano *leg* had to be a piano *limb*. I wonder why women are supposed to be filled with some kind of shame for being female, when this is never accorded to a male. I wonder why they call "ladies of the night" wicked and horrible other things like "whores," when they are there to service the male. Aren't their customers also "whores," or at the least, "whore seekers?" And blaming the fall of man right out of Eden - on Eve, *and every other woman*, always raised my temper. If Eve went to hell for presenting Adam with the apple, why didn't he trundle along right after her for eating it? I certainly did not approve of the science of my time that said women were inherently stupid, and if they put anything into their brains aside from child rearing, husband and house pleasing, their brains would turn to chocolate pudding, and they would not even have the further ability to blink their eyes shut.

Elizabeth Humphreys, wrote of me, "Her features were not *regularly* beautiful, but she was certainly very pretty with her clear blue eyes, lovely complexion and soft brown hair, with a bright intelligent face that having once seen you could not easily forget. Her form was fine, and no old master ever modeled a more perfect arm and hand." She, too, said I could be sarcastic, was impulsive and made no attempt to hide my feelings, and that my "face was an index to every passing emotion." I always did show my feelings. I never hid one emotion, which real ladies were supposed to do with all of them, as they glided wraith like and angelically from child birth to childbirth and soon right off to heaven.

"If Molly would curb her tongue and keep her *mind* within a *respectable* boundary," they said, "she is charming and delightful company. She should smile and show her dimples and *keep hidden* what bubbles up from her brain."

Well, I did say what I thought, and I saw no point in being some demurely *stupid*, to tremble or flutter behind some belle-of-the-South fan. I was intelligent and I knew it, and books had never turned my brain to chocolate pudding, and I could argue politics with the best of any man. I thought what I thought, and I knew what I knew, and no one was going to talk me out of either one. Even - if I had been born *female*.

My brother in law said, "Molly would turn a saint away from his prayers, being so alluring." I liked that. His sister in law said of me, " She is so jolly, filled with fun, merry. The sunshine in her heart is reflected in her face."

I *was* a happy person now, *blossoming into womanhood*, as they called it. If I was charming and alluring, and considered pretty, that was *wonderful*. I was a true romantic; even if politics were my real passion, I was daydreaming of a great love that would magically come into my life, a *highly intelligent* man, of course, and he would sweep me away into a *perfect* marriage. For him I wanted to be alluring, charming and pretty. And I would be pleased if he told me about it, too. Often.

I had a great affinity and affection for the so - called *servants* of the South. I always hated and despised their enslavement. I admired their ingenuity in escaping to the northern free states, even if they had to mail themselves north nailed up in a box. I admired the great colored funerals, wherein the mourners were legally allowed to follow the deceased to the colored cemetery, and their marching on right on by it, corpse in the coffin, and wailers on their way north by the Underground Railroad. Dear Mammy Sally really raised me, and I did not believe in slave *servants* any more than she did. *Our* family *slave servants* were supposed to be freed, *some day*. The word *nigger* was never used for one, and it was thought very uncouth and trashy for anyone to use that word.

I don't remember *not being* drawn to the colored, and when I was home, I helped Mammy Sally smuggle corn bread and bacon out for the run away slaves following the North Star to freedom. It was I who helped mark our back gate so they would know we would give them food. My father and *Betsy* would have been horrified. When I was older, I gave away some of my clothes to escaping mulattoes, so they could pose as whites traveling north. That way one "white" lady could take reams of black servants along with her to freedom - well, not reams, but plenty, a Mammy, a carriage driver, a footman, at *least*.

When I was thirteen, in 1832, my sixteen- year old sister Elizabeth, we all called Lizzy, made a very good marriage. It was to Ninian Wirt Edwards, the son of Ninian Edwards, a Senator, and the third governor of the Illinois Territory. The bridegroom was very wealthy, and soon he and Lizzie lived in the finest house in Springfield. From his house high on what was called *aristocratic* hill, Ninian could look down on the town and the *lower* people. He was quite a snob, and so my sister became, right along with him, and after that magnificent marriage, Lizzy and I were never as close as we were before it. And soon she was saying the *worst* she could say about me, that I was a *radical abolitionist,* and so, honestly, I was. I said, and often, no man has the right to enslave another man, and that you can *not* justify the unjustifiable.

When I was close to fourteen, in 1832, I entered the select boarding school of Madame Leclerc Mentelle, and her husband, Monsieur Augustus Mentelle. The school was on the Richmond Pike, and across the street was the beautiful mansion of Henry Clay, *Ashland.* Away at boarding school during the week, I was taken home on the weekends in the elegant family carriage with driver and footmen Nelson, all done up in his blue swallow tail coat with huge brass buttons. Dear old Nelson. He also mixed the mint juleps for company. The Todd carriage had *three* folding steps; its interior, I remember, was of wine velvet. I remember rides in it, the wearing of white organdy dresses with blue sashes and the large leghorn hats used to keep the whites ever- pure white.

I spent four years at Mentelle's, and all of our lessons were in French. We did not speak *anything* but French. At Mentelle's it was recorded I had the highest marks and was quote, "the star actress of school dramas." I was seen and recorded as a "merry companionable girl with a smile for everybody. She was really the life of the school, and there she learned to dance so gracefully." I read the finest French books in French all the rest of my life. If possible, I became more enraptured with poetry, and the poems I loved I committed to memory to always have them with me. I loved the writings of a poor unknown English poet who died too young to become famous. His name was John Keats. His writing put me in mind of Shakespeare, whom I could recite along with lines of John Keats.

I was most carefully taught, and most carefully learned, all of the social graces, and all of the dances, the polka, the schottische, and the new and *daring* waltz. Dancing the waltz made me day dream of that great romance to come, where my *true* love who would look right at me, in as pretty a dress as could be, and fall in love with me *at first sight*. And, naturally, I would fall in love with him *at first sight,* too. All of this wondrous new world for me beginning to the music of the romantic, *romantic* waltz!

Then another sister of mine, Frances, went to Springfield, upon Lizzie's invitation, to find herself a good husband, for Lizzie believed this was where all of the good husbands were. Frances went, and she did find a good husband, a prosperous druggist and physician, Dr. William Wallace. We Todds had many relatives in Springfield; I recall three lawyer politician uncles, and no sooner was Franny married off, then Lizzie thought she would work on me. In 1837, when I was nineteen, I was invited to her mansion on aristocratic hill for a visit, and though I liked the town, the raw frontier *energy* it had, I only stayed there three months. I wanted more schooling, what you would call in your present time - *post- graduate courses,* for two more years in the advanced school of Dr. John Ward.

In 1839 Springfield became the state capital, and by this time the Ninian Edwards knew and entertained all those *who mattered*, as Lizzie said, and she invited me to stay with her, to meet some of them, and marry into this sky -high class. "Molly," she said, " you have already dithered your time away at this education *thing.* It is time for you to settle down and marry - the sooner the better."

"I will marry for the better," I smiled. "But the *sooner* has nothing to do with it, Lizzie. Nothing."

"What are you talking about, Molly? Your *sooner* is already almost too late!"

How I remember when I returned to Springfield! It was in October of 1839; fall leaves were flying before the wind in showers of red and gold; the prairie twilight was a lingering lovely lilac. Lilac was always my favorite color, and the lilac was always my favorite flower. The days were bronzed as only a fall day can be, as bright as a new minted penny, and absolutely, totally, *humming* with life's energy. Summer has slumbered sweetly away, those fall days said, but here I am, bearing the energy of all spent summers past - to color the maples red and gold, oaks into flame, as if God has taken my brush to them all - dipped into no more than glory. How graciously rose that harvest moon, touching stubbles of grain long gone for winter bread, gently silvering the prairie, the town and our slow meandering stream, as if the moon whispered down, I can paint enchantment, too!

I *loved* Springfield!

I joined the exclusive "Edward's" club of the wealthy and highly cultured young people, called by themselves the *coterie, click* in French, and it was filled with men who were up and coming and would surely be famous lawyers or politicians. Or both. There was the brilliant and handsome Stephen Arnold Douglas, who was not too much taller than I, but so cultured, intelligent, and refined. He seriously courted me, and although I could easily concede his charm and brilliance, he lacked a certain sense of humor, and *certainly* seemed humorless about himself. Mr. Edwin Webb, the wealthiest man in Illinois, proposed marriage, and Lizzie was ecstatic, but I was *not*. "Molly, oh, Molly! " she lamented. "You are an old maid of *twenty one!* Doesn't that worry you?"

"No."

"What *is* the matter with you?" Lizzie had blue eyes like mine, and they all but filled with tears.

"You ask me that *all of the time* since you married Ninian!"

"Well, what *is* the matter with you? Why don't you marry Mr. Webb?"

Lizzie," I said crossly. "I have not found the man I *want* to marry."

"What *is* the matter with you? Molly, what do you want in a man, anyway?"

"I want to fall in love with him."

"At first sight, I suppose," she said sarcastically.

"At first sight," I said sincerely.

Other young men in our *coterie* were dear Edward Baker, handsome James Shields, (courting me, but too in love with *himself*) Lyman Trumbull and James Conkling, the beau of my best friend, Mercy Levering, who was visiting her brother, Lawrason. He had a home on the hill next door to Ninian's, but it was not as grand. No house in Springfield was yet as grand as Ninian's. That fall and winter Mercy and I became best friends. Her beau, James Conkling, wrote of me saying, "She is the very creature of excitement, and never enjoys herself more than in society and surrounded by a company of merry friends." I was now recorded as having a *merry laugh*, always being in *good humor* and *full of fun*. I keep putting this in because, according to the noxious little man, my innate temper was usually one of rage. *My natural nature was a merry one. I loved* life. I loved its every cranny right into the years lying ahead of me. I was filled with excitement and the joy of just – *being!* The memory of my mother's face frozen in death was put away, deep, deep down, and I guess I thought no death would ever cause me such pain again. Fine clothes she had taught me to equate with earning approval. So I loved fine clothes. Material things, their luxuries, I frankly enjoyed. I loved the Edward's great house, their finest carriage, and I probably would fall in love with a wealthy man - that would be nice - I just had not run across him yet.

While I was brought up in luxury and had such a grand education that few women, *or men,* of my time had, the man I would love had the grimmest beginning. It was hard-scrabble, and it was pain and deprivation, and it made him strong, and it made him iron-willed, and it made him educate himself. He always said he had no more than a year of formal education, that his education came in fleeting *littles-* as he called it – the few times his father would allow him into a school, and he spent his life in making up for this deficit. He was a self- taught man, and I will say that nowhere on earth could he have found a better teacher.

They say a tree that bears the cruelest winter delivers the sweetest summer fruit. They also say a tree is best measured when it is down, but I won't think of that now.

It was important to us then – where our ancestors came from and what they did. On his maternal side was the Hanks family, his mother was Nancy, and his grandfather was Joseph Hanks who was born in 1725 and died in 1793. Joseph Hanks had two wives, names not recorded, and they produced for him ten children in a thirty-year period. In order of their birth they were Anna Maria, Thomas, Joshua, Lucy, William, Charles, Mary, called Polly, Elizabeth, Nancy, and Joseph. Joseph Hanks was the son of John Hanks, and Joseph started out in Berks County, Pennsylvania; in 1780 he was in Hampshire County, West Virginia, and in 1784 he was in Nelson County, Kentucky. It is still important to get the family tree straight as my husband is so loved and yet so revered every little schemer tries to attach itself to the tree and remove its roots to dig in their own.

On his paternal side it is known his family followed the trade of weaving, and when his ancestors came to America in 1637, the line here was founded by Samuel Lincoln, from Hingham England to settle in Hingham, Massachusetts. I think a Mordecai came next – not sure – then a Mordecai Jr. and I am sure this was my husband's great, great grandfather who lived from April 24, 1686 to May 12, 1736, dying at age fifty. Here Joseph Hanks brother, named John, became best friends with Mordecai's son, John Lincoln, and they migrated to Virginia together to what was then Augusta County and now is Rockingham County. In this period the Hanks and the Lincolns became friends with Squire Boone, the father of Daniel Boone.

John Lincoln, a Quaker and great grandfather to my husband, lived from May 3, 1716 to November of 1788, dying at age seventy-two. He had a successful farm in the fertile Shenandoah Valley and was wealthy enough so he could give his son Abraham two hundred and ten acres of the best land in Virginia. There were eight other children, birth years from 1744 to 1767.

The Lincolns had spread out from Massachusetts to New Jersey, to Pennsylvania, and to Virginia. They fought in the American Revolution, as my ancestors had; one had participated in the Boston Tea Party - became an artillery captain, and a first cousin, Hananiah, fought at the Battle of Brandywine, a captain of the Tenth Pennsylvania Regiment, and his brother, Jacob, was with Washington at Yorktown.

My beloved was named for his grandfather, Abraham, born in Berks County, Pennsylvania on May 13, 1744, who married Bathsheba Herring on June 9, 1770, and they farmed in the Shenandoah Valley. They had three sons, Mordecai (1771-1830), Josiah (1773-1835), and Thomas (1778-1851), and two daughters, Mary (1775-?), and Nancy (1780-1845). Abraham was a good friend of Daniel Boone, and when Boone moved into Kentucky, Abraham followed in 1780. Land was cheaper there, going for $.42 cents an acre. Abraham followed the Wilderness Road to Lexington, and traveled beyond Lexington to the Green River where he bought two thousand acres.

On a beautiful day in May of 1786 Abraham, then forty two, wanted to burn out some stumps on his land and took his three sons along. Three Indians swept down on them and Abraham was killed instantly. Mordecai, fifteen, and Josiah, thirteen, ran for the family cabin as fast as they could run, and Thomas, eight, sat and cried over his father's dead body. An Indian picked Tommy up and was about to break his neck when Mordecai found the family shot gun and killed the Indian. Tommy ran for the cabin and reached its safety. Josiah had slipped away to a nearby fort seeking help, and men came to the cabin and saved the boys from the Indian attack upon it. Mordecai inherited his father's land and money, and Bathsheba went to live with relatives. Bathsheba lived to be ninety. She was born in 1746 to die in 1836 at Mill creek Union, Illinois. She was the *only* wife of Abraham Lincoln. Many try to sneak in another wife, but that twig wasn't on the tree.

Mordecai lived from 1771 to December of 1830, known as the winter *of deep snow.* In 1792 he married Mary Mudd of a very prominent Catholic family. He prospered, becoming the sheriff of Washington County, Kentucky, and a respected member of the state legislature.

I don't know what happened to Josiah, but Thomas had a very rough time of it. He did not tell the funny stories his brother Mordecai was noted for, but he was a powerful wrestler. He was five foot ten inches tall and weighed one hundred and seventy five pounds, had hazel eyes and thick black hair, and always wanted to be, it was said, *where work wasn't*. Still, when he was twenty- five, he bought a farm in Hardin County, Kentucky, and continued getting into fierce fights, one time biting a man's nose off. He could read a little and sign his name, and he opposed slavery and became a Baptist because they did, too. He fell in love with Sarah, "Sally" Bush, but she married Daniel Johnston, the Elizabethtown jailer, and Tom then married a pretty girl, Nancy Hanks, who was the illegitimate daughter of Lucille Hanks. I heard Lucille had fallen in love with a man, who had promised to marry her, and he didn't, and the Hanks family always said he was a highborn Virginia aristocrat who was not given permission by his parents to marry Lucille. My husband told me this, too, that his maternal unknown grandfather became a well bred Virginia farmer and planter, no name noted. From the love affair Lucille's illegitimate daughter Nancy was born and was given to Lucille's barren sister, Betsy, Mrs. Thomas Sparrow, to raise. Lucille became what they termed *wild*, so much so, she was told by the grand jury of Mercer County to get married or leave the area. At the age of twenty- six she then married her brother in law, Herbert Sparrow, and had nine more children, teaching them all how to read and write.

Another sister to Betsy Sparrow, Nancy Hanks, also got into "trouble" –where a child was said to come into the world by nature's back door -and gave her fatherless boy, Dennis Hanks, to Betsy to adopt along with Lucille's daughter, Nancy Hanks. So Nancy Hanks had an aunt named Nancy Hanks, and Dennis had a mother named Nancy Hanks and a first cousin named Nancy Hanks.

The Sparrows adopted both children.

It is important to remember that Tom *did* marry Nancy Hanks, daughter of Lucille Hanks, for that odious little man said later in a lecture that they did not marry and *their two children were illegitimate*. In my time this was a disgraceful thing, a scalding, burning lie of the odious wicked man, and, believe me, when I married, I *did not* become Mary *Hanks*. Tom, 28, had married Nancy, 23, on June 12, 1806, and the Methodist Reverend Jesse Head married them. There was a notation of this marriage in the family Bible. For a long time the Bible was lost, but when the odious little man said Tom had never married Nancy, my son, Robert, found it, and also got a sworn written statement by a witness to the marriage, Christopher Columbus Graham. Graham, then one hundred, wrote that he was in the woods gathering roots for his medicines when he was invited to Tom's wedding, and what he remembered the most about the wedding was the food that was served after it. He must have loved that food, for he itemized the whole meal. What was served was bear meat, wild turkey, venison, duck eggs, maple sugar on a string that could be dipped into whiskey or coffee, peaches with honey, all placed on a great eating table that became the floor of the cabin the next day, and he continued, "Well if yer going to press me about the *wedden couple,* Nancy was a fresh looking girl, and Tom, he was a respected carpenter, so that made her respected." Tom worked as a carpenter in Elizabethtown making cabinets, door frames, and coffins. Nancy had been employed as an expert seamstress and was remembered as deeply religious and "loved and revered by all who knew her." This was from her cousin, John Hanks. She was tall, five foot seven, and slender, one hundred and twenty pounds, and had hazel eyes and dark brown hair. No photo of her exists.

Dennis Hanks well remembered Tom and wrote of him, "He warn't lazy, nor afeared of noth'n, but he was kind of shiftless and couldn't get ahead no-how, and he didn't care pa–tick-ular. Lots of them kind of fellers in those days, druther hunt or fish, and *I guess the clearings just had no use for him.* They had their uses, too, they did kill off all of the varmints for other fellers to go into the woods with axes. Well," continued Dennis, "we was all poor, but Tom, he was poorer than anybody - reckon his line just warn't as smart as the Hankses. Nancy - she was a pretty as a picture, tall and slender, with gray eyes and dark hair and quiet, not the *persterin* kind, and she knowed Tom was doing his best, even if it just warn't no good. Tom did think a heap of Nancy, and he didn't drink or cuss none, and them was cussen quarrelsome days. Tom, he was popylar and could beat up any man he had a mind to, but he just could not get ahead - never - no-how. And he didn't care pa-tickular."

Tom's history of farms is varied and extensive.

One year after he moved to Hardin County, Kentucky, he purchased two hundred and thirty acres on Mill Creek for one hundred and eighteen pounds. When Nancy became pregnant he bought a lot in Elizabethtown where he worked as a carpenter and where their daughter Sarah was born on February 10, 1807. The next year Tom bought a three hundred acre tract on the South Fork of Nolin Creek, often termed the "Sinking Springs Farm." It was here that Nancy and Tom had a son named for his paternal grandfather.

Betsy Sparrow and her husband and Dennis lived two miles away, and

Dennis recalled, in writing, the birth of Tom's son. "I ricollect how Tom cum over to our house one cold,cold morning in February and he said, kind of slow-like, 'Nancy's gone and got herself a baby boy.'" While Aunt Betsy hurried up with her work so she could go and see the baby, Dennis wrote, "I didn't have nuthen to wait for, so I cut and run the hull two mile to see my baby cousin. You bet I shore was tickled to death for babies warn't as common as blackberries in the woods of Kaintucky. Mother come over and washed him and put a yeller flannen petticoat on him and cooked some dried berries and honey for Nancy and went home and that's all the fuss'n either one of them got. I rolled up in a bar rug and slept by the fire so's I could see the little feller when he cried and Tom got up to tend him. Nancy even let me hold him pretty soon, and as you know, *that boy never was one for looks."* Dennis had other memories of his cousin - that "he just *growed* right out of his clothes, faster than Nancy could *make 'em,* and he had *these here fits* of *cutten up,* looking all sober at something, or someone, and then laughing *fit to kill.* He liked to fish and make traps for rabbits and go on coon hunts with Tom and me, and he would drop corn for his pappy, follow bees to the honey tree for honey, but never, never would he take a gun to large game." Dennis said that Tom just could not get him to do it, even with a good licking. And Dennis thought there *was* many *more* ways in which his cousin was *"more peculiarsome, most peculiarsome* - he had this *here* passion for *larn'in,* and three months of it in *Kaintucky,* and three more months of it in Indiana just made the *whole thing get worse.* He read the Bible, over and over, and *could get* a lot out of it, even recited passages, and he read some *shaking spearman* from England and recited him, too, just as if he was the Bible! He *writ* his name everywhere, all over the walls with charcoal, or with a stick on the crek sand, and I seen him." said Dennis, "walk miles to borrow a book to read and walk back miles to return it. He said, 'My best friend is a man who has a book I ain't read.' If he could've tied a book on to the handle of a plow he would be read'en while plow'en when his Pa rented out his work for thirty cents a day, which Tom kept for hisself. When he took a lunch break from plow'en, he would sit on a snake rail fence and read while eat'en his corndodgers. If Tom saw him at that, he grabbed a board and knocked him clean off the fence!"

Dennis recalled that Tom's son read *every* night by the only light in the one room cabin, the fire, all stretched out on his shoulder blades, his legs going up the wall, wherever there was still room for them, for they were growing so long, so fast, it was a *frightening thing.* "He read to us some danged fool tales of Ar-raabs running their trails at night, laughing over them fool things fit to kill, and I said, 'Why do you read them? Them fool tales are *lies* from beginning to end!' "

There had another son, Thomas, born in 1811, and he lived only a short time. That year Tom moved ten miles away to another farm, two hundred and thirty acres on Knob Creek, eight miles from Hodgenville. This was paid for by the sale of his land at Mill Creek. Here his son lived from the age of two to seven. Tom had thirty acres, fourteen tilled, in a beautiful valley where a stream called Rolling Fork flowed into the Salt River that flowed into the Ohio. The stream was full of fish, the cedar woods filled with game; corn was the main crop planted, and Tom's son not only dropped the corn but rode the horse to plow with a bull tongue plow between the corn rows. Tom raised pumpkins, potatoes and onions, and as Tom prospered he had a stallion and several brood mares. The cows grazed in the hills and voluntarily came home at night to their calves.

There was no school of any kind except during the warm weather, and for three months Tom's son walked eight miles *each way* to the Knob Creek School. Then Tom, ever restless, having as little use for the clearings as they had for him, moved on to his Pigeon Creek farm in Indiana, government land which he bought for two dollars an acre. It was an unbroken forest. The War of 1812 had bought hard times to Kentucky, and it was in the summer of 1816 that Tom left Knob Creek, and as usual, Nancy's Aunt Betsy, her husband and Dennis would follow when they could sell out their land. Tom seems to have loved the wilderness, even if he did not enjoy clearing it. Indiana had only three people per square mile, and Tom had to cut a trail out for their wagon. Later Tom built for his family a very crude log cabin near the pole shed they had first used. They were near the future village of Gentryville, and Tom was always digging for a spring that he never found, and they had to haul water from the creek. The area was thick with great oaks, beeches, the sugar maple, and walnut trees. There was a salt lick for deer nearby, and when Tom's son had the time to read, he went there with a book while the deer silently slipped by, and the creek murmured beside him into dark thickets and deep tree shadows.

He was allowed by his father to go to a school again, for two months where the emphasis was on oral teaching, and so they called it a *blab* school. It was Nancy who pushed Tom to allow their son at least *some* education. His Indiana school was run by Nathaniel Grigsby who remembered Tom's son as being the first at school and the last to leave. He was always quick to learn and was at the head of the class on all subjects, even when his father interrupted them by hiring out his labor.

In October of 1817 Tom's family was happy to see the arrival of Aunt

Betsy, her husband and Dennis. Now, at last, the family was together again. The frontier was a lonely place; miles and miles around them there were only seven other settlers. If the wolves howled through the night, and the bears came close enough to cast a huge black shadow, and in the darkness the lions screamed, the frontier was bountiful to them in many ways. In their season there was plentiful food to be gathered, currants, blueberries, wild grapes and persimmons, walnut, hickory and hazel nuts. They planted corn, beans, potatoes and onions, and for meat they had deer, coon, bear, wild turkey and fish.

In 1818 tragedy engulfed the little family; it was milk sickness from Tom Sparrow's cow, and he and his wife died from it a few days apart. When they were buried and Dennis came to live with Tom's family, Nancy, 34, took sick from the same thing, and for a week faced her death with the sweet grace in which she had faced the harshness of her life. The autumn leaves were turning, and Nancy loved the beauty of it and said she loved to see how they made splashes of gold in the forest, and left a long trail of gold on the dark forest floor.

From her bed of poles covered with corn husks, she tenderly caressed the face of her children. "I am going where we all must go," she said. "You must not grieve and think that I am in any grave. I will be with Aunt Betsy in a beautiful, beautiful place, where there are no graves and grief over them. I will be where angels sing, but you two will always be with me."

"How?" had asked Sarah, unable to stay her tears.

"The angels sing very, very close to earth," she said softly. She looked at her son, into his anguished eyes. "You must care for your father and your sister," she said.

"I will," he replied. I can so clearly imagine his agonized face. He was so closely bonded to his mother, and not to his father. How he must have tried to ease and comfort her as she was taking her leave from life. When she died, she closed her eyes peacefully, as if she had heard the singing of the angels so close to earth. His unthinking father had him help build his mother's coffin and help put her into it and down into the cold dark ground when Dennis was there to help. "He has to learn to be a man," Tom said of his nine-year old grief stricken son. That was Tom. Make a man out of a boy who was already one.

On the crude little grave marking by the forest path to the salt lick were carved her name, her birth date of February 5, 1784, and the date of her death, October 5, 1818.

The autumn leaves flamed more brightly in the colors she loved, and then the trees stood grim and bare as the wind carried away the last brightness of fall, and the sky darkened more and more and the wind grew colder and colder. He must have listened to its lament, nature echoing the sadness of man in loving and in losing what is loved, and he grieved for his mother out in the night alone, cast from the fire shadows on their cabin wall, and out to where the wolves howled for companionship, and the lions screamed for whatever reason.

When the first snow fell, it was said Tom's son tried to shield his mother's grave from it with his own body. He wrote his first letter to an old Kentucky friend, Parson Elken, and asked if he could come to their farm and say some words over his mother's grave.

The next summer Parson Elkin came to do just that, and two hundred lonely people gathered from miles around to attend Nancy's funeral. Weddings and funerals were important social gatherings, and it did not matter if anyone knew the bride and groom to be married, or the deceased to be buried. I can picture all of those frontier women, with their hard chapped hands and weather beaten faces, from being outside as much as in, women who gathered food, milked the cows, hoed, planted and harvested the vegetable garden. And there they stood with their homemade cornfield bonnets, the homemade linsey woolsey dress, the same size for all women, waist under the arms, with no lace, no puckered frills of any kind, and certainly, no buttons. At a funeral, before their own, these *always* tired women had a day of rest. At home they never had that. Every minute was as precious as gold, and taking the time to bathe was sheer luxury. I *can see* all of those gaunt and tired women standing still and silent at the grave, and I see Nancy as she must have been, always busy, always gentle, like her son. And probably her daughter, but I never saw her daughter. The days and the nights rushing on - outside chores - inside chores - birthing and caring for babies, cooking meat, vegetables, corn dodgers, corn pone and hoe cake, the sewing of the family clothes, the tanning and the working of buckskin, *every day* at the loom or wheel, spinning the years away, weaving into a life the joy of a new baby, of a child's happy laughter. And now Nancy was free of all of that, but did she not know the grief of her children? Did she not yearn to hold and comfort them, even if she were where the angels sing?

By her grave under the dogwood, on the shadowed deer path to the salt lick, the women silently remained, living about as she had done, and the wind must have rustled back their bonnets, their plain dresses, and near them stood their husbands Nancy had never known either. In low voices the men talked of the weather, what it had been and might be, and how their crops would fare. And as the minister said *dust to dust* and *ashes to ashes,* they all wondered what Nancy had been like, if she had been pretty, if she had been content in her brief thirty-four years. And if they noticed the bright summer day blooming all around them, they might have thought - days like this will come, when I, too, will be under the earth; the sky will be as clear a blue, and the birds will be singing in the same way, and I won't hear them, and I will not see this light or feel the warmth of the sun. And when dusk falls, the stars will come out and march, as usual, across the night sky, and I won't see them either, and the full harvest moon will rise unseen over *my* grave when I have harvested my life away.

The Parson Elkin said words from the Holy Bible, straight from God Himself, and as they listened, others thought, *God did not create life for it to end. Life cannot be renewed for the earth in the spring and not to me.*

And so on a warm summer day, when the birds were singing among high tree shadow, Nancy got her day of appreciation and loving remembrance, all because of the tender heart of her son.

Chapter Two

Thirteen months after Nancy's burial, Tom, forty-one, found he could not take care of his family alone. Sarah did her best, but the cooking, sewing, and the cleaning were too much for her, and Tom heard the girl he had first loved, Sarah Bush Johnston, was now a thirty one year old widow. He lost no time in getting to her at Elizabethtown. He arrived there on December 2, 1819, and he also lost no time in proposing, *that day*, right in front of the clerk of the court, one Samuel Haycraft, who recorded its every word. I guess he had a habit of recording things. Tom said, "Well, *Miss* Johnston, here I am, a lone man, and here you are, a lone woman. I have no wife and you have no husband. I came a purpose to marry you. I have knowed you from a girl, and you have knowed me from a boy. I have come all the way from Indiana to ask if you will marry up with me right off, if you are willin, as I have no time to lose." They were married *a few hours later*. After he had paid all of her bills. Sarah had three children, two girls, Elizabeth Sarah, and Matilda, and a son, John. There was room in Tom's wagon for them. But Sarah also had what she saw as very fine furniture, and she wanted to take all of it with her. "What?" gasped Tom. *"What?"*

"I have a real bed," she said, and it is not one of poles and corn husks and bear skins, but a *real* bed!"

"Good!" said Tom. "We can get good money for it!"

"And," Sarah continued, not hearing him at all, "I have a table, *with chairs,* and two bureaus, *with drawers.*"

Tom's face lit up, and he rushed to see the furniture. "Why this *one* bureau alone will fetch forty dollars *cash!*" he said in triumph. "It would be a crime against the Lord Almighty and the laws of the United States of America *not* to sell all this furniture for cash dollars!"

Sarah finally heard him and she did not like what she was hearing. "Tommy," she said, " you take me - you take my furniture."

"You cannot mean this!" Tom was stunned. Things, so far, had gone so well in their getting married. Since the Indians had almost killed him, everyone else did his bidding. "Move along -*furniture?*"

"Yes! Indeed - *yes!*"

"Woman," said Tom, "my poor wagon is weak and my poor lame old horse is weaker, (aging by the minute) and I can never get you, me, and your children to Indiana with *furniture!*" The furniture he had loved at first sight he now hated at second sight. If it could not become cash, what excuse did it have for going on?

Sarah firmly pursed her lips, and he knew this woman was not a *non-pestering* kind like Nancy. "My former brother in law, Ralph Krume, has a large wagon, and he has *four* horses that can pull it, and he promised he would bring me my furniture *wherever* I go," said Sarah.

"You won't change your mind?" Tom pleaded, almost weeping for the furniture cash.

"Where I go - *there goes my furniture.*"

"Sarah, cash is *good.* Cash is a *good* thing."

"Tommy, not as good as my furniture."

"Then, I guess it is the will of the Lord." Tom sighed, not agreeing with the Lord's will at all.

Sarah met Tom's children, and immediately loved them. They immediately loved her, but she did *not* like Tom's cabin. It was *not* as described.

"Tommy," she said. "Your cabin is *awful.* It has no window."

"Well, I know that," he replied. "I built the thing."

"I want a window."

"Why?"

"To see outside."

"Well, if you want to see outside, I reckon you can walk out *into* it!"

Sarah pursed her lips. With the same furniture firmness. "If I don't get a window, I will go back to Kentucky," she said, and so Tom put a window in, and now the sun could warm the furniture when it arrived in its wagon pulled by *four* horses.

"And your door is only a deer skin," said Sarah. "An *old* deer skin. It will let in varmints, rain, and winter snow."

"Well, then," soothed Tom, "you just put another log on the fire. Sarah, fires are not only for cooking. We warm up with them."

"Not in *this* cabin in the middle of a blizzard, Tommy."

"Sarah, that door is *fine.* It gets us *in,* and it gets us *out.*"

"Tommy, I will have a *real* door to keep the cold and the varmints out, and the heat in, or I will go *right* back to Kentucky," said Sarah.

Tom put in a wooden door. Rapidly. A woman could be a pestering kind, but he had already learned the alternative.

"And you have no floor but dirt, and I am not going to place my fine furniture on *dirt!*" said Sarah.

19

Tom did not cuss for he thought cussing wicked, and if Tom did not cuss out loud, his thoughts leaned in that direction. His cabin got a wood floor to make the furniture right out of hell happy.

Sarah looked at the pegs nailed to the wall that led to the children's loft, and here Tom stopped her short. "No room for stairs," he said, and as there was not, the pegs remained.

The furniture arrived, the miracle of the frontier, *two* bureaus with *drawers,* a table and *six* chairs, and the bed, and miracle of the frontier or not, Tom never looked upon them as anything else but cold blooded cash murderers.

Sarah scrubbed everything but the cabin ceiling, and when lines of footprints suddenly appeared there, she found that Tom's son had created them by holding all of the children, dirty shoes up, so they could walk across the ceiling. Sarah laughed, as Dennis said, *fit to kill,* for anything Tom's son did, was all right with her. He could easily lift the children to the ceiling, for by the time he was fifteen, he was as strong as an ox and towered at six foot four. Sarah had as hard a time as had Nancy keeping his clothes caught up with him, and when he was allowed, for a short time, to go to the Crawford school, both of its teachers remembered that his buckskin pants failed *by at least twelve inches* to meet the tops of his shoes. They also remembered he wore a home made linsey woolsey shirt, a coonskin cap and was always laughing, always being both in good humor and good health. He was still the fastest learner in school. He won every spelling bee, and had to be left out of them to even up the odds. During one spelling bee, the class floundered and flubbed, and the teacher, Master Andrew Crawford, grew mightily in temper. "I am disgusted with you," he said. " I am disgusted and angry and angrier, and I am going to call on *just one more person* to spell a word, and if the word is missed, school will *not* be dismissed!" And it was already past time for that to have happened. "*One* person misses the next word, you *all* miss going home!" Mr. Crawford repeated, swelling up in growing fury.

Not to go home for supper? No supper, no bed, parental wrath added to teacher wrath? A shudder of horror swept the class, and in it little Kate Roby was shaken the most. As she was so visible about it, Mr. Crawford pounced on her to spell the word to save the class from damnation. "Miss Kate Roby," he said, a spider reeling in its quivering prey, " *You* may now spell the word *defied.*" Miss Roby had no clue to such a word, and she bit her lip, trying to remember if she ever had *heard* of it - while the great spider was opening its jaws. She knew *by sound* the word began with a d. And she knew *by sound* probably an e - f followed, but after that she was lost. "*Defied,*" snapped Mr.

Crawford. The class groaned over *no supper, no warm bed*. "D-e -f," she began bravely, on a trail of some kind, but it forked, and she did not know which fork to take. Was it def-y-ed? Or was it def-i-ed? She was leaning toward the Y trail when she saw that Tom's son was looking at her with a gentle smile upon his face, and he slowly began to rub his eye. Taking his hint, she immediately switched to the I trail. "D-E-F-I-E-D," she said. "That is *correct*," the teacher said. She had saved herself. She had saved the class! She had saved the day! What was left of it, and she wrote, years later, she remained grateful to Tom's son for his rescue of her on that dreadful day for the rest of her life.

Tom's son was reading and writing on anything he could find, still mostly on the walls, and Sarah let him do it, too, saying Tom's son was the best boy she ever saw or expected to see. "I can say he never gave me even a cross look, or word, and never refused in fact or appearance anything I asked him," she remembered. So he could charcoal up the walls and lift the children to walk upside down across the ceiling any time he had a mind to. He still read at night by the firelight. When the fire was out, if there was a full moon, he read by its light. He still walked miles to borrow a book to read and miles to return it. And he was growing into what Tom called, "the gangliest most *awkwardest* boy who ever stepped over a split rail fence - he appeared all jernts." He lifted a six hundred pound hen house on a bet, and he could throw *anyone* in wrestling. He split rails faster than anyone in the state. He was to write about himself and say he had handled an ax from age eight to twenty three, the ax, "that most useful instrument." He could shuck corn faster than anyone he met, and he shucked corn three days for no pay to keep Josiah Crawford's book by Parson Weems on George Washington.

He also wrote later, that in his tenth year he had been kicked in the head by a horse, and was "apparently killed for a time." Another day Tom sent him to buy a horse for fifty dollars, but if he could not get it for fifty dollars, he was supposed to offer sixty. His son went to the neighbor and said to him that he was to offer fifty for the horse, and pay sixty if he had to, but he saw the horse was worth no more than fifty, and that was *all* he was going to pay. Tom got the horse and saved himself ten dollars.

Tom's son now wrote on the wall, "My hand and pen, they will be good, but God knows when." He *never* read while sitting on one of Sarah's chairs. He still loved to lie on his shoulder blades at night before the fire, his legs up the wall as he read to the family *Robinson Crusoe, Pilgrim's Progress, Aesop's Fables*, (more and more *lies*, moaned Dennis) *Benjamin Franklin's Autobiography*, and even the *Statutes of Indiana*. Of course he continued to read the family Bible and could quote it better than any minister I ever knew. Where he found the works of Shakespeare I do not know, but he read, memorized and quoted favorite passages that were balm and music to his soul. Shakespeare, the Bible - he always carried with him all of his life, and had them with him in his White House office.

The fireplace was the heart of the log cabin. Its outside chimney was the usual cut and clay, cut grass mixed with stiff clay and laid in alternate layers with split laths of hard wood. Inside, its hooks and a long crane suspended pots that served for the cooking. The heat of the fire was next to food in importance, and in the winter it came first. Tom's son took care of the fire that was *never* to go out. Chips for a low fire, brush for a blaze, and the night big log to pack in the coals to stir up as kindling in the morning. Sarah had brought along her Dutch oven, a big iron pot with long legs that was never removed from the coals. She also had brought along her long handled frying pan for the cooking of venison, wild turkey and rabbit. In the frying pan she also made what she called meat cakes, and she had a clay oven for bread baking. In the hot summer she had Tom build her an outside fireplace that she could use for cooking, and into the Dutch oven was mixed soap, but Tom would not waste tallow on candles. Tom's cabin never saw a candle.

Tom's sister, Sarah, also remembered as very bright, was hired out as a maid for the Crawfords, and Tom's son became their hired hand, for thirty cents a day from working from sunrise to sunset. Tom still kept the money his children earned.

One icy morning, before Tom's son went out to the field, he told Mrs. Crawford a story about his family. "My late uncle was the most polite man in the world. He was making a trip on the Mississippi when the boat sank. He got his head above water just once, took off his hat, and said, 'Ladies and gentlemen, will you please excuse me?' and down he went!" Then warmed by the stove fire and Mrs. Crawford's laughing, he looked out the window at the sunrise and said, "Well, this won't buy the child a coat!" and went outside to work. "Yes," he said, and often, "my family and I were the *scrubs*, looked down upon because slaves did not do our labor, but I would not want what the sweat of another man has earned." In his autobiographies, he always told how dirt poor he was, the non education of his father and his education by *littles* - to read and write and cipher to the rule of three - "I have not been to school since. The little advance I now have upon the store of education I have picked up from time to time under the pressure of necessity." He then went on to describe himself as he was in 1860 - "I am in height six feet four inches, nearly, lean in flesh, weighing on an average of one hundred and eighty pounds; dark complexion, with coarse black hair, and grey eyes - no other marks or brands recollected."

When he was eighteen, he walked fifteen miles to the Booneville Court to see lawyers in action. There he saw a fine handsome lawyer deliver a magnificent summation, and afterwards he went up to shake his hand in congratulation, all but struck dumb in wonder. The lawyer told his friends this *ugly huge* beardless *clodhopper* had no *right* to assume a *handshake*, and he swept indignantly by him. Later, in 1862, when they met again, the President of the United States shook hands with this very, very little man, and remembering the *exact* date, the case, the summation, finished his congratulations.

When he was nineteen, his sister, twenty-one, died in childbirth. She had married Aaron Grigsby when she was eighteen, on August 29 of 1826, and that family allowed her to die in labor on January 21, 1828. No one in it sought for her help of any kind. She was buried with her stillborn child in her arms. Tom's son never forgave Aaron Grigsby. He and his sister had been very close, and he grieved deeply at her death. He is quoted as saying then, "I go into melancholy moods. The death of one so young, and so loved, makes me wonder why such a thing has to be part of a divine plan. It is a melancholy thing - trying to figure this out. I reckon I am not good at losses when it comes to those I love - and lose."

That was another thing we had in common. But when deaths threatened us, found us, he found an inner strength, I found not. He bore the burden of saving the sacred flower of democracy - the blood, the agony, the young men dying minute after minute - he bore it all. He comforted me. He rose above his grief. I became mine, and I freely own, I let him down. That was the sorrow my soul bears yet. I tried so hard to make things light and merry in our personal part of the White House, and I did, until death took our Willie. And in all of the time - now become timeless- I see the flaw I had then, and it is here, now, in this page, in this story I am telling you. My beloved rose above grief. I repeat – I became mine.

Tom's son was well liked and respected. He could sink an axe into wood deeper than any man, could carry the heaviest post, and still out wrestle any challenger, but what he became noted for, like his Uncle Mordecai, was his talent for story telling. When he helped out at the William Jones store in Gentryville, a mile and a half from Tom's cabin, the store trade picked up because so many came to the store just to hear his stories. And when he operated a ferry on the Ohio, the passengers were " happily and mightily" entertained, and when he took a flat boat as bow hand to New Orleans for eight dollars a month, from April to June of 1828, his stories were said to be the best part of the journey. When he returned upstream by steamer, he was the most popular and most *listened to* passenger on board. He had learned that he could draw an audience and hold it spell bound. He was not interested in following his father in carpentry or farming. "I want to do something else with my mind," he told his step -mother. He said little to Tom. Their paths always remained strange to each other.

After fourteen years at Pigeon Creek, on March 1, 1830, Tom took his family away to Illinois, about ten miles west of Decatur, to farm ten acres near the Sangamon River. They traveled the two hundred mile journey for two weeks in a home made wagon drawn by a team of oxen that Tom's son drove. The oxen struggled the wagon across an icy prairie stream and the family saw that their dog had been left behind, and he was running up and down the bank, yelping in great distress. Tom said, "Leave the cur be!" His son paid no heed, stopped the oxen, pulled off his shoes and socks and brought the shivering animal back to the wagon. He always loved animals. Once on his way to court with other lawyers, dressed in the best clothes he had, he saw a pig struggling to get out of mud hole, and dismounting, he pulled the pig free, and got covered with mud. "How *could* you have done that?" asked a shocked fellow traveler.

"How could I have *not* done that?" he replied.

Tom's son helped clear his father's ten acres, and he helped build Tom his new cabin, and even put a snake rail fence around it. Then, at age twenty- one, he left to be on his own. He had helped his father, as his mother had asked him to do. He had tried to care for his sister, and now he said a tender goodbye to his step -mother, little to his father, and was gone from the new cabin on the Sangamon. He took no money. He had nothing but his poor clothing and set about splitting rails for a new pair of pants, and as he was so tall, his pants took forty yards of material, and for forty yards of material, he had to split four hundred rails. That winter was bitterly cold and remembered as the *winter of deep snow,* and I hope he split enough rails for warm pants and a warm coat.

Tom's son was hired by Denton Offutt to take a flat boat of produce to New Orleans. He helped build the boat, and in New Orleans bitterly opposed slave auctions and was told by a colored fortune teller *he* would free all of the slaves. "How?" he asked. "When you are President," she replied and John and Dennis Hanks, with him, laughed *fit to kill,* as Dennis recalled. On his return from New Orleans, in July of 1831, Tom's son clerked for the Offutt Store and mill in New Salem, a village of log cabins, and soon met the local gang of bullies who called themselves the Clarys' Grove Boys. They lived in the woods called Clary's Grove where they drank heavily and learned to be accomplished ruffians. They could out wrestle and beat up any stranger they took a mind to, and their mind generally ran in that direction, and then they heard about Tom's son clerking at the Offutt store. They took a crowd along with them and went to the store to size him up. "What do you want?" Tom's son asked.

"We come to wrestle you down," said the gang leader, Jack Armstrong.

"*We* - all of you?" asked Tom's son.

"Well, one at a time, of course," said Jack.

When Tom's son went out back to oblige, as he was so big, they decided they had all better jump on him at once. This was a mistake, for Tom's son did not respect bullies, and he angrily picked out Jack and shook him around like a rag doll, taking him up so high it took sometime for him to fall back down. When he did, finally, and when he got the coordination of his head with the rest of himself, he shook his head in real admiration. "Why, this here is the *most cleverest* feller that ever broke into this settlement!" he gasped. "I really *like* you!" he said to Tom's son, still straightening out the kinks from his travel on high. The whole gang became as devoted, and in 1832, when Tom's son ran for the Illinois General Assembly and was defeated by my cousin, John Todd Stuart, wherever he spoke from the stump, the gang was there to cheer him on. If *any* man in the audience uttered a *sign* of disrespect, the boys were all over him, fists swinging. Tom's son constantly had to jump off the stump and pull the boys away. "Now boys, this man has a right to be wrong," he would say. Amiably.

"Well, he should keep it to himself," would reply Jack.

"And not sicken us with it," said Jack's vice president in ruffian heaven.

Tom's son now found his passion for books but increased; he walked six miles to borrow a book on grammar, and when business was slow, he would leave the store, and go outside to, as he said, *wrestle* with the grammar of the English language. He would lie on his shoulder blades in the shade of a tree, and as the sun moved the shade around, he moved with it, somehow managing to keep his book steady and his feet up the tree trunk. He met and was fascinated by the semi colon that he termed a *friendly little fella,* and he used it often.

When Tom's son needed new jeans he split new rails. He slept in the loft over the store and took his meals at a nearby farmhouse, and he gained a reputation for three things - being a champion wrestler, telling funny stories as no one else could, and being honest. One day he overcharged a woman six cents for tea he had weighed improperly, and he walked four miles to give her the six cents. If he found he had overcharged a penny, he walked miles to return it. People around soon put the word *honest* before his name.

When he was asked about his religion he said, "This reminds me of a man I met in Indiana who said of his, 'When I do good, I feel *good;* when I do bad, I feel *bad.*' I reckon that's my religion, too."

He loved to tell a true story about a preacher and a blue lizard. The preacher attached his pantaloons to his shirt, and his shirt was attached by a single button at his collar. So *one button* held the whole thing up. The preacher got to preaching, all hell fire and everyone else falling into it, when a blue lizard began to crawl up his leg under his pantaloons. He let it go, for he was talking for the Lord and told his audience so. "I am the Christ whom I represent this day!" he thundered, and this made the blue lizard scurry up to his waist, so he loosened his pantaloons there to give the creature more room. But as the sermon went on, so did the blue lizard, crawling all over under his shirt. Furious, the preacher loosened the shirt button, the *lone* button that held everything up, and down went everything, and he stood stark naked before his stunned congregation. There was a long silence, and then an old woman stood, took a *good* look and said, "If *you* represent Christ, then I 'm through with the Bible!"

The Offutt store failed, and Tom's son was without a job. He enlisted for the Black Hawk War from April 21 to June 16, 1832, and then he enlisted for another thirty days. In this war prominent men were engaged, Jefferson Davis, Zachary Taylor, Albert Sidney Johnston, General Winfield Scott, and Robert Anderson. As Tom's son was leaving for the war, one of the Clary's gang asked if he were not afraid of Black Hawk. "Why?" came the quick reply. "I'm no chicken." The Clary's gang followed him to the war, too, and followed right behind him in it. The men got to choose their own captain by lining up behind him. Of course that was where the gang headed, and as Tom's son had the longest line, he became a captain. All of his men said they picked him because he told the funniest stories around the campfire. In the Black Hawk War he did not kill one Indian and saved the life of one who came into camp starving, and while men were drawing straws to see who would get to kill him, Tom's son gave him food and said, " No man is going to kill this Indian, and if he has a mind to try, he will have to wrestle me down first."

"That ain't fair, Cap," grumbled his company. "You can throw anybody!"

But Tom's son did run into trouble. He was marching his rifle company and all twenty were doing fine, formation perfect, in perfect step, heads high, and then they came to a fence with a gap that only could be cleared *single file*. Tom's son did not know any command for *single file,* so as they all approached the fence, he shouted, "Company halt!" It did. He went on, "Break ranks!" They did. Then he shouted, "You are dismissed for two minutes, after which you will fall in again on the other side of the fence!"

In the Black Hawk War he met two of my cousins who were prominent men, John J. Hardin and John Todd Stuart. They both were impressed with this rough young man's keen mind, friendly personality and a dignity and magnetism that were just an innate part of him. John Stuart told him to study law, pass the bar and then he could join his firm *as a partner.* "I reckon I will do just that," Tom's son said, and finally, he did. He always used that frontier word, *reckon* and another I never head before, by *jenks!* And I think he made up the word *skedaddle.*

He had run for the state legislature and lost in 1832, and he wrote it was "the only time he was beaten on a direct vote of the people." He ran again in 1834 and won, and won every time until he decided to retire from politics.

He had returned to New Salem where he stayed at the Rutledge's Tavern. He read their twenty-four books and met Ann Rutledge, who was engaged to his good friend, John McNamar, and he and Ann also became good friends. They did *not,* could *not* and would not *become lovers!* There was no man with a higher moral compass than Tom's son, and he would not and could not and *did not* betray a friend by a love affair with his fiancee. Only that wicked odious little man of *no character* would make up this *lie,* too, along with saying Tom's son was *illegitimate,* an *atheist,* loved Ann Rutledge and *despised* his own wife! Only a wicked odious man of *no moral compass* would do this to the memory of a man who had taken him in as a *clerk,* nevertheless splitting legal fees with him *half and half,* and putting up with his drunkenness that landed him in jail over and over. *Odious* Billy would get drunk and attack a store, usually its front door, when he found he could not enter it through its front wall. Tom's son had to get up early in the morning, find money to pay for the damages, his fine, or bail, or all three. I like to think that every man has the sacred within his soul, but this lying, coarse, *odious* little man was so low in the gutter he thought that was where life went on.

On August 25, 1835, Ann Rutledge, twenty- six, died when McNamar was away. Tom's son grieved, and he grieved deeply that such a fine and lovely young woman had been given to death, just as his mother had been given to death before her time, and his sister before her time. He never was able to stay tears for those he loved when they died. When the lying odious little man lectured of his *love affair* with Ann Rutledge which *never* was, the denials of the Rutledge family did no good; the denials of all who knew him then did no good, and the denials of John McNamar did no good, and the love affair that *wasn't* - even made its way into American poetry! It *was* a lie and it *is* a lie!

Tom's son was working on becoming a lawyer, and he began going from New Salem to Springfield, twenty miles away, to borrow my cousin's law books, but he had to figure out a way of getting there, as he had no horse. There are many stories about this, and most are, *generally*, true. On the Springfield road one day, he hailed a man in a wagon. "Would you have the goodness to take my cover coat to town for me?" he asked.

"With pleasure," said the man. "But, how will you get it back?"

Tom's son pondered over this. "Well," he said, "I reckon I'd better stay with it," and got into the wagon. When he got to the town and got the books, he decided to go to a hotel for some food. It was served, and he was very puzzled. He got the waiter and said, "I hate to hurt your feelings, but if this is coffee, bring me tea, and if it is tea, bring me coffee," and as he had been served some ice cream, never having seen that before, he said, "And did you know your pudden's froze?"

He soon found he was able to borrow a wagon if he would transport goods to Springfield in it, and this he often did. On one trip he met a wagon on the road, and in it were an old man and an old woman. The old woman stared at him so much she all but fell out of the wagon trying to follow what her eyes were seeing. He stopped his wagon and asked her why she was staring at him so hard. "Why, I declare - you are the *ugliest* man I ever seen in my *whole* life!" she exclaimed. He could not agree with her more, and did, saying, "Now, can I help it if I am so ugly?"

"Well," she said, thinking on it, "you could at least stay to home!" He told this story many times, laughing with absolute glee. No one in this world had a more contagious laugh. Sometimes he was even on a horse when he met the old woman, and it could be that he met a woman on a horse who said the same thing, but how he enjoyed telling stories about his ugliness. In another borrowed wagon he was riding alone against the sunset. It had been pouring rain and the mud was high on each side of the narrow road, and once a wagon got into it, it was hard for the horses to pull it out. He was all hunched up in his seat, as he always tried to hunch away his great height, and he met another wagon with a lone driver. There was not room on the road for the two wagons to pass each other. "You pull right out!" said the man to Tom's son. "*You* pull out!" replied Tom's son. "I said for *you* to pull out!" said the stranger. Tom's son began to unravel himself, saying, "Now, if you don't pull out, I'll tell you what I am going to do - " And he began to unravel himself more and more, getting taller and taller, just as if he intended to go right up past the setting sun. The stranger watched the great unraveling before him in horror. "My *gawd!*" he cried. " *Stop that*! Don't go no higher! *Don't go no higher!* I'll pull out!" And he did. Tom's son patiently waited to see that he got his wagon through the mud, and when he did, heaving as much as his horses, he looked back at Tom's son. "What *was* you going to do if I didn't pull out?" he asked.

"I reckon I was going to, " said Tom's son.

Tom's son had been postmaster of New Salem since 1833, and he had on hand, from the United States Government, eighteen dollars. The United States Government forgot to call it in and did not remember it at all until years later when it decided it needed the money and presented Tom's son with a draft for it. Every cent was returned, kept all the years in an old blue sock, silver and copper coin, the *same* silver and copper coin.

When he was delivering mail, Tom's son came across an old frail man, shoeless and shivering in the snow, trying to chop some wood. "Why are you out here without shoes?" he asked.

"Chopping wood to buy myself some," said the old man.

"How much do you need for the shoes?"

"What this chopped wood will bring," said the old man, and Tom's son quickly chopped the wood and the old man got the dollar to buy new shoes.

Tom's son soon became a businessman. The Clary's gang liked to do what they called, *booze it up.* One night they descended on the town store owned by Reuben Radford, who was at home, and asked the store clerk, Reuben's brother, for some whiskey. The clerk knew the gang and gave them two rounds free, thinking this would make them all warm and cozy and they would leave in good spirits, once filled with them. But that idea did not fly. The gang wanted more free whiskey and when it was not given to them, they became irate. The whiskey bottles they did not empty, they shot up, and finding that so pleasurable, they shot up as much of the store as long as there was still a lamp left to see by. Before dawn, out of lamps, bullets and whiskey, they rode home, drunkenly singing of life's pain, passing right by Reuben's house. Reuben put two and two together and rushed to his store. Seeing its condition, and what had happened to his prize stock of whiskey, he said, "I am going to sell this wreck." He did and right away, to the first man who wandered by, Billy Greene. "Sir," he said, "you can have my store for four hundred dollars - payable in six months."

"I'll take it *right now,*" said Greene, for he had shopped at the store and thought he was getting a real steal. As the day further dawned, Green saw Tom's son shaving outside of where he roomed, and he asked him to help inventory his new store's stock. Then Greene and Tom's son went into the store to take inventory, and in full daylight Greene saw the mess he had bought. "The Clary's boys have done all the inventorying I want!" he said. "I am going to sell this wreck!" Just then Noah Berry rode by. "Do you want to buy my store?" Green asked him. "You can have it for a good horse and saddle and two hundred and fifty dollars later to me and four hundred dollars later to Reuben Radford." Berry eagerly jumped to buy the store and took in Tom's son as a partner. When the store was stocked with whiskey again, Berry drank most of it, died shortly thereafter, January 10, 1835, leaving Tom's son with what he called his national debt, now seven hundred and five dollars. It was at this time, when he was serving whiskey across the counter, a drunk came in and asked Tom's son to pour him some booze. As he was pouring the drink, the drunk drew out his pistol and held it at Tom son's head. "Now, *why* are you doing such a fool thing?" asked Tom's son, very annoyed, for he was swamped with customers.

"Well, I swore if ever I seen a man uglier than me, I would kill him and put him out of his misery!"

Tom's son looked at him and said, "Well, if I'm uglier than *you*, go ahead and shoot, for I don't want to live!"

Tom's son was still having trouble with home made jeans, for they was said to fail by at least a half foot to meet the top of his socks. And the jeans that were too short were not in good shape otherwise, made of flax and tow, they were usually coming out at the knees. When they went out at both back pockets, he kept them, anyway, and called them his *spectacle* pants. Obviously poor, he was well liked, and wherever he ate, men gathered around him to hear a funny story. One of his favorites told at this time concerned a young swain sparking the farmer's daughter, with a little too much spark, and the farmer came home in time to see the conflagration. The swain jumped out the window and running across the cabbage patch scared up a rabbit he kicked up in the air, grunting, "Git out of the road and let someone run who knows how!"

Another story he loved to tell then was of a balloonist in New Orleans sailing gloriously in the sky until he suddenly had to drop down in a field where slaves were working. The sky master got out of his balloon, his coat decorated in shiny spangles, wearing golden slippers, and the slaves, watching him descend from heaven and exiting a sky craft all a-sparkle, ran for the woods as fast as they could run. They weren't prepared to meet their maker. But an old slave, who could hardly walk, was not going anywhere, so he had to make the most of his situation. He politely removed his hat and said to the heavenly shining one, "Howdy, Massa Jesus! How's yo Pa?"

In 1834 Tom's son was elected to the Illinois General Assembly, he and my cousin, both Whigs, won, not having run against each other this time. In 1836 Tom's son was elected again, received his law license, and as he rose rapidly in his profession, more stories began to circulate about his honesty. A client temporarily needed thirty thousand dollars in legal tender for a land claim. The client said, "I have no thirty thousand, and there is no way I can get it."

"I can get it," said Tom's son. And he did. They went into the bank, and Tom's son said to the cashier, "We just want to take thirty thousand dollars to make legal tender with; I'll bring it back in an hour or two," and without even a signature from him, the cashier handed over the thirty thousand, and in two hours the money was returned.

He was doing well enough to buy himself a new coat, but a short one was all he could afford. When he left the clothing store, a friend met him in the new coat and said, "Isn't that coat too short?" and the reply was, "Perhaps so, but it will be long enough before I get another one." He really paid no attention to what his clothing looked like - *ever*.

On his way to court in a bitter ice storm, he stopped at a tavern to warm himself up and saw fellow lawyers doing the same. "It is colder than hell," he observed.

"Oh, you have been there, too," said another lawyer with sarcasm.

Tom's son looked at him. "Oh, yes, and the funny thing is that it's like it is here - all lawyers nearest to the fire."

On another cold night he came to a tavern with no money on him, and he was hungry. He went inside and ordered some catfish for his horse. "Horses don't eat catfish!" said the tavern owner.

"Mine certainly does," said Tom's son. "Just cook some up for him and see for yourself!" The fish was cooked, and all in the tavern rushed to the stable to see a horse eat catfish. The horse vehemently refused to do so. Tom's son sighed and said, "Well he is not in the mood for it *now*. But it is a shame to waste it, so shouldn't I eat it myself?" He got the catfish and enjoyed it very much.

He was before an uncertain Judge Harriet of Pekin, Illinois, who said after *every* argument made by Tom's son, "I don't know about that!" Finally, Tom's son turned to him and said, "I know your honor did not know about it, and that's why I am telling it to you!"

He illustrated in court how it is possible to settle a dispute in a non -violent way. "Now this reminds me of a grocer in Juliet who had a violent quarrel with a neighbor. The neighbor was not a violent man, but he wanted to get *back* at the grocer who had been so impossible to deal with. The next day the grocer was busily making sausage, his store filled with favorite customers waiting to buy some. The disgruntled neighbor marched in with two huge dead and decaying cats which he put down by the sausage in progress, saying, 'This makes seven today. I'll call 'round on Monday and get my money for them.' " This story, he said, made the jury decide in his favor.

He was always making fellow lawyers laugh in court, and Judge David Davis did not like this at all. One day a lawyer laughed too loud at one of his jokes, and the judge fined both of them. Later, the judge asked for the story, roared with laughter and remitted the fines.

Before Judge Davis one day, Tom's son was asking the members of a jury if they knew his opponent. The judge found this a waste of time. "The mere fact that a juror knows your opponent does not disqualify him!" groused the judge.

"No, your honor," came the quick reply. " But I am afraid some of the gentlemen may *not* know him, which would place me at a disadvantage." He won that case, too.

In defending a man who had harmed a man in self-defense, Tom's son said, "Now this reminds me of a story. A man was walking down the road with a pitchfork over his shoulder and a farmer's dog attacked him, and the man used his pitchfork in self-defense and killed the dog. The farmer was furious. 'What made you kill my dog?' he asked. 'What made your dog bite me?' asked the man. 'Why didn't you go after him with the other end of the pitchfork?' asked the farmer. 'Why didn't your dog come at me with *his* other end?' asked the man." It was another successful defense.

Tom's son made a bet with an Illinois judge for a horse swap the next morning with *no backing out,* or there would be a forfeit of twenty–five dollars. The judge found the worst horse he could find, and waited for Tom's son who would *not possibly* find a worse horse. A crowd had gathered and restlessly awaited Tom's son and a worse horse. Finally, he appeared carrying a wooden saw-horse. The crowd hooted in laughter. The judge took the saw horse and Tom's son looked at the judge's horse and said, "Well, judge, this is the first time I ever got the worst in a horse-trade."

A rich man was pursuing a poor man who owed him two dollars and fifty cents and was going to court over it. Tom's son took on the case, charged the rich man a ten-dollar fee, gave the poor man five dollars of it, from which he paid back the rich man and the claim was satisfied. Tom's son got five dollars and the poor man got two dollars and fifty cents and the rich man was happy because he had won the suit.

Around a tavern fire men were betting and a man called *Know All*, because he always thought he knew everything, said, "Any man who asks a question he cannot answer *himself* has to set up our drinks." Tom's son entered the room and the contest, not for free drinks, but because he loved contests. His question was, "What is the reason there is no dirt in the mouth of those ground squirrel's dens?" No one could answer this, and they waited for free drinks from Tom's son, who said, "The reason is that they begin to dig at the *bottom*." There was a puzzled silence and then *Know All* said, "And how do they get at the bottom to commence?" and Tom's son said, " *Know All,* that is *your* question! Now answer it, or set up the boys' drinks!"

In 1832, when Tom's son had lost his first try to be in the Illinois Legislature to my cousin, John Todd Stuart, it is no wonder he lost. As he appeared on the stump, here was the written description of him. "He wore a mixed jean coat, short in the sleeve and bobtail- so short in the tail he could not sit on it - flax and tow linen pantaloons, and straw hat and pot metal boots." And as he started his first speech, a ruffian insulted him and started to beat up one of the Clarys' boys who had jumped on him, and Tom's son leaped from the platform, pushed through the crowd, broke up the fight, and threw the ruffian at least "twelve feet away." He then leaped back up on the platform, having lost his straw hat, but went on with his speech, anyway. "I have been solicited by many friends to become a candidate for the legislature. My politics are short and sweet like the old woman's dance. I am in favor of a national bank. I am in favor of the internal improvement system, and a high protective tariff. These are my sentiments and political principles. If elected, I shall be thankful; if not, it will be all the same." This was the only time he was to lose when running for the State Legislature, and even then he carried his precinct 277 to three.

In 1834-35 he had served as a Whig in Vandalia, the first state capital, a twenty-four-hour run by coach from Springfield. When he had been elected, he went to a prominent supporter, Coleman Smoot. "Smoot," he said, "did you vote for me?"

"Most certainly I did."

"Do you want me to make a good appearance in the Legislature?"

"Most certainly I do."

"What do you think of what I am wearing - the best I have?"

"It is awful. Most certainly and truly - *awful.*"

"Then what about a loan of two hundred dollars so I can look good, and I will pay you back as soon as the state pays me."

He got the loan, but knowing him, I doubt if he spent too much of it on clothes. The loan was promptly paid back from his *first* check.

In 1835 he wrote of his political principles, "You may burn my body to ashes, and scatter them to the winds of heaven; you may drag my soul down to the regions of darkness and despair to be tormented forever, but you will *never* get me to support a measure which I believe to be *wrong*, although by doing so I may accomplish that which I believe to be *right*."

He was elected again for the term 1836-37, and in 1837 he wrote of the corruption of money in politics. "It is an old maxim and a very sound one that he who dances should pay the fiddler. I am decidedly opposed to the people's money to pay the fiddler."

On April 12, 1837, Tom's son left New Salem where he had lived for six years, where he had mused over the works of Shakespeare, Burns, Byron, and as usual, the Bible. He left behind many friends. Those friends said of him that if he grew *beyond* them, he never grew *away* from them. He rode a borrowed horse to Springfield to practice law with my cousin, John Todd Stuart, who was always more of a politician than a lawyer. Their law address was Number Four, Hoffmann's Row, and office upstairs.

But back in the summer of 1836 Tom's son got himself into a pickle. I am going to tell this as he told it to me, and as he wrote to the lady in question and his whole written account of the matter in a letter dated April 1, 1838, to our friend, Mrs. Orville Browning. Here is the jist of the pickle. In 1835 Tom's son had met an intelligent and nice looking young woman named Mary Owens, who was visiting her sister, Mrs. Bennett Abbell, in New Salem. Mrs. Abbell was a good friend to Tom's son, and he found her sister pleasant and agreeable. (Note this was the *same* year he was supposed to be having that *passionate* love affair with Ann Rutledge - made up by that *odious* man) Miss Owens left to return to her home in Kentucky. Then in the fall of 1836, Mrs. Abbell decided to visit her sister in Kentucky and told Tom's son she would bring Miss Owens back with her "on condition that I would agree to become her brother in law with all convenient dispatch," he wrote, accepting the proposal as "I could not have done otherwise." Still, he was pleased to do so, as he "thought her intelligent and agreeable, and saw no good objection to plodding through life hand in hand with her." But alas, when Miss Owens arrived once more in New Salem, the groom to-be got very cold feet. Miss Owens had gained over eighty pounds and had lost all, or most of her teeth. "She did not look as my imagination had pictured her," Tom's son continued in his letter. "I knew she was oversize, but now she appeared a fair match for Falstaff. I knew she was called an 'old maid', and I felt no doubt of the truth of at least half of the appellation, but now, when I beheld her, I could not for my life avoid thinking of my mother; and this, not from withered features - for her skin was too full of fat to permit of its contracting wrinkles - but from her want of teeth, weather beaten appearance in general, and from a kind of notion that ran in my head that nothing could have commenced at the size of infancy and reached her present bulk in less than thirty five or forty years; (he was twenty seven - actually she was only twenty eight) and, in short, I was not at all pleased with her. But what could I do? I had told her sister that I would take her for better or for worse, and I made a point of honor and conscience in all things to stick with my word, especially if others have been induced to act on it, which in this case I had no doubt they had, for I was now fully convinced that no other man on earth would have her, and hence the conclusion they were bent on holding me to my bargain." So when he went off to Springfield, he continued, he tried to find in Mary Owens *something* he still liked, and he solaced himself in that she did not have an inferior mind, her mind "much more to be valued than the person." Tom's son would stand firm to his promise, when he clearly did not want to. He wrote he would stand as "firm as the surge repelling rock . . . continually repenting the rashness which led me to make it." He wondered how he could postpone what he dreaded, marriage to Miss Owens - "how I might procrastinate the evil day for a time, which I really dreaded as much, perhaps more, than an Irishman does the halter."

From Springfield he wrote her two letters in 1837, on May seventh and August sixteenth. In the May letter he tells her she would not like to live in Springfield. "I am afraid you would not be satisfied. There is a great deal of flourishing about in carriages here, which it would be your doom to see without sharing in it. You would have to be poor without the means of hiding your poverty. Do you believe that you could bear that patiently? Whatever woman may cast her lot with mine, should any ever do so, it is my intention to do all in my power to make her happy and contented; and there is nothing I can imagine, that could make me more unhappy than to fail in the effort. I know I should be much happier with you than the way I am, provided I saw no signs of discontent in you . . . My opinion is that you had better not do it." He had addressed her as *Friend Mary*, and had signed off *Yours, etc.* No 'dear' - no 'love.'"

The August letter was also addressed to *Friend Mary*, and he signed it, *your friend*. No *love* or *affection* again. It seems at their last meeting they had "but few expressions of thoughts." He does not see or think of her with "entire indifference." He writes she may be mistaken as to his real feelings toward her, but he avoids saying what they are. What he wants is "to do right by you;

and if I knew it would be doing right, as I rather suspect it would, to let you alone, I would do it." He is squirming harder. "I now say you can drop the subject, dismiss your thoughts (if you had any) from me forever, and leave this letter unanswered, without calling forth one accusing murmur from me ... if you feel yourself in any degree bound to me, I am now willing to release you ..." He still wanted her to be happy; he still would be miserable if he made her the same way. He closed: "If it suits you not to answer this, farewell. A long life and a merry one. But if you conclude to write back, speak as plainly as I do. There can be neither harm nor danger in saying to me anything you think, just in the manner you think it."

No wonder she turned him down, a blessing and great relief to both of them.

The Panic of 1837 had left Illinois deeply in debt and the Whigs had to soft pedal the idea of government internal improvements, the building of new bridges, railroads, and canals to unite the Northeast with the Northwest. The Whigs stood for what Henry Clay called the American System, with raw materials from one section of the country going to the manufacturing sections, to their mutual advantage. By this time, Tom's son was the unquestioned leader of the Whig minority party in the Illinois State Legislature.

When I arrived in Springfield in October of 1839, it had become the state capital. I was to stay, Lizzie insisted, until (1) I found a wealthy husband, (2) turned Democrat, and, (3) stopped my radical abolitionist talk. On November 2 my cousin, John Todd Stuart, defeated Stephen A. Douglas for the seat in the National House of Representatives, and Tom's son did all the work of his law firm and split the fees he earned fifty-fifty. I heard my cousin had this *rough-hewn tall* man for a partner who seemed to be very intelligent. John Todd Stuart said, "*No*, he is very *brilliant*, and that is why he is running my law practice." John Todd Stuart said his partner had so quickly mastered the science of law, had unerring judgment, could quote forever from the Bible, Shakespeare and Burns, and how eloquently he could express a thought! Lizzie's husband served with him in the State Legislature and said he was also very amusing. He could make an audience roar with laughter, and he had the physical strength of a giant.

I really heard all of this in 1836. This man was quite the talk of the town, if not in the upper cream of its society. Of course, due to this, he was not presented to me.

When I returned to Springfield, it seemed half of Kentucky's upper crust had moved there along with my two sisters. My father's brother was Dr. John Todd, and his two daughters, Elizabeth and Fanny, became my dearest friends. Now I heard again and again of my cousin's law partner - this *very* rough-hewn man. That is - he was careless of his personal appearance, wore jeans and did not care about dancing. That is all I heard now of Tom's son - brilliant, amusing, very, very tall, *and very, very rough- hewn.*

I was young, and filled with what I was termed as having, *joie de vivre.* I knew they were saying I *was more than* pretty, and I loved it. I was happy with the bronze glints in my brown hair, the long dark lashes, the deep blue of my eyes, dimples when I smiled, perfect teeth and what they called a *peaches and cream* complexion, a *perfect* figure, *perfect* neck, arms, and shoulders. It was thrilling. I loved it. I loved to hear that more men said I was a "fascinating and alluring creature." Lizzie even wrote of me, "She has an adorable crooked slow coming smile, violet eyes with incredibly long lashes, and pink cheeks." This was fun - *marvelous.* I wanted to be this- *more than pretty* - for this love of my life. Lizzie wrote that I was brilliant, witty, audacious and well bred. Why not - all these things? Like her, I was a Todd. I was now said, more than once, to have a joyful "bubbling" personality, a fine mind, even if still used in *erring* ways, for its passion about politics. This bubbling bit was nice, too. I flirted and I danced, and did both very well - with Southern grace and charm. I wrote home that I was on "the wings of expectation." What *did* I expect? *The beginning of my charmed life! Charmed by what? My true love, my wondrous wealthy brilliant true love!*

As 1839 closed, after Lizzie's magnificent Christmas for all of us, I heard that John Todd Stuart's law partner, the *rough- hewn tall* one, was going to speak at the Springfield House of Representatives, refuting Stephen A Douglas and Martin Van Buren and all the Democrats on earth, I guess, on the need for a renewed national bank. It was to be the evening after Christmas, and I wanted us to go see him. Ninian was a politician. He was in the legislature with him. And he was the law partner of John Todd Stuart. "Let's go hear that Whig speech," I said eagerly. "I want to see what he says about Jackson's failed banks."

"Molly, you will *have* to learn ladies do *not* do politics," said Lizzie.

"I do," I replied, "and I am going to attend that Whig speech."

"You cannot go without an escort!"

"Mr. Edwards will go with *us, "* I said.

Ninian looked cross and said firmly, "Mr. Edwards will *not.*"

"And certainly *not,* Mrs. Edwards," said Lizzy.

Chapter Three

The speech by Tom's son was published in the *Quincy Whig,* January 4, 1840. I read every word, and then I read them over and over, and I thought, he *is* brilliant. I read the speech when the cold made it too miserable to leave the house fire, and again when the rains fell and fell and fell - until I almost knew it by heart. The Whigs were distributing it in their campaign for General Harrison against President Van Buren as an important political document.

Here is what Tom's son, or my cousin's *rough- hewn* law partner, said about the Sub-Treasury the Democrats had given us for the last ten years, contrasted to the National Bank they had killed with the withdrawal of government funds.

His three major points were (1) the Sub Treasury cuts down the national money supply, (2) it costs more, (3) and it was a less secure depository of the public money. The Sub Treasury - what I call the S. T.- collects the government revenues, stores it *out of circulation* until the government needs it, where it does nothing but rust in iron boxes in the meantime. The revenue is to be collected in *specie* that takes more than half of what the nation has, cutting down paper circulation based on specie, and with the quantity of money reduced, the whole country suffers. The former National Bank established and maintained currency for forty years, a sound and uniform currency with *no* shrinking of the money supply.

The S.T. is more expensive to run, for the National Bank not only safely kept, transferred, and disbursed revenue received, but made *an annual payment* to the government of $75,000 for doing so. The difference in the expense of the two systems was around $405,000 a year.

The National Bank was more secure for public funds, for it answered to sworn officers of the government. Not one cent had been stolen from the National Bank system and thievery was grossly fed by the Sub Treasury scheme, and a list of the thieves and the money stolen was provided. Money lying around awaiting spending is a great temptation, and a national bank with government checking and control reduces this temptation. Of course, he digressed, one never knows about people and their temptations. Look at Jesus and his twelve disciples, and among these men chosen *with super human wisdom,* there still turned up a Judas - the sub treasurer of the Saviour and his disciples. "The interest of the Sub-Treasurer is *against his duty*- while the interest of the Bank is *on the side of its duty*. If it proves faithful to the government, it continues its business; if unfaithful it forfeits its charter, breaks up its business . . . "What if the Democrats have tacked on a Penitentiary Department to the Sub Treasury? Have jails stopped robbery? Gallows stopped murder? Why did they build a cage if they expect to catch no birds? Will punishment of the thief, if he has not fled to another country, bring back the money stolen?"

He then refuted in careful detail all the claims made by Stephen A. Douglas, all the excuses made for Van Buren spending more money in 1838 than *all of our previous presidents*. Washington could have gotten the country through twenty years with what the Van Buren Administration had spent in 1838.

His closing was magnificent, and, I was to learn, the very core of his political thought: *Liberty, sanctified by the rule of the people.* He would not be the last to desert the cause of liberty - he would *never* desert it. "Here, without contemplating consequences, before High Heaven, and in the face of the world, I swear eternal fidelity to the just cause as I deem it, of the land of my life, my liberty and my love . . ." And if he were joined by others of the same mind, and they all should fail to keep liberty alive - "We shall have the proud consolation of saying to our consciences, and to the departed shade of our country's freedom, that the cause approved of our judgment, and adored of our hearts, in disaster, in chains, in torture, in death, we NEVER faltered in defending."

"Magnificent," I whispered, every time I read those lines.

They actually brought tears to my eyes. *Land of my life, my liberty and my love.*

I grew sick of the rain. I could not bear to stay in the house another day, and sent a servant to Merce's house. I had to get outside. Why shouldn't we take the carriage to town?

Merce sent a message back. "It is still raining."

I replied, "Not as much. *Please?*"

So we went down the hill into Springfield. I didn't care if the horses and the carriage had to *swim* through the mud. I had brought shingles along so we could walk on them from the carriage to the board sidewalk. As we reached town, the sun came out, and then it went away and left gloomy skies, but at least rain had stopped falling from them. I was dressed in my favorite color, lilac, as always, with my shoes to match in color. "You look lovely," Merce said to me, and I hoped I did, for something told me that this was going to be a *special* day, or why did I ache so much to get outside and be in it?

The carriage stopped as close to the walk as it could, and we put down our little path shingles and made it to the boardwalk without getting even our shoes muddy. "Mary, you are so clever!" enthused Merce, as happy to be away from the house as I was.

"Sometimes I am clever," I replied, but, generally, I thought I was clever *most* of the time.

As we walked along the boardwalk, we passed the store of Joshua Speed, a wealthy young man from Kentucky, who was a member of our exclusive *coterie*. Inside his store men were sitting around a warm fire, and we heard from them the merriest laughter. It seemed so warm and inviting in there, we just went in! I saw the men were all listening raptly to a very tall man in very humble clothing, and I had never seen clothing so humble or a man so tall. When we entered, they all stopped laughing, and took off their hats to us, those that had hats, and we spent some money, I don't remember what for, and the tall man went on with his story. I stopped to listen. It was about a greedy farmer. "I ain't greedy," the tall man said, being the farmer. "Who can say I am greedy? I only want all the land that joins mine!" Then he laughed louder than anyone, and went on about the same farmer. It seems his house burned down, and then down went his barn in the same fire, and the good neighbors gathered and built them both all over again. When the house and barn were finished, another good neighbor brought him a bag of oats, and the greedy farmer frowned at the oats and said, "Sorry, I am only taking cash now."

I laughed myself and so did Merce, for it was not just the story. It was the way it was told, the accent, the voice inflection, the *drama!* And no one enjoyed the story more than its teller, and his laugh was the most *unconditionally* enjoyable laugh I had ever heard in my life.

I looked at him, and he looked right at me, and I thought, goodness, Merce and I should not have been in that store without gentlemen escorts, and we should not leave the house without them, as Lizzie told me all the time, and here we were, the only ladies present, and laughing, probably too loudly, too. We were both embarrassed, Merce and I, and we hastily left the store, the warmth, the cheery stove fire, and I thought to myself, the tall man *must* be John Todd Stuart's partner - for tall men like that just cannot be found everywhere. "Oh, Mary," said Merce as we left the store. "We should never have gone in there alone!"

"If we hadn't, we would not have heard about the greedy farmer!" I said, and we both laughed. But when we saw our carriage, we stopped laughing. Our mud boards had sunk down into it, and the coachman did not seem aware of our predicament. I was not about to ruin my lilac shoes and skirts in glucky mud for a ride home. "Mary, we cannot get to that carriage unless we swim to it!" moaned Merce.

Before I could reply, the tall man in the shabby clothes was by us because he saw the sunken boards and our dismay. The most beautiful smile transformed his rugged face, he had *perfect* teeth, and with his gray eyes twinkling, he said, very gently, "Ladies, this will *not* do," and he picked up Merce, put her into the carriage and came back for me, getting mud all over his jeans. As he carried me to the carriage, I never had sensed so much *power* in a man in all of my life. It was a *very* shocking thing for the shabby man to do, but we were glad for it, anyway. Merce and I were embarrassed that we had made for ourselves such a mud calamity just to get into town, and so neither of us spoke of it again. *Ever.*

It *was* a special day, for that was my first meeting with Tom's son and my cousin's law partner. No proper introduction. No word alone to me, just a kind gesture to help Merce and me, even if it covered his jeans with street mud.

That kind man, that strong *gentle*man, who dared to do what no other man would *properly* do, haunted me. The laughter from his story telling, his own joyful laughter as he told his story, haunted me. *I just could not get him out of my mind.* I kept seeing those tender lips, the twinkling of humor in those beautiful gray eyes, and I found out his name from Lizzie, who still did not think much of it, or of him.

"Molly, why on earth do you want to know *that?*"

"That?"

"His name. It will never concern you!"

"He seems so kind. And gentle. He helped Merce and me -"

"What? *How?*" asked Lizzie. She looked white faced with shock.

I dared not say.

"He had better not!" said Lizzie angrily. "He had better not have helped you - about *anything!*"

"Why not?"

"He is not of our class, and never will be."

Frankly, I thought this to be a compliment, for when aristocrats get too aristocratic, I don't like them. And the tall man in shabby clothes, his jeans probably still muddy, I thought was just *glorious.* I found and read another speech he had made in 1838 before the Young Men's Lyceum. He talked of the gift of freedom that our forefathers had left us and of our duty to cherish and nourish it. "Our forefathers," he said, "were the pillars of the temple of liberty, and now we are to be the new pillars, hewn from the solid quarry of reason, general intelligence, morality and in particular, a reverence for the Constitution and the laws, and upon these the fabric of freedom will rest, and the gates of hell will not prevail against it." I loved his speeches. I asked Lizzie why their author could not be invited to the Edwards' gatherings, and she said he would not know how to act among them, and that was why his friend, Mr. Speed was a member of the *coterie,* and he was not. I asked Mr. Speed why he did not bring his friend along to the *coterie* Saturday night dances, and he said his friend had never danced because he didn't know how, and probably never would. I then asked if his friend was married, and got basically the same reply. I then gave up on meeting the tall man again, but *I very much* wanted to meet him again. Then, on a clear Saturday there was a great hay wagon ride, where, for a lark, the elite could play act simple farm folk and ride in a hay wagon and sing songs and bundle with each other against the night, in a very proper but informal way. My escort was Stephen Arnold Douglas, who, everybody kept saying, would surely be the President of the United States. *The* Mr. Douglas my cousin's law partner had meticulously dissected in his national bank speech. When Mr. Douglas and I finally reached the hay wagon, we were the last 'on board', and the wagon bed was very high to reach for both of us. Mr. Douglas was trying to figure out my ascension, before his own, and as he pondered, the shabby giant of a man leaped from the wagon, and lifted me right up into it. "This is getting to be a regular habit," I smiled, and he said, "Well, I reckon, good habits ought to continue," and then he pulled Mr. Douglas into the wagon. He went back and sat with men without lady friends present, and I thought, *very* unhappily, this *will* be the last time I will see him.

I was still courted by the grandson of Patrick Henry, a most "agreeable" lawyer, and I still received Mr. Webb *and* Mr. Douglas, to Lizzie's delight.

Whig rallies for General Harrison were starting very early, right down the main street of town, with the beating of drums, wagons bearing log cabins, and hard cider barrels, and when the wagons stopped, the barrel contents were drunk by the white males who yelled, "Tippecanoe and Tyler, too!" General Harrison had killed many Indians in the Battle of Tippecanoe, so that became his campaign name.

Or they chanted,

> "Without a why or a wherefore,
> We'll go for Harrison there fore! "

Or,

> "Van, Van, little man,
> Is a burned up squirt,

Wirt! Wirt! Wirt!"

There were fireworks at night, great outdoor bonfires where Whigs danced around them, drinking from little glass log cabins filled with whiskey, and the Whig whiskey was put there by the Booze company, and that is where we got the word *booze* for whiskey. The little log cabins were to give the impression that General Harrison was a poor man and lived in one, but he was rich and lived in a mansion.

During all of the Whig marches and celebrations, I went out to see if *he* would be there, but he wasn't, and I found out he would be making speeches all over the state for the Whigs, while Mr. Douglas would go with him to the same places, making speeches for the Democrats.

When did I see the shabby man again? What was the meeting again that changed my life, and made it richer than it ever could have been?

When was that night, that magical night of light and the waltz - when love danced into my life, love that is as ageless as creation, yet ever new - like an old melody that haunts you forever before it is ever heard. *When was that night?*

It was at Lizzie's. It was at a *Coterie* ball, and I remember it was snowing - as usual; I had all of my dances taken, and during one, as I seemed to whirl by Joshua Speed, I saw he was entering the room with *him,* the *him* who did not dance, could not dance, would never dance! He stood stalk still by Mr. Speed, in his poor clothes and his great Conestoga boots, and he smiled that beautiful smile, and he said, "Oh - boy, how *clean* these girls look!" Everyone heard and everyone laughed, except Lizzie, who was being told by Mr. Speed his friend wanted to be *formally* presented to *me.*

"Oh - my *goodness,*" said Lizzie. She had turned white faced with shock.

"Is it all right?" Mr. Speed asked Ninian who heard and rushed up to defend his wife from this grossness. "*Present* him - *him* - to Miss Todd?" asked Ninian in even greater shock than Lizzie.

"Yes," said Mr. Speed. "He has asked to be *formally* presented to Miss Todd."

Mr. Edwards looked at Mrs. Edwards, and she finally shrugged, as if she were shrugging off an annoying fly. What harm could a *presentation* do?

"All right," said Mr. Edwards. "It is all right," he repeated, swallowing hard.

When the dance ended, Mr. Speed *formally* presented Tom's son to me, and very shyly, he said, "Miss Todd, I would like to dance with you the worst way."

That was *not* very reassuring. He would like to dance with me the *worst* way? Mr. Speed had said he did not know how to dance, and I looked down at his great Conestoga boots, *huge-* and they grew larger and more menacing with each second. "Miss Todd?" he asked anxiously. I looked up into those beautiful gray eyes and immediately forgot the size of his boots. I slipped my hand into his, and he held me around the waist, while with my other hand, I held up my gown train, but even that did not save it. He stepped on it, and true to his wish, he did dance with me in the *worst* way. I quickly suggested that if we could not *reasonably* (safely) share a waltz, we could sit down and *reasonably* share some punch. He laughed that merry infectious laugh at my semi joke, and we sat down to drink the non- booze punch. "Miss Todd," he said, as he handed me my glass. "What would *you* like to talk about?" How unsure he was around me, how shy he was, and I saw his hands tremble that held his glass of punch. He was holding his glass with *both* hands! I had never seen that done before. I looked into his anxious face. "What on earth is the matter?" I asked, very politely.

"The matter?" he quavered. The punch was rocking its way up to the top of the glass.

"Yes. Why are you shaking so much?"

"Because I am scared," he said promptly, and had the good sense to put his glass on a table near us.

"Afraid of me?"

"Yes, and you are so *little!*"

I laughed as much at this as I had at his greedy farmer. But I saw he did not join in my laughter and looked really terrified. "Women are not *bad* things," I said, smiling in a friendly way and trying to put him at ease, or at least, encourage the panic on his face to go away. "We really aren't."

"No, no," he agreed. "But the young ones I find very frightening."

"Why? Why on earth would you be frightened of us?"

"Because I think I frighten them - you?" He jested, but he did not.

"*You* frighten *me?*" And I laughed again. Then I saw his eyes for I looked boldly into them, and I saw how I *did* frighten him. "No, no and *no*," I said. "You do *not* frighten me."

"I mean by the way I *look*."

"*I like the way you look*," I said, very positively.

How *bright* the room had become, how ethereally and magically bright, and the music, the romantic, *romantic* waltz playing all around us - made me in a different place. I was in the great ballroom, and I was not in the great ballroom. I was already in some enchanted isle where loneliness is ended when the seas withdraw for the appearance of love. He was stronger than any man I could imagine. I knew that right away, back at the mud carriage, and it was not just physical strength at all. I saw the depths of his being in those beautiful gray eyes, and they had lights in them when he looked at me, and I knew that I had captured this man's heart, and no more than he had captured mine. *Fudge on Victorian courtships and silly necessities that are not necessary at all!*

"Miss Todd?"

"Yes?"

"You *like* the way I look? I have never heard any one say that in my entire life!" He stretched out his long legs and sighed in joy, and I gave thanks we were far enough from the dance floor to afford the room, both for his legs and for the waltz to continue. With him here - sitting next to me - I felt more and more - *cherished.* I looked at him more closely, more boldly, and the room, the moment, *the time,* shimmered more and more beyond reality. "I want to thank you for saving me from the mud and saving me for the hay ride," I said.

He smiled his beautiful smile, that I discovered always began in his eyes. "I reckon it was my pleasure," he said.

"And I want to thank you for your speeches on our national treasure - or, our national *goal* - man's *inherit* right to life, liberty, and the pursuit of happiness."

His smile broadened, and I saw it was one of approval, and he looked at me, very happily, and then he quickly looked away.

"I refer to your closing argument on our Sub Treasury and your magnificent speech - in 1838 - to the Boys' Lyceum."

"You read them?"

"Every word."

He sighed in about ecstasy. I was feeling the same, and if I was ever alluring, I wanted to be more so; if I was really enchanting, I wanted to be more so. I wanted to be all that brought that expression of joyful admiration into his eyes - and, I thought, *I already am!* "I would very much like to talk about the writings of Thomas Jefferson," I said. "You quote him, and he is one of my heroes."

"Mine, too," he replied. "Obviously." His eyes were filled with such feeling, such energy - and I was to forever see for me - love. "I never dreamed I would be sitting by you, talking to *you,*" he said gruffly.

"Why not?"

"Me - here? By *Miss Mary Todd?*"

"Why not?"

"*Miss Mary Todd,* courted by great prominent and wealthy men - Miss

Mary Todd - as removed from my earth as the most beautiful star - so far, far away."

I laughed, and if I never flirted before, I flirted then. "Well, here I am, right next to you and not stuck in the sky - all remote - and certainly *not* far, far away."

He swallowed and looked at the non -booze punch.

"I am not removed from your earth," I said. "Or earth," I added. "Now - about Mr. Jefferson -"

He pulled at his collar and began a rapid discussion on Jefferson's *Notes on Virginia*.

I knew every word. There was no place he could lead me about Jefferson that was foreign to me. "This is wonderful," he sighed, that beautiful smile making my heart sing.

"What is wonderful?"

"Finding a beautiful young girl who is interested in Thomas Jefferson. And has read his writings."

"And yours," I added, impishly.

"And by some wonder - mine!"

"I love politics," I smiled. "And I am also a Whig."

"Living in the home of Ninian Edwards?"

"Yes, and I know the saying - Ninian Edwards hates democracy as much as the devil hates Holy water."

He laughed again, such a merry *whole-hearted* laugh. When I looked into that ruggedly gentle face, at the tender lips and the expressive eyes that I had thought of so much, I knew I was in love. But that might have even been when he first touched me, carrying me to the mud ensconced carriage, or when he lifted me into the hay wagon - or when I first heard the merriment in his voice when he was making all of the men at Joshua Speed's store laugh at the greedy farmer.

Neither of us touched the punch. It spent the remainder of the evening lying quietly on the elegant side table of the Edwards' ballroom, absorbing its shavings of ice. The music of the waltz seemed to be made in Heaven; the lights of the room stardust fallen to where the angels do sing so close to the earth.

I thought I loved this man before either of us was born, for it seemed to me, that here was a man so safe, so cherished in my heart, we could never have been strangers. I believe there is one man for one woman, and when they happen to meet and fall in love, it is something so sacred - it must have been decreed, even before the dawning of the first light.

Chapter Four

Lizzie and Mr. Edwards were horrified when the man who lived for *no pay* over Joshua Speed's store had asked to call on me. "Do you know what he told me, Molly, when I reminded him you were a *Todd?*" asked Mr. Edwards. "I even spelled your name for him - T-O-D-D. And do you know what he said?"

"What was that, Mr. Edwards?" I asked.

"He said, 'How is it that God can get by with one D - but the Todds have to have two?'"

I laughed until tears rolled down my cheeks, but Mr. and Mrs. Edwards were not amused. "I hate to have him in my house," said Mr. Edwards. "I cannot see him *here* calling on *you*, Mollie."

"Why not?" I asked. The Todds needing one more D than God was marvelous, and I was still laughing over it.

"Even if he serves in the Legislature with me, he is poor white trash."

Now he had gone from *rough- hewn* to *white trash*. I stopped laughing, and I looked at Lizzie. Anger scalded my throat, as if I had burned it with the hot coffee. "He may not call on me here?" I asked, keeping my voice quiet. After all, when I was away from home, Ninian was acting as my guardian.

Lizzie and Mr. Edwards looked at each other, and I thought, clone to clone, and then Mr. Edwards used his napkin to wipe away a stray muffin crumb, and really, his dislike of a social inferior daring to call on his sister in law. "He may come here," he said shortly. "I do not like it, but if you wish, Molly, I will tell him he may call on you here."

"I thought it was going to be just a *presentation*," moaned Lizzie. "He surely is not *daring* to court you," and Lizzie trembled at the thought. "Even without *any* social grace, he has the intelligence not to do *that!*"

"He just asked to *call* on me, not *marry* me," I said.

However, from the start, it was a mutual courtship, and before he said a word about it, I knew he had fallen as deeply in love with me. It was so thrilling that I seemed not to walk, but to dance, and not to speak, but to sing. Or maybe it was time spinning by in a dance and a song of its own. "Molly," he said soberly to me one night, "I would like to court you."

"*Court* me?" I wanted more specifics. "Court me for *what?*" I teased.

"I would like to court you toward marriage - if you would have me, of course." His face looked very, very sober.

I looked at him silently, filled with joy and speechless for the first time in my life.

"Do you think you could ever marry me?" he asked, so softly and so shyly, I could hardly hear him. He could speak to hundreds, and brilliantly, but to me, now, he all but strangled out each word. "Can you stand the idea?" he asked, *imploringly*.

"Oh, yes, yes, *yes!* I can."

"Can what?"

"Stand the idea. *Glory* in it!"

"Marrying me?" He looked shocked. He actually looked *shocked.*

"Not another person!"

"Me?" he repeated.

"Yes, you silly man. *You.* I *want* to be courted by *you.*"

"Toward *marriage?*" he asked huskily. He seemed to be catching after his breath, wherever it had gone.

"How can I accept more plainly?" I giggled.

"I don't know," he said in a kind of wonder, as if he did not know just exactly where and what he was.

"Well, I do!" I said and flung myself into his arms and got my first kiss from him. It was tender and it was gentle, but with the kiss, and then kisses, I felt the power of his emotions. "I fell in love with you as soon as I saw you," he said. "Molly - Molly," and my name sounded like a caress. "As soon as you walked into the store - I *knew.*"

"Did you forget the greedy farmer? You did *not!*"

"He was left on his - to rote, " he sighed, still replenishing his breathing ability.

I touched those tender lips, and kissed his face near them. No proper woman would do this of course, but no one in my time allowed a proper woman to do too much. "I don't know when I fell in love with you," I said, "but I did, and maybe it was even when the greedy farmer was on rote."

"*You* - in love with - *me?*" He beamed and seemed to be trying to get the idea of the earth's rotation all straightened out.

"Miss Mary Todd, of the family with one more *D* than God, is wholly, completely, and *joyously* in love with *you!*"

"Ninian told you about the Todd - d's?"

"Yes. And without one *d* - you are a *most* glorious man!"

He looked at his image in the mirror over the fireplace. "Glorious?" he asked, perplexed. "I - I - *glorious?*"

"Believe it," I smiled and arranged for more kisses that I never wanted to end. There was energy between us, wonder, that made *the whole world* ours.

"I cannot believe that you could love a poor nobody like me," he said softly. "I cannot believe it. I had dreamed - hoped - and then scoffed at myself for reaching too high - reaching for that *remote* star so far away - and I did not even envision a *polite* refusal." He had his arm around my shoulders, and again, there was this feeling of his physical power as I had first felt it when he carried me through the mud to the Edwards' carriage. "Molly, Molly," he said again, as if the word were new and wondrous. He gently stroked the curls back from my face, and it was the sweetest caress I had ever known. I touched his hand, held it, and took it to my face, in a caress of my own. "I have never loved another man, nor shall I," I said, and was startled at how my voice trembled.

"I have never loved another woman, nor shall I," he solemnly repeated.

Our caress in kissing and holding would not have been stayed if all the rest of life on earth was.

The musical clock on the mantel chimed a quarter hour, and it might have been for one hour or twelve hours, or, maybe, it just felt like singing along with my heart.

We were sitting on the plain horsehair sofa of Lizzie's back parlor, and we watched the fire before us burn beautiful fire castles away, and, finally, cast shadows to move upon the ceiling. "I am so happy," I said.

"Who would *ever* have guessed?" he asked himself. And there was the sweetest wonder upon his face.

"That I would be so happy?"

"In loving me." That sweet wonder never left his face, even as we parted.

He wrote to my father in Lexington for permission to court me, and after many inquiries about him, my father gave his consent, although Lizzie did every single thing she could do to get our father into her house to take me back to Lexington where I would no longer be tempted by Tom's son. Back to the house of Robert Smith Todd she wanted me to go, with all of its gold-framed mirrors, luxuriously appointed rooms, fine china and silver on the sideboards, and the fan shaped window over the house entrance. Back, back to go- to be solidified into *upper class* elegance. "What can you possibly see in *him?*" asked Lizzie.

"Everything," I replied.

"He is too tall - and so *ugly!*"

"Because he is so tall, there is just more to be *glorious*. I think he is the most glorious man alive."

"Oh, God!" said Lizzie, and she was praying I am sure, for Lizzie would never take the name of the Lord trivially.

"He is a fascinating man," I said. "I love his intelligence. I love his humor. And we like the same things. We have so much in common."

"You have *nothing* in common," snapped Lizzie. "He is, and you *are not.*"

"I am a poor man," he had told me from the first. "As if you cannot see that. I rode a borrowed horse to Springfield from Vandalia, the only member of the legislature without his own horse, and wearing a suit of clothes a man who had voted for me bought. And I have the national debt of seven hundred and nine dollars."

"He is in debt to *seven hundred and nine dollars!*" said Mr. Edwards to me. He looked at me as if he expected that news to "elegant" me right up to marching down the aisle with Mr. Edwin Webb. Under a cascade of American flags - all made of Webb dollars.

"Oh, he told me that right away," I said. "He is incapable of lying or of *any* deceit."

"Molly," said Lizzie. "If he *truly* loves you, he would never expect to give you a life of hardship and poverty. It will *never* be different. He is not going anywhere as Mr. Douglas is, and he will never have a hundredth of the money of your Mr. Edwin Webb!"

"He is not *my* Mr. Edwin Webb!"

"He surely sees that in *no way* are you two matched," said Mr. Edwards. "Look at your fine education, and he goes around saying he has had no more than a *year* of formal schooling!"

"Mr. Edwards, he has educated himself," I replied tartly. "And *nowhere* in this world could he have found a better teacher!"

Man and wife looked at each other for strength.

"As well as his being a man of incredible honesty, integrity and generosity, he is brilliant. I have never known a man as brilliant. He is a *genius!*"

"*Molly!*" said Lizzie, as if I were about to fall into a bottomless pit.

"*Molly!*" said Mr. Edwards, as if I had already done it.

Lizzie and Mr. Edwards were determined to drive my beloved away. *Look how he hangs on Molly's every word,* Lizzie lamented to all of our relatives in Springfield, and she wrote of it to our relatives in Kentucky and Missouri. *She hangs on his every word, looking at him so adoringly, it is not proper to say the least! And the way he looks at her - it is worse than improper!* "Mary leads the conversations, and he listens and gazes at her as if he is drawn by some *superior* power, scarcely saying a word."

Lizzie was desolate. She had married herself and her other sisters off so well, one to a well to do druggist and physician and the other to well to do store owner. Frances Todd had become the Mrs. William wealthy physician Wallace, and Ann Todd had become the Mrs. Clark wealthy storeowner Smith, and here I was, in love with a poor man in serious debt with no roof of his own over his head!

Frances and Ann did not share aristocracy hill with Lizzy, but they had fine beautiful homes and fine beautiful carriages with fine beautiful horses to pull them. "I deeply fear they are secretly engaged," said Lizzie to her husband, in constant tears over the tragedy unfolding right before their eyes. "They have *nothing* in common!" She kept saying this.

But we had *everything* in common! We both loved politics and we were both staunch Whigs. We both hated slavery, and thought it an abomination against God. We both saw the salvation of every man, here, in the whole world, to be free to earn his own bread, and control his own government. We both passionately believed Jefferson's eternal truth as he explained for all time the (unrealized) ideal of the American Revolution - *We hold these truths to be self evident, that all men are created equal, that they are endowed by their Creator with certain unalienable rights, and that among these are the right to life, liberty and the pursuit of happiness.* My beloved said the hope for our democracy, for self-government, was in the *Union* of the United States of America. He was passionate in the possibility that our new and radically liberal experiment in democracy held for *all* mankind; he hoped the desire for self-government, the north star of liberty, would flame forever in the human soul.

Was this not based upon the gospel of Jesus Christ? For - if all may be equal before God, surely, they must be equal before their government. It was the Pilgrim concept going back to Martin Luther and Jesus Christ - the *God-given opportunity* for *equal* salvation.

We both loved to read, and we both loved poetry and the same poets, and what I could not recite, he could - Shakespeare, Bobby Burns for his love of the common man, and we both loved that poor looked over poet, John Keats. We loved stage dramas, the opera, music, and *we loved people.* We loved the joy of friends. We loved to tease each other; his teasing of me was a form of his constant affection. His teasing of me, and his marvelous sense of humor never failed to delight me.

But what we knew of love, Lizzie never saw. I know Lizzie married Ninian when she was sixteen, and the marriage was not as much between them as much as between their high social positions. And they seemed amiable enough to each other. But - I did not sense the passion, the tenderness, the *ecstasy* - I felt - but, perhaps, no other woman alive could feel it.

When was our courting period? In our talks before the back parlor fire, in hay rides in the fall and sleigh rides in the winter and in our long walks along the town stream when the season turned the prairie sky into its special lilac of a soft summer gloaming.

We went to the dinners at our friends' houses, picked fresh strawberries for the seasonal strawberry parties with the berries and ice cream, and my beloved was accepted with appreciation everywhere, *everywhere*, but in the house of Ninian Edwards. You see, he was accepted there as a casual visitor, and a friend of Joshua Speed who was rich, a Democrat, a member of the exclusive *coterie*, but this ugly poor man as a prospective brother in law? Never. *Ne-ver!*

"When I come into the Edwards' home," he told me one night, "I feel as if I am entering through the portals of hell."

"They are just snobs, not devils," I said.

The rain was drumming so hard against the widows. The musical clock on the mantel chimed long enough to send its little villagers in a walk around a church and back into it. He kissed me, and he said he loved me, and I said I loved him, and then he looked at the fire, and tears were in his eyes. "Love is eternal," he said.

"Will you have that put into my wedding ring?" I asked.

"Yes," he said. "I will put that in your wedding ring."

And we kissed upon that.

How tender and gloriously gentle a man he was.

How gloriously 1840 turned out to be for us. It was simply *our* year, and if the rest of the world lived in it, too, that was nice, but it was *our* year and *our* wonder world. He enjoyed every one of my collected books, and in the small back parlor of the Edwards' mansion we discussed them, and never once were we to be invited into the elegant front parlor that was reserved for the Edwards' *distinguished* guests.

"I love your slow sweet smile," he said, caressing the curls around my face again. "I love your merry laugh, the dimples, the joyful sparkle that comes to your eyes - you are so - *enthusiastically- alive!*"

"Especially now," I said, snuggling closer to him.

"You can carry on a conversation about anything," he said. He looked at me, adoration bringing those lights of love into his eyes. "Such a melodious - soft cultured voice - such *sharp* intelligence."

"I wish I were not so sarcastic," I said, not wanting to swell up with too much pride.

"I love your imitations," he said. "And they usually are of fools."

"I guess fools do have the right to be fools," I said.

He laughed. "As long as they do not think we are, too."

I stretched, and got back into his arms. "How falling in love changes life!" I said. "It just creates no more and no less than the whole world being ours!"

"It has changed my life and my world," he said, his fingers still caressing my curls. "I never knew such happiness as in the time I spend with you."

The rain drummed harder against the windows. The fire leaped from wind gusting down the chimney, pressing to its screen a beautiful showering of sparks, and at the quarter hour, the little villagers peeped from the church door and went back inside. I was beloved of my beloved. I was safe in all the eternity of love with my protector. Never would I be fearful of anything again. "You have made my life safe," I said.

"You have made my life a miracle," he replied.

"Time is *ours*," I said. "I am glad that I am young, and with you, and we can share so many more sunrises with the joy of another day. When we are together, night holds only a sky of beautiful stars, a beautiful waxing or a waning moon. I used to be so *afraid* of night."

He smiled, and his caress went from my curls to my cheek. "Molly," he said. "I will always love, shelter and protect you. But you should know that my nature has a very melancholy side."

"What do you mean?"

"I am not always cheerful and buoyant as you are."

"I have seen no melancholy side."

"My spirit falls into deep valleys of depression. I had a terrible time in accepting the deaths of my mother - my sister."

"My mother's death took away my childhood. I felt as if all love and any pride in me - was gone. Maybe that is why I so love beautiful clothes - my mother loved to dress me in them - with beautiful clothes - I do like feeling - admired."

"Beautiful, anyway."

"I have never seen you in your valley of despair."

"Maybe you have vanished the blues away forever," he smiled.

To see his long legged stride up the drive, to go to the door and find him there, to look up into his tender face, and know that later I would kiss those tender lips - it was incredible, beyond anything I had ever imagined.

Surely, in some long night, we must have sought the other part of ourselves, our other half, our own completion. *That* must have brought light to the lonely dark. That must have brought forth the stars themselves to sing in the joy of creation.

We must have sought the opening of our shuttered self to a lover, to share the jeweled light within, for union, is the sacred rapture of love's totality.

Chapter Five

I waited for him to set our marriage date, and I was in a panic that Ninian would get to him and increase the morbidity of his growing self- doubts. I was *always* fighting his self doubt now about not deserving me. He was so strong in every other way. No man could change him when he knew the truth and its right, but about me, it was different. "I am *not* a weak woman," I said. That was my way of saying I would go wherever he was, live as he was living. "I am not a weak woman," I repeated.

"You are certainly a very tiny one," he smiled.

"And strong," I said. "Strong!"

He looked down at me quizzically. "But not poor," he said. "Poverty has a way of killing women early."

In July I went to Columbia, Missouri, to visit my uncle Judge David Todd and my dear cousin, his daughter Ann. Merce was in Baltimore, and we kept in touch by the post. I had only told her about my beloved. I did not want anyone else to know. She shared with me her growing love for James Conkling, but that did not have to be kept secret, for he was wealthy. My first *preserved* letter is the one I wrote to Merce from Columbia on July 23, 1840. In my letters I did not bother too much with periods, and leaned instead toward commas by the dozen and plenty of dashes. I never learned to spell *pilgrimage* and *villainous,* and probably more words. I did not mention Tom's son by name, for who knows who might share a letter? He had visited me earlier in Columbia and on a Sunday, we had gone to church together. He was in Missouri to make a Whig speech at Rochester, but as I recall, he never made it to Rochester at all. In my letter I spoke of the social whirl I was in, an excursion to Booneville on the river, (a lovely, lovely place) attending four parties there, dancing until almost three in the morning in the *festive halls of mirth*, dancing the gay and old Virginia reels - and how exhausting it was to keep pace with the music! And so many "beaux" were dancing attendance on us. I was referring to my beloved when I wrote of my *life* to come, "I fancy it is to be a *quiet* lot." I would be sharing his struggles to pay back his debt and make a living as a young lawyer and a member of the state legislature. But, I wrote, "happy indeed I will be, if it is, only cast near those I so *dearly* love ..." Then I *indirectly* told Merce that I had been receiving letters from my beloved.

"When I mention *some letters*, I have received since leaving S- you will be somewhat surprised, as I *must confess* they were entirely *unlooked* for - this is *between ourselves*, my dearest, but more of this anon." And then I mused on those who come and go in a life, and wrote, "to me, it has ever appeared that those whose presence was the sunlight of my heart have departed - separated far and wide to meet - when?" I noted the men courting me, one "An agreeable lawyer and grandson of *Patrick Henry - what an honor!* Shall never survive it - I wish you could see him, the most perfect original I had ever met, my beaux have always been *hard bargains* at any rate, Uncle and others think he surpasses his *noble ancestor* in *talents*, yet Merce, I love him not, & my hand will never be given where my heart is not -"

Those that are the sunlight of my heart - depart. How strange that I wrote that - then. How bitterly true those words were to become.

I did not write Merce again until the middle of December. I apologized and I trusted our "future correspondence may be more punctual." I wanted to spend all of my time with my beloved, I did *not* note in a letter, but I would have in person. I made the excuse that I did not write for so long as I was doing "sewing necessary for winter comfort." I noted that Ninian's cousin, Matilda Edwards, had joined the household, "a lovelier girl I never saw." Mr. Edwin Webb who "dances attendance very frequently," was still courting me. I wished that Merce and I could live next door to each other again, "that our hearts will acknowledge the same kindred ties," and noted in a *clue*, that I was still seeing my beloved. I then gave a list of all our single friends who had married, Harriet Huntingdon to James Campbell (I attended this wedding as did James Conkling) and that she seemed to be "enjoying all the *sweets* of married life." Mary Lamb was about to marry Joseph Bouman on the twenty- first and I wrote, "I am pleased she is about to commit the *crime* of matrimony." Merce knew how my beloved was disdained in the Edwards' mansion, and my desire to marry him was the *crime* of the century. I asked, "Why is it that married folks always become so serious?" referring to Lizzie. I went on, "This fall I became quite a *politician*, rather an unladylike profession - but the crisis warranted it." I noted how we had loved to walk along the town stream which we called the *Lionel*, how "the icy hand of winter has set its seal upon the waters," and to Jacksonville "a pleasant jaunt" was contemplated, as was a nine person sleigh ride, including my beloved. "We are watching the clouds most anxiously trusting it may snow - Will it not be most pleasant?" Our State House was near completion, enough so that the Legislature could meet within it; The Second Church had another bell; Lizzy had been ill with a cold, but "I am the same ruddy *pine knot*," although, "the weather is miserably cold." I signed off, "ever your attached friend."

The weather *was* miserably cold, and it did snow for our sleigh ride. Now, my beloved and I were on a sleigh ride of our own.

A wind was ruffling through the trees. I loved the sound of it, the feel of it, the *energy*. My beloved had said little. He looked sober - really grim, and above all, *miserable*. I felt an ominous chill, as if this winter had just fallen from a summer sky, and I was not prepared for it. The ice particles in the air went through my furs and chilled my heart. There was something wrong - terribly, terribly *wrong*. He looked defeated, in the deepest despair, and I had never seen him look like this before. I shuddered. "Molly, are you cold?" he asked, and took my gloved hand in his. He never wore gloves; I had never seen him wear gloves. "Aren't *you* cold?" I asked. "Your hands must be. Why don't you wear gloves?"

"I don't have any, and I don't like them. I guess my hands are too large for gloves, anyway."

Soft snow flurries rustled down from the trees around us. He fell silent, clicking the horse on, staring moodily at the road ahead. And talk was *always* eager and easy between us. "What is it?" I asked finally.

"I am not doing right by you."

"What are you talking about?" As if I did not know.

"I have done wrong asking you to marry me."

Ninian. "You have been talking to Ninian," I said. I was in total panic. Ninian would wear him down, Ninian, with the diamonds on his wristwatch, his custom made suits - his air, as if he were always within his magnificent mansion -or more realistically - as if the world outside were but an extension of it.

"Molly, I can figure this for myself," he said shortly. He had never been short with me before.

"But Ninian *did* talk to you."

"In his office. Yes."

"And he told you that I could *not* be poor. And you would cause me to die from poverty - or wish I were dead from it - this being poor for the first time in my life -"

"Yes."

"And you believe that?"

"Yes." Tears were suddenly in his eyes, and he made no attempt to stop them, or even to wipe them away.

"You set me up too high," I said. "And you must *never* let Ninian speak for *me*."

"Molly," he said gruffly. "I would give away my very life before I would bring any suffering into yours."

His voice always deepened when he was emotional. And I had learned his emotions could move him to tears, and he *never* would try to hide them. "My real suffering would be in not being with you," I said, "in *my* not spending the rest of my life with *you.*"

"You have never been poor, Molly. You could never stay poor. It would kill you. I saw poverty kill my mother and my sister, and I could not live through it killing you. Ninian is right."

"You cannot let *Ninian - or Lizzie -* decide what is good for *me - for us!*" I was terrified - then angry, and my voice showed it.

"I always make my own decisions," he said curtly, and he had never been curt with me before, either.

"Why would you even *listen* to Ninian? Speak to him?"

"He is your guardian when you are away from your father."

"You know he and Lizzie are determined to break us up! They will do anything, short of murdering both of us, to do it!"

He looked forlorn, *and* he looked *indomitable.* "Molly, you have always been wealthy. Your family is wealthy. You do not know what *not* having wealth is. And women who are poor -"

They die young, at twenty one, in the first child birth, or at thirty four from being worn and tired - "Is Ninian making you believe that I can only live in a mansion filled with servants, and wear the latest fashion in clothes - French embroidered swiss and muslims from New Orleans? Silks and satins from the pages of *Godey's Ladies Book?*"

"That is what you wear now. And shoes to match each gown."

"And Ninian makes you feel - inferior -"

"I know what Ninian thinks of me," he said quietly. "And I think *all of the time* - of what you are used to having. Ninian makes good sense -"

"*He* makes sense. I don't?" Tears were rushing into my own eyes. He stopped the horse, and there we were, alone in the night, with the lonely, *lonely* wind, the lamenting, *sorrowing* wind that had lost all of its charm. And the snow gleamed into moonlight as blanched as blanched lives finally given away to bone. If there had been a moon it had set, and would not rise in its own sweet grace for me again. *I will not change him,* I thought. How terrible is this night, and how filled with desolation I am!

"Molly, love is shown in cherishing and protecting the loved one. A man, who is not a cad, will not hurt any woman, and especially, not the woman he loves." His voice was so deep I could hardly hear it. And his tears still came, and were still not brushed away.

"How have things changed?" I cried. "Are you any more poor? *Am I any richer?*"

"Maybe you are," he said, and he clicked the horse on, and he said no more to me that night. He took me to the door, and he did not touch me, and he hardly looked down at me. It was nearing end of 1840, our *own* magical year, and I thought Ninian has reached him and has taken all of the magic right out of my life.

January 1, 1841, turned into a *terrible* New Years Day. Lizzie had a huge family gathering - seven guests I think - Judge *John* Todd, or was it Judge *David* Todd and his dear daughter, Ann? Or was it my cousin Stephen Logan, and was the witty and handsome James Shields, who was supposed to be a beau - also present? I don't know, because I do not remember. I do remember a dread growing and growing inside of me as we ate the perfect food served perfectly in the newly done, in Victorian furniture, dining room. "Molly," asked Ninian, "why are you so quiet?"

"Molly," asked Lizzie. "Are you ill? Did you catch my dreadful cold?"

"I am fine," I murmured, not being so at all.

I knew that I was going to hear something I could not bear. That evening, when my love finally entered the front door, he did not bend down for me to kiss his face. In our private little room before its fire, he kept himself distant from me, even gently withdrawing when I went to cover his face with kisses. He even got up from his chair and moved away from me. "Molly," he said hoarsely, "We cannot get married." When I looked up at him, so hurt I could hardly breathe, I saw in his eyes the extent of human pain. I sat down, for my legs would not hold me up. "Say that again," I whispered, for surely those words could never have been uttered between *us*. "*You* do not want to marry *me*," I said, finally.

He groaned, and tears flooded his eyes, and again, he made no attempt to brush them away. "Molly," he said, his voice shaking, "I *am* poor white trash. I have no money and I owe close to eight hundred dollars. Ahead of me is a life of grim poverty. I have no way to buy us a home. I have no way to buy us a carriage. I cannot make you share this -"

"What I *want* is to share your *life!*"

"I cannot let you do it. I will not let you do it." His facial expression said it all. "Ninian is right. I *did* fall in love with the wrong girl," he said, "and I love her too much to just satisfy myself."

I burst into sobs. "How little you must think of me to believe you would only be satisfying *yourself!*"

"Molly, don't cry," he said in anguish. "I cannot bear to see you cry!" He lifted me from the chair and held me on his lap, stroking the disheveled hair from my tear-streaked face, and he kissed the side of my lips, and I felt his tears mingle with my own. "Dearest Molly," he said, "You love me, but you *live here,* in the most elaborate home in Springfield. You travel in the finest carriage; you wear the finest clothes, and you always have. Your *coterie* - the dances you love so much - all of the brilliant parties - I fell in love with the wrong girl, as Ninian so rightfully pointed out."

My grief turned to rage. I got away from him, and paced like a cat before the fire. "You let Ninian decide what is good for me! Ninian - the *snob!*"

"I told you, I make my own decisions." That iron expression was back on his face - that look of - *you will not change me on this* - "I have decided this for myself," he said. "It was hard, and I should never have started courting you, but I will not see you destroyed in a marriage to me. I cannot. I *will* not."

I stopped my pacing and looked at him, at all of his suffering, and I thought, he loves me enough for me to change all of this around! I *could* change this all around! I *could!* I ran to him and I covered his lips and his face with kisses, but the fire that was always in his response was gone. He had shut a door between us. I finally moved away from him and sat in a chair alone, shivering before the fire, for its warmth was gone, as was looking upon all my tomorrows with joy.

Desolation darkened his face. "Molly, I am a poor nobody and will always be."

"You *cannot* believe that!"

He started to leave. "I reckon - that for now, it seems so."

"You are not being *kind* to me. You are being *cruel.*"

"Molly, you are the only woman I have ever loved. I will always love you. I will always remember this year, the way we shared it - *always.* It has become a part of my heart." His voice broke.

I got up, too, and stood as high as I could, which was not very high at all, being five foot two inches to his six foot four inches. "You are being *very* cruel to me," I repeated.

Tears remained unchecked in his eyes. "You will thank me for this."

"I will *never, never* love another man," I said. "Never, never, *never!*"

He bent and kissed my forehead, ever so gently. "Molly, you will. You will choose a fine young man who can give you what you have always had and deserve."

"And what is that?"

"A *safe* life," he said. "At least, a secure roof over your head, your own home, carriages, fine clothes - all that you have taken for granted and should never lose."

The clock began to strike its musical tune, and the villagers were beginning to leave the church, *couple* by *couple.*

"Those things *are* important to you, Molly," he said softly. "I will say that you broke the engagement. It will be in the papers that you broke the engagement necessary," I replied. "I do not see it as broken."

"Good-by, Molly," he said, and left the room, the house, me. The last thing I saw of him was the grim determination on his lips and the tears that were still in his eyes.

The clock was winding down the hour, and the villagers were going back inside of the church. "Don't you fools get tired of going around in circles?" I asked aloud, as if they could hear, and if they could, they would.

Chapter Six

And so we moved apart in our lives. I want it clearly understood that Ninian did persuade my love he was not good enough for me, and his son, Albert Edwards said the Edwards broke our engagement, as, *also,* did recall Mrs. John Todd Stuart. There is the vicious tale told by the odious little man that said there was to be a great wedding that day, wedding cake and all of the proper upper crust present, of course, and I was waiting in bridal white and my love came to run away from the wedding. How stupid. *How stupid!* Only a cad would do such a thing, and my love was never in his life, and in any shape or form, a cad. Then there is the error that I was in a fury and stamped my feet, or foot, I guess - or both - one at a time, of course, and said - "I never want to see that detestable face again!" *How stupid!* And then there is another story, equally as untrue, that my love was late to pick me up for a dance and I went to it alone (imagine - so *improper!*) and flirted so with Douglass, that when my love arrived, wearing a *satin* vest, he was so jealous that I flirted so, he broke the engagement. It was as I have said, and I never stopped loving him for one minute because, for a short while, my love had lost faith in himself and thought he would be poor all of his life. Or that *he* could ever be a nobody! I did not go giddy and flirt all over the place with another man. And when I heard how our break up had gravely broken his health, I shed many a quiet tear - over all I had so richly had and all that he had taken away - or had *allowed* taken away.

I would not go out to be courted by another man. The *coterie* seemed vacuous and silly, and if I danced to be polite and hospitable, the music had no charm. I do not know if I even heard it. I just twirled around like a wound up toy doll, dress stylish, hair in perfect curls and eyes that were as bright as my merry facade. *I wasn't there among those things.* I was still in the small back parlor, with *him,* listening to him read, with his long legs stretched toward the fire, his head braced against the bottom of the sofa, near my lap. "I always like to read lying on the floor before a fire," he said, and I could see him as a boy doing this, in a one -room cabin that had no other light, and probably no sofa. I explored again all of the ideas and the abstractions we had loved to explore together. This seemed to keep him close to me when he was not.

Stephen A Douglass (he dropped the last s later) and Mr. Edwin Webb continued to call. Handsome men of good breeding and money called, and left, for I went nowhere with them, any more than they went anywhere with me.

"Molly, all of your friends are married with at least *two* children," said Lizzie impatiently. "What is the *matter* with you?"

"I am waiting for the President of the United States to ask me to marry him," I replied.

On January 13, the town gossip was that my beloved was very ill, that he was filled with a deep *spiritual* and *physical* melancholia. He did not attend the legislature for the first time since he was elected. I heard Mr. Edwards tell Mrs. Edwards that my beloved was *in a bad way.* "He is as crazy as a loon," Ninian said. "He has gone as *crazy as a loon!*"

"As long as he keeps his *promise*," Mrs. Edwards whispered. But I heard her. She then looked at me and said, "*He*, at least, has the sense to know he fell in love with the wrong girl!" Where had I heard *that* before?

I thought, she is not my sister. She is not my friend.

I never forgave Mr. and Mrs. Edwards for this.

From January thirteenth- to January twenty first, 1841, I heard that he was too ill with the flu, or depression, or both, to attend the legislature, except for one day, the nineteenth. The town gossip was that he was close to dying. He lost weight. He took little food and could not sleep. "*Crazy as a loon!*" Ninian kept repeating, rather joyfully. On January 20 my beloved wrote my favorite cousin, John Todd Stuart, saying he wanted Dr. Anson Henry to have the postmaster-ship to keep him in town. "I have, within the last few days," he wrote, "been making a most discreditable exhibition of myself in the way of hypochondrianism and thereby got an impression that Dr. Henry is necessary to my existence." He closed poignantly in a bursting of pain, "Pardon me for not writing more; I have not sufficient composure to write a long letter." He wrote my cousin again on January 23, and that letter reveals more suffering. I am quoting lines from it, the ones I was shown that tore at my heart. "Yours of the 3rd. Inst. is recd. & I proceed to answer it as well as I can, tho' from the deplorable state of my mind at this time, I fear that I will give you little satisfaction. (The matter was an act fixing the manner of Congressional elections) His conclusion was: "For not giving you a general summary of the news, you must pardon me; it is not in my power to do so. I am now the most miserable man living. If what I feel were equally distributed to the whole human family, there would not be one cheerful face on the earth. Whether I shall be better I cannot tell; I awfully forebode I shall not. To remain as I am is impossible; I must die or be better, it appears to me . . . I fear I shall be unable to attend to any business here, and a change of scene might help me. If I could be myself I would rather remain at home with Judge Logan. I can write no more."

In 1841 Joshua Speed left Springfield and seemed to have fallen in love, after at least twenty women thinking they were the one he would marry. Tom's son wrote to him about the sacredness of love between a man and a woman, but apparently, as far as I was concerned, Tom's son still believed he had fallen in love with the *wrong* girl.

I knew *my* suffering because of it, and I well knew his, and so did his friends. Mr. Conkling wrote about our break up to Merce, who was visiting in Columbus, Missouri. "How the mighty have fallen!" he wrote of Tom's son. "He was confined for a week, but though now he appears again, he is reduced and emaciated in appearance and seems scarcely to possess strength enough to speak above a whisper. His case at present is truly deplorable, but what prospect there may be for ultimate relief, I cannot pretend to say."

I have deep valleys of depression. When my heart loses a loved one, my body cannot bear it - How had he said it?

On March 7, 1841, Mr. James Conkling and Merce announced their engagement, and Mr. Conkling wrote to her again of Tom's son, "Poor helpless simple swain who loved most true, but was not loved again. I suppose he will now endeavor to draw his cares among the intricacies and perplexities of the law. No more will the merry peal of laughter ascend high in the air to greet his listening and delighted ears . . ."

How I missed Merce when she left Springfield, but I could not write, as I should have. My spirits were too low. I was too depressed to take pen to paper. I took long afternoon naps, and before my unquiet sleep, then or at night, *his* beloved face was before me, and when I would cover it with kisses again, it vanished, and I would awaken to desolation, and bitterly know that from my life he was gone. Finally, in June, I did write to Merce, now so happily about to marry, while I never would. I told her that I would have written sooner, but my letter would only be flat, stale and unprofitable, "the past two or three months have been of *interminable* length." I wrote I had "lingering regrets over the past, which time alone can overshadow with its healing balm, thus my springtime has passed and summer in all of its beauty has again come, the prairie looks as beautiful as it did in the olden time, when we strolled together & derived so much happiness from each other's society - this is past and more than this." I wrote that I had heard from Joshua Speed, and "*His* worthy friend, deems me unworthy of notice, as I have not met *him* in the gay world for months. With the usual comfort of misery, imagine that others were as seldom gladdened by his presence as my humble self, yet I would that the case were different, that he would once more resume his station in Society, that *Richard* (I called Tom's son this to Merce) should be himself again, much, much happiness would it afford me..." I wrote that Stephen A. Douglas "talented and agreeable, sometimes countenances me." Of Mr. Edwin Webb I wrote, "...in your friendly and confiding ear allow me to whisper that my *heart can never be his*, I have deeply *regretted that his constant visits, attentions* & I should have given room for remarks, which to me were unpleasant, there being a slight difference of eighteen or twenty summers in our years..." Merce knew my heart belonged to "Richard." If Mr. Webb were my age, it would not have mattered. Even if he did have more money than Ninian!

I could not have described how totally miserable I felt, how terribly, terribly lonely I was with the Edwards' rooms overflowing with the cream of Springfield society. Life seemed to move vigorously and happily on, in the vibrancy that was Springfield itself, but not for me. The fall of night was dreaded; the next day's dawning, tolerated.

On March first, 1841, Tom's son had left John Todd Stuart to form a law partnership with Judge Stephen T. Logan. I guess he wanted nothing to do with the name Todd, with two d's. I heard that in August he went to Lexington to visit Joshua Speed, and met the girl Mr. Speed had decided to marry. Her name was Fanny Henning, and when Mr. Speed expressed written doubts to Tom's son that he had somehow *reasoned* himself into a marriage proposal, Tom's son replied, "Was it not, that you found yourself unable to *reason* yourself *out* of it? . . . Were not those heavenly *black* eyes, the whole basis of all your early *reasoning* on the subject?" Miss Henning and Speed were married on February 15, 1842, and theirs was to prove a happy marriage. Tom's son wrote them a letter of congratulation on March 27, and in it said that he, too, could be happy were it not for the "never absent idea, that there is *one* still unhappy who I have contributed to make so. That still kills my soul. I can not but reproach myself, for even wishing to be happy while she is otherwise -" But he had written the previous February 25, "I tell you, Speed, our foreboding (about happy marriages) for which you and I are rather peculiar, are the worst sort of nonsense." My *Richard w*as being rescued from his morbid self-doubts of being worthy of me.

He wanted to visit Speed in Kentucky again but wrote him a letter instead on July 4, 1842. He did not have the money for traveling. "I am so poor," he wrote, "and make so little headway in the world, that I drop in a month of idleness, as much as I gain in a year's rowing."

But he did not want to leave Springfield, and neither did I. We had our reasons for not wanting to leave Springfield.

Each other.

For eighteen months we were apart. Dr. Anson Henry was my physician, and he was the physician of Tom's son, and he saw what our broken engagement was doing to both of us. We also had as close friends the editor of the *Sangamo Journal,* Simeon Francis and his wife, and they were seeing the same thing. "What are we going to do about their misery?" they asked each other.

"Why don't I give a party for them?" asked the doctor.

"At our house," said Mr. and Mrs. Francis.

"But we must *not* let them know it is to get them together," said Mrs. Francis.

"I will invite each separately," said the doctor. "I promise, it will be a complete surprise to both of them!"

And it was. I was in the glooms. Winter was gone; the prairie was blooming its lilac summer skies, but in my loss, summer had not come at all. Lizzy was going religious where she was beginning to think dancing as a sin, parties the same, and in the great house no more music was played, for that was approaching sin, too. "A party?" I asked the doctor when he came to see me.

"A dinner," he replied.

"I don't think I want to go out at night -"

"You have a strong family carriage to get you through it," the doctor teased. "We will all be very disappointed if you do not accept."

I smiled. "All right. And I will be light hearted and - happy."

"That is the idea," the doctor said. "That is the idea," he repeated, smiling to himself.

I had arrived and was in the entrance hall when Tom's son was shown in the door. He looked at me and into his face came *life,* for it was so - *distant -* from it before. "Molly!" he said, almost breathlessly, if that can be so over one word. "Molly!" he repeated, and he opened his arms to me, and in a second I was within them. I think our host and hostess and the good doctor actually clapped and laughed in joy, in a very un-Victorian way. He continued to hold me, and I knew that he would never let me go again.

"We *thought* you two would still be friends," said the doctor dryly.

This time our engagement was *not* shared with Lizzie and her husband, and we met in the Francis home, and our trysts were kept *totally* secret. *Private things should remain private, anyway.*

During our renewed courtship, occurred the *James Shields* affair. There is a dreadful story about the whole thing, and I must correct it. Mr. Shields was a member of our *coterie,* and for a while he was even courting me. I always thought him rather pompous and unappealing in spite of his Irish good looks. He was a Democrat, and my beloved was his Whig political adversary. Tom's son had told me of Shields that he was so conceited he was the only man in the world who could strut sitting down. He wrote a teasing letter about James Shields to the *Sangamo Journal,* from a "Rebecca" to "Dear Mr. Printer," dated August 27, and it was published. "Rebecca" lived in the backwoods of *Lost Townships,* and she is a nosey old lady who goes about finding out any business but her own. She talks to a backwoodsman named Jeff who says, " 'Why, I'm mad *as the devil,* Aunt Becca!' " Aunt Becca wonders if his new baby had been born with the wrong features. " 'What about,' says I, 'ain't its hair the right color? Now none of that nonsense, Jeff - there ain't a honester woman in the Lost Townships than -'

'Than who?' says he. 'What the mischief are you about?'

I began to see I was running the wrong trail, and so says, 'Well, then, what *are* you mad about?'

'O nothing, I guess,' says Jeff."

He then takes the Whig position against the Democrats on state taxes and state bank paper, castigating Shields by saying, " 'far as getting a good bright passable out of him, you might as well strike fire from a cake of tallows. I seed him when I was down at Springfield last winter. They had a sort of gathering there one night, among the grandees, they called a fair. All of the galls about town were there, and all of the handsome widows, and married women, finicken about trying to look like galls, tied as tight in the middle, and puffed out at both ends, like bundles of fodder that hadn't been stacked yet, but wanted stack'en pretty bad. " 'Shields dashes from one lady to another,' and on his features could be read his thoughts: dear girls, *it is distressing,* but I cannot marry you all. Too well I know how you suffer, but do remember, it is not *my* fault that I am *so handsome* and *so* interesting."

Tom's son wrote *only* this third Rebecca letter about Mr. Shields, which was published on September 9, 1842. I wrote the fourth letter myself with the help of my friend, Julia Jayne. We did ridicule Shields, but admitted he was "rather good looking than otherwise." *We* became the widow Rebecca, and now *our* Rebecca decided to marry Shields! "And I don't think" our Rebecca says, "upon the whole, that I'd be sech a bad match neither - I'm not over sixty and I'm not much over four feet three in my bare feet, and not much more around the girth...isn't marrying better than fight'in, though it does sometimes run into it?"

Then I had Becky and Shields married in my poem that was published

September 16:

> *The combat's relinquished, old love's all forgot,*
> *To the widow he's bound, oh! bright be his lot!*
> The footsteps of time tread lightly on flowers-
> *May the cares of this world ne'er darken their hours.*

Mr. Shields did not like my poem at all. He rushed to the paper and demanded of Simeon the author's name, and as he was bound to find it, Tom's son said *he* was the author. Then he forgot all about the incident and went off on the circuit court. Mr. Shields did not forget. On September 17 he wrote to Tom's son that he had been "the object of slander, vituperation and personal abuse," that the *Rebecca Letters* had degraded him, and he and his friend, General John Whiteside, rushed to Tom's son in Tremont to get personal satisfaction. Whiteside went to challenge Tom's son as Shields' second.

Here is how the vulgar version goes: "A duel?" asked Tom's son. Why would I be dumb enough to fight a duel?"

"Then, Sir," said Whiteside. "You have no honor!"

"Why is that?"

"Because, Sir, you are a coward!"

"Why is that?"

"Because you will not face Mr. Shields in a duel for slandering his good name."

"He is hell bent on this thing - this *duel* thing?"

"Absolutely!"

"Well, as I am the challenged, the challenger has to use the weapons of choice."

"Indeed."

"I choose the weapons."

"I said that. You said that. What is your choice of weapons, and Mr. Shields will be happy to oblige."

Tom's son shifted his feet on top of his desk, and the feet on the desk part is probably true. If he were sitting at a desk, his feet would be on top of it, and he *is said* to have said, "Tell Mr. Shields that for weapons I choose cow dung at ten paces."

That is absolutely untrue. For weapons he chose *broadswords*, and with his long arms Mr. Shields would not have come close to him, and so he decided that his honor could live on without a duel with Tom's son. The seconds got so mad at each other they challenged each other to a duel – which they didn't fight either.

We planned to be married on Christmas Day, and as we talked before the parlor grate at the Francis' home we could not have been happier. The cozy crackling and popping sounds of the fire - the sound of the wind swooshing the rain against the windows, the showering of sparks against the fire screen - and here we were - warm and safe inside, in love and with each other. I knew it would be *forever.* I thought there was more joy in me than the world could contain.

"I love you, love you, love you," I said, "and I loved you before we were even born!"

"Where?" he smiled.

"In Eden. When we walked with God."

"We did that, too?" he asked, but not as a question.

"*You* said it. Our love is eternal; it always was and always will be. How *did* you say it?"

"We can march our bodies off to dust, and comets may fall and stars may be formed and they may vanish, but love is eternal," he said softly.

"It is as if we can *always* touch the face of God, but still look for him somewhere else -"

"What is created would bear the energy of the Creator," he said. "I am not comfortable with organized religion. As an *individual,* I love to study the Bible. The symbols in it stretch beyond mere words -"

We were silent. We were companionably, *joyously* silent. "Two fold silence is the song of love," I said. That was from a poem, or should have been.

The fire was almost gone before he replenished it.

"Let's not wait for Christmas, " I said. "Let's get married right away!"

"When?"

"Tomorrow!"

"Tomorrow?"

"Or the day after. Oh - just - *soon.*"

He sat by me again, kissed the side of my face, and caressed some curls away from my cheek. "I will have to tell Ninian."

"No! *No!* He will find some way to stop our marriage! As he did before!"

"No, Molly," he said. "I heard what he told me, but I thought it all out *for myself.*"

"But now we are to marry."

"Yes. I hurt you more by breaking our engagement, and I realize it now. I was a fool. And I hurt myself more than I did you, for being such a fool." He still touched the curls. "You should have a fine wedding, with a house full of lights and fires and all of your friends." He kissed me, and he held me, as I held him. "You will be such a beautiful bride," he said. "How could you marry an ugly nobody like me?"

I touched his face, caressed it near those beautiful, beautiful eyes, and then kissed the gentle lips, and I said, "You are the handsomest man in the world."

He sighed. "And how is that?"

"Because you are the most glorious man in the world."

He smiled. "I heard I was ugly even as a baby. Aren't all babies supposed to be beautiful?"

"They are," I said. "And ours will be."

A shadow crossed his face. Never could a face reveal changing thoughts as his did. " Molly, I have an absolute horror of childbirth for you. My sister died in childbirth," he said, "and so did your mother."

"Yes."

"It seems so grotesque that if a man loves a woman with all of his heart and shows it to her in a physical way, that it could cause her to die." His eyes became wet. "I could not lose you Molly," he said.

"Nor I you," I replied.

"I am ten years older than you. You probably will."

"I won't live beyond you," I said. "I positively *will not allow it!*"

"But Molly, love is eternal."

And that is what he did have engraved inside of my wedding ring.

We had planned a simple wedding at the home of Dr. Charles Dresser of the Episcopal Ministry. Tom's son stopped by his home on Eighth Street, the home we would later purchase and live in for seventeen years, and he said, "Miss Todd and I would like you to marry us tonight." The family was at breakfast, and they were overjoyed. "I thought that is why you seemed so happy," said the Reverend. "I could not be happier for you both."

Tom's son met him and told him we were to be married that night, and Mr. Edwards gave his consent as my guardian. He accepted what was to be - as a killer toothache that will come along, but Lizzie was not as stoic.I went into to Lizzie's room to tell her, for I certainly did owe that to her, and another sister, Frances Todd Wallace, was there, too, and then Ninian, and I had three thunderclouds bursting over me all at once. "*You are a Todd!*" screamed Lizzie. To get away I rushed to the home of my cousin, Elizabeth Todd, and asked her to be my bridesmaid.

"Molly, I have nothing to wear!" she lamented.

"You have a beautiful white dress of your own - have it pressed and wear it."

"All right. I can do that. I *want* to do that!" And then we hugged and kissed, and some of my own joy shone on her face.

I returned to the Edwards' battlefield, where Lizzie held up the white flag of surrender, and said she would be disgraced in all of the high society of Springfield if her sister married in a minister's home and not in the Ninian Edwards' home.

I rushed to my beloved's office. "Lizzy wants us to marry in her home," I said.

"She has hated me since I asked for your hand in marriage."

"You don't want to marry me there?" I asked.

"Miss Todd, I will marry you anywhere."

"In Ninian's house, right through the gates of *hell?*" I jested, but was anxious for us to marry where he wanted to.

"Through the gates of hell. Do *you* want to be married at Ninian's?"

"Yes. I think it would hurt Lizzy dreadfully if we did not. "

"All right, Molly."

"Ninian is not so bad -"

"About me - he *is* that bad."

"We are just marrying there - not staying there -"

"Molly, it is *all right.*"

I left his office and rushed home to get ready for the happiest night of my life.

My three bridesmaids were Miss Julia Jayne, Miss Rodney and my cousin, Miss Elizabeth Todd. For our marriage, Tom's son and I would be allowed, together, and *at last,* in the elegant Edwards' front parlor, and a blazing fire was set there and the room made cozy with many lighted lamps. I found a lovely white hand-embroidered muslin dress to wear. Lizzie was lamenting it was too late to have the cooks bake a wedding cake, and she sent for one from the only bakery in town, but it now had only cheap ginger cakes. "Why, that will do," I said sarcastically to Lizzie. "Ginger cakes will do fine for us *plebeians!*" But Lizzie set her cooks to baking a huge wedding cake, and when it was served it was still warm, and its caramel frosting was melting down its sides.

Tom's son was boarding at the home of his good friend William Butler, and when he told them he was going to get married that night, the children began to tease, and Mrs. Butler decided to help him get dressed properly for his marriage. She saw that his thick black hair was tamed as best as she could tame it, brushed down his suit, and tied his necktie for him. When he left the house a child called after him, giggling, "Where are you going?"

"To the devil!"

"Where is he?" asked the child.

"Behind the gates of hell, of course," replied Tom's son. *In jest. In reference to Ninian's opposition to him as a member of his family* - stating the fact he had *never been received* in that house as a possible member of the family.

Of course this was half remembered and used against me. The odious little man used it - Tom's son did not want to marry me but only did so because I expected it, *(no one* could *ever* make him do what he chose not to do) and I married him because I wanted *revenge!* This is because, according to lying Billy, on January 1, 1841, there was to have been that *huge society* wedding, and when it was time for me to march down the aisle, the groom ran away! Perhaps, back to the grave of Ann Rutledge.

I must add that whenever she is described, she is given *auburn* hair and deep *blue* eyes - I fill in for looks, and she fills in for my beloved's love interest - if you believe that odious - *evil* - noxious little man.

I hadn't noticed the lowing sky that day, but that night, as the thirty guests gathered in the Edwards' formal front parlor, it began to rain. I saw that Lizzie had had set a beautiful table, with a linen cloth of turtle dove design, using the best of her china and silver, for after all, I was still a Todd. For a while. I think she had even found flowers to place among her new *modern* Victorian furniture. It was November 4, 1842. I was almost twenty- four and Tom's son was thirty- three. How gravely happy he looked. And yet, in a way, he looked boyish, too, when I entered the room in my white wedding gown. He looked as if he was awakening from a wondrous dream and found himself still within it.

We were to be married before the fireplace. Wordlessly, we took our positions. No one stood up for us. The Reverend Dr. Charles Dresser wore his clerical robes, and as he commenced the marriage ceremony, I was aware of *each word* in a room reverently hushed except for the sounds of the fire and the rain striking hard at the windows.

My friends were all long married and on their third childbirth, but here, being married to my beloved, I had chosen the right man in this time, this perfect, *perfect* time. The wedding vows did go on and on with all of the legalities involved until our guest, old Judge Brown, impatiently burst out, "Lord *Jesus Christ* and *God Almighty,* the Statutes of Illinois fix all of that!" There was laughter, the most from Tom's son, and then Dr. Charles Dresser pronounced us man and wife. My husband bent and kissed me, and then I cut the wedding cake, and we all had cake and coffee. I was so excited; I spilled my coffee down the bodice of my beautiful white gown. We quickly took our leave, and outside my husband had a carriage waiting for us. He all but put me into it, and I thought of that other time when he had as gently placed me into another carriage. The wind had grown fierce, and through a blinding storm we were driven to the Globe Tavern at the bottom of the Edwards' aristocracy hill. There we both would room and board for four dollars a week.

The Globe Tavern was a two - storied hotel, of the old frontier type, and all night long, when new carriages arrived, the clerk rang the bell on the roof for the stableman to come and get the horses. It was not too conducive to sleep, but neither is a honeymoon.

I was not shy with my husband, embarrassed in any way at intimacy. There was no consideration between us that a man and woman in love married into *any* kind of shame. It was nothing but the most *natural* feeling in the world between us - the yearning for union, and its fulfillment. *Possession* is mutual *giving*. Possession is a bond - as light as diamond lights sparkling on water, and as strong as the sun that creates them.

How marvelous it was to hear his quiet breathing next to me as he slept, to finally sink into sweet sleep myself, and to awaken to the sounds of the outside - wind rushing the rain against the windows - and within - with him - warm, *safe*. Tender lover. Tender, beloved husband. We had captured time and held it stilled. I could not have described my rapture. Perhaps, that is thought to be only for God, but when we love, I think we join the rapture of our love for God.

Our love, our sensual attraction to one another lasted all of our marriage. I never was to find my husband anything but a *romantic, sentimental* lover, steadfast friend, and a fascinating and affectionate companion. He always made me feel that I was the most beautiful and desirable woman who had ever walked the face of the earth. Of course I was not as brilliant as my husband - how did my little sister, Emilie Todd, put it? "Molly found a young man with a mentality dominating her own, yet in accord with her own." I wrote to Merce what this new bride thought of *him*, "My husband's heart is as big as his arms are long, and there is a kind of poetry in his soul." I said this many times, and I wrote this many times.

On November 11, my husband wrote to Samuel D. Marshall, "Nothing new here except my marrying, which to me, is a matter of profound wonder."

On February 25 of this year, 1842, he had written to Joshua Speed about *his* new wife. "You owe obligations to her ten thousand times more sacred than any you can owe to others." How true he saw this to be with us. When I married Tom's son, in no way did I become poor, and *in all ways*, I became the richest and most blessed of women.

Chapter Seven

Springfield had no streetlights, mud so thick and deep it would stop a carriage, but the rain could pour, and the wind could send ice sleeting across the prairie, and we were aware of neither. In our new life together at the Globe Tavern, it was always spring and the moon was always a full moon. Together we had made our first *home* right in our rented rooms at the Globe. He told me home was where I was, and I told him that home was wherever he would return to me. I loved to talk with him about his day, about what was new in politics, about a new poem I had discovered, or new lines in Shakespeare I found that delighted both of us. When he was impressed with a poem he learned it, it seemed to me, while he was reading it!

We loved; we talked over our dreams before sweet sleep, dreams of a future together that all young lovers have and will always have. Sharing the ending of a day with him made the night glorious, and night was dark and had always frightened me. I used to see death in darkness, and I remembered the still face of my mother, frozen in death downstairs in her own eternal silence now, and not hearing me cry for her, or kissing my tears away. *Mama, how can you be so cruel? Don't you care for* me *anymore? Don't you care that I am terrified at the ticking of the clock – shadows in every corner of the room?*

Childhood haunts us all. But now with him, I was safe. I was centered in strength he always gave to me. How glorious it continued to be to hear his breathing next to me, to feel his warmth close to me through all the long night, to know he accepted me for what I was, and loved what I was without any conditions imposed whatsoever. Dearest lover, dearest man, dearest friend, love's enchantment was never lost to either of us in the twenty-three years of our marriage.

I am so thankful for that.

I became pregnant right away. He treated me as if I were walking on eggs; he all but cared for me as if I were a child wife. "Molly, be *careful*," he said when he went to the office. "Molly, be *careful*," he said, if I tried to lift anything, or move anything. I told him how strong I was, but I loved the pampering. I gloried in his worry for me. I gloried in it, and in many ways, I was a child wife. I always admitted his maturity and innate wisdom to be far superior to my own.

And I always thought of his political truths as acorns that would some day plant roots deep into the heart of America.

We celebrated his first birthday after our marriage with our friends, and I raised a glass of fruit punch and toasted my husband. "I am so glad you have a birthday. I feel so grateful to your mother!" We revealed our emotions. We never kept an emotion hidden away when it should be out in the open. "I give thanks to your mother!" I said again, and the love in his gray eyes brought tears of joy to my own. Yes, I knew I had my *perfect* lover, husband and marriage. No fantasy of a fairy tale princess living happily ever after with a fairy tale prince in a charmed world could be better. My husband, my lover and my best friend - was my all, the completion of me. Without him I had half lived. Without him, I would half live.

You think when you are safe and you are revered - that the every day commonness of it will go on, and on. You think that the terror of night will never ever, ever come again. It is so good that you feel the sun always will be in the sky; night won't come - even when you *are* governed by a physical sun that does set, and allows the night to fall.

Young lovers – kiss your beloved, for time is hungry.

My husband warned me again that he did not have a continual happy nature - that he sank into moods of deep depression. He said that dark mood had almost killed him when he felt he had to break our engagement. "Molly, I was the most miserable man alive," he said. "When I saw ahead no life shared with you - I wondered if I would ever laugh again. I knew I would never love again."

"It was the same with me," I replied.

"And I caused us both pain."

"You were thinking of me."

"Yes. But I did in the wrong way. You *are* strong to share a life with me. And here we are, in two cheap rented rooms, and you are as bright and cheerful as ever. The sunnyness of your nature has driven all my glooms away."

"And you are the balance and the light of my life."

We *never* hid our love for each other.

Among his most endearing characteristics was his humor. No one could tell a humorous story as he did. One day our friend, who was always talking about the fast approaching Day of Judgment, was doing it again. My husband, who thought that day came every day in a life, got what I learned to be a *pre-story* twinkle in his eyes, and he said, "Now this reminds me of Paddy, and Paddy was told the same thing by his friend as he was stealing a spade. 'Paddy, better lay down that spade you are stealing. If you don't, you'll pay for it at the Day of Judgment.' Paddy thought on this, brightened and said, 'By the powers! If ye'll credit me so long, I'll jist take another!'"

During my pregnancy the world was supposed to come to an end, or so the Millerites said. They were buying Ascension Robes for that exact date, which was April 23. It was a fearful time for me, too, for I secretly dreaded death in childbirth. I was relieved when my husband returned from the circuit courts on the fifth of May. He took away my fear of dying. "I will not allow that *at all,* Molly," he said, and I was convinced he would not.

Our first child was born at the Globe Tavern on August 1, 1843, nine months less than three days after our marriage, if you figure that way. It was *not* an easy birth. It was a hard birth. I suppose most of them are, and during all of the excruciating agony my beloved stayed by my side, and the love and the concern that was on his face I cherished all of my life. "Molly," he said, when I felt as if I were being torn in two. "You will have this baby and *not leave me.*"

I looked up at him, and fire was burning me up, or agony was, and through it I saw him, those beautiful eyes so filled with love. "I will never leave you," I whispered, my strength draining away.

And I didn't, wouldn't, couldn't.

Our first son, Robert, was named for my father. None of my sisters had even visited me during my confinement, and it was Mrs. Bledsoe, who lived at the Globe, who helped care for me and cared for Bobbie until I could. But my father came to Springfield to see his new namesake and found that he liked and admired his new son-in-law very much. He wrote, "I hope Mary can make as good a wife as she has a husband." Lizzie must have been shocked when she heard that. My father gave my husband and me, with property and cash, about $1,157.50, but my husband was still paying off his "national debt" and was sending money to his father and his step mother.

Our first seven years together were very, *very* lean. In 1843 we wanted to visit Joshua Speed in Kentucky, but did not have the money to do so. I will not lie and say this was easy on me, for I had been spoiled, as far as having money goes, all of my life. I did miss a fine carriage, the latest clothes right out of *Godey's Lady's Book,* "servants" galore, and when we would buy our own home, *someday.* I had no idea how to prepare a meal, much less than shop for one. The only thing I had learned that might help a wife was the ability to sew, which all women of the South learned, some sewing in a more *gentile* way than others. I did not know how to *mend* anything. And there was no way I was going to learn to milk a cow.

The poverty did bother me. It bothered me very much, *for I was vain* about having no social standing. My rich sisters lived nearby in their mansions and gave magnificent parties, to which *we were not invited,* and this hurt me. They were saying, without saying it, you married poor white trash and are banished right out of the world of Todd.

My husband, I soon learned, did not care *a fig* about money or about the resultant social position gained from it. Even when he became President of the United States, he said, "Money? I don't know anything about money. I never had enough of my own to fret about, and I have no opinion about it in any way." He was a lawyer, and he never even made a will! Money was certainly more abstract to him than his political ideals.

At nights Bobby never seemed to stop crying. When the carriage bell rang, it woke him up, and when he woke up, he yelled and yelled *and yelled,* and *everybody* woke up. Out of consideration to our fellow boarders, and to ourselves, we moved to where Bobby could sleep all night with no carriage bell to wake him up. The winter of 1843-44 we rented a three - room cottage at 214 South Fourth Street, and saved money for our own home. Dr. Charles Dresser, who married us, put his home at ighth and Jackson up for sale, and my husband made an offer, drawing up a contract for a deed in January of 1844, and in May we moved in. My husband paid one thousand two hundred dollars for our home, plus trading a lot he had, valued at three hundred dollars. The house was a story and a half, light brown with dark green shutters, and I called it our little brown *dream* cottage. It was not like the stately brick mansions of my family in Lexington, and it was not like the mansions in Springfield owned by my sisters, but it was a special house because in it were the happiest days of our lives. It was my husband's first *home*, and he loved it. He could comfortably walk the seven blocks to his law office. After he had milked our cow. And a neighbor's cow, both kept together down the street in a pasture. My husband's income was from one thousand five hundred dollars to two thousand dollars a year; he paid off all the "national" debt and continued sending money to his father.

Springfield got city lights, oil lamps, and I learned to cook, with very, *very* much difficulty. I looked unhappily at our big black stove, and it looked more balefully back at me, and I knew, from the first, we were not destined to become amiable partners. I called the stove *Evil Eva.* My husband would get her all fired up, and as soon as he left the house, she would send out billows of smoke but *no heat* at all. Or, if I wanted a *slow* fire, she would suddenly roar into life as if she were the sole energy of hell. Then she burned up my custards, pies, cakes, roasts, and still managed to snarl licking flames out at me. I burned up meal after meal. Fire poured from our kitchen so many times that if the whole house should burn down, my husband said, the neighbors would just drink another cup of coffee and say, "There goes Mary - cooking another roast."

"Molly," teased my husband, "you have to aim for a fire *inside* the fire box." And he showed me about Evil Eva's damper, which I never got straight, for she always froze it all up with my husband's departure. She let it slide and coo to his touch, and to mine, she sent it right into rigor mortise.

I learned to shop, and even how to make soap, wherein Bobby tried to eat the lye before I could get it into the soap. This sent me off into a hysterical fit, and a neighbor heard the screams and came and washed Bobby's mouth out. The neighbors all agreed that we spoiled Bobby. They were right. My husband said, *and I quote,* "It is my pleasure that my children be free, happy and unrestrained by parental tyranny. Love is the chain whereby to bind a child to his parents." I am sure he was thinking of the beatings he received from his own father- for refusing to shoot an animal.

Soon, *halleluiah!,* gas was piped into our back yard and into the house, and *we had gaslights!* Trains were now careening by at *twenty- eight miles* an hour, and then you could buy soap! In *bars! Perfumed* bars! I thanked God for that, for I hated, hated and *hated* to make soap. I hated that as much as I hated Evil Eva, for making soap on her foul moods was a life-threatening thing.

Houses still had no screens; in the summer windows were propped open with boards, which children promptly removed to squash their fingers; water was carried into the house from a pump in the back yard, and there was a serious winter problem of keeping the house warm enough to survive in it. To avoid occupants freezing into snowmen, every house needed *mountains* of wood for its fires. My husband was an excellent woodchopper. He chopped up the big wood and Bobby chopped up the little wood, but still, the bitter cold would creep in from outside and stay around in the corners of every single room. I know my sisters scorned me for this, but I kept only the rooms warm that we used, and the rest of them were shut off for the winter. And I would *not* spend the money for matches. They were too expensive and just went up in smoke when you could bank your coals and use *them* for the morning fires. That was the household task of my husband, aside from milking the cows, trying to placate Evil Eva, and chopping our wood - banking the coals. But my husband usually forgot to bank the coals. "Father," I would ask. "Have you banked the coals for morning?"

"Yes, Molly," he would reply, *thinking* of it, *meaning* to do it after - another book - or brief, and in the morning the house would be iced over - Evil Eva all black ice, we would be iced over, and there would be no banked coals to change the situation. "Father!" I would shiver. "There are no coals! Not a single one!"

He would pick up his coal bucket, put on a wool shawl and run down the street to come back with neighbor coals. The neighbors amiably greeted him as he ran down the street with his empty coal bucket and he was warmly received into any house to fill it.

I did scrimp to save. My husband said I pinched our dollars so tight I made the eagles on them scream. He knew I needed help with the children later, and he knew I would pay *no more* than one dollar a week. He sneaked by me another dollar right into the help's pocket. He sneaked around me on money again. Into his office came members of Springfield's volunteer fire department asking for help for a new hose. My husband told them that he had to talk it over with his wife, and here is how he would do it. He would tell her he wanted to give fifty dollars, and she would say twenty- five was quite enough, and they could stop by tomorrow for the twenty- five - which they did.

Our life in *our own* home at Eighth and Jackson was all we had dreamed a home together would be. My hands, no longer dainty and soft, were hard from hard work, and I did not care. Our house was always swept clean, and they said of me I even scrubbed the corners of every room, which I did. Our home was furnished in good taste, not extravagance, with flowers kept on the tables and pictures in the *right* place on the walls. Ultimately, our front company parlor, to your left when you entered the house, had a stuffed rocking chair and foot stool for my husband, a *lovely* sofa, a marble table between the windows, and a velvet chair on each side. By the fireplace there was a large stuffed chair and footstool, and on the other side of the fireplace was an ornate curio cabinet with six shelves. In the front corner to the right of a window was another corner curio, also with six shelves. The mantel carried crystal prisms for candles, with a large three armed brilliant in the center. Our family parlor, across the way with my husband's library, had two rocking chairs, a large table, my sewing stand, many occasional chairs, a two drawer stand underneath a fine mirror, and on the fireplace mantel another large brilliant with five arms. This fireplace had no ornate heating stove in front of it as did the company parlor fireplace.

In time, when my husband was able to hire help, here is what a little Portuguese girl wrote of me: "She is a good woman who will taka no sassy talk, but if you good to her, she good to you. You gotta good friend." As for my husband, she wrote, "He so kind. He choppa the wood for fire and little Robert choppa the little wood. When he passa me, he patta my shoulder . . .

he kind with no verra style. He just common like someone that is poor."

I loved the colored help. I told them of my dear Mammy Sally, of those kind eyes and gentle hands and how she would tell us *chillens* that there was *this ole man Satan* with horns and a long *green* tail, just waiting down in hell for the bad *chillens,* and a black bird went to him *every* week (Friday night) carrying a report on the devil's future roomers and boarders. There was not a colored helper that did not praise me, call me a *kind* woman, a *very nice* lady who did all of the cooking and sewing of the house while they scrubbed the floors and their corners. They recalled I sewed on *inexpensive* material, and that Bobby's little pants were filled with patches. So you see, I did learn to mend, and very well, too. I stitched, and also very well, my husband tucked shirt bosoms, and I made *all* of my children clothes, and my own, not out of silks or satin, but out of calico, still following *Godey's Lady's Book* you can be sure.

I loved it when they said my husband had such a pretty, vivacious and intelligent wife, for he enjoyed hearing this more than I did. Yet, so proud of the impression *I gave,* he was *never* concerned about the way *he* looked. He kept saying he was too ugly to do much about it anyway. I told him he *had* to take *some* concern about his appearance. "All right, all right, Molly," he said. "I will let *you* take that job on." So before he left for the office, he would always bend down and say, "Now, Molly, slick me all up." He was forever running his hands through that thick black hair of his and making it look caught in a cyclone. Or two. When I slicked him all up, my main effort had to be to tame down that head of hair. I got his brush and brushed and brushed it all down to my will, but no sooner was he out of the gate, than it bounced back into its old mess with a will of its own. If I did finally get enough oil on it to slick it down, when he came back from the office it was mussed up more than ever. He was also so careless about his pants; it would not surprise me to see one leg of them rolled up and the other down, as I heard was their style when he lived in New Salem. I now saw that he wore decent looking black suits, with a swallowtail coat and a tall silk hat, with my bosom-tucked shirts, but when he came home in them, they were always in as bad a muss up as his hair. He carried most of his important legal papers around in his hat, or he probably would not have worn one at all. I had to see that he carried an umbrella and wore a raincoat in the rain, or a shawl in the cold, and I joked about it - how had he managed to survive long enough for a wife to take care of him?

"Fate saved me, Molly, for you to do it," he would say with his eyes twinkling. "It was all fate." And then he gave me a kiss because fate had been so kind.

I thought he didn't know one color from another until I made myself a white dress with little deep blue flowers in it, and he said, "Molly, those flowers *just match* the color of your eyes." Maybe it was the reds and the pinks he could not tell apart. Or maybe he remembered I was said to have deep blue eyes.

So I learned that my husband had little concern for money, did not care too much, or at all, about his appearance, would seldom remember to bank the coals - and there *was* one more thing. *He had no idea of time.* He would get into a law book and disappear, vanish - *swoosh* off the face of the earth and any revolution on its axis. I think the sun could rise and set over those pages, and until he knew them all, he would not know what the sun was doing. The book or the legal brief were all that mattered - and whatever the day did outside of them became a total mystery. I had enough trouble with Evil Eva, and I had to learn that he would come home for lunch, maybe past the supper hour, or home for supper when the sun had set and the stars and moon were about to follow. I could not go to the office and fetch him, for I could not leave the baby and the malevolence of Evil Eva, and after 1844, I would seldom go to the office even if I could leave baby and Evil Eva. For that was the year, 1844, he took in as a law clerk that odious little man, that skunk, that shiftless drunken skunk, that *drunk skunk,* Billy Herndon. This odious *lying* little man had no idea of time, either, or anything necessary for a decent life - I disliked him from the first, and he disliked me. I thought he was coarse, uncouth, a crazy drunk and that he took constant advantage of my husband's kindness to him. He had no sense of humor at all, and never did understand my husband's. My husband even got tired of that, and said he grew weary of Billy's *"meaningless metaphysics* and *gaseous generalities."* Billy had God all figured out. There was not one. He knew this for a fact from some secret part of his brain that was usually in the gutter with the rest of him. He was as dour and as sour as a bad pickle, and that was basically from boozing his brain into one. He was a law clerk, and *just getting* his license, and my husband split his fees *equally* with him! And when he got drunk and attacked a store front, or any other building, my husband would have to get up at dawn and raise one hundred dollars to get him out of jail *before eight o' clock in the morning.* I *hated* drunks. So did my husband. He had one for an uncle and I had one for a brother, and we *never* served liquor in our home, or at the White House.

When Billy became a lawyer, he bragged *he was a better one than my husband. He* was the *real* brain behind the partnership! No, at first sight I did not like Billy, and he did not like me. He thought I was a snob because I thought of him as white trash, which I certainly did.

There they both would be - *without a clue* as to time, in my husband's upstairs law office, not far from the *sacred* shop where he bought my wedding ring. My husband's office was in the back of the brick building on the public square, and Judge Logan and his new partner, Milton Hay, had the front office. Their office was always neat and tidy as a pin. My husband's office was another story - sort of a horror story. It was a normal room, *in size,* anyway. And it had two tables forming a T with green baize on each table and inkstands, which were to later give our sons so much pleasure. Two windows looked out on the back yard; in one corner was a secretary with pigeonholes and a drawer for law papers. There was a bookcase with my husband's two hundred law books, but there was *no record* book, anywhere, concerning their cases, the fees, or costs.

I remember *the* office, Billy and my husband sitting in it with paper legals piled up around them, the two hundred books teetering on the edge of their shelves, my husband chewing on cheese and crackers, mice eagerly coming out of their numerous mouse holes to share in the falling crumbs, the hair falling out of the office hair sofa, so worn and tired it could not stand unless propped against the wall, my husband reading, as usual, on his shoulder blades, feet on the table, or on a chair in front of him, and Billy thinking how he could get drunk as soon as my husband left the office. The floor was not only accommodating to the crumbs for the office mice, but grew its own organic garden. When my husband wrote local farmers, he would drop in some seed, spilling some on the floor, and there they sprouted *and grew.*

The only thing we really ever fussed about was Billy who was about my age. It was his decision to keep the odious little man, but I was never expected to have Billy Herndon in our house, or to eat at our table, and he did neither.

As time went on, my husband, still uninvolved in it, had to be pushed or pulled home if he was ever going to eat again. When our children could walk to his office, that was their job. One would pull from the front, the other push from the back, and that way he could continue on with his reading, if the sun had not yet set. There was no use complaining. His way was his way, and he was so gentle, loving and kind to me, I could not *stay* mad. Oh, I did have a temper. I flew into it many times. I remember when I went to church on Sunday, he would pull the baby around in a wagon while studying a law book. One time I came out of church, met him, and he had his book, and the wagon, but *the wagon was empty!*

"Where is Bobby?" I screamed. We found him soon enough, for as Bobby got older he could yell even louder. I had a real fit over my baby yelling a few houses down the street, sitting all alone on a snow bank. "I don't mind Molly's little fits," my husband always said amiably. "They do me no harm and do her a lot of good." I did have a quick temper, and I always regretted losing it, and apologized, and even wept because I had what my husband called *That Todd Tantrum Tendency.*

So my husband ate in his shirtsleeves; I could not change that; he even answered the door in them, and I could not change that. He dropped papers about the room just where he was through reading them, usually forgot to bank the coals, cared not a fig about money or his appearance, and was totally oblivious to time - once he started reading. As I said, *his* way was *his* way, and he was so endearing in it, my fits at his little flaws flew right by us both. If they didn't, he patted me out of them, and if he couldn't, he took the boys on a walk. In minutes the fit was flown, and when they came home something marvelous would be baking in Evil Eva, that is, if she were so inclined.

Husbands of my day never baby-sat. They never tended the children even if their wives were already half way into heaven. But *my* husband *loved* to baby-sit. When the babies were too big to pull about in the wagon, he took them to the office with him. He was so *proud* of them! He thought Billy was equally appreciative, but Billy was not. They did not like Billy at all, and Billy did not like them at all. To show this they covered Billy with giant ink splashes and my husband did not mind, as he did not see it, hear it or know it. They then used Billy's pens for darts to throw at the wall, and when that got boring, they threw his papers into the stove, after they had covered them with ink. My husband did not see it, hear it or know it, for he had abdicated within a law book. When the stove was not in summer use, they set Billy's papers on fire outside of it and danced and whooped like little Indians around them. I do not think their father even *smelled* the smoke. Billy ducked the pens, the ink splotches and put out the fires and dodged the teetering books they took off the shelves, for they would play catch with them, and when Billy showed a hysteria of disapproval, they threw his papers out the window. "Look! Little white birds!" they would squeal in delight, as the papers fluttered away in the wind. Billy told all of this. He might even have told the truth for once. If this happened, I do know my husband would not know it unless the fire burned away his organic rug and reached his shoes - oh, but it couldn't, as they would be on the table above the fire line.

I heard that after work, when Billy reached his own children, he strapped them as soon as they got close enough.

They said I was brave about the big things and terrified of the little things, and this was true. Thunderstorms sent me into a blind panic. Whenever one threatened, my husband closed the office, or left it to that *odious* little man, and rushed home so he could comfort me through my terror. When he had to travel on the Eighth Judicial Circuit, wherein the lawyers followed the judges to the varying courts, he was gone twice a year for three months each. It was *terrible* for me. I was afraid to stay alone at night, and so when he was gone, he saw that someone stayed in the house with me. Our neighbor, Mr. James Gourley, then milked our cow as well as his own, looked into Evil Eva, and calmed me down during thunder -storms. One time, one of my house companions, a female, turned out to be a *lady of the night*, and when so many men came rushing into our house to share it with her, I woke up and thought they were all robbers and screamed so loudly, Mr. Gourley ran over and kicked them all out. I kicked *the lady of the night* out myself. By the way, when *lying, drunk skunk* Billy said I was a hellcat and a foaming fiend, and tried to get Mr. Gourley to agree, he did not and said I was a *very good wife and woman.* And Mr. Gourley ate at our table many, *many* times, and I would sit on Evil Eva when she was roaring hell fire and memorize *everything* Shakespeare ever wrote, or *thought of*, before Billy would eat a bite of food cooked on her.

We were so happy together. Even Lizzie had to recognize this. My little half sister, Emilie Todd Helm, was to later write, "They understood each other thoroughly, and he looked beyond the impulsive words and manner, and knew his wife was devoted to him and his interests." My sister, Frances Todd Wallace, was to later write of my husband, "He was devoted to his home and his wife . . . and they certainly did live happily ever after - as much so as any man and woman I have ever known." My husband's long time friend, Henry B. Rankin, was to write that my husband, "thoroughly loved his wife." All the neighbors knew how we adored each other and our children. When I sent the boys to push /pull their father from the office, I met him at our front gate where we would walk hand in hand into our home.

When we had the money and we attended the theater or the opera, he *always* held my hand. He never grew embarrassed to show his love for me. He never thought the tenderness of a man for his woman to be anything but manly. He told complete strangers how he loved me, loved my dimples when I smiled, and that he had a wife with a sweet Southern melodious voice, and a very sharp mind. He was proud to say he had a wife who was Southern to the core and hated slavery as much as he did.

The country *was* sick over the question of slavery. With the sentencing of John Punch in 1640, the English colonists turned slavery here into something unique. In that year three indentured servants had run away - two white men and one black man, John Punch. They were all caught. The white men had years added to their service, but John Punch was made a slave *for life.*

For the first time in the history of world slavery, slavery was not based upon misfortunes of war, but on a *physical characteristic*. Skin color. *Black* skin color. And for the first time in the history of slavery-it was *inherited*. Through the condition of the mother, and in that way, when a white slave owner used a black woman as a concubine and produced a mulatto, the child was neither free nor legitimate. And for the first time in the history of world slavery, it was not considered an *unfortunate* accident of war - but *a good fortune!* The 'savages' were "gentled down," dressed, more or less, taught English and introduced to God through Jesus Christ, and to heaven, a black one of course, for heaven would be as segregated as a Southern graveyard. So the great civilizations of the African Sudan - Ghana, Mali, and Songhai, went into the dust bin of history, with the fact that during the great Elizabethan Age, *white* doctors came to study eyes surgery under *black* doctors in Timbuktu, at the University of Songhai. Into the dust bin of history went the advanced cultures of Benin, Kush, Ethiopia, and the blacks of Egypt, including *black* pharaohs. Into the dust bin of history went the fact that there were *Christian* Africans, Ethiopians, and *Muslim* Africans, in the kingdoms of Mali and Songhai. The first slave brought to Portugal was a devout Muslim prince. The Africans were hardly naked bloodthirsty eating each other all up savages, and they had already found their way to God - without any guidance from the slave owners of Europe or the European colonists.

My husband and I agreed the unjustifiable cannot be justified. Now my husband was saying that the country would be all slave or all free, and that it could be no other way. Of slavery he was quoted as saying, "If slavery is right, then nothing is wrong." Of slavery he wrote, "When I see strong hands sowing, reaping, and thrashing wheat into bread, I cannot refrain from wishing and believing that those hands, some way, in God's good time, shall own the mouth they feed."

He wrote this about the Missouri Compromise: "It used to amuse me some to find that the slaveholders wanted more territory because they had not room enough for their slaves; yet they complained of not having the slave trade because they wanted more slaves for their room."

On July 4, 1845, my husband was the orator of the day in the cupola of the Statehouse, and I, twenty six, was a rapt listener, even with Bobby, not quite two, squirming on my lap. It was not just *what* he said, although what he said was always very clear and concise, it was the *way* he said it. When he spoke, he not only had his usual personal magnetism, but he spoke as neighbor to neighbor. Billy was to say he had a high piping voice. *He did not.*

On March 10, 1846, our second son, Eddy, was born, named for our dearest friend, Edward Baker, a fellow Whig and a fellow enthusiastic player with my husband of handball, then called *playing fives*. My husband excelled at *all* sports.

Bobby, almost three, grew very jealous of the baby, and began to run away to get our attention. We were always scouring the neighborhood for him, and the neighbors soon got wise to Bobby and returned him home. Soon my cry, "Bobby's lost!" just rallied them into a quick Bobby catch and return. One time, when he ran away for the *third* time in one day, both my husband and I *thought* about spanking him, and in a letter to Joshua Speed my husband said Bobby had actually *been* spanked by his mother, but I said I would and didn't.

On August third of 1846 my husband was elected to the United States Congress. We rented our house, beginning on November 1, 1847, to Cornelius Ludlum for ninety dollars a year, keeping the north upstairs room for our furniture. I did all of our packing, and a lot of packing it was. Just for a woman, it took sixteen yards of silk, lined, for one dress, and with hoops, thirty yards of silk. There would be also twelve to fifteen yards of whalebone and sixty-three yards for cotton underwear.

In October of 1847 we were on our way to Washington. We took the stage-coach to St. Louis where we stayed at the Scott's Hotel and were joined there by Joshua Speed. We wanted to visit Lexington, for my father was anxious to see us, and we were anxious to see him. Traveling from St. Louis to Lexington took a week, by packet steamboat down the Mississippi to Cairo against the current of the Ohio, up the Kentucky River to Frankfort, and then on by the Lexington and Ohio Railroad to Lexington. The trip was *glorious*. Bobby, four, was exploring everything, and about everybody, but he did climb too far over the deck rail once, and my husband saved him from falling into the river by grabbing the seat of his little pants. Eddy, one and a half, was enjoying himself as much as the rest of us. My husband and I *loved* to travel. In Lexington we had a wonderful three-week visit with my father. The Todd carriage met us at the train depot, and I remember exactly how my father's household received us. The whole family, and behind them all of the *servants*, awaited us in the great entrance hall. I carried Eddy and my husband carried Bobby and there was my precious half sister, four year old Emilie Todd. She wrote later that she thought I was beautiful, but my husband terrifying because he was so tall. But after Bobby squirmed to the floor, my husband bent down and lifted her gently up into his arms and said, "So *this* is little sister!" Right then, she recalled, she knew he was not the giant threatening Jack from his beanstalk.

My stepmother's nephew, Joseph Humphreys, was on the train with us, and had almost run to the Todd house to complain about two *brats* on the train that pestered the passengers and how their long legged father just *smiled* about it. "I was never so glad to get off a train in my life!" he sighed in relief, and then, behold, he saw us alighting from the Todd carriage and after saying, "Good Lord! There they are now!" ran out of the house and so was not in the hall to greet us. I do not recall his ever coming home while we were in it.

While we visited, my husband gloried in the Todd library, found the poem *Thanatopsis* by William Cullen Bryant and memorized it. He also saw manacled slaves chained together being marched down the street, and the slave 'pens' by Grandmother Parker's house. He saw the difference between the house slaves and the field slaves - *servants,* and told my father, not self righteously, that he was glad he had been raised a *scrub.* My father understood that a *scrub* had no slaves and did his own manual labor. He told my husband all of his *servants* would be freed -in that great *someday,* of course. Grandma Parker had in her will that her *servants* would eventually be freed at her death.

I was proud to show off my two sturdy boys and their intelligent father, beginning a career in *national* politics. My father liked his son in law as much as ever and made him the lawyer for his will.

After our Lexington visit, we went by coach to Winchester, Virginia, took the Winchester and Potomac Railroad to Harper's Ferry, the Baltimore and Ohio Railroad to Relay Station, Maryland, and from there we went by coach to Washington. There we stayed at Mrs. Ana Spriggs' boarding house on Capitol Hill, facing the capitol, just some fifty feet from Capitol Park. Most of our fellow boarders were members of Congress. I met so many wonderful and important people, did so much sightseeing - how exciting were those days and nights when we were first in Washington!

Our supper table was always filled, not only with the boarders, but strangers came in from the near by bowling alley to sit with us and hear my husband tell a funny story. "Another one! Another one!" they kept saying. "Your husband leaves a trail of laughter wherever he goes," they said to me in real appreciation.

I thought my husband should have his first picture taken with the new daguerreotype process, for after all, he was in the Congress of the United States. He objected, but I poured lots of oil on his hair and the picture was taken. He then wanted one of me, and as I did, too, I put on a striped silk dress with a lace scarf at my shoulders fastened with a cameo pin, and waited and waited *and waited* for the picture to be taken, and froze like Evil Eva's rigor mortise damper in every single picture ever taken of me. In photos my husband's kindness and inner strength showed up, but in my photos, none of my zest for life. Before a camera, my so-called *joie de vivre* flew away, as did my best part, the rosy cheeks, violet/blue eyes, auburn hair, and I looked stern and believe me, I was never stern! I was still filled what was called "Mary's bubbling fun," and had more than ever, "the soft Southern drawl of Mary's cultured voice." I was twenty- nine and my husband not yet thirty-nine. These two photos were hung in our home as a pair, but never were we to be photographed together.

My husband had written to Billy on December 13, 1847, about money matters, and he ended his letter by saying, "As you all are so anxious for me to distinguish myself, I have concluded to do so before long. "

He did. He had the courage to attack President Polk for lying about why we were at war with Mexico. On December 22 he introduced into the House of Representatives the "Spot Resolutions." He quoted the President in his war message of May 11, 1846, as saying, "The Mexican Government not only refused to receive him (the peace envoy from us) or listen to his propositions, but after a long series of menaces, have at last invaded our *territory*, and shed the blood of our fellow *citizens on our own soil.* Then on December 8, 1846, the President said again that Mexico was the aggressor, "by invading *our soil in* hostile array, and shedding the blood of our *citizens.*" And, in his message of December 7, 1847, President Polk had said Mexico refused to even hear our minister of *peace,* and "under wholly unjustifiable pretexts, involved the two countries in war, by invading the territory of the State of Texas, striking the first blow, and shedding the blood of *our citizens* on *our own soil.*"

My husband wanted the President to inform the House how this was true by replying to eight questions. Was the spot where American blood was shed on American soil given to Spain by the treaty of 1819? Was it in the territory wrested from Spain by the Mexican Revolution? Had the inhabitants of that spot fled from the approach of the American Army? Was the spot isolated from any settlements and surrounded by uninhabited regions? Was the spot inhabited by people who submitted to the laws of Texas, or the United States by consent or compulsion? Did the people of this spot flee from the approaching American army, leaving their homes and their crops *before* blood was shed? Were not the American citizens, whose blood was shed on the spot, *armed* officers and *soldiers* sent there by the President? Were they not sent to that *spot* after General Taylor, more then once, told the War Department that no such invasion of the *spot* was necessary for the protection of Texas?

On January 12, 1848, my husband gave a magnificent speech to the House in which he took all of the President's justifications for the Mexican War and proved them false. He concluded by saying about the President, "He is a bewildered, confounded, and miserably perplexed man. God grant he may be able to show there is not something about his conscience more painful than his mental perplexity!"

Billy had written on January 29 objecting to my husband's Spot Resolutions and his speech about them on the twelfth. My husband wrote back, "Allow the President to invade a neighboring nation whenever *he* shall deem it necessary to repel an invasion, and you allow him to do so *whenever he may choose to say* he deems it necessary for such purpose - and you allow him to make war at pleasure... your view...places our President where kings have always stood."

My husband was in Washington to serve the *Union,* the Union of the United States of America - the land he held dear. How had he said it in 1839? *"The land of my life, my liberty and my love."*

At night we talked over everything, what was new, what was important, what was wondrous in our lives, and our life *was* wondrous! Warm before a nice fire, in love and together, while near us our babies slept peacefully - how could our life have been better?

Chapter Eight

In April of 1848 I returned to my father's home, as Mrs. Spriggs was not too compatible for our two sons. Bobby kept taking things apart, even if he *generally* put them back together again, a trait his father had with the children's toys, and Eddy was bringing stray cats that were outside - inside.

My husband wrote me a letter on April 16. It began, "In this troublesome world, we are never quite satisfied. When you were here, I thought you hindered me some in attending to business; but now, having nothing but business - no variety - it has grown exceedingly tasteless to me. I hate to sit down and direct documents, and I hate to stay in this old room by myself." He had received my second and third letters, and he wrote, "Dear Eddy thinks his father has *gone tapila*." He had been shopping for some plaid stockings "for Eddy's dear little feet," and he had bought for himself some shirt-bosom studs, jet set in gold, paying $1.50 for the set, continuing, "Suppose you do not prefix the "Hon" to the address on your letters to me anymore. I like the letters very much, but I would rather they should not have that upon them...Are you entirely free from head-ache? That is good - considering it is the first spring you have been free from it since we were acquainted. I am afraid you will get so well, and fat, and young, as to wanting to marry again . . . What did Bobby and Eddy think of the little letters father sent them? Don't let the blessed fellows forget father." He signed off, "Most affectionately."

My husband was the kindest and most loving of fathers. We both could get into the mind of a child, with pleasure, and enter their untapped kingdom of wonder. My children were always clean, and I dressed all of them very nicely. I saw that they loved good literature, reading to them Sir Walter Scott, and making Bobby yearn to become a good knight. Later, when Little Sister Em, or Emilie Todd, was visiting our home, we heard a ruckus outside of the window. When we looked out, there was Bobby dressed as a knight, a fence poling as a lance, shouting to a little adversary, done up the same way, "This rock shall fly from its firm base as soon as I!" We laughed, Em and I, and I shouted down, "Gramercy, brave knights. Pray be more merciful than you are brawny!"

My sons could quote poetry, too, and I taught them manners, even if Billy wanted to wring their necks and toss them out of the office windows. If their father had *told* them to stop with the ink, papers, fires and books, they would have done it. We always kept our word to our boys, just as we did to grownups. They were our dearest sons, their presence among us no less than a cherished miracle.

When we had the money and I wanted something, my husband would say, "You know what you want. Go and get it." And I could do the same for our boys. Whatever they wanted, if it did not hurt them or anyone else, they got.

Now, May of 1848, the boys and I were at *Buena Vista*. This was my father's summerhouse in the country, a great rambling house high on a knoll, and from the house portico there was a sweeping view of the countryside. It was one-fourth a mile from the Leestown Pike, down the Pike several miles from Lexington. There were acres of green land around us, locust trees, magnolias, and the sweet smell of lilies and honeysuckle. From the stone spring house came a stream flowing right outside my window and by the long side porch below me that connected to the "servants" quarters. The rising moon was large and made the hot night appear filled with romance. Yearning for my husband, I looked out of my window, the green of the grass getting more vivid as the darkness fell, the moon shining in more and more splendor as it did, and I thought how beautiful is this earth. The stream murmured by in liquid silver, the lights of the "'servant" quarters shone like fireflies lost to the night - *all of my dreams had come true.* I was so lonesome for my husband. I went to my chair and read his letters again and again. Just seeing his writing brought him close. I found pen and paper, turned up my lamp for better vision and began a letter to my *My Dear Husband.* Our babies were peacefully asleep down the hall; the hall clock was ticking in its old familiar and cozy way - saying time *is sweet and safe.* I wrote a long cheerful letter, full of family gossip and news. I dated it *Lexington May - 48 -* (I was bad with *exact* dates) It is the only surviving letter I wrote to my husband in this period, and of all the letters he wrote to me then, only three survive. Our son, Robert, burned most of our letters to each other.

I had important news of my sister Franny Wallace. I had wanted her to send me some discarded children clothes to save me some summer sewing, but she thought they might be lost in the mail and the cost was not worth it. Her husband and daughter had been sick, and Springfield was as dull as usual. Then I wrote about our boys, called by my husband, his *dear little codgers.*

"Our little Eddy, has recovered from his little spell of sickness - Dear boy, I must tell you a story about him - Bobby in his wanderings to day, came across in a yard, a little kitten, *your hobby,* he says he asked a man for it, he brought it triumphantly to the house, so soon as Eddy, spied it - his *tenderness,* broke forth, he made them bring it *water,* fed it with bread himself with his *own dear hands,* he was a delighted little creature over it, in the midst of his happiness Ma came in, she you must know dislikes the whole cat race, I thought in a very unfeeling manner, she ordered the servant near, to throw it out, which, of *course,* was done, Eddie screaming & protesting loudly against the proceeding, *she* never appeared to mind his screams, which were long & loud, I assure you - Tis unusual for her *now a days,* to do anything quite so striking, she is very obliging & accommodating, but if she thought any of us, were on her hands again, I believe she would be *worse* than ever - In the next moment, she appeared in good humor, I know she did not intend to offend me. By the way, she has just sent me up a glass of ice cream, for which with this warm evening, I am duly grateful."

I went on to tell my *dear husband* of a family member thinking about going to Philadelphia, (where the Whig Convention would be held to nominate Zachary Taylor for the Presidency) and it would be a good chance for me to pick up and go with them.

"You know I am so fond of sightseeing, & I did not get to New York or Boston, or travel the lake route - But perhaps, dear husband, like the irresistible Cl Mc, (Colonel John McClernand) cannot do without his wife next winter, and must needs take her with him again - I expect you would cry aloud against it - How much, I wish instead of writing, *we* were together this evening, I feel very sad away from you." I teased him about my seeing Mr. Webb again at the closure of his daughter's school the first of July and wrote, " I must go down about that time & carry on quite a flirtation, you know *we* always had a *penchant* that way. With love I must bid you good night - Do not fear the children, have forgotten you, I was only jesting. - Even Eddy's eyes brighten at the mention of your name - My love to all -

Truly yours -"

And I was.

On June 12, having just returned from the Whig convention, my husband wrote me a short letter from the House. He addressed me as his *dear wife.* I was to join him, "as soon as possible. . . I shall be impatient till I see you. . . Come on just as soon as you can. I want to see you, and our dear, dear boys very much. Every body here wants to see our dear Bobby." He signed off, *affectionately.*

In Congress my husband was working on a bill to bar slavery from the District of Columbia, and he said before the House that those who denied that our war with Mexico was one of aggression reminded him of the Illinois farmer who said, "I ain't greedy about land; I only want what joins mine." I had heard that story before!

On July 2, he again wrote to *My dear Wife.* He worried that a draft of one hundred dollars for my trip to Washington might not have reached me before I left. (it did) Had I made preparations to forward my mail from Lexington? (I had) I was to give his kindest regards to my family. (I had) Then he was dunned for two unpaid Washington bills I had left behind, which I had completely forgotten. One was for $5.58 and the other for $8.50. When I had been too frugal for my husband in our seven years of poverty, he now worried about me going the opposite way. (I was, and it would get worse.) Then with his usual humor he said that according to Mr. Richardson, Mrs. Richardson had had a baby, "and he ought to know." The Capitol grounds' music on Saturdays was dwindling because interest in it was. He had no letters from home but business letters "which have no interest for you." They didn't. Men managed the money in my day and women had to work around that as best they could. He closed with his usual tender concern for me,

"By the way, you do not intend to do without a girl, because the one you had has left you? Get another as soon as you can to take charge of the dear codgers. Father expected to see you all sooner; but let it pass; stay as long as you please, and come when you please. Kiss and love the dear little rascals."

Later in 1848 my husband was to make speeches in New England for the election of Zachary Taylor, and the boys and I joined him. We took the steamer *Globe* to Chicago, and we had a marvelous opportunity to see the Niagara Falls. My husband was awestruck by them. He told the boys how the earth's water forever goes around and around the earth. He looked at the roaring falls and said, "Boys, that very water might have sustained Jesus."

On October 10 we were back in Springfield where we stayed at the Globe Tavern. In its dining room my husband shook many hands, *frontier style,* with both hands, "like my sons," he said. He used the western *Howdy* to about everyone he met, took the wood up to the rooms where widowed women stayed, gave his seat at the table for them, and on our railway passenger car, it was he who had seen that the elderly couples got settled in a comfortable double seat. He was of the people, always. "I am a common man," he would say, "but God must love the common man, because he made so many of them."

I stayed on at the Globe while my husband left for Washington for the inauguration of President Taylor, after which my husband misplaced his hat and had to walk to his lodgings bare headed at four in the morning. He still was *so* careless with his clothes. Gloves and he were as compatible as Evil Eva and I. We would agree they were proper for dignity, and I would buy the best for a man in the Congress of the United States of America, and where did they go? When out of *my* sight, they landed deep into a pocket. All of his pockets held gloves, one on top of the other, too. "Molly, they don't like me and I don't like them," he would say.

In 1849 he was offered the governorship of Oregon, but we decided his political future was still in Springfield where he was so well known. In 1849 he was resuming his law practice and riding the circuit. I still would have liked to have had a continent between us and that odious little Billy whom my husband was again getting out of jail for drunkenness, *still paying his fines.* We were getting begging letters about my husband's father from his stepbrother, John D. Johnston, who often kept the money my husband sent to Tom.

On July 16, 1849, my father died suddenly of cholera. I had never been close to him, but he was strength and security, even if he was so remote. I grieved for the loss of him in my life. It seemed, in a strange way, that my mother had died all over again.

My husband was the lawyer for his estate as my father had a lawsuit in progress and one of his sons was objecting to his will. My husband represented four of his daughters who lived in Springfield, Lizzie, Frances, Ann and me. In early November we began our eight- day journey to Lexington, and on the Ohio, our steamer got into a race with another one. My husband loved the race, and did the pitching of the wood, which he did magnificently. But we still lost.

In January of 1850 my beloved Grandmother Parker died, and I thought, *death comes by threes!* It was an old superstition, but who would be next in my family?

The previous December my boys had become ill. I always was a good nurse for them. From our local drugstore, *Corneau and Diller* I always kept a supply of castor oil, cough syrups, vermifuge for worms and drops of cough candy. I kept their room warm and saw they had warm clothing through the winter, but Eddy took ill after Christmas, very ill. I thanked God my husband was not on circuit, and together we nursed and tenderly cared for our precious son. We brought his collection of kitties into his room, and how his little face brightened when he could pet them, and they snuggled against him. Robert saw how drained we both were, my husband and I, and he probably felt neglected, isolated and alone, for my husband and I sat by our son for fifty two long days of absolute anguish. *Be well, my darling! You did not come to us to leave us so soon! See – another little kitten Bobby has found for you!*

When we could see how gravely ill Eddy was, we sent Bobby off to my stepmother in Lexington. We did not want Bobby to see his brother die, and it was all we could do to see it ourselves. Day and night for *fifty- two* days my husband and I stayed with him, and when Eddy went peacefully to his death, looking like a sleeping little angel, it was on the morning of February 1, 1850.

My husband wrote a letter to his stepbrother, John Johnston, on February 23, and in speaking of our Eddy's death, he said, "We miss him very much." Words. How empty, vague, *indifferent* they are - *our son died. We miss him very much.*

How can anyone understand the loss of a child unless that bitter brew has been shared? Our house became empty and desolate, as if it were grieving with us. I kept listening for the sound of Eddy's quick footsteps, the sound of his voice saying, "Ma, I am home!" I went to his room and stayed there as quiet as could be, waiting for him to enter it again with another stray kitten in his arms. As I did my housework - in every shadow, I thought - there he is, *alive,* with that sunny smile of his that no one on earth would ever have again. At nights I dreamed *so clearly* he was sleeping down the hall in his little bed, and I woke up, so *sure* that he was, tears of joy ran down my face. And then, in the silence of the dark, with the clock downstairs ticking its own time away, the bitter truth came back. Our Eddy is gone. He will never call me again. I can never hold him again, and wipe away his tears, or treat a skinned knee. And then I thought - why are we created but to die?

I could not eat. The sight of food made me physically ill, for all I could think of was I lived and Eddy did not.

It rained and rained; how it rained and rained, and I thought that the skies were weeping with us. The earth was so sodden, *so cold,* and around our house came a ceaselessly mourning sorrowing wind. The days grew darker; the sky glooming over with constant black clouds. The light of the sun was gone. Maybe Eddy had taken it away with him.

My husband went into his own deep melancholia. He never ate much anyway, and now he stopped eating, too. He grew more and more haggard until our concern for each other made us try to move apart from the galling pain. "We have to live for Bobby," we said to each other. "We *have* to live."

Dr. James Smith, a dear Scottish friend, had given Eddy's funeral service, and I later joined his congregation. He visited our home as if it were his own; so grateful were we for the comfort he gave us in facing what never should be faced.

There appeared an unsigned poem in the *Illinois Journal* of four stanzas after the notice of our dearest son's funeral. It ended with these words,

Bright is the home to him now given,
For such is the kingdom of Heaven.

Somewhere, where the children do go, maybe our son would say, *"Look! I am home!"* And an angel of the Lord would hold him tenderly as I loved to do, until I could do it again.

I wrote that unsigned poem, and its last line was added to our child's tombstone, our dearest Eddy who lived to be almost four.

Within one month after we lost Eddie, I found I was pregnant, and our joy was as the sun returned to the sky. My husband saw that I had help with the house chores, hovered over me like a mother hen, even *more* tender and loving to me, as if that were possible! "Mother," he said, "you must rest, and not do too much. Maybe you could just sit by the fire, and sew?" About this time he did begin to call me *mother* as well as *Molly*, for the word mother was reverenced by him. Now he remembered to come home for meals, and generally, even when they were prepared. As the baby grew within me, my headaches went away, and when I would shed tears for our little Eddy, and see his kittens grow when he was not allowed to, the baby I carried moved, and I said, "My dearest little darling - be here for us by Christmas!"

And he was. A perfect beautiful little boy, born December 21, 1850, and there could be no present for Christmas more wonderful. We named our new son William, for our family doctor, William Wallace, married to my sister, Frances.

December now was *special* to us with Willie's arrival on the twenty- first and my own birthday being the thirteenth. The *expectation* of the season! The sweet carols of Christmas - the extra lights, extra candles and lamps, the fires in *all* of the house fireplaces, holiday desserts and friends in to share the season's joy - to hear the church bells, ringing crisp and clear, snow silently falling to make everything so luminous, so pure - oh, we claimed December and its holy Christmas season as *ours*.

It was the ever-renewing miracle of our very first Christmas at the Globe - our two rooms - *home*, because we shared them.

Then we heard from Dennis Hanks, John Johnston and Dennis's daughter, Harriett, (Dennis had married Sarah's daughter, Elizabeth Johnston) and the news was that Tom was dying. My husband did not reply to the first letters, but on January 12, 1851, he wrote to John Johnston and explained why.

"It is not because I have forgotten them, or been uninterested in them - but because it appeared to me I could write nothing that could do any good. You already know I desire that neither Father nor Mother shall be in want of any comfort either in health or sickness while they live; and I feel sure you have not failed to use my name, if necessary, to procure a doctor, or any thing else for Father in his present sickness. My business is such that I could hardly leave home now, if it were not, as it is, that my own wife is sick-bed (It is a case of baby-sickness, and I suppose it is not dangerous) I sincerely hope Father may yet recover his health; but at all events tell him to remember to call upon and confide in, our great, and good, and merciful Maker; who will not turn away from him in any extremity. He notes the fall of a sparrow, and numbers the hair of our heads; and He will not forget a dying man, who puts his trust in Him. Say to him that if we would meet now, it is doubtful whether it would not be more painful than pleasant; but if it is his lot to go now, he will soon have a joyous meeting with many loved ones gone before; and where the rest of us, through the help of God, hope ere-long to join them."

Tom died on January 17, 1851, having been born January 6, 1778 - age - my husband noted in the family Bible - 73 years and eleven days.

John Johnston was always short of money and wanted my husband to share his, and for his mother to share hers. My husband heard that John was thinking of going to Missouri and his mother would be getting the short end of the stick when Tom's land was sold. This is how he handled this situation in a letter to "Dear Brother," dated November 4, 1851. The John Johnston idea of going off to Missouri he found "utterly foolish," and continued,

"What can you do in Missouri better than here? . . . Will any body there, any more than here, do your work for you? If you intend to go to work, there is no better place than right where you are; if you do not intend to go to work, you can not get along anywhere. Squirming & crawling about from place to place can do no good. You have raised no crop this year, and what you really want is to sell the land, get the money and spend it - part with the land you have, and my life upon it, you will never after, own a spot big enough to bury you in. Half you will get for the land, you spend in moving to Missouri, and the other half you will eat and drink, and wear out, & no foot of land will be bought. Now I feel it is my duty to have no hand in such a piece of foolery. I feel that is so even on your account; and particularly on *Mother's* account. The Eastern forty acres I intend to keep for Mother while she lives - if you *will not cultivate it*; it will rent for enough to support her - at least it will rent for something. Her Dower in the other two forties, she can let you have, and no thanks to me.

Now do not misunderstand this letter. I do not write in any unkindness. I write it in order, if possible, to get you to *face* the truth - which truth is, you are destitute because you have *idled* away all your time. Your thousand pretenses for not getting along better, are all non- sense - they deceive no body but yourself. *Go to work* is the only cure for your case."

He added a note to Sarah, "A word for Mother" from "your Son." He told her to try living with her granddaughter, Harriett, and her husband, Augustus Chapman, "I have no doubt he will make your situation very pleasant." Then, if she did not like it she could return to her own home. "If son John has not sold *that*," I said sarcastically.

On November 25, 1851, my husband wrote to "Dear Brother," for again Johnston wanted to sell the east forty acres which were really my husband's. My husband wanted Sarah to have them and said so.

"I want her to have her living, and I feel that it is my duty, to some extent, to see that she is not wronged. She had a right to Dower (that is, the use of one third for life) in the other two forties; but, it seems, she has already let you take that, hook and line. She now has the use of the whole East forty, as long as she lives; and if it be sold, of course, she is entitled to the interest on *all* the money it brings, as long as she lives; but you propose to sell it for three hundred dollars, take one hundred away with you, and leave her two hundred at 8 per cent, making her the *enormous* sum of 16 dollars a year. Now, if you are satisfied in treating her in that way, I am not. It is true, that you are to have that forty for two hundred dollars, *at* Mother's death; but you are not to have it *before.* I am confident that land can be made to produce for Mother, at least $30 a year, and I can not, to oblige any living person, consent that she shall be put on an allowance of sixteen dollars a year."

"*Halleluiah!*" I said to him, to myself, and even to Evil Eva while I stirred her up to cook supper.

On April 4, 1853, we were blessed again with another son, Thomas, named for my husband's father. This birth was the *worst* on me and left me with "female problems" that would stay with me the rest of my life. I was not able to have any more children.

My husband called our last son Tad, for he said, that as a baby, he looked like a little tadpole with his large head and sleek little body. My husband was to say Taddie reminded him of me, with his high emotions and enthusiasms, *gift of gab,* fun loving impulsive nature, and *dare.* I called Taddie my little *troublesome sunshine.*

Willie, on the other hand, was a copy of my husband, quiet, spiritually reflective, gentle, writing poems and making drawings for them, and he imitated his father as much as he could possibly do, even holding his head cocked to one side when he made an earnest argument. I just knew that Willie would be the comfort of our old age. Willie and Taddie were as different as night from day, but they were fiercely devoted to each other.

Bobby soon became Robert, and I always thought that when he stayed at the Todd mansions in Kentucky, he came back more Todd each time. As Robert grew older, I knew he was ashamed of his father for his backwoods' manners, his use of *reckon,* and even *ain't,* and when he studied Latin and his father studied it along with him, I felt *Robert* was a little snobbish about the whole thing. I know that, compared to the Todd wealth he so revered, he thought his father a financial failure. Robert just grew more and more different from the rest of us, reserved - *restrained* and so *private,* as if he never wanted to be a part of our family. It was as if he was indignant that he was put down the wrong stork chimney, that it should not have been the one at the plain old farmhouse, the Globe, but one of the Todd's. He seemed to show every restraint for life, while Taddie and Willie gobbled it up as fast as they could. He loftily scolded us and said to his father and me that we were spoiling the boys *rotten.*

My husband also felt the difference between Robert and our other sons. He wrote to Joshua Speed that Robert was "short and low," and "he is quite smart enough. I sometimes fear he is one of the little rare ripe sort, they are smarter at about five than thereafter."

My husband was a most sensitive man. He hid his sensitivity behind humor, but he knew, even when elected President of the United States, he had not yet earned Robert's approval.

But the fifties grew into golden years in our house on Eighth and Jackson. In the 1850's my husband's law practice was earning him good fees, and we even had a one-horse buggy. My husband carefully curried our horse he named *Buck,* and if I needed a carriage, he paid for someone to drive me at five cents a ride. We still pastured our cow with the Gourley cow, just east of our house. My husband still milked both cows before going to the office, and it was now Taddie's job to bring the full milk pail to me in the kitchen, and to take another full pail next door to James Gourley. I now had steady help with the house chores. I began to make my dresses out of silk and satin and was able to buy new clothes for the boys, instead of mending hand me downs. When my husband was off on circuit, I completed the second story of our house at about the cost of the original house. When my husband came home to a different one, he rang up each neighbor and asked him if they knew what had happened on the street. "What happened to *my* house?" he joked. I even had bought us a fine carriage, and he did not joke with the neighbors about that.

His law office was on the west side of the public square, and in the center of its green was the state capitol. When my husband walked the seven blocks to the office, he knew every neighbor on the way, and they were all our good friends. Their children played with our children, and our house was the most popular house for children in town. Across the street from us, the Solomon Wheelocks lived, and their teen-age daughter was at our house more than her own. She remembered that one night my husband and I were all dressed up to go to a party and Taddie yelled to go with us, and then Willie cocked his head to one side, like his father, and eloquently, and more quietly, joined Taddie's pleas. Of course, we let the boys come along. What they wanted they got, if it does not hurt them or anyone else, was *our* mantra. She also recalled an elegant party in our company parlor when Taddie peeked around the door in his red flannel nightdrawers. "Pa!" he hissed. "I want to be in the party, too!"

"Of course, son," my husband said. He picked him up, brought him into the room and gravely introduced him all around. Taddie groaned about it later. "Pa! You should have let me change out of my drawers first!"

"Son, that is not the way you asked to join the party," my husband gravely replied.

We did not fuss at Willie or Taddie *ever*. After Eddy left us, in their bright sweet faces, he was with us again.

When Willie and Taddie were small enough, their father used to lie on the floor, reading, with one or both boys balanced on a leg, which he rocked back and forth to their delightful squeals. When they were tired of that, they sat on his stomach, patted his face or pulled at his nose, and never did he lose a line of his reading. When they were older and had pushed/ pulled him home for lunch and supper, other children would run from their yards and clamor to be lifted up in those great arms and get a ride on his shoulders. There never was a parade in town that the little neighbors did not take turns to see it perched from there. One time, coming back from the office, our two sons were fighting, even as both were riding along on their father's shoulders. "What is the matter with your boys?" called out James Gourley.

"Just what's the matter with the whole world," my husband replied. "I have three walnuts, and they each want two."

My husband continued to baby-sit for me, now taking Willie and Taddie along to work. While he read his law books, sitting on his shoulder blades, as usual, they did everything Bobbie and Eddy had so enjoyed, and did it more thoroughly. They tore up the office so much they even terrified the office mice into scurrying back for their mouse holes, and trampled the organic floor garden into mush. They made cunning designs of splattered ink upon the walls, Willie being the more artistic, and Billy's legals continued to soar out of the window to fly away with the wind. Willie and Taddie did not see these as cunning birds but as their own little precious clouds. Sometimes, if it were cold, Billy's papers went into the fire instead, and then they did a little Indian dance of warmth appreciation, just as Eddy and Bobby had done. Of course, their father still had no clue to any change in his surroundings, and Billy's children had learned by now to run away from Billy at first sight.

To the office Willie and Taddie began to bring along our dog, Fido, and their many cats. Billy told everyone the boys could have also brought along the family cow, providing they could have pushed her up the stairs. *I could wring their necks* said Billy. *I could toss those brats out of the window!* he said in the old mantra with a new child basis. Being as I was such a hell-cat, naturally I had spawned forth demon children.

Willie loved toy trains, and he and his father would take each one apart and put it back together, and they both started up a house railroad. Willie took over the job, and excelling at math, drew up meticulous timetables for his trains. They ran from Chicago to New York and the trains were never *one minute* late. When my husband had to try a case in Chicago, he went by train and took Willie along. Never was a son happier to see that the railroad outside ran as efficiently as his own.

Taddie developed a lisp and did not like to read or study, so he didn't. He, like Willie, was most affectionate, and when their father came home, if they were not pulling/pushing him home, they jumped on him like a thunderbolt. Sometimes he would be reading, and they would jump right through his paper. And many times, when we were entertaining, Taddie would burst into the room, give his father a fierce hug, and then burst back out, leaving behind a wake of swaying *dented* hoop skirts.

On night, the boys just could not get their father away from an office chess game with Judge Samuel Treat. "Ma," said Taddie to me, "he says he will be right home, and then when I return, he is still playing the game!"

"Go try again!" I insisted before Evil Eva burned the house down with the meal she was working on to make ashes.

"*Ma!*" moaned Taddie.

"Taddie, you *can* do it," I said, not being entirely sure he could.

Taddie went into his father's office and did not say one word about coming home to supper. Instead, he kicked the chess board high into the air, and my husband mildly looked at its descent and that of all its brethren and said, "Well, Judge, I reckon we'll have to finish this game another time."

I tried to take Taddie to church, but it did not work, for Taddie had to listen for *so long* to someone else, when he mainly liked to listen to himself. He got so restless and was about to pull on nearby bonnet bows that when his father passed by, reading a book, and *actually glanced up*. I desperately signed for him to take Taddie home. My husband came in, picked up Taddie, put him on his shoulders and said to the startled congregation near the door, "Gentlemen, I entered this colt, but he is kicking so much I better withdraw him."

One night I remember my husband and I were at a party. The boys were home with a baby sitter. The party was wonderful, and the laughter from my husband's stories filled the room. But I suddenly felt a panic, and it would not go away. "Father," I said before another joke began. "Father!"

"What is it Molly?" he asked, worried as I as so agitated.

"There is something wrong at home!"

My husband immediately excused us and we went home. A fire had spread from a fireplace and the sitter was fast asleep. "If Molly had not had *known*," my husband told friends, "we could have lost everything!"

Let me quote again my sister, Emilie Todd who stayed with us for so long so many times. "Mary seemed almost clairvoyant; her intuitions were so clear and strong. She felt that Billy Herndon was detrimental to her husband and urged him to form a more desirable partnership. She distrusted Herndon and she did not believe in the sincerity of his friendship for her husband. The type of man was abhorrent to Mary and, honest above all things, she could no conceal her distaste for him and his very unfortunate habits, therefore incurring his bitter enmity. *Her intuitions were fully justified when Herndon became a Lincoln historian.*" (Emphasis by me) What ghastly *untrue* things the odious little man said about me, our *miserable* marriage! *He who was never in our house* - What if I do keep saying this? You keep hearing that I was a hellcat, made my husband's life hell etc and etc. Here is Emily again, "Mary was inordinately proud of him with every fiber of her being. She wanted his success because she wished the whole world to see him with her eyes, a great and glorious human being, the master spirit of his day and his generation. She was thrilled as she saw his greatness being recognized by his fellow citizens." Emilie noted I loved to wear white roses in my hair, that I flirted with my husband; that I met him at the gate of our fence and we walked into the house "swinging hands and joking like two children." Emile again, "Anyone could see that Mr. Lincoln admired Mary and was very proud of her - she took infinite pains to fascinate him again and again with pretty coquettish clothes, a dainty air and graces. She was gay and light hearted, hopeful and happy." As for my temper? "It was soon over, and for it her husband loved her none the less - and oh, how she did love this man! ...Mr. Lincoln enjoyed his home and he and Mary idolized their children. So far as I could see there was complete harmony and loving kindness between Mary and her husband, consideration for each other's wishes and a taste for the same books. They seemed congenial in all things."

My sister, Mrs. Frances Todd Wallace, wrote, "Mary fairly worshipped him. The story of their unhappiness is absolutely false."

So there I was in that - *then* - having our little parlor parties, the house filled with flowers, flowers in my hair, "happy, charmed and charming," they said, even if I continued to read novels in French!

Those golden years of the fifties - those cherished years, the best of our lives - our front gate might have been crooked with children swinging on it so much, but that made no difference to either my husband or to me. He always said, *let the little codgers have their fun, and run free.* For every single thing Eddy would never have, we wanted Willie and Taddie to have. It was at our house where all the block children came for toffee pulls, my husband putting on a big apron and making the toffee himself, and although I kept a neat and a clean house, the house was for the children and us, and not the other way around.

Our home was ever warm with childish squeals of glee, with our little boys at our table in deep content, with a mother and a father deeply in love, and the world wonderful beyond a most cherished dream.

Chapter Nine

Henry Clay died on June 29, 1852. In Springfield all businesses closed and there were two July 6 memorial services in his memory, one at the Episcopal Church given by Reverend Charles Dresser, who married my husband and me, and the other at the State House of Representatives given by my husband. It was a long speech, beautifully delivered, and here are excerpts from it.

Clay and the new Republic had had a life together since Clay's birth in 1777, and "As on a question of liberty, he knew no North, no South, no East, no West, but only the Union, which held them all in its sacred circle." . ." Clay had quelled civil commotion three times, and in the last one, "when this Union trembled to its center - in old age, he left the shades of private life and gave the death blow to fraternal strife . . . He exercised the demon which possessed the body politic, and gave peace to a distracted land . . . Mr. Clay's predominant sentiment, from first to last, was a deep devotion to the cause of human liberty - a strong sympathy with the oppressed everywhere, and an ardent wish for their elevation . . . He loved his country partly because it was his own country, but mostly because it was a free country; and he burned with a zeal for its advancement, prosperity and glory, because he saw in such, the advancement, prosperity and glory, of human liberty, human right and human nature. He desired the prosperity of his countrymen partly because they were his countrymen, but chiefly to show to the world that free men could prosper." Jefferson had noted the danger of a *geographical* line dividing the country with the Missouri Compromise of 1820, and wrote: "But this momentous question, like a fire bell in the night, awakened, and filled me with terror. I considered it at once as the death knell of the Union . . . A geographical line, co-including with a marked principle, moral and political, once conceived, and held up to the angry passions of men, will never be obliterated; and every irritation will mark it deeper and deeper. . ." What to do? Jefferson said of the question, "But we have the wolf by the ears and we can neither hold him, nor safely let him go. Justice is in one scale, and self preservation in the other." My husband noted that Clay was always opposed to slavery, that he had favored *gradual* emancipation of the slaves in Kentucky. "He did not perceive, that on the question of human rights, the negroes were to be excepted from the human race." Yet, immediate emancipation, my husband said, "would shiver into fragments the Union of these states," and the opposite extreme, to perpetuate slavery, mocked our charter of freedom, the declaration that "all men are created free and equal." (denied by John C. Calhoun) Henry Clay opposed both extremes. "We both then believed in *compensated* emancipation." My husband wanted slavery to end; he wanted our country freed from its *dangerous presence*, and if negroes could be restored to their father land, (as the Jews had been freed from Egyptian bondage of four hundred years) and *if* they had "bright prospects for the future," this to be done so gradually that "neither races nor individuals *shall have suffered* by the change, it will indeed be a glorious consummation."

In January of 1854 Stephen Arnold Douglas, who had been elected to the Senate the same year my husband had been elected to the House, introduced his Kansas Nebraska Bill, and that year it became law. Mr. Douglas was chairman of the Senate committee on territories, and he was anxious to organize the territory of Nebraska. We all knew a railroad to the Pacific West was coming, and he wanted it to be built from the North through the Nebraska Territory and not from the South. The Gadsden Purchase of 1853 made a Southern route from New Orleans very possible. To get Southern support in Congress for his organization of the territory of Nebraska, Douglas proposed to also create a territory of Kansas, and open up both to popular sovereignty, wherein the people there could chose for themselves whether their territory, and thus its subsequent states, would be slave or free.

This would allow at long last the spreading of slavery outside the fifteen slave states of the South. My husband always noted that our forefathers legalized the heinous thing in our Constitution without once using the word SLAVE, as if they were ashamed of the word and its vile practice. My husband said the Kansas Nebraska Bill nullified the intent of our forefathers, for in their 1787 Northwest Ordinance slavery was forbidden in the states that would form in the Northwest. Douglas's bill even nullified the Missouri Compromise of 1820! By that year the Senators from North and South were even, but the House stood at 105 Representatives for the North and 81 for the South. When Maine was admitted as a free state to balance the admittance of Missouri as a slave state, the division of the free and slave states to be in the Louisiana Purchase Territory was set at 36-30, except for the Missouri southern boundary. And even then, way back in 1820, a strong tide of nationalism helped prevent North/South fighting over the extension of slavery. I remember reading Tom Cobb of Georgia said then a controversy of fire had been kindled "that all the waters of the ocean cannot put out, which seas of blood can only extinguish." Now the embers of this conflict were stirred up again by Mr. Douglas. My husband sighed, "Why didn't he just leave well enough alone?"

I really think that our friend, Mr. Douglas, certainly a brilliant man, wanted to be elected the Democratic President in 1860, and his bill was courting the Southern vote in allowing slavery to spread beyond its present borders. He already had the support of Northern Democrats.

His bill set the country on fire. It was sparks to dry tender of the South's defense of slavery and that of the majority of those in the North disliking it and opposing its extension. The Kansas Nebraska Bill simply caused a spontaneous eruption, and from its flames emerged a whole new political party, *too strong in one year* to be delegated to a third party status. It was the new Republican Party, and into it flocked former northern Whigs and Democrats, Free Soilers, Quakers and Abolitionists, all who did not want the spreading of slavery beyond where it had been accepted as legal. My husband changed from Whig to Republican. He was on fire with determination that slavery would not spread beyond where it had to be legally accepted. He made endless speeches against the bill. In September of 1854 he spoke in Bloomington, in October he spoke in Springfield, making speeches against the bill from October 15 to November 1 - in Chicago on the 27, in Quincy on November 1. He never could let it go. In 1856 he spoke in Petersburg, Jacksonville, Bloomington, Olney, Belleville, Quincy, Vandalia, and on December 10, he spoke at a Republican banquet in Chicago. I loved this speech. *The central idea of this country* - what rested in public opinion (the basis of our government) *was the equality of men,* or the "steady progress towards the practical equality of all men." Now the pro-slave party is to substitute for this "the opposite idea that slavery is right, the workings of which, as a central idea, may be the perpetuity of human slavery, and its extension to all countries and colors. . . let us re inaugurate the good old central ideas of the Republic. . . . We shall again be able to declare that 'all states as States, are equal,' nor yet that ' all citizens as citizens are equal,' but to renew the broader, better declaration, including these and much more, that 'all *men* are created equal.' "

Joshua Speed, of course, opposed the stand my husband was taking, as he was a firm believer in slavery. My husband had written a letter to him on August 24, 1855. So, in the *abstract,* Speed admitted slavery was wrong. "But you say," my husband wrote, "that sooner than yield your legal right to the slave . . . you would see the Union dissolved. I am not aware that *any one* is bidding you to yield that right; very certainly, I am not . . . I also acknowledge *your* rights and *my* obligations, under the constitution, in regard to your slaves . . . I do oppose the extension of slavery, because my judgment and feelings so prompt me; and I am under no obligation to the contrary." About the Nebraska law - "I look upon that enactment not as a law, but as *violence* from the beginning. It was conceived in violence, passed in violence, is maintained in violence, and is being executed in violence. I say it was *conceived* in violence, because the destruction of the Missouri Compromise, under the circumstances, was nothing less than violence. It was *passed* in violence, because it could not have passed at all but for the votes of many members, in violent disregard of the known will of their constituents. It is *maintained* in violence because the elections since, clearly demand its repeal, and this demand is openly disregarded . . . The slave-breeders and slave-traders, are a small, odious and detested class among you; and yet in politics, they dictate the course of all of you, and are as completely your masters as you are the masters of your own negroes." Where did he stand? "I now do no more than oppose the *extension* of slavery." . . . I am not a Know Nothing. That is certain. How could I be? How can any one who abhors the oppression of negroes, be in favor of degrading classes of white people? Our progress in degeneracy appears to me to be pretty rapid. As a nation, we began by declaring that *"all men are created equal."* We now practically read it *"all men are created equal, except negroes."* When the Know Nothings get control, it will read, "all men are created equal, except negroes, *and foreigners and Catholics."* When it comes to this I should prefer emigrating to some country where they make no pretence of loving liberty - to Russia, for instance; here despotism can be taken pure and without the base alloy of hypocrisy." He closed, "And yet, let me say I am, Your friend forever."

My husband had the rare ability to separate a person's ideas he did *not* like from the person he *did* like.

Because of its *peculiar institution*, the South remained mainly agrarian with the importation of most of its manufactured goods. It was the large land and slave owners who ruled the South for the number of their slaves increased their political representation. Henry Clay's great American System was largely trade of raw materials from the North*west* for manufactured goods from the North*east*, with the South lagging behind in not only the North's manufacturing boom of the 1830's but the North's transportation boom as well. Importing many manufactured goods from Britain, the South opposed a high tariff; the northern industrialists wanted a high tariff to protect their industries from foreign competition. For its domestic trade, the North wanted increased and publicly financed transport; the South did not. The North supported immigration for the cheap labor of its factories, the South opposed immigrants as mainly being (Irish) Catholic plots. The *Know Nothings,* more powerful in the South, *hated* Catholics and declared the

Pope digging a tunnel under the Atlantic Ocean to start up the Vatican in the Mississippi Valley. This would increase American nun/priest orgies with more of their babies tossed down into the church well. A free press, widely read penny newspapers, public schools, and working men's unions were plentiful in the North and scarce in the South. I believed the very roots of democracy that were flourishing in the North were poisoned in the South by its defense of slavery. Not only had the slaves lost their right to liberty, also those who dared to write or preach against it.

The churches had already divided into north and south over the very morality of slavery. *Uncle Tom's Cabin* had been published in 1852. Harriet Beecher Stowe might not have written a great novel, but it had a great impact in showing the horrors of slavery. Her book swept the North, selling 3,000 copies on its first day, and 300,000 before the end of the year. Soon the story was drama in the theaters, and below the Mason Dixon line it was *not* read, and it was not dramatized. In the South they said in the North Uncle Tom would be out of work, out of luck and on the street without a cabin.

In 1856 my husband campaigned for the first Republican Presidential candidate, John C. Fremont, running against Democrat James Buchanan. The South was solid in support of Buchanan, but in the North he won only five states, while Fremont won eleven. And two days after the inauguration of Buchanan came the *dreadful* Dred Scott Decision of the Supreme Court in which it adopted the Southern view of slavery IN FULL. Of the nine justices, seven were Democrats, one a Whig and only one a Republican. Of the seven Democrats, five were from the South. Chief Justice Roger Taney wrote the court opinion - the black man had NO rights the white man had to respect. The black man was property, and the ownership of him was protected by the Fifth Amendment. (At least in the Constitution - "those who owed service" - the slaves - were counted as 3/5th of a white man for representation and taxation) *Slavery could not be declared illegal in a territory,* and Congress had exceeded its authority to make it illegal in the Louisiana Purchase, except for Missouri, north of thirty-six degrees thirty minutes. The Missouri Compromise had not created any free states? Neither had the Ohio River and the Mason-Dixon line? There were *no* free states? Now - was it the law of the land that slavery could spread to the territories, or *anywhere* north of Dixie?

What *had* been said in Jefferson's ideal for the American Revolution? Who had the *inalienable* right to life, liberty and the pursuit of happiness? Did the Declaration of Independence declare *all* men equal? Negroes to whites? All whites to whites? Here is what my husband had to say when he discussed the Dred Scott Decision in a speech given in Springfield, June 26, 1857.

"I think the authors of that notable instrument intended to include *all* men, but they did not intend to declare *all* men equal *in all respects*. They did not mean to say all were equal in color, size, intellect, moral developments, or social capacity. They defined with tolerable distinctions, in what respects they did consider all men created equal - equal in "certain inalienable rights, among which are life, liberty and the pursuit of happiness" . . . They meant simply to declare the *right*, so that the *enforcement* of it might follow as fast as circumstances should permit. They meant to set up a standard maxim for free society, which should be familiar to all, and revered by all, constantly looked to, constantly labored for, and even though never perfectly attained, constantly approximated, and therefore constantly spreading and deepening its influence, and augmenting the happiness and value of life to all people of all colors everywhere." It was *not* just to explain our separation with Great Britain, it was "meant to be a stumbling block to those who in after times might seek to turn a free people back into the hateful paths of despotism." Douglas has argued - " 'They were speaking of British subjects on this continent being equal to British subjects residing in Great Britain!' Why, according to this, not only negroes but white people outside of Great Britain and America are not spoken of in this instrument. The English, Irish, and Scotch, along with white Americans, were included to be sure, but the French, Germans and other white people of the world are all gone to pot along with the Judge's (Douglas was briefly a judge) inferior races.

I had thought the Declaration promised something better than the condition of the British subjects; but no, it only meant that we should be *equal* to them in their own oppressed and *unequal* condition. According to that, it gave no promise that having kicked off the King and Lords of Great Britain, we should not at once be saddled with a King and Lords of our own."

If it *were just* a justification for our revolution, then as that has passed some eighty-one years ago, "the Declaration is of no practical use now - mere rubbish - old wadding left to rot on the battlefield after victory is won." He gave the Douglas version of the Declaration, "We hold these truths to be self-evident that all British subjects, who were on this continent eighty one years ago, are created equal to all British subjects born and *then* residing in Great Britain." Is our declaration no more than "an interesting memorial to the dead past? Not a germ, or a suggestion, of the *individual rights of man* left in it?"

So here, about the *extension* of slavery, we have the Douglas bill opening the territories to popular sovereignty; the Supreme Court nullifying that and the Republican Party opposing the spreading of slavery out of the established slave states.

Civil war broke out in the territory of Kansas. Anyone could have seen that it would. Slavers sent in armed men from Missouri to make Kansas a *slave* territory, and Free Soilers sent in armed men from the Northeast with "Beecher Bibles" (guns) to see that Kansas was a *free* territory. Armed Free Soilers formed the anti-slavery camp of Lawrence, and armed Missourians formed the pro-slave camps of Atchison, Leavenworth and Lecompton. The Lecompton paper, *Squatter Sovereign,* announced that pro slavers would "lynch and hang, tar and feather and drown every white livered abolitionist who dares to pollute our soil." In May of 1856 they pillaged the free town of Lawrence, and John Brown came down from the mountains of New York with sons and what he saw as a God-given crusade to fight slavery wherever he could. Buchanan, pro - South, worked to have Kansas admitted slave and did not support Douglas's popular sovereignty at all, for the majority in Kansas voted free, and that was how, in 1861, Kansas eventually came into the Union. Free.

In 1857 there was a panic in the North that did not hit the South. With the Democrat weak banking system over extending credit, there was northern over speculation in the railroads with railroads going where there would not be profits for years to come. Manufacturers and farmers over expanded right along with the railroads. But the Crimean War kept the European demand for Southern cotton prosperously high, and the South felt more secure than ever with an economy of *King Cotton* wedded to its *peculiar institution.*

The Illinois Legislature had met in February of 1855 to choose a second senator, and my husband worked to get Lyman Trumbull the nomination. Trumbull was now married to my friend, and bridesmaid, Julia Jayne, who had helped me write the *Rebecca* letters. After the election of Mr. Trumbull, my husband devoted all of his time to his growing and successful law practice. We both loved to entertain, and now we could afford it. During the season we gave strawberry parties, with the usual combination of fresh berries and ice cream, seventy guests the norm, sometimes the most influential people in the state, but mostly our guests were our friends and relatives. We made calls on our friends, too, for the *proper* three-hour visit, and went often to the theater, now brilliant with gleaming new gas lamps. We never lost our love for the theater.

At the close of 1854, my little sister, Emilie Todd, now eighteen, the same age as Bobby, came to Springfield for a six-month visit with her four married sisters. My husband still affectionately called her "Little Sister," and he and I both conspired to see that she had prettier clothes than the governor's own daughter. We bought her a beautiful white bonnet with white feathers that got more attention from the Sunday church congregation than the minister! She was with us long enough to observe and *record* our very happy marriage. She also noted I had taught Robert *impeccable* manners, that when we went out to the country on wild flower hunts, that he helped the ladies into and out of their carriages, just like his father. Emilie left us in the late spring of 1855 and married our dear friend, Ben Harden Helm. Ben was the son of Governor Helm of Kentucky.

On February 5, 1857, after I had made *all* new curtains for our downstairs, we invited in five hundred guests! But the weather turned foul and only three hundred came. We could not have squeezed more into our house, anyway. It was recognized in Springfield that dinners at our house were special and coveted events. Isaac Arnold wrote of a "kind and genial hostess," and "the wit, humor anecdotes and unrivaled conversation of the host made a dinner at his house one to be remembered."

My favorite cousin, John Todd Stuart, attended our parties with my other relatives, but as his daughter grew into womanhood, he *gravely* feared its consequences. When he took her away from home, to ours, or *even to church,* she was *not* to look at *any* young man. And if she felt the inclination to do such a thing, she was to shut her eyes *tight!* Such was the fear of the normal in my day.

My husband had worked for the Illinois Central Railroad for an agreed *large* fee of $5,000, (the odious little man taking half) and he had gone before the Illinois Supreme Court on February 28, 1854, arguing against his two former law partners, my cousin, John Todd Stuart, and Stephen Logan, and when the case was continued, he won for the railroad in January of 1856. He then waited for his payment. It did not come. The only thing he heard from the railroad, in May of 1857, was that they wanted him to continue working for them! Still, *no payment.* On June 18 my husband went to the McLean Court to sue the railroad and won by default. Their lawyer appeared that afternoon and asked that my husband's judgment be set aside for his fee being unreasonable. My husband won again; still no payment. In late July my husband went to see the railroad powers that be in their high and mighty New York City office, and the railroad directors treated him very coolly. He came home on August 1 and got a court execution for the sheriff of Mclean County to begin seizing enough railroad property to satisfy his judgment. The railroad then paid him his $5,000, kept him on as a lawyer, and when he went east to do some more business for them, he had the money to take me along! It was a honeymoon of a trip; we visited Niagara, Canada and in New York; we saw the great ships coming in from Europe or going out to it, and

I said, "Father, will we travel like that some day?" And he smiled in content; sea smells of summer mixed with the first brightness of autumn, and he said, "Mother, I reckon we will. That is a *promise.*"

On August 29, 1857, a man had been beaten to death by two men, so said the state's chief witness, Charles Allen. His testimony had already sent to jail for manslaughter one of the assailants, James Norris. The other accused was the son of Jack Armstrong, William Armstrong, or *Duff.* His trial was to be in the spring of 1858 in Beardstown, Cass County. Jack Armstrong was dead and Duff was the sole support of his mother, Hannah. My husband was asked to defend Duff, which he did, and the manner in which he did it became famous. At Duff's trial, Allen repeated his story. He had seen the murder. *You saw it?* asked my husband. *From 155 feet away? At eleven at night? That exact time - eleven at night?* "Indeed, yes." *How could you see so clearly at eleven at night?* "The moon was so bright." *Was it full?* "Yes, as high in the heavens as the sun at ten a.m." My husband then had the 1857 almanac presented to Allen and asked him to read to the jury what the moon was doing that night. He had to read that the moon was barely past its first quarter, and at eleven it had completely disappeared from the sky.

A huge crowd had gathered to see and hear my husband. It was a very, very hot day; the courtroom was sweltering but not a person left it. My husband had taken off his coat and his vest and even his neck stock. As he talked, it seemed more likely the deceased had taken a fatal fall from his horse, and as my husband told about Hannah being such a good kind woman and how she would be destitute if Duff were put in jail, he had tears in his eyes. So did the audience. So did the jury. I heard they were sobbing outright when they acquitted Duff on the first ballot.

On June 16, 1858, at the close of its Illinois state convention, the new Republican Party chose my husband to run for the Senate against Stephen A. Douglas. His acceptance speech became known as "The House Divided Speech." It was published in the *Illinois State Journal* on the eighteenth and in the *Chicago Daily Tribune* on the nineteenth. In his early lines he said that agitation about the slave crisis had been "constantly augmented" and "will not cease, until a crisis shall have been reached and passed.

A house divided against itself cannot stand.

I believe the government can not endure, permanently half slave and half free.

I do not expect the Union to be dissolved - I do not expect the house to fall - but I do expect it will cease to be divided.

It will become all of one thing, or all of the other.

Either the opponents of slavery will arrest the further spread of it, and place it where the public mind shall rest in the belief that it is in course of ultimate extinction; or its advocates will push it forward, till it shall become alike lawful in all of the States, old as well as new - North as well as South."

He pointed out that the Nebraska Bill had opened to slavery the territories where Congress had prohibited it. That was the first point gained by the pro-slavers. This, he said, was to be based on squatter sovereignty, the sacred right of self government perverted to mean, "*That if any one man, chooses to enslave another, no third man shall be allowed to object.*"

Then, my husband continued, came the Supreme Court's Dred Scott Decision, right *after* the election, the day *after* Buchanan's inauguration, supported by both Douglas and Buchanan, *astonished that any different view had ever been entertained!* Squatter Sovereignty had been squatted out of existence. Then came the squabble between Douglas and Buchanan over the rigged pro slave Lecompton Constitution for the territory of Kansas - was it made by the majority there? No, and so Douglas, to his credit, opposed it, and Buchanan's support of it.

My husband continued. The Supreme Court has said that neither "Congress nor a territorial Legislature can exclude slavery from any United States territory . . . thus to enhance the chances of permanency to the institution through all the future." Therefore, the freedom for the people to choose was no freedom at all.

Does the court apply this *also to the states?* my husband asked. The justices "all omit to declare whether or not the same Constitution permits a state, or the people of a state, to exclude it . . . In what cases the power of the states is so restrained by the U.S. Constitution, is left an open question." Will there be another Supreme Court decision "declaring that the Constitution *of the* United States does not permit *a state* to exclude slavery from its limits?

And this may especially be expected if the doctrine of 'care not whether slavery be voted down or voted up' (Douglas's view) shall gain upon the public mind sufficiently to give promise that such a decision can be maintained when made . . .

We shall lie down pleasantly dreaming the people of Mississippi are on the verge of making their State free, and we shall awake to the reality instead, that the Supreme Court had made Illinois a slave State . . .

To meet and overthrow the power of that dynasty is the work now before all those who would prevent that consummation.

That is what we have to do.

But how can we best do it?

Would it be through Senator Douglas, because he has quarreled with Buchanan over popular sovereignty, in that Buchanan wants Kansas a slave territory in spite of the opposition of its majority?" my husband asked. But Douglas does not oppose the extension of slavery. "His avowed mission is impressing the 'public heart' to care nothing about it.

A leading Douglas Democratic newspaper thinks Douglas' superior talent will be needed to resist the revival of the African slave trade.

Does Douglas believe an effort to revive the slave trade is approaching? He has not said so. Does he really think so? But, if it is, how can he resist it? For years he has labored to prove it is a sacred right of white men to take negro slaves into the new territories. Can he possibly show that it less a sacred right to buy them where they can be bought cheapest? And, unquestionably they can be bought cheaper in Africa than in Virginia.

He has done all in his power to reduce the whole question of slavery to one of a mere right of property; and as such, how can he oppose the foreign slave trade - how can he refuse that trade in that 'property' shall be 'perfectly free' - unless he does it as a protection to the home production?

The cause of the Republican Party had to be entrusted to and conducted by its own undoubted friends "who do care for the result . . .

We shall not fail- if we stand firm, we shall not fail.

Wise councils may accelerate or mistakes delay it, but sooner or later the victory is sure to come."

My husband's speech won him national recognition and to increase it, on July 24, he challenged Senator Douglas to debate him, and seven debates were scheduled. He was asked to give a bibliography for publication, and here is what he wrote:

Born, February 12, 1809 in Hardin County, Kentucky.
Education defective.
Profession, a lawyer.
Have been a captain of volunteers in the Black Hawk war.
Postmaster of a very small office.
Four times a member of the Illinois legislature and was a member of the lower house of Congress. Yours, etc.

Because I had to be home with the children, I could only attend his last debate at Alton on October 15, 1858.

The first was at Ottawa on August 21, and my husband made many speeches while the debates were going on and I read them all in the *Chicago Press and Tribune,* certainly NOT in the vicious Democratic Party *Chicago*

Times! How proud I was of my husband. He never stooped to the personal attacks that Mr. Douglas did. I cannot imagine that Mr. Douglas, who knows my husband never drinks *any* liquor could have the nerve to say right off that my husband "could ruin more liquor than all of the boys of the town together!" Mr. Douglas likes booze and drinks plenty of it, and when he cited all of the failures of my husband at about everything he has done, farming, liquor selling, the law, my husband replied to him, "It's true, every word of it. I've tried a lot of things, but there is one thing that Douglas forgot. He told you that I sold liquor, but he didn't mention that while I had quit my side of the counter, he has remained on his." The laughing and clapping was tremendous.

During all of the debates Mr. Douglas had his own special train of cars, his own band, his own bodyguard of friends and his own cannon to boom, boom out his arrival when he did that at a town. On this, which my husband called "fireworks and fizzle gigs," Douglas spent $50,000. My husband rode freight trains, or the caboose of the train, and even then he spent five hundred dollars of our money, and with no income, that was a lot and we were hurting when it was all over.

There was great scorn among the Democrats because my husband was so tall, his legs so long. One came up and asked my husband what he thought the *proper* length of a man's leg should be. My husband looked down at the man and said, "I reckon it should be long enough to reach from his body to the ground."

Chapter Ten

On Saturday, August 21, in their first debate at Ottawa, Mr. Douglas called my husband an *old friend,* but said he was a failure at everything but dividing the country and seeing to the demise of the old Whig Party. A new party had been formed in its stead, the BLACK Republican Party, the ABOLITION Party of FRED Douglass. And, said Douglas, the only thing my husband had done in Congress was to oppose the Mexican War, "taking the side of the common enemy against his own country." This, said Douglas, made him so disliked he had "to retire to private life forgotten by his former friends." He then dredged up the horrors of Negro citizenship, Negro equality - free Negroes pouring into Illinois - EQUAL TO YOURSELVES! This caused moans and screams among his admirers, and Douglas compounded the travesty by saying, "I believe this government was made on a white basis. I believe it was made by white men, for the benefit of white men and their posterity for ever, and I am in favor of confining citizenship to white men of European birth and descent, instead of conferring it upon Negroes, Indian and other inferior races." Neither the Declaration of Independence nor God decreed the negro as equal or a brother. In fact *God* never intended the Negro to be equal to the white man, for *wherever* the negro went he was an *inferior* race. Each territory and each state must decide the slavery issue consistent with their public good on the basis of popular sovereignty. Under *self-government,* said Douglas, we have grown from a nation of three or four million to one of thirty million, replacing the *savages* and their *barbarism* with churches and schools.

When my husband came forward to speak, *both* the Democratic papers covering the speeches had to admit that he got two thirds of the audience cheering for him. *Protracted* cheers the papers called them. My husband attacked popular sovereignty and the repeal of the Missouri Compromise. "I hate it because of the monstrous injustice of slavery itself," he said. "I hate it because it deprives our republican example of its just influence in the world - enables the enemies of free institutions, with plausibility, to taunt us as hypocrites - causes the real friends of freedom to doubt our sincerity, and especially because it forces so many really good men amongst ourselves into an open war with the very fundamental principal of civil liberty - criticizing the Declaration of Independence, and insisting there is no right principle but *self interest*." He went on to say that he had no prejudice against the Southern people. "They are just what we would be in their situation. If slavery did not now exist among them, they would not introduce it. If it did now exist amongst us, we should not instantly give it up...When southern people tell us they are no more responsible for the origin of slavery than we; I acknowledge the fact . . . I surely will not blame them for not doing what I should not know how to do myself. If all the earthly power were given to me, I should not know what to do, as to the existing institution." If the slaves were freed, what to do with them? Certainly sending them to Liberia could not be done, for their survival would be in doubt, as well as the means to send them there. Free them and make them our equal? The universal feeling would not accept this now and a universal feeling cannot be safely disregarded. Without it, the Negro cannot be made equal. Perhaps gradual emancipation was the answer, "but for the tardiness of this I will not undertake to judge our brethren of the South. But all this; to my judgment," he continued, "furnishes no more excuse for permitting slavery to go into our own free territory, than it would be for reviving the African slave trade by law."

If the negro cannot be made equal to the white man, with the physical difference between the two, "there is no reason in the world why the negro is not entitled to all the natural rights enumerated in the Declaration of Independence, the right to life, liberty and the pursuit of happiness. I hold that he is as much entitled to them as the white man." The negro is not considered equal in many respects, certainly not in color, "But in the right to eat the bread, without leave from anybody else, which his own hand earns, *he is my equal and the equal of Judge Douglas and the equal of every living man*."

As for my husband's opposition to the *reason* given to the Mexican War - this did not stop him from supporting our soldiers sent to it. In that way, he voted the same as Douglas.

It is good that our nation has diversity of soil and climate, my husband said, that it has different goods to trade, and this diversity forged bonds of union, not discord, unlike the slave question. It is on that question the house is divided against itself, the *spreading* of slavery, and its *perpetuation*, its *nationalization*. This is what Douglas and his supporters are doing now, placing slavery on this *new* basis, when our forefathers fought its extension by restricting slavery from the new territories where it had not gone and cutting of its source by cutting off the slave trade. The new plan is making slavery "alike lawful in all of the States, old as well as new, North as well as South. Now, I believe if we could arrest its spread, and place it where Washington, Jefferson, and Madison placed it, it would be in the course of ultimate extinction...The crisis would be past and the institution might be left alone for a hundred years, if it should live that long, in the States where it exists, yet it would be going out of existence in the way best for the black and white races."

"Popular Sovereignty is humbug!" the crowd shouted. My husband gave it his own definition. "My understanding is that Popular Sovereignty, as now applied to the question of Slavery, does allow the people of a Territory to have Slavery if they want to, but does not allow them *not* to have it if they *do not* want it . . . as I understand the Dred Scott Decision, if any one man wants slaves, all the rest have no way of keeping that one man from holding them."

Why did Douglas vote down an amendment to his Nebraska Bill giving people the right in that territory to exclude slavery if they wanted to? Why did he say his bill was not an attempt to "legislate slavery into any Territory or *State?*" So why *did* Douglas put - *or State* there? "The law they were passing was not about States, and was not making provisions for States. What was it placed there for? After seeing the Dred Scott decision, which holds that people cannot exclude slavery from a *Territory*, if another Dred Scott decision shall come, holding that they cannot exclude it from a *State,* we shall discover that when it was originally put there, it was in view of something that was to come in due time; we shall see it was the other *half* of something." Is the course of Douglas to make slavery national? Will this be accomplished by the next Dred Scott decision? Douglas has disagreed with decisions of the Supreme Court many times, but upholds the court on Dred Scott because the court made it, in a "Thus saith the Lord attitude with no say whether the decision is morally right or wrong. "The next decision, as much as this, will be a *Thus saith the Lord."*

What influence is Douglas making on public opinion? With it nothing can fail; without it nothing can succeed. When Douglas says he 'cares not whether slavery is voted down or voted up, ' - that it is a sacred right of self government - he is in my judgment penetrating the human soul and eradicating the light of reason and the love of liberty in this American people." Here, my husband received *long* and *enthusiastic* applause.

I do not think that Mr. Douglas did himself well by saying that my husband had set himself up above the Supreme Court and two Presidents, (all pro-slave) and that without fact or proof, he was trying to bring down and destroy "the purest and the best of living men." He called my husband "an ignorant man."

Any man, who dares to call my husband ignorant, is, indeed, a *fool.*

The second debate was at Freeport on August 27. Mr. Douglas had asked my husband to reply to seven key questions, which he did clearly and right away. He then asked four questions of his own, and the key ones, in my opinion, were (2) "Can the people of a United States Territory, in any lawful way, against the wish of any citizen of the United States, exclude slavery from its limits prior to the formation of a State Constitution?" and (3) "If the Supreme Court of the United States shall decide the *states* can not exclude slavery from their limits, are you in favor of acquiescing in, adopting and following such decision as a rule of political action?"

The applause for this question was tremendous. Even the Democratic *Chicago Times* admitted this.

And here is how Mr. Douglas evaded the issue. Of course slavery could be excluded from a territory. What matters the Dred Scott Decision? Said Mr. Douglas: "It matters not what way the Supreme Court may hereafter decide as to the abstract question whether slavery may or may not go into a territory under the constitution, the people have the lawful means to introduce or exclude it as they please, for the reason that slavery cannot exist a day or an hour anywhere, unless it is *supported by local police regulations.* Those police regulations can only be established by the local legislature, and if the people are opposed to slavery they will elect representatives to that body who will by *unfriendly* legislation effectually *prevent* the introduction of it into their midst. If, on the contrary, they are for it, their legislation will favor its extension. *Hence, no matter what the decision of the Supreme Court may be* on that abstract question, still the right of the people to make a slave territory or a free territory is perfect and complete under the Nebraska Bill."

So much for the decisions of the Supreme Court! Or any court! We can pass local laws *against* court decisions? Doesn't the court ultimately decide what *is* lawful and what *is not?* Aren't the decisions of the Supreme Court *Constitutional* ones? And is not the Constitution the law of the land? The law must be obeyed until it is changed, surely, under a changed judiciary.

And Mr. Douglas becomes *amazed* that my husband would ask about a *state* having the *right* to exclude slavery! Why a school -boy should know better and to not cast an imputation upon the Supreme Court! Mr. Douglas had denounced such an idea himself, and the Supreme Court would not violate the Constitution of the United Sates! "I tell him that such a thing is not possible. It would be an act of moral treason that no man on the bench could ever descend to."

But hadn't that *same* court, with the *same* men, already nullified self - government, regarding slavery, in the territories?

My husband made many speeches in between his seven debates with

Mr. Douglas. In Carlinville on August 31, he said again he had no wish to interfere with slavery where it was already established and lawfully exists. But he pointed out that although the Constitution supports slavery in the South, no where in it is the word *slave* mentioned- "and Madison says it was omitted that further generations might not know such a thing ever existed - and that the Constitution might yet be called a 'national charter of freedom.'" If things had been left alone we might have had peace over the issue, "But it is now advancing to become lawful everywhere ... This change in our national policy is decided to be constitutional ... a territorial legislature cannot exclude slavery in behalf of its people, and if their premise be correct, a state cannot exclude it - for they tell us that the negro is property anywhere in the light that horses are property ... It only requires another case and another favorable decision from the same court to make the rights of property alike in *states* as well as territories ... The compromises of the Constitution we must all stand by, but where is the justness of extending the institution to compete with white labor and thus degrade it?

Are only white Englishmen to have the right to life, liberty and the pursuit of happiness?" my husband asked. "Are Jeffersonian Democrats willing to have the gem taken from the magma charta of human liberty in this shameful way? ... We can no longer express our admiration for the Declaration of Independence without their petty sneers. And it is thus they are fast bringing that sacred instrument into contempt ... to gain their end they will endeavor to impress upon the public mind that the negro is not human, and even upon his own soil he has no rights which white men are bound to respect .. . If Douglas can make you believe that slavery is a sacred right - if we are to wallow in Dred Scottism that the right of property in negroes is not confined to the states where it is established by local law - if by special sophisms he can make you believe that no nation except the English are born equal and are entitled to life, liberty, and the pursuit of happiness, upon their own soil, or when they are not constitutionally divested of the God-given rights to enjoy the fruits of their own labor, then may we truly despair of the universality of freedom, or the efficacy of those sacred principles enunciated by our fathers - and give in our adhesion to the perpetuation and the unlimited extension of slavery."

On September 11 in Edwardsville, my husband was requested to state the difference between the two parties in this campaign. "The difference between the Republican and the Democratic parties on the leading issue of this contest, as I understand it, is, that the former consider slavery a moral, social and political wrong, while the latter *do not* consider it either a moral, social or political wrong . ." He pointed out that Douglas did not invent popular sovereignty; it was enunciated in our Declaration of Independence - the right of the people to govern *slaves* is not the right of a people to govern *themselves*. To put slaves under the lash is not a sacred right of self-government. "Now, when by all these means you have succeeded in dehumanizing the Negro; when you have put him down, and made it forever impossible for him to be but as a beast in the field; when you have extinguished his soul, and placed him where the ray of hope is blown out in the darkness like that which broods over the spirits of the damned; are you quite sure the demon you have roused *will not turn and rend you?* What constitutes the bulwark of our own liberty and independence? It is not our frowning battlements, our bristling seacoasts, the guns of our war steamers, or the strength of our gallant and disciplined army. These are not our reliance against a resumption of tyranny in our fair land. All of them may be turned against our liberties without making us stronger or weaker for the struggle. Our reliance is in the *love of liberty* which God has planted in our bosoms. Our defense is in the preservation of the spirit which prizes liberty as the heritage of all men, in all lands, everywhere. Destroy this spirit and you have planted the seeds of despotism around your own doors. Familiarize yourselves with the chains of bondage, and you are preparing your own limbs to wear them. Accustomed to trample on the rights of those around you, you have lost the genius of your own independence, and become fit subjects of the first cunning tyrant who rises."

In Greenville, on September 13, my husband addressed Douglas's support of both the Dred Scott decision and his own popular sovereignty. "This position and the Dred Scott Decision are absolutely inconsistent. The judge furiously indorses the Dred Scott Decision and that decision holds that the United States Constitution guarantees to the citizens of the United States the right to hold slaves in the Territories, and that neither Congress nor the territorial legislatures can destroy or abridge that right. In the teeth of this, where can the judge find room for his unfriendly legislation against their right? The members of the territorial legislature are sworn to support the Constitution of the United States. How dare they legislate unfriendly to a right guaranteed by that Constitution? . . . But can members of a territorial legislature, having sworn to support the United States Constitution, conscientiously withhold necessary legislative protection to a right guaranteed by that Constitution?"

At Freeport my husband had asked Senator Douglas if he would support a court decision *making slavery legal in all of the states*, and my husband said, "To this question the judge gave no answer whatever. He disposes of it by an attempt to ridicule the idea that the Supreme Court will ever make such a decision." But the Supreme Court in the Dred Scott Decision protects slaves in the territories as property under the Fifth Amendment - that "no person shall be deprived of life, liberty, or property without due process of law. The guaranty makes no distinction between persons in the states and those in the territories; it is given to persons in the states certainly as much as, if not more than, to those in the territories. 'No person,' under the shadow of the Constitution, 'shall be deprived of life, liberty, or property without due process of law.' No state can override the Constitution. The Constitution is the supreme law of the land. There is no escape from this conclusion but in one way, and that is to deny that the Supreme Court, in the Dred Scott case, properly applies the constitutional guarantee of property."

When my husband debated Mr. Douglas at Jonesboro on September 15, it was Mr. Douglas's turn to speak first. He pointed out again the demise of the old Whigs into the northern Republicans due to *ambitious* politicians taking advantage of the *temporary* excitement over his Nebraska bill. The new Republican Party sought to abolitionize both Whigs and Democrats in a crusade against Democracy, and this effort was led by my husband for the Whigs, and his friend, Lyman Trumbull for the Democrats. These two were aiming at warfare between the North and the South. They even brought FRED Douglas to Freeport "in a carriage driven by the white owner, the Negro sitting inside with the white lady and her daughter." SHAME called the Douglas section! Trumbull and his men were out to abolish democracy. They were in a conspiracy to abolish democracy in the name of the BLACK Republican Party, and wage a war on one half of the Union. My husband's House Divided speech made this clear to Mr. Douglas. To the South my husband says, "If you desire to maintain your situations as they are now, you must not be satisfied with minding your own business, but you must invade Illinois and all the other northern States, establish slavery in them and make it universal; and in the same language he says to the North, you must not be content with regulating your own affairs and minding your own business, but if you desire to maintain your own freedom you must invade the Southern States, abolish slavery there and everywhere, in order to have the states all one thing or all another." Our country had been created half slave and half free. And we rose from a weak nation "to become the terror and the admiration of the civilized world." Was my husband wiser than the framers of our government? Did the Declaration of Independence include the Negro? Only white men of European birth and European descent our fathers declared to be equal "and had no reference either to the negro, the savage Indians, the Fejee, the Malay, or any other inferior and degraded race when they spoke of the equality of men." So we must keep our government the way it was created, and on the question of slavery "that is a question which each State of this Union must decide for itself." Then, to my astonishment, Mr. Douglas declared, "The Dred Scott decision covers the whole question, and declares that each State has the right to settle . . . all questions as to the relation between the white man and the negro." I could not believe my eyes. If I had been there, I would not have believed my ears! Now, Mr. Douglas decreed his own precious popular sovereignty, when we should take them, to "any portion of Mexico or Canada, or of this continent or the adjoining islands, we must take it as we find it, leaving the people to decide the question of slavery for themselves, without interference on the part of the federal government, or any state government of this Union." And apparently Mr. Douglas saw us taking all this new territory, *when it becomes necessary.* He concluded in saying that each state should mind its own business and regulate its own domestic affairs and thus preserve the Union. "Why should we not act as our fathers who made the government?"

My husband's reply included the following points: He had repeated *again and again,* "I hold myself under constitutional obligations to allow the people in all the States without interference, direct or indirect, to do exactly as they please, and I deny that I have any inclination to interfere with them, even if there were no such constitutional obligation."

Why couldn't we leave the slavery question as our fathers had placed it? "That is the exact difficulty between us; I say that Judge Douglas and his friends have changed (slavery) from the position in which our fathers originally placed it. I say in the way our fathers originally left the slavery question, the institution was in the course of ultimate extinction, and the public mind rested in the belief that it *was* in the course of ultimate extinction . . . I have no doubt that it *would become* extinct, for all time to come, if we but re-adopted the policy of the fathers by restricting it to the limits it has already covered - restricting it from the new Territories."

As for the Douglas lamentation at the passing of the old Whig party, he had called *them* abolitionists, but now "it has got an extremely good name since it has passed away." (laughter)

My husband said the Compromise of 1850 did not repeal the Missouri Compromise and Douglas wrote his Nebraska bill so it would. "When he came to form governments for the territories north of 36 degrees 30 minutes, why could he not have let that matter stand as it was standing?...When we had peace under the Missouri Compromise, (turning to Douglas) could you not have left it alone?"

As for what my husband saw as a house divided, it was not due to the diversity of its landscape or climate. That bound the union together with trade from one part of the country to another. What was divisive was the conflict over the spreading of slavery. On this my husband said, "What right have we then to hope that the trouble will cease - that the agitation will come to an end - until it shall be placed back where it originally stood and where the fathers originally placed it, or on the other hand until it shall entirely master all opposition."

My husband said he had answered all of the questions at Freeport that Mr. Douglas had asked him at Ottawa. But Mr. Douglas did not give his interrogatories the same consideration. The stickler was the *Freeport Doctrine* of Douglas - "As I understand him, he holds that it can be done by the Territorial Legislature refusing to make any enactment for the protection of slavery in the Territory, and especially by adopting unfriendly legislation to it . . . In the first place the Supreme Court of the United States has decided that any Congressional prohibition of slavery in the Territories is unconstitutional . . . the Constitution of the United States expressly recognizes property in slaves, and from that other constitutional provision that no person shall be deprived of property without due process of law... I understand also that Judge Douglas adheres most firmly to that decision; and the difficulty is how it is possible for any power to exclude slavery from the Territory unless in violation of that decision? That is the difficulty." First Douglas had said the people could *not* decide the issue, that it was up to the Supreme Court, and now that the court has decided it, Douglas says "that it is *not* a question for the Supreme Court . . . When he now says the people *may* exclude slavery, does he not make it a question for the people? Does he not virtually shift his ground and say that it is *not* a question for the Court, but for the people?"

Unfriendly police regulations can keep out slavery? Slavery began here without police regulations. Hadn't Dred Scott been held in slavery in the Minnesota Territory, and claimed his freedom because an act of Congress prohibited his being held as a slave there? *"Will the judge pretend that Dred Scott was not held there without police regulations? . . .* This shows that there is vigor enough in Slavery to plant itself in a new country even against unfriendly legislation."

And what about Douglas's *unfriendly legislation?* "How could you, having sworn to uphold the Constitution and believing it guarantees the right to hold slaves in the Territories, assist in legislation *intended to defeat that right?*" And "how long would it take the courts to hold your vote unconstitutional and void. Not a moment."

And doesn't Congress have to give legislative support to the Constitution?

He asked Mr. Douglas, "If the slave holding citizens of a United States Territory should need and demand Congressional legislation for the protection of their slave property in such territory, would you, as a member of Congress, vote for or against such legislation?"

My husband concluded with a quote from Mr. Douglas saying he overpowered him so much at Ottawa he "made him tremble at the knees so that he had to be carried from the platform. He laid up for seven days..." "Well," my husband said, "I can explain it in no other way than by believing the Judge is crazy." My husband *had* been carried away from the platform *on the shoulders* of his cheering supporters. As for his being laid up for seven days, the judge "knew that I had made speeches within six days of the seven days at Henry, Marshall County; Augusta, Hancock County, and Macomb, McDonough County, including all of the travel to meet him at Freeport at the end of the six days. Now, I say, there is no charitable way to look at that statement, except to conclude he is actually crazy. (much laughter)...Now, how little do I look like being carried away trembling? . . . I don't want to quarrel with him - to call him a liar - but when I come square up to him I don't know what else to call him, if I must tell the truth out." (cheers and more laughter) "My time, now, is very nearly out, and I give up the trifle to the Judge to let him set my knees trembling again, if he can."

He did not. He surely, surely did not. Douglas said he was just *teasing* in his Joliet speech about making my husband tremble enough to have to be carried from the platform, even if it was printed all over the state, and there was no word added saying, *This is a* joke. Douglas went on with the people of a new territory or new state deciding slavery for themselves, and if he were a senator, would he vote to admit a new slave state? No more slave states is a BLACK REPUBLICAN doctrine, and my husband is trying to cover up his true *abolitionist* heart, and as for my husband's question of Congressional protection for slave holding in territories, he said, "The Democratic party have always stood by the great principle of non-interference and non-intervention by Congress in the states and territories alike, and I stand on that platform now."

And yet he concluded with his support of the Constitution!

And of course, the Dred Scott Decision, which was as incompatible to his popular sovereignty, as I now was to him.

Chapter Eleven

At two forty five on September 18, my husband and Mr. Douglas met in Charleston for their fourth debate. In his beginning, my husband denied he was preaching racial equality or inter-marriage with the Negro. "I say upon this occasion I do not perceive that because the white man is to have the superior position the Negro should be denied everything. I do no understand that because I do not want a negro woman for a slave I must necessarily want her for a wife. My understanding is that I can just leave her alone." As Mr. Douglas was in a horror about racial mixture, and this can only be controlled *by states and not Congress,* my husband suggested Douglas skip Congress and stay with the state and fight against his case of horrors. (Much laughter and applause) Then, as well as I could understand the debate from the *Press &Tribune,* and I *never* would read the Democratic *Chicago Times,* my husband, in order to defend himself, had to defend our other Senator and good friend, Judge Trumbull. Judge Trumbull had returned to Illinois and in a speech said this against Mr. Douglas: "Now, the charge is, that there was a plot entered into having a constitution formed for Kansas and put into force without giving the people an opportunity to vote upon it and Mr. Douglas was in the plot." And as my husband had endorsed the character of Judge Trumbull for veracity, Douglas held *him responsible for Trumbull's slanders!* In my opinion my husband clearly showed that Judge Trumbull did *not* lie, and in his last three minutes my husband said this, "The point upon Judge Douglas is this. The bill that went into his hands had the provision in it for a submission of the constitution to the people; and I say its language amounts to an express provision for a submission, and that he took the provision out. He says it was known that the bill was silent in this particular; *but I say, Judge Douglas, it was not silent when you go it* . . .How could he infer that a submission was still implied, after its express provision had been stricken from the bill?… I insist upon knowing why he made the bill silent upon that point when it was vocal before he put his hands upon it."

Mr. Douglas then spoke for an hour and a half, and said again, and again, my husband was for social and political equality of the races, and Judge Trumbull's charge against him was two years old, made in 1856, and instead of reading Trumbull's speech at Alton, why wasn't my husband "capable of making a public speech on his own account or I should not have accepted the banter from him for a joint discussion." Well, Mr. Douglas was not going to waste his time upon these personal matters, these *petty and malicious* assaults that only began when he was showing up my husband's "Abolitionism and negro equality doctrines" all so "I would not be able to show up the enormity of the principles of the Abolitionists." Douglas went back again to the BLACK Republicans tearing up the Union, discarding the forefathers by "slander and not by fair means," and he thought he was running against my husband and not Judge Trumbull! My husband also refused to discuss the issues, and "has not uttered one word about the politics of the day… It turns out that his only hope is to ride into office on Trumbull's back, who will carry him by falsehood." *The Chicago Times* gave Mr. Douglas rousing cheers, and I wonder if the audience did.

Again Douglas gave us the BLACK Republicans with their mad and revolutionary schemes, how they destroyed *the perfect peace* over the slavery question, all settled by the Great Compromise of 1850, (until his own bill!) and we must remember my husband's ally, his own brother, "the negro hunting me down," said Senator Douglas of FRED Douglas. My husband makes the negro equal to the white man when he believes the Declaration of Independence includes them; but the "negro, belonging to a race incapable of self government, for that reason ought not to be on equality with white men." So why can't we continue half slave and half free? asked Mr. Douglas. "We can if we will live up to and execute the government upon those principles upon which our forefathers established it."

Once more the *Chicago Times* gave him applause, *deafening* applause.

My husband had a half hour response preceded by three *rousing* cheers. My husband stated he was not in favor of negro citizenship, (*clearly public opinion would not allow it*) and Douglas alone has stated my husband's objections to the Supreme Court's saying a negro never could become a citizen. "Judge Douglas tells people what my objections were, when I did not tell them myself. (Loud applause and laughter) Now my opinion is that the different States have the power to make a negro a citizen under the Constitution of the United States if they choose. The Dred Scott Decision decides they have not that power. If the State of Illinois had that power I should be opposed to the exercise of it."

With public opinion behind you, you can do anything. Without it, you can do nothing. That was the stated belief of my husband. That is why he saw the road ahead for the political rights of the Negro a long one. And what if the hatred and the bigotry in this country are too entrenched *ever* to be changed? I asked him this, and many times, too.

"I hope it is not," he always replied. "You can't make racial hatred illegal, but with the people behind you, you can make its negative results illegal."

"And *if* the local laws and the police are a part of the problem?"

"Then there would have to be federal legislation, and I would hope in the federal government the negro haters would be in the minority. Ultimately, it is not a question of *states'* rights, but *peoples'* rights."

"When?"

"In time. And in appreciation for the stated cause of our revolution."

"The *uncompleted* revolution."

"But its ideals are stated."

"Giving the negro his alienable rights?"

"In a rebirth of freedom, so that we do have a government of the people, by the people and for the people."

"All the people?"

"That is Jefferson's glorious North Star of Freedom."

" . . . in regard to the latter portion of the Judge's speech, which was a sort of declamation in reference to my having said I entertained the belief that this government would not endure, half slave and half free . . . Have we ever had any peace on the slavery question?...How are we ever to have peace upon it? To be sure if we will all stop and allow Judge Douglas and his friends to march on their present career until they plant the institution all over the nation, here and wherever else our flag waves, and we acquiesce to it, there will be peace. But let me ask Judge Douglas, how he is going to get the people to do that? Has his own bill settled the slavery agitation? Has the voting down of the Lecompton Kansas constitution settled it? If Kansas sank into the earth, would it be settled? I say, then, there is no way of putting an end to the slavery agitation amongst us but to put it back upon the basis where our fathers placed it, no way but to keep it out of our new Territories - to restrict it forever to the old States where it now exists. (*Tremendous* cheers) Then the public mind *will* rest in the belief that it is in the course of ultimate extinction."

My husband said he endorsed Judge Lyman Trumbull's veracity because he never knew him to break his word or to lie. They were not out to *sell out* the Whigs or the Democrats. And they had not attacked Douglas personally. But, "Judge Douglas, in a general way, without putting it in a direct shape, revives the old charge against me, in reference to the Mexican War . . . That charge is more than ten years old . . . the more respectable papers of his own party throughout the State have been compelled to take it back and acknowledge that it as a lie." My husband said he would not endorse the reasons for the war but never failed to vote for supplies to our soldiers fighting it. To prove

128

this, he reached into the audience and brought to the platform a startled Orlando Ficklin, who had served in the House with him, and he verified what my husband claimed.

My husband said that about the Trumbull issue, where *he* was held responsible for the so-called *slanders and lies* of *Trumbull,* on the whole issue Douglas was playing *cuttle fish* that leaves a black fluid trail so no one knows where it is going. What did Trumbull say that was *not* true? "Trumbull says that Judge Douglas had a bill with a provision in it for submitting a Constitution to be made to a vote of the people of Kansas... Then Trumbull says that he struck it out." The question now was, *why Judge Douglas took it out? . . .* If he can explain all of this, but leaves it unexplained, I have the right to infer that Judge Douglas understood it was the purpose of his party, in engineering that bill through, to make a Constitution and have Kansas come into the union with that Constitution, *without it being submitted to the vote of the people . . . I suggest to him it will not avail him at all that he swells himself up, takes on dignity and calls people liars."*

On Saturday, September 25, my husband came home. The Republican Club came to our house with their band, and played several songs until my husband appeared and made a short speech. They all cheered him, and with the cheers echoing into our house, he closed the front door and swept me up into his arms, and then Willie and Taddie, and he said, "There is no place this side of heaven like my *home."*

Heaven was complete for me when he was where I was.

There were, of course, the *religious* justifications of slavery. My husband had read Reverend Frederick Ross's *Slavery Ordained by God,* and in October of that year he wrote, "Suppose it is true, that the negro is inferior to the white; is it not the exact reverse of justice that the white for that reason, take from the negro, any part of the little which has been given him? '*Give* to him that is needy,' is the Christian rule of charity; but '*Take from him that is needy,'* is the rule of slavery."

But so many were saying slavery *helps* the Negro, *is good* for him. "As a *good* thing," my husband said, "slavery is strikingly peculiar, in this, that it is the only good thing which no man seeks the good of, *for himself.*

Nonsense! Wolves devouring lambs, not because it is good for their own greedy maws, but because it is good for the lambs!"

The fifth debate was at Galesburg on October the seventh. Mr. Douglas spoke first for an hour in which he repeated he was doing the right thing in defending the right of each state and territory to regulate its own domestic concerns under the Constitution. He repeated that the Republican Party was sectional, abolitionist and couldn't state its case in *all sections* of the country. He repeated again the racial inferiority of the negro and *how only white men of European descent* are given the God given rights of the Declaration of Independence. Then he introduced a new slander against my husband; that he was deceitful, for in the northern part of the state he talked abolitionist and in the southern part he was pro slave. He noted that both Washington and Jefferson had slaves and that our forefathers had given us a government of the whites, for the whites *forever*. Even Christianity supported slavery. Again, we could skirt the Dred Scott decision and not allow slavery in the territories with unfriendly territorial laws. (No extension of slave codes) He concluded by saying that he was for the great principle of self-government, and the country divided slave and free, just as the fathers had created it.

My husband spoke for an hour and a half. He had replied to *all* of Douglas's questions in printed speeches of his own. He made the point the Declaration of Independence does not read FOR WHITE MEN OF EUROPEAN DESCENT ONLY, no one ever declaring that it excluded negroes. Jefferson did have slaves and he detested the practice and said of slavery that "he trembled for his country when he remembered that God was just, and his justice cannot sleep forever."

My husband smiled when he said: "When the Judge says in speaking on this subject that I make speeches of one sort for the people of the northern end of the state and of a different sort for the southern people, he assumes that I do not understand that my speeches will be put in print and read *north and south*. (laughter)

The Judge will have it when we do not confess that there is a sort of inequality between the white and black races, which justifies us in making them our slaves, we must, then, insist that there is a degree of equality that requires us to make them our wives (laughter) . . . but the so called inferior are our equals to the right of life, liberty and the pursuit of happiness."

As to the Republican Party being a sectional one because it is not popular in all of the country - "Is the test of the soundness of a doctrine, that in some places people will not let you proclaim it?" Is the party sectional because "in the southern part of the Union the people did not let the Republicans proclaim their doctrine amongst them?" Does this make the Republican doctrine wrong? "The only evidence he has of their being wrong is in the fact that there are people who won't allow us to preach them . . . is that the way to test the soundness of a doctrine?" Does the *South* agree with Douglas? "I see the day rapidly approaching when his pill of sectionalism which he has been thrusting down the throats of Republicans for years past will be crowded down his own throat." (*tremendous* applause)

Judge Davis and his party *see nothing wrong with slavery.* Having due regard for the difficulties of getting rid of it in any satisfactory way, "what is desired is this *wrong* be ended."

In the Dred Scott Decision the Supreme Court concluded: *The right of property in a slave is distinctly and expressly affirmed in the Constitution.* My husband said this is not true, "the falsehood in fact is a fault of the premise. I believe that the right of property in a slave is *not* distinctly and expressly affirmed in the Constitution and Judge Douglas thinks it is. I believe that the Supreme Court and the advocates of that decision may search in vain for the place in the Constitution where the right of property in a slave is distinctly and expressly affirmed." But if you accept the decision as true, no State law or constitution can destroy the right to have slaves. (Unfriendly laws or not!) Would the decision have been made at all if Buchanan had not won the election? "The new Dred Scott Decision against the right of a people of the *states* to exclude slavery will never be made if that party is not sustained by the elections." Jackson and Jefferson did not see *a political* obligation from a Supreme Court decision. Jefferson said that whenever a free people submit to any department of government without any recourse of appeal they have given up their liberties. In the political climate fostered by Douglas and his allies the goal is to make slavery *national* and *perpetual.* In saying the negro has no rights enumerated in the Declaration of Independence this is not only *not* true but Douglas is blowing out the light of reason and the love of liberty. It is the agitation over the extension of slavery that has always menaced the Union - "that has ever disturbed us in such a way as to make us fear for the perpetuity of our liberty..."

In his half hour reply Douglas again sneered at my husband's patriotism for his questioning whether the Mexican War had started on the *right spot,* (their land, or ours) that he was bringing the Supreme Court into disrepute so mob rule can be produced and on its crest he can ride into the Senate by avoiding the public issues and to "not get there on his own principles and merits." And then he asked, "Is it possible that you Republicans have the right to raise your mobs and oppose the laws of the land and the constituted authorities, and yet hold us Democrats bound to obey them? ... all I have to say is this, that I am bound by the law of the land ... and any man who resist them must resort to mob law and violence to overturn a government of laws."

I reached the conclusion that for my husband to reason with Mr. Douglas would be as futile as his visiting the Niagara Falls again, watch them thundering down from above, and say, *now you stop that!*

Chapter Twelve

The debate at Quincy began at two in the afternoon on October 13, and my husband spoke first. Clearly, concisely he made these points: He could not be held responsible for what Republicans had said at their convention or any local meetings in which he had taken no part. He did not double deal with one kind of speech in the northern part of the state, and another in the southern part. He had never preached negro equality, "*that even if my own feelings would admit of it, I still knew the public sentiment of the country would not, and such a thing was an utter impossibility.*" He did not see that this deprived the negro the rights of the Declaration of Independence; "in the right to eat the bread without leave of anybody else which his own hand earns, he is the equal of Judge Douglas, and the equal of any man." The Supreme Court has *not* said that a *state* could exclude slavery. The Republicans consider slavery a *wrong;* the Democrats do not. About the Dred Scott ruling - "We do not propose that when Dred Scott has been decided to be a slave by the court, we, as a mob, will decide to set him free. . . but we, nevertheless do oppose that decision as a political rule which will be binding on the voter . . . which shall be binding on the members of Congress or the President to favor no measure that does not actually concur with the principles of that decision. We do not propose to be bound by it as a political rule in that way, because we think it lays the foundation not merely of enlarging and spreading out what we consider an evil, but lays the foundation for spreading that evil into the States themselves. We propose so resisting it to have it reversed if we can, and a new judicial rule established on the subject." If Douglas says that any one can have slaves who wants them, "he is perfectly logical if there is nothing wrong in the institution; but if you admit it is wrong, he cannot logically say that anybody has a right to do wrong."

Mr. Douglas repeated the *same lies* about my husband - he was firing up the North against the South; he was saying one thing in the northern part of our state and another in the southern part, and - how does he intend to end slavery? Shall all of the states be free so the house is not divided against itself? Of course, his intent is to make them *all free,* just *saying* he is not going to interfere with slavery in the South. He is going to worry the South out of it, and if slavery cannot expand, the victim will be the Negro. That is because without slave expansion and new soil, they will starve to death. That is how my husband will end slavery in the South, "he can extinguish slavery only by extinguishing the negro race." *Will Douglas now say* whether slavery is *right or wrong?* No, he doesn't have to say it, because that is up for the states to decide. And Congress has no right to interfere with the decision of judicial tribunals. *(idiots* cheered him for this) Then we are back again at the Republicans being lawless and the Democrats being law abiding, and on again to his popular sovereignty, the local *laws* being necessary to protect slaves as property, and if they are not there, neither will be the slaves! This will exclude slaves "from the territory just as effectively and as positively as a Constitutional provision would." Thus our great Republic can exist forever half free and half slave to become the "admiration and the terror of the world." (Not be a beacon of liberty for all of the world and all mankind, but to be the *terror* of the world!)

My husband in his half hour rebuttal said four major things. Douglas *"contemplates that slavery shall last forever."* When he assumes this as desired by the fathers, "he assumes *what is historically a falsehood.* It was on the course of ultimate extinction." Why didn't Douglas just "let it remain as our fathers made it?" (tremendous cheering from the intelligent in the audience) His third point - he never intended interference in slavery in the South, and about this Douglas "knows it's all humbuggery." And here, we have the Dred Scott case again. Neither it, nor Douglas, has said if the *States* can exclude slavery. If the court says they can't, Douglas has not said whether he would support such a decision. Why does Douglas shudder at disagreements with the Supreme Court, when he himself worked against it on the question of a National Bank? As for his *unfriendly* territorial laws - they would be *illegal.* How can you *nullify* a *Constitutional* right? "Doesn't he know you cannot do indirectly what you cannot do directly?" *The Supreme Court just went ahead and squatted out his popular sovereignty.* (great laughter and applause, and even some of the dummies laughed) Isn't the whole argument that it did *not,* "as thin as the homeopathic soup that has been made by boiling the shadow of a pigeon that has been starved to death?" (cheers and laughter - from our side)

For the last debate at Alton, the train from Springfield allowed those who wanted to go a price of half fare. Robert and I went, for the boys' health allowed it, and there, before he spoke, I got my husband *all slicked up.* I had seen my husband at home on only two Sundays since the debates began, and for this last one that I could finally attend, I wanted to dress up and look *my* best. I wore lilac velvet, and shoes and bonnet to match. I wore a deep purple brooch at my throat. "Molly," my husband said. "You just keep on stealing my heart away!"

There was such energy in the air, not to mention a comet in plain sight! I had had no idea of the exciting endless parades, the fireworks, the barbecues, ice cream parties, the marching bands, the music, the voters' *fever* from reading the *Press & Tribune*. That October 15 was so glorious. My husband was known, *admired*, and so brilliant. It was thrilling that others acknowledged what I had seen from the first conversation I had with him at the *coterie* dance. No one could state the issues more clearly, and no one could better deflect stupidity with humor. I recall when Mr. Douglas had said my husband was such a failure with his life - failing at everything but dishing out booze from a failing store, and my husband had said, with a twinkle, it was all true, every single word, but the only thing Douglas had left out, was that while he had abandoned his serving side of the counter Douglas had not abandoned his receiving side. Douglas was quite a boozer, and I was told he sipped from his ever-faithful flask even during the debates.

Mr. Douglas spoke first and I counted that he made eight points, if you can call them that. First, we must have the nation half free and half slave *as our fathers created it*, so the house is not divided against itself at all. Second, since the Dred Scott case, my husband has been crusading *against the South*. Third, my husband is preaching *racial equality*. (groans from the Douglas idiots) Fourth, any creed is wrong that cannot be proclaimed in *every* state. Fifth, the Union was established with each state doing what it wanted to do regarding slavery. Six, my husband is an *Abolitionist* who wants war with the South. Seven - again brings forth the gem in the Douglas crown for victory, *popular sovereignty*. The Great Compromise of 1850 "rested on the great principle that the people of each State and each Territory should be left perfectly free to form and regulate their domestic institutions to suit themselves." For this compromise Whigs and Democrats had united. *His own Kansas Nebraska Bill did the same as the Great Compromise of 1850.* As to the *friendly* and *unfriendly* local laws for the protection of property, the Honorable Jefferson Davis agrees with him. So does Alex Stephens, and of course, these men later became the President and the Vice President of the Confederacy. "I say to you," said Douglas "there is but one hope, one safety for the country, and that is to stand immovably by that principle which declares the right of each State and each territory to decide these questions (of slavery) for themselves." When he came to his eighth point, he was back again *and again* on the *racial inferiority of the Negro* and all the other so-called *savage barbarians*. It had been nauseating enough for me to read, and it was worse hearing it in person.

My husband's party was one of *Abolitionists* hell bent in including the negro in the Declaration of Independence when it clearly referred to *whites only* of *European* birth and *European* descent. (his idiots cheered themselves speechless over this) "Our government was established for white men and they should run it forever." As to how the dependent people are to be treated - it is up to the States to decide that for themselves. "If all the people of all of the States mind its own business, attend to its own affairs, take care of the negro and not meddle with its neighbors then there will be peace between the North and the South . . . Why should we thus allow a sectional party to agitate this country . . . merely that a few ambitious men may ride into power on a sectional hobby . . . the moment the North obtained the majority in the House and Senate by the admission of California, and could elect a President without the aid of Southern votes, that moment ambitious Northern men formed a scheme to excite the North against the South, and make the people be governed in their votes by geographical lines, thinking the North, being the stronger section, would outvote the South, and consequently they, the leaders, would ride into office on a sectional hobby."

I was furious at this dig at my husband, but when I looked at my husband on the speaker's platform, he just uncrossed his legs and smiled. Then to the great cheering of the intelligent part of the audience, (ours) he took his position, and right away he set the audience, even the dumb Douglas ones, to laughing. He was saying how delighted he was that Douglas and Buchanan were still having such a great fight over the Kansas Lecompton Constitution - "I say to them again - 'Go it, husband! Go it bear!'" Once Douglas had been a valiant advocate of the Missouri Compromise, my husband said, and then his Kansas Nebraska Bill went ahead and repealed it! He asked if Buchanan didn't have the right to be as "inconsistent as Douglas has? Has Douglas the *exclusive right* in the country, of being *on all sides of all questions?*" (laughter and cheering from our side, of the *humans*) My husband complained that Douglas was constantly saying he said things that he did *not* say, and instead of calling him a liar, observed, in a most gentlemanly way, that Douglas "has strongly impressed me with the belief of a pre-determination on his part to misrepresent me."

Here are the points made by my husband: First, the Dred Scott Decision was "a portion of a system or scheme to make slavery national." Second, about the ideals of the Declaration of Independence - while slavery existed in the founding of our country - "We had slaves among us; we could not get our Constitution unless we permitted them to remain in slavery; we could not secure the good we did secure if we grasped for more; and having by

135

necessity admitting to that much, it does not destroy the principle that it is the charter of our liberties." It was meant to include *all* men, but did not mean to declare all men equal in all respects as to "color, size, intellect, moral development or social capacity." The equality is in the "certain inalienable rights, among which are life, liberty and the pursuit of happiness. This they said, and this they meant. They did not mean to assert the obvious untruth, that all men are actually enjoying that equality, nor yet, they were about to confer it immediately upon them. In truth, they had no power to confer such a boon. They meant simply to declare the right so that the enforcement of it might follow, as circumstances should permit.

They meant to set up a standard maxim for free society which should be familiar to all: constantly looked to, constantly labored for, and thereby constantly spreading and deepening its influence and augmenting the happiness and value of life to all people, of all colors, everywhere." (humans applaud and cheer) "As for negroes being included in the all men are created equal I reassert that today." The first man who contradicted this was Chief Justice Roger Taney in the Dred Scott case, and Douglas. This is evil in dehumanizing the negro, "to take away from him the right of ever striving to be a man," and "to prepare the public mind to make property, and *nothing but property* of the *negro in all the States of the Union.*" (tremendous cheering from the humans and hisses from the non humans)

As for the intent of the fathers: Slavery was not seen as a right and therefore *introduced* into the Constitution. They had to leave slavery as they found it because of the "absolute impossibility of its immediate removal." To say the government was *deliberately* created half free and half slave is a falsehood. But if it were the marvelous policy Douglas claims it was - and here my husband turned to look at him, saying, "*I turn to him and ask him why he could not let it alone?*" (prolonged cheers and much laughter on our side of the intelligent humans) Douglas himself says he has introduced a new policy. In the way the fathers had left it, there was no war, so if we return to their policy why should we have the war that Douglas threatens? "I have proposed nothing more than a return to the policy of the fathers," my husband said to more cheering of the humans. The *Yahoos* booed. Like Yahoos.

I know ladies were not supposed to show emotion about a single thing, and never, never about politics, for such deep thoughts were to send their minds into chocolate puddings. But one of their Cretins had wondered amongst us, and he was so nasty and so obnoxious in yelling insults at my husband, I removed my brooch and stuck him at his nearest point to me, which happened to be his back end. It was so huge; I could not have missed

136

it. When he whirled, grabbing, with both hands, the seat of his pantaloons, I gave him a look of shock, indignation and *horror*, and I said, "Sir, *where* are you putting your hands?" And those around me looked from my husband to the Cretin holding the back of his pantaloons and they were also shocked. "You don't do that *here*," one of the gentlemen said, and his lady began to fan herself to keep from fainting. I thought this was such a good idea I began to do it myself.

Then my husband was on the platform, so tall and so magnificent, and so *vulnerable* to a mad man's gun. It was hardly into fall, but a winter chill went all through me, and I wondered if it was wise for my husband to pursue *anything* to do with politics.

My husband's fourth point was to explain he held no ill will for the South. "I propose nothing but what has a most peaceful tendency."

Of course the country has different crops in a different geography, he said, and the cranberry laws of Indiana, the oyster laws of Virginia, the sugar laws of Louisiana do not apply to Illinois. That is good, for then we can trade our surpluses to our mutual benefit and bonding. But this does not apply to the question of slavery. Our disputes between states have *always* been when slavery struggles to spread itself where it is not. And has this not gone *beyond* political circles? "Does it not enter into churches and rend them asunder? What divided the great Methodist Church into two parts, North and South?" It had done the same for the Presbyterian and Unitarian churches; the question of slavery agitates in politics, in religion, in morals, in all of the manifold relations of life and, "Is this the work of politicians?" Are we not to talk about it? Care about it? To cease being agitated about it? "Is it not a false statesmanship that undertakes to build up a system of policy upon the basis of caring nothing about *the very thing that everybody does care the most about?*" (tremendous cheering from our humans)

"Douglas is but fighting a man of straw when he assumes that I am contending against the right of the *States* to do as they please about it. Our controversy with him is in regard to the new *Territories.*" The Republican Party was *not* "warring upon the right of the States. What I insist upon is, that the new Territories shall be kept free from it while in the Territorial condition." There was no Republican war against the South. The point is, "it is the sentiment on the part of one class that looks upon the institution of slavery *as a wrong,* and of another class that *does not* look upon it as a wrong. Seeing it wrong, the Republican Party *"is to make provision that it shall grow no larger."* My husband said it was a clear choice between *right* and *wrong,* and that the Dred Scott decision avoided that issue in *seeing humans as no more than property.* "That is the real issue. That is the issue that will continue in this country when these poor tongues of Judge Douglas and myself shall be silent. It is the eternal struggle between these two principles - *right and wrong* - throughout the world. They are the two principles that have stood face to face from the beginning of time; and will ever continue to struggle. The one is the common right of humanity and other is the divine right of kings. It is the same principle in whatever shape it develops itself. It is the same spirit that says, 'you work and toil and earn the bread, and I'll eat it.' (tremendous applause from humans and the dummies hissed like the snakes they are) No matter what shape it comes, whether from the mouth of a king who seeks to bestride the people of his own nation and live by the fruit of their labor, or from one race of men as an apology for enslaving another race, it is the same tyrannical principle."

Judge Douglas had said here - *"that he looks to no end of the institution of slavery.* That will help the people to see where the struggle really is. It will hereafter place with us all men who really do wish the wrong may have an end."

My husband's last point was in retaliation to what was now called Douglas's *Freeport Doctrine*, that the people of a territory can still *somehow* exclude slavery. "Before the decision, Douglas said the Supreme Court was to decide the question, and when it did, he now says, 'it is not a question for the Supreme Court, but for the people.' (laughter and applause from the humans) How are the *people* to do this? With "unfriendly legislation." Now, how can a Territorial Legislature do this? Have not the members taken an oath to support the Constitution of the United States? So how can they pass unfriendly legislation and violate their oath? "Why this is a *monstrous* sort of talk about the Constitution of the United States!" my husband said with great indignation. (More human cheering and laughter) *"There never has been as outlandish or lawless doctrine from the mouth of any respectable man on earth.* (great, *great* cheering from our side) I do not believe it is a constitutional right to hold slaves in a Territory of the United States. I believe the decision was improperly made and I go for reversing it. Judge Douglas is furious against those who go for reversing a decision. But he is for legislating it out of all force while the law itself stands. I repeat that there has never been so monstrous a doctrine uttered from the mouth of a respectable man." (Cheers and laughter-our humans) And if the Dred Scott decision can be so easily nullified, what about the Fugitive Slave Law? Can the North just ignore it? And my husband had even most of the dummies laughing when he concluded, "Why there is not such an Abolitionist in the nation as Douglas after all!"

In his reply Mr. Douglas went back to my husband being against his country and taking the side of Mexico during the Mexican War, even being a part of a Mexican party in Congress! "He voted that the war was wrong, that our country was in the wrong, and consequently that the Mexicans were in the right . . ." (All over the war starting on the wrong *spot* - which happened to be in Mexico, so it was *not a Mexican invasion)* "It is one thing to be opposed to the declaration of war, another and a very different thing to take sides with the enemy against your own country after the war has been commenced. (Douglas dummies yelled, "That's the truth! He is a *traitor!*") That a man who takes sides with the common enemy against his own country in time of war should rejoice in a war made on me now is very natural." (Douglas demented waved their American flags and cheered over them, if they were not soaking them up with tears of patriotism) Then Mr. Douglas went on to say that my husband had cut Henry Clay's throat by choosing Zachary Taylor to run for President at a Whig caucus at Ninian's house in 1847, that my husband, who really admired Henry Clay, (always against slavery and a dear friend of my own father) was all the time his bitter enemy, bitter and *deadly* enemy, who left his mangled and murdered Whig remains before him. My husband voted for the Wilmot Proviso (no slavery in land taken from Mexico which never passed the Senate, anyway) with all of the other *Abolitionists* and got up this sectional strife Clay worked so hard to quell.

Oh, it was *terrible,* and I was so happy that I witnessed only *one* of these monstrous attacks upon my husband by a man of our *coterie,* and one who had courted me. He tried to compare the fever against slavery extension with the nullification of the tariff in 1832, and the Hartford Convention in opposition to the War of 1812, to show, I guess, that politicians like to disagree now and then. Then he went back to the same old thing. "I care more for the great principle of self-government, the right of the people to rule, than I do for all of the negroes in Christendom. I would not endanger the perpetuity of this Union. I would not blot out the great inalienable rights of the white man for all of the negroes that ever existed. (His idiots nodding their heads in a shared tick) Hence, I say, let us maintain this government on the principles that our fathers made it, recognizing the right of each state to keep slavery as long as its people determine, or to abolish it when they please." (Idiot cheering for this great *immorality*) He even went back to my husband talking one way in the southern part of our state and one way in its northern part, and he asked how my husband could advocate non interference with slavery in the states and see it off on the course of ultimate extinction. "His idea is that he will prohibit slavery in the territories, and thus force them all to become free

States, surrounding the slave states with a cordon of free States, and hemming them in, keeping the slaves confined to their present limits whilst they go on multiplying until the soil on which they live will no longer feed them, and he will put slavery in a course of ultimate extinction by starvation . . . And he intends to do that in the name of humanity and Christianity, in order that we may get rid of the terrible crime and sin entailed upon our fathers holding slaves." (Imbecilic laughing and cheering over this) And Mr. Douglas returned to local laws doing what they would with slavery- "If the people want the institution of slavery they will protect and encourage it; but if they do not want it they will withhold that protection, and the absence of local legislation protecting slavery excludes it as completely as a positive prohibition." ("That's so!" chanted the Douglas demented) Then Mr. Douglas said slavery is a bone of contention only because "agitators have combined in all the free States to make war upon it. Suppose the agitators in the States should combine in one half of the Union to make war on the railroad system of the other half?"

Tears suddenly stung my eyes. *Rights of railroads* compared to *rights of human beings!* I thought of this denial of Negro *humanity*, the pitiless cruelty of the whole slave system, and I thought of the dear sweet face of my Mammy Sally, all of my black friends, and I looked at Mr. Douglas and his supporters who hated the negro so much they had lost the sense of right and wrong. My husband noted my anguish and his look said to me, *they are doing this, not you, not me, and don't waste any tears on them.* Mr. Douglas concluded with saying we must "sustain the decisions of the Supreme Court and its constituted authorities."

I could not believe it. But I could not believe any of his tortured reasoning - he says we *must* do A - by *not doing* A!

My husband could have said to me, this is just the same old politics, or, the man wants to become President in 1860, and he is just working for the Southern vote - but my husband would *not* say that to me, for he does not think that way.

On October 30, there was a great torch lit parade in Springfield for my husband, and on that date he gave his last speech of the campaign. The *Illinois State Journal* said it "was one of the most eloquent appeals ever addressed to the American people."

And it was. He kept only the conclusion, the only part he had written down. And this is a part of it. But the words are little compared to the way I saw them delivered.

"I stand here surrounded by friends - some *political*, all *personal* friends, I trust . . . I have born a laborious, and, in some respects to myself, a painful part in the contest. Through all, I have neither assailed, nor wrestled with any part of the Constitution. The legal rights of the Southern people to reclaim their fugitives I have constantly admitted. The legal right of Congress to interfere with their institution in the states, I have constantly denied. In resisting the spread of slavery to new territory, and with that, what appears to me to be a tendency to subvert the first principle of free government itself, my whole effort has consisted. To the best of my judgment I have labored *for and not against* the Union. As I have not felt, so I have not expressed any harsh sentiment towards our Southern brethren. I have constantly declared, as I really believed, the only difference between them and us, is in the difference of circumstances."

He noted how painful the contest had been for him, to be constantly accused of being out to destroy the Union - "but I have cultivated patience, and made no attempt to retort," he said.

"Ambition has been ascribed to me . . . I claim no insensibility to political honors; but today could the Missouri restrictions be restored, and the whole slavery question replaced on the old ground of 'toleration by *necessity*' where it exists, with unyielding hostility to the spread of it, on principle, I would, in consideration, gladly agree, that Judge Douglas should never be *out*, and I never *in*, an office, so long as we both, or either, live."

How little sister Emilie was right - *how I loved that man!*

Chapter Thirteen

On November 2, my husband lost the election for the Senate to Mr. Douglas. He won the popular vote, but the Democrats gerrymandered the electoral districts for victory. Neither of us really thought he would defeat Douglas, with his *popular sovereignty* smoke in your eye, pie in the sky, for slavery *up* or slavery *down*. I had had a feeling in Alton that we would lose.

My husband was worn down, and had a very bad cold until well after the fifteenth of November. He went into such a deepening gloom, it was almost as if we had just lost our precious little Eddy. It rained and rained, just as if the skies were weeping for the death of our dear child again. It rained so hard that the street fights stopped, but the drunks in jail increased. (I don't remember if Billy was there that time) "Molly," he said to me, "My whole campaign was no more than fizzle-gigs and fireworks." His depression lasted at least until the twentieth. He had been deeply hurt, but his hurt never contained malice, and he wrote to his friend Norman Judd about it, "But let the past as nothing be." We were *very short* of money. He had earned no salary and had paid all of his own expenses for the political speaking. He wrote to Mr. Judd on the sixteenth, "I have been on expenses so long without earning any thing that I am absolutely without money now for even household purposes." When *he* was concerned about money, we *really* did not have any.

On November 19, he wrote about the election to our dear friend, Dr. Anson Henry. "Of course I *wished*, but I did not *expect* a better result . . . I am glad I made the late race. It gave me a hearing on the great and durable question of the age, which I could have had in no other way; and though I now sink out of view, and shall be forgotten, I believe I have made some marks which will tell for the cause of civil liberty long after I am gone."

He was wrong about sinking out of view. He was invited to speak, and did, for he felt too much for the inalienable rights of *all men to life, liberty and happiness* to abandon the issue.

He wrote to B. Clarke Lundy on November 26. "There will be another 'blow up' in the democracy. Douglas managed to be supported both as the best instrument to *break down,* and to *uphold* the slave power. No ingenuity can keep up this deception - the double position - up a great while."

To H. D. Sharpe he wrote on December 8, "I think we have fairly entered upon a durable struggle as to whether this nation is to ultimately become all slave or all free, and though I fall early in the contest, it is nothing if I shall have contributed, in the least degree, to the final rightful result."

On March 1, 1859, he made a speech in Chicago, and about slavery he said, "I do not wish to be misunderstood upon this subject in this country. I suppose it may long exist, and perhaps the best way for it to come to an end peaceably is for it to exist for a length of time. But I say that the spread and strengthening and perpetuation of it is an entirely different proposition. There we should in every way resist it as a wrong, treating it as a wrong, with the fixed idea that it must and will come to an end."

In April he had been invited to Boston to honor the birthday of Thomas Jefferson, and in his letter saying he could not attend, he wrote that the Democrats "while claiming political descent from him have nearly ceased to breathe his name everywhere.

Remembering too, that the Jefferson party was formed upon their supposed superior devotion to the *personal* rights of men, holding the rights of *property* to be secondary only, and greatly inferior, and then assuming that the so called democracy of to-day, are the Jefferson, and their opponents, the anti-Jefferson parties, it will be equally interesting to note how completely the two have changed hands as to the principles upon which they were originally supposed to be divided.

The democracy of today holds the *liberty* of one man to be absolutely nothing, when in conflict with another man's right to *property*. Republicans, on the contrary, are for both the *man* and the *dollar*; but in cases of conflict, the man *before* the dollar . . .

All honor to Jefferson - to the man who, in the concrete pressure of a struggle for national independence by a single people, had the coolness, forecast, and capacity to introduce into a merely revolutionary document, an abstract truth, applicable to all men and all times, and so to embalm it there, that to-day, and in all coming days, it shall be a rebuke and a stumbling block to the very harbingers of re-appearing tyranny and oppression."

This letter was given wide circulation in the Republican press.

No, my husband did *not* sink out of sight.

We had had a great party in early February. I arranged it to cheer up my husband, to get our house filled with his friends and political supporters, and the Edwards even came, although they were not and never would be political supporters.

Then in late February our Taddie became ill, very, very ill. My husband was in Chicago on a business trip and I heard that our friend, Ozias Hatch, was going to Chicago and on Monday morning, February 28, I wrote him this letter:

"If you are going up to Chicago to day, & should meet Mr. L- there, will you say to him, that our *dear little* Taddie, is quite sick. The Dr. thinks it may prove a *slight* attack of lung fever. I am feeling troubled & it would be a comfort to have him *at home.* He passed a bad night, I do not like his symptoms, and will be glad, if he hurries home."

My husband got the news on a Wednesday, and he was home the next day. We sat by Taddie's bed, and we watched his struggle to breathe while the rain battered at our house. Alone with my husband while Taddie slept, I said in panic, "Father, we can not lose another son!" He took me gently in his arms and kissed away my tears. "Mother, we will not lose him because we *can't.* Taddie will not leave us."

And he didn't. The doctors said he had pneumonia and that his lungs were left weak, but we did not hear that. Our Taddie stayed with us, and in time he and Willie were at play, and Robert again could go on grousing, "You two spoil the boys *rotten!*"

"I hope we do," said my husband. "It is so much fun for them and for us."

Willie began to deliver his own church sermons and had seen a preacher smoking a cigar, and so got a cigar for himself to try along with Taddie and the two Dubois boys. They all got sick and had to be *seriously* nursed back to health. Willie then decided he would be a preacher without a cigar and Taddie said no matter what he did with his life, it would not include cigars.

In the summer of 1859, when he was sixteen, Robert decided to leave home and enter Harvard University. The main problem with that was he failed fifteen out of sixteen subjects on the entry exam, and so he entered the Exeter Academy in New Hampshire. Here, he had to enter at a sub-freshman level. We had to put up a bond for payment that was signed by Judge Julius Rockwell who knew my husband in Congress and was a brother in law to our friend, Judge David Davis. Robert was said to be popular at Exeter, quiet, intelligent, and like me, and *unlike* his father, *a good dresser.* And he was very popular with the girls.

In June of 1859 my husband had to try a case in Chicago, and he took Willie along. Willie delighted in the trains still running right, and in the hotel room he and his father shared. He wrote a friend all about it, how the room was *very grand,* with a *small* bed for him, a *large* bed for his father, a *large* water pitcher for his father, a *small* one for him, and even the towels were small and large. His father took him to *two plays* in one night, and Willie loved the theater as much as did his father and I.

On August 28 I wrote to my dear friend, Mrs. Hannah Shearer, who had moved to Wellsboro, Pennsylvania for her husband's health. They had lived directly across the street from us for a year. I apologized for my two-month delay in response, and that is usually how I began all of my letters. I told her I had expected to spend a quiet summer at home, but on July 14 my husband took me on a long trip. "Within a week, after we had started unexpectedly on an excursion, (to assess some property for the Illinois Central Railroad in regard to some litigation) we traveled *eleven hundred miles,* with a party of eighteen." I noted that my dear first cousin Ann Todd of Columbia, Missouri, was one of the eighteen guests. She was now Mrs. Campbell. "*Words* cannot express what a merry time, we had, the gayest pleasure party, I have ever seen." You will well note how I still loved to sprinkle in unnecessary commas.

In September my husband took me to Cincinnati where he was to make a political speech, and every trip with him was like a new honeymoon. We had the money for reliable women to stay with the boys, and we both loved to travel, to see new people and new places. "Father," I said, "we will go to Europe when we can afford it?"

"We will," he said.

"Where will we go?' I asked, happily daydreaming.

"Maybe Germany, maybe Scotland, maybe Italy, Britain and France. Or all of them!"

And how wonderful 1859 was, and how deeply I was in love with my husband, and how deeply he was in love with me. A good marriage just gets better and better.

I gave a *huge* birthday party for Willie on his ninth birthday, December 21, 1859, with fifty or sixty children attending. I *fancifully* wrote all of the invitations and made all of the Christmas puddings. Even Evil Eva got into the Christmas spirit and happily baked them allowing sweet cinnamon and ginger smells throughout the house.

My husband was approached for running as President in 1860, but he said he was not fit for the Presidency. "Imagine a sucker like me as President!" he laughed. And being known politically, did *not* pay the bills. And that *odious* little man, Billy Herndon, was getting drunk more often, and my husband had to keep him out of the office as much as possible.

My husband wanted to go to Robert's school to see him, but felt we could not afford it. Then in February of 1860 some men in New York invited him to speak at the Cooper Union Institute in New York City, and agreed to pay for his trip. After his speech he could visit Robert in New Hampshire, where he was also engaged to make political speeches.

I believe it was his February 27 speech at the Cooper Union that won him the Republican presidential nomination. I know someone who attended that speech, and she wrote that my husband totally captivated the audience and held it so spellbound that no one stirred, no one sneezed or coughed and the only sound with his speech was the hissing of the gas lamps. She wrote he would have held his audience spellbound if he had spoken all night.

I cannot explain what happened to my husband when he took the speaker's platform. There was just something of such brilliant light of *character* and *reason* it totally captivated all but the most bigoted human haters. I think it was the inner fire of his very soul that once his natural shyness was immersed in his passion for justice, transformed him to be a man above most men.

That night my husband sought to explain the policy of the framers of our Constitution and reconcile that with the policy of the new Republican Party. He asked, "Does the proper division of local from federal authority, or anything in the Constitution, forbid our *Federal Government* to control as to slavery in our *Federal Territories?*" Douglas says yes; my husband says no. What was the understanding of our founding fathers, twenty- one of the thirty-nine men who framed and signed the Constitution? Our Constitution dates from September 17, 1787, was ratified by all the states, except North Carolina and Rhode Island, in 1788, and went into operation on the first Wednesday of January 1789. (Rhode Island smelled a rat and was not even represented at the convention) Britain had recognized the loss to us of the land termed the Northwest Territory. In 1787, *before* the Constitution, while the convention was *still in session* framing it, while the Northwest Territory was *the only* territory owned by the United States, was there to be *no* federal control over this territory? There was *not*. And in the territory what was decided about the presence of slavery? It was *prohibited* into law by the Ordinance of 1787. "In 1789, by the first Congress that sat under the Constitution, an act was passed to enforce the Ordinance of '87, including the prohibition of slavery in the Northwestern Territory," said my husband, continuing, "This shows that, in their understanding, no line dividing local from federal authority, nor anything in the Constitution, properly forbade Congress to prohibit slavery in the federal territory... Again, George Washington ... then President of the United States, and, as such, approved and signed the bill, thus completing its validity as a law, and thus showing that, in his understanding, no line dividing local from federal authority, nor anything in the Constitution, forbade the Federal Government, to control as to slavery in the federal territory. . . The Supreme Court in the Dred Scott case, plant themselves upon the Fifth

Amendment, which provides that no person shall be deprived of 'life liberty or property without due process of law,' while Senator Douglas and his peculiar adherents plant themselves on the tenth amendment, providing that 'the powers not delegated to the United States by the Constitution, are reserved to the States respectively, or to the people.'" The same Congress, the *identical* men who wrote it, passed the Northwest Ordinance and framed the Constitutional amendments - "Is it not a little presumptuous in any one of this day to affirm that the two things that Congress deliberately framed, and carried to maturity at the same time, are absolutely inconsistent with each other?" Were not the framers of the Constitution and the seventy-six members of Congress "our fathers who framed the government under which we live?" If the argument be made that this authority and this history do not exist, a man has the right to his own opinion, "But he has no right to mislead others, who have less access to history, and less leisure to study it … thus substituting falsehood and deception for truthful evidence and fair argument …

This is all Republicans ask - all Republicans desire - in relation to slavery. As those fathers marked it, so let it be again marked, as an evil not to be extended, but to be tolerated and protected only because of and so far as its actual presence among us makes that toleration and protection a necessity. Let all the guarantees those fathers gave it, be, not grudgingly, but fully and fairly maintained."

He then spoke directly to the people of the South, although he doubted if they would listen. When they denounce Black Republicans as reptiles and outlaws, are they fair to even themselves? Because Republicans have no existence in the South, does that make the Republican Party sectional? "The fact that we get no votes in the South, is a fact of your making, and not of ours." Accept the challenge of telling us how we threaten your section; meet us "as if it were possible that something may be said on our side." Washington had written to La Fayette that he considered that {slavery} prohibition a wise measure, expressing in the same connection his hope that we should at some time have a confederacy of free states." (In that *same* letter Washington had called slavery a social and political evil, and in a letter to Robert Morris he also wrote of slavery: "I can only say that there is no man living who wishes more sincerely than I do to see a plan adopted for the abolition of it; but there is but one proper and effective mode by which it can be accomplished, and that is, by LEGISLATIVE AUTHORITY, and that, as far as *my suffrage will go, shall never be wanting.")*

My husband said the South considered itself conservative and the Republicans radical - but was not conservatism "adherence to the old and tried, against the new and untried?" Was not the South unanimous in rejecting

147

and denouncing the old policy of the fathers in not accepting the prohibition of slavery in the territories? How do Republicans cause insurrections among your slaves? my husband asked. John Brown was no Republican, nor was there a single Republican at the Harper's Ferry enterprise, and "persisting in a charge which one does not know to be true is simply malicious slander." Slave insurrections have not increased since the formation of the Republican Party - did the Republicans cause the revolt of Nat Turner? "John Brown's effort was peculiar. It was not a slave insurrection. It was an attempt by white men to get up a revolt among the slaves, in which the slaves refused to participate." And what would be gained in the destruction of the Republican Party? Can you change human nature? "There is a judgment and a feeling against slavery in this nation which cast a million and a half votes. You cannot destroy that judgment and feeling - that sentiment - by breaking up the political organization which rallies around it." Will a change be made from the peaceful channel of the ballot box- "But you will break up the Union rather than submit to a denial of your Constitutional rights." ..."But no such right is specifically written in the Constitution" ... "even by implication" ... "You will rule or ruin in all events." Has the Supreme Court in the Dred Scott Decision settled this for you? The decision made by a *divided* court by a *bare* majority, *not in agreement among themselves*, its own supporters disagreeing as to its meaning, but the decision "was based on a mistaken statement of fact- the statement in the opinion that 'the right of property in a slave is distinctly and expressly affirmed in the Constitution.' " *Not true at all,* said my husband. Not once is the word *slave* used in the Constitution, nor the word *slavery.* The word property is not used either in connection to slaves or slavery, "and that whenever in that instrument the slave is alluded to, he is called a *'person'* - and wherever his master's legal right in relation to him is alluded to, it is spoken of as 'service or labor which may be due,' - as a debt payable in service or labor . . . this mode of alluding to slaves and slavery, instead of speaking of them, was employed on purpose to exclude from the Constitution the idea that there could be property in man." AND "When this obvious mistake of the Judges shall be brought to their notice, is it not reasonable to expect that they will withdraw the mistaken statement, and reconsider the conclusion based upon it?" If the court decision is not a final rule of *political* action, *you* will break up the Union? "But you will not abide the election of a Republican President! In that supposed event, you say, you will destroy the Union; and then, you say, the great crime of having destroyed it will be upon us! That is cool. A highwayman holds a pistol to my ear, and mutters through his teeth, ' Stand and deliver, or I shall kill you, and then you will be a murderer!' . . . The threat of destruction to the Union, to extort my vote, can scarcely be distinguished in principle." How *do* we satisfy the South? "We must not only let them alone, but we must, somehow, convince them that we do let them alone." The attempt over and over to do this has not met with any success. What *will* convince them? "This and this only; cease to call slavery *wrong,* and join them in calling it *right.* And this must be done thoroughly - done in *acts* as well as *words.* Silence will not be tolerated - we must place ourselves avowedly with them. Senator Douglas's new sedition law must be enacted and enforced, suppressing all declarations that slavery is wrong, whether made in politics, in presses, in pulpits, or in private . . . The whole atmosphere must be disinfected from all taint of opposition to slavery, before they will cease to believe that all their troubles proceed from us . . . Holding, as they do, that slavery is morally right, and socially elevating, they cannot cease to demand a full national recognition of it, as a legal right, and a social blessing . . . all they ask, we could readily grant, if we thought slavery right; all we ask, they could as readily grant, if they thought it wrong. Their thinking it right and our thinking it wrong, is the precise fact upon which depends the whole controversy."

My friend who attended that speech wrote me that there was an *electrical* energy from him to the rapt audience as he was finishing with these words,

"Wrong as we think slavery is, we can yet afford to let it alone where it is, because that much is due to the necessity arising from its actual presence in the nation, but can we, while our votes will prevent it, allow it to spread into the National Territories, and to overrun us here in the Free States? If our sense of duty forbids this, then let us stand by our duty, fearlessly and effectively. Let us be diverted by none of those sophisticated contrivances wherewith we are so industriously plied and belabored - contrivances such as groping for some middle ground between the right and the wrong, vain as the search for a man who should be neither a living man nor a dead man - such as a policy of 'don't care' on a question about which all true men do care - such as Union appeals beseeching true Union men to yield to Dis - unionists, reversing the divine rule, and calling not the sinners, but the righteous to repentance - such as invocations to Washington, imploring men to unsay what he said, and undo what Washington did.

Neither let us be so slandered from our duty by false accusations against us, nor frightened from it by menaces of destruction to the Government nor of dungeons to ourselves. LET US HAVE FAITH THAT RIGHT MAKES MIGHT, AND IN THAT FAITH, LET US, TO THE END, DARE TO DO OUR DUTY AS WE UNDERSTAND IT."

At his conclusion, the audience gave him a standing ovation. I said I can not explain what transformed my shy husband when he gave a public speech. Some magic reached out, probably from the magnificence of his soul, sharing its own inner light in his belief that this country was conceived in liberty and dedicated to the proposition that all men are created equal.

Chapter Fourteen

My husband arrived at Robert's school on February 29, and I can well imagine that Robert was ashamed of his father and feeling he did not come up to his high toned friends. They did think my husband rather grotesque, for one of them, Marshall Snow, wrote about it later. He said they pitied Robert, for his father had such a tall angular *odd* figure, being six foot four when the gentlemanly thing to do was to stay five foot nine or ten. And of course, the unruly head of hair was noted, as I was not around to get it all slicked up, and his clothes *always* looked as rumpled as his hair. Isn't it too bad that Bob's father is so *homely?* they queried among themselves. Then Bob's father was asked to speak at the school that Saturday night, with a Judge John Underwood of Virginia, and there was press coverage in the *Exeter News and Letter.* It was noted that the judge's feet did not quite reach the floor from his chair, and that my husband "had difficulty arranging his long legs *under* and *about* his chair." And then my husband went into his speech, and the old magic worked, and when he was finished, all of the high toned friends of Robert were on their feet, cheering, they recalled, like wild Indians. My husband was sharing Robert's room, and it was so filled with eager *worshipping* young men who wanted to take him to dinner on Sunday, I guess Robert could look upon his father's visit as a good thing. "Why didn't you ask me questions after my speech?" my husband asked the young men. "Don't you folks jaw back at a fella as they do out West?"

My husband gave nine other speeches, and took Robert along. Trustee Amos Tuck said that after one year at Exeter Robert was at the top of the ladder as a student, that he was brilliant, showed great promise and behaved himself in every way to be *worthy of his father.*

In Springfield, *just* at noon on May 18, 1860, I heard the firing of one hundred cannon. My husband rushed into the house, lifted me off my feet in a great hug and kisses, and said that the Republican Convention in Chicago had nominated him for the Presidency on the third ballot! Taddie and Willie clung to him. "Will we get to be President,too?" they asked. "Can I make President speeches?" Willie asked, already deciding to switch from preacher speeches to Presidential ones.

"All you want!" my husband said.

"But I don't make speeches," said Taddie. "I have this lisp thing."

"Talk to the folks *your* way," my husband said. "Just charm them, like your mother."

The weather had turned very hot. I *hate* hot weather, but I hardly minded this heat spell, for Springfield went wild over my husband's nomination. Crowds flocked to our house; *parades* came to our house, and when night fell, *torch lit* parades came to our house. I dressed up Taddie and Willie in white pantaloons, and they got to greet the crowds along with my husband. What they did was to join in the cheering, and their own cheers were, "Hurrah for Pa!" Officials for the *official* nomination arrived and Willie gravely said to them, "I am my father's son," and Taddie shook all of their hands and said, "So am I, and I have given up cigars forever."

All that night *all* of the houses in Springfield had lamps in their windows. On the streets were giant bonfires and then rockets were flamed into the air, and you would think it was the glorious Fourth. Soon Willie and Taddie organized *children* parades for their father. These followed the continuous adult parades, and Willie, who had written his Presidential speeches by now, managed to deliver them in between his marching. He held his head *exactly* like his father, and gestured just like his father, and *more or less,* said the same things he heard his father had said. The so called *Republican* cannon never seemed to stop their booming, and the constant *hurrahs* for my husband outside of our house, day and night, the smell of bonfire smoke and the kerosene smells in the night air - all of this made my soul sing. *He was doing it.* He was going to popularize what America at least *stood for* - the inalienable God given right of every man to life, liberty and the pursuit of happiness. If we did not have that right yet, and if we would not have it for a long time, or ever, the words of Thomas Jefferson were ingrained deep within America. *Let the light of liberty be the North Star of freedom within the human soul,* I heard my husband say. *The country must live up to its revolution, complete it, as a flower must open to the sun,* I heard my husband say. A man asked my husband what he would like to be remembered for when he was gone. I watched my husband's face, the gray eyes so filled always with *just* what he was thinking - and he slowly said, "I would like to be remembered for this - that I found a thistle and put in its stead a flower, where I thought a flower would grow."

Like Taddie, I wanted to fling myself on him and kiss his face.

My husband had to have an official portrait painted. He even hated to pose for a *photo,* so he did *not* relish a *painting* done of him. When the painter came to paint his portrait, he went on working at his desk in the State House, and did not pay any attention to the poor painter at all. Then Willie and Taddie came into the room, and he didn't pay any attention to them either, exited totally into his papers by now. While the poor painter watched in horror, Willie and Taddie joined him in the painting, doing each other all up first, and then the walls all around them. Finally, the painter gasped loud enough (probably a near death tone) to make my husband look up, and when he saw all of the varying colors on our sons and on the walls, he said fondly, "Now boys, you must not meddle with Mr. Hicks' paints; go home and have your hands and faces all washed up."

I did that. I think their father did the same for his office walls. And Mr. Hicks got to do his portrait of my husband and I thought it turned out to be rather good.

Mark Delahay visited us on his way home from the Republican Convention and brought along two convention flags, and he told Taddie he could have one. Mr. Delahay was a strong supporter of my husband and published an antislavery paper, the *Kansas Territorial Register*. He was even a distant relative of my husband's step-mother. *Nevertheless,* he forgot to leave Taddie his flag, and Taddie let me know all about it. About continuously. I wrote Mr. Delahay the following letter with the usual *Dear Sir:*

"One of my boys, appears to claim prior possession of the smallest flag, is inconsolable for its absence, as I believe it is too small to do you any service, and as he is so urgent to have it again - and as I am sure, the largest one will be quite sufficient, I will ask you to send it to us, the first opportunity you have, especially as he claims it, and I feel it necessary to keep one's word with a child, as with a grown up person - Hoping you reached home safely, I remain yours respectfully."

Taddie got his Convention flag and he and Willie added it to their children parades. Willie made so many street corner speeches for his father he lost his voice. Then that summer he got scarlet fever, from which he rapidly recovered, so he could resume his public speaking by July 24. Now his speeches came *immediately after* the children parade. Willie had set up as efficient children parade timetable as he had for this trains.

Robert shrank from the publicity that now befell him, and when he was asked to read the Declaration of Independence at Exeter he declined, saying he had to get his father's consent first. A wire was sent to his father and his father wired back, "Tell Bob to read that immortal document every chance he has, and the bigger the crowd, the louder he must holler." Robert then had to read the document and hated every minute of it. I think since his *Todd* stay he was always a recluse. Well, he wasn't *before* then.

In July of 1860 Robert entered Harvard University.

In August Springfield celebrated my husband's nomination with a parade down Eighth Street that took two and a half hours to pass by our home. Six thousand people were in it; float after float passed, *even one* having the *same* flatboat on which my husband had floated down the Mississippi to New Orleans, and another float had a man on it splitting rails as my husband once did!

Not as well, of course.

Robert was soon dubbed "the prince of rails," and did he ever hate that.

Letters started pouring in, and we were most delighted with this one:

"Dear Sir

My father has just home from the fair and brought home your picture and Mr. Hamlin's. (Vice President on my husband's ticket) I am a little girl only eleven years old, but want you should be President of the United States very much so I hope you wont think me very bold to write such a great man as you are. Have you any little girls about as large as I am if so give them my love and tell her to write me if you cannot answer this letter. I have got 4 brothers and part of them will vote for you any way and if you let your whiskers grow I will try and get the rest of them to vote for you would look a great deal better for your face is so thin. All the ladies like whiskers and they would tease their husbands to vote for you and then you would be President. My father is going to vote for you and if I was a man I would vote for you to but I will try to get everyone to vote for you that I can. I think that rail fence around your picture makes it look very pretty I have got a little baby sister she is nine weeks old and is just as cunning as can be. When you dir[e]ct to Grace Bidell Westfield Chatauque County New York

I must not write any more answer this letter right off Good by Grace Bidell"

My husband's reply went out as soon as we received the letter.

Private

"Miss Grace Bidell   Springfield, Illinois
My dear little Miss,   October 19, 1860

Your very agreeable letter of the 15th is received.

I regret the necessity of saying I have no daughters. I have three sons - one seventeen, one nine, and one seven years of age. They, with their mother constitute my whole family.

As to the whiskers, having never worn any, do you not think people would call it a silly affection if I were to begin it now? Your very sincere well-wisher. A. Lincoln

But my husband began to grow the whiskers, silly affectation or not.

In October my husband's political headquarters were his offices in the State House. He went there every day for his reading and replying to *mountains* of mail, dealing with artists who came to draw or sculpture his features, journalists who came to look at him first hand and wonder if *this* unassuming and *common* man could save the republic. Important men appeared at our home, men I had read about, and now, I was their hostess, and received them with Southern grace as they studied my husband, me, our home.

Here is how one reporter saw our home. It was a brown frame two storied cottage, easy to find, clearly marked with the name of its owner and he was ushered into it by a servant, while he waited for my husband to come down from upstairs. It was neatly furnished without being extravagant, and "an air of quiet refinement pervaded the place . . . there were flowers on the tables and pictures on the walls. The adornments were few but chastely appropriate . . . the hand of the domestic artist was everywhere visible. The impression was one of a very pleasant home." When he saw my husband enter the room he saw him as "tall and arrowy, with a profusion of wiry hair lying about loose on his head, and he had a pair of gray eyes that made you feel right at home . . . his whole face indicative of goodness and resoluteness . . . his face was one of the most eloquent I have ever seen. None of his pictures do him the slightest justice. His presence is commanding - his manner winning to a marked degree. After a few minutes of his company you cease to think he is either homely or awkward . . . I found him to be one of the most companionable men I have ever met. Frank, hearty, and reassuring, one feels irresistibly drawn toward him." The visit was on June 21, 1860, and its account was published in both the *New York Herald* and the *Sacramento Daily Union*. In early November, I was described by Thomas Webster, a visiting politician, as "'having a soft sweet voice," being "dignified, self possessed with undemonstrative manners, graceful and easy and unembarrassed." But he thought my husband appeared "lean and ugly in every way."

So much for *his* powers of observation!

A poet friend of Robert's, Albert Leighton, was our guest and he observed a warm happy family, and how we took turns saying grace before meals. He admired my own love of poetry, and left me the little book of his own poems that I kept all of my life. He also recorded that when crowds came to cheer my husband, Willie and Taddie, even if barefoot, ran out to join in on the cheers.

I wrote to friend Hannah on October 20 and expressed some feeling about the campaign. "Fortunately, the time is rapidly drawing to a close, a little more than two weeks, will decide the contest. I scarcely know, how I would bear up, under defeat . . . You must think of us on election-day, our friends will feel quite as anxious for us as we do ourselves."

And so had ended the 1850's, except for the loss of our dear little Eddy - sweet golden years of love and marriage, and children, and on November 6, 1860, that was all to change. My husband had been elected President of the *United* States, and, on December 20, South Carolina led the exodus from the Union, with Georgia, Alabama, Mississippi, Florida, Texas and Louisiana to follow, and we were in the greatest crisis since the American Revolution.

There was to be hate I had never believed to exist on earth. I had to defend every action I took, swallow being despised and reviled, lied about constantly, hated in the North for being born in a slave holding state, and hated in the South for politically supporting my husband, spat at, cursed at in person and prayer, and live in terror for my husband's very life.

You see, on November the sixth, 1860, I had become the First Lady of the land.

Chapter Fifteen

My husband did not vote for himself on November 6. He cut the Presidential electors off from the ballot and voted only for the state officers. That day I remained home and he spent most of it in his office at the State House. I teasingly told him if he were not home by ten I would lock him out of the house. I wanted to know the results immediately and not wait all night for them. As night fell, he went to the telegraph office to get the latest returns. It grew later and later. Anxious crowds gathered outside, some ten thousand. Inside Lyman Trumbull said, "If we take New York, that settles it." Jesse Dubois fell asleep and was asleep when the news clattered in that New York had gone for my husband. They all walked down the stairs; word had already reached the crowd of my husband's victory. "Speech! Speech!" they shouted. They began to throw their hats into the air, slapping and hugging each other. My husband did not cross over to them. "I guess I'll go down and tell Mary about it," he said to Lyman. He laughed. "That is if I am not locked out."

I had gone to bed and was asleep. My husband gently shook me awake. "Molly," he said. "We are elected!" I could hear the yelling of the crowds and a band marched right up to our door. Taddie and Willie rushed to join us, and Taddie said to Willie, "We are *all* elected!" Taddie always thought that Willie's many political speeches had turned the tide.

All of the lights were lit in the State House, and soon, like giant fireflies, house lights went on all over the town. My husband took me to *Watson's Confectionery* where the Republican women were holding a "victory supper." We were cheered and we were hugged, and my friend, Ada Bailache, said and wrote later, "I could hardly realize that I was sitting in the presence of a *real live President!*" She also remembered that the election never changed me or my husband, that we were both as down to earth and agreeable as ever, and did not "put on any airs at all."

That night we could not sleep, and in bed there was silence between us, the shared silence so common to those happily married. I thought of the silence between us in our courtship days, in the Edwards' back parlor - when we knew we loved and would marry, when we knew life to be right and forever, love eternal, and in content beyond words we watched the fire castles burn down into glowing coals, and I said, "two fold silence is the song of love," from some poet I had forgotten.

And on this night, this *sacred* night, that odious little *liar*, Billy Herndon, made up a most vicious and cruel story about me, and my husband, too. He said that *on this night* I chased my husband out of our house with a butcher knife in my hand, or a chair, or a table, or perhaps, and *why not?* - Evil Eva, and my husband was to have yelled to me, as he *dragged* me back into the house, "Now stay in there and don't be a *damned* fool before the people!" This lie even was to make itself into a Sherwood Anderson play about my husband! In fact, I was to play such a heinous witch in American drama, I cannot even believe it yet. My husband never would *drag* me anywhere, and I never heard him *yell* at me, or ever swear a single cuss word, and the idea of my taking a knife, or *anything*, to my beloved is as silly as my having the ability to crown *Billy* with Evil Eva, which I would have been delighted to do.

On February 6 we gave the last reception we were to give at our home. Dear Mercy came and she said it took her twenty minutes just to reach our hallway, and just as long to get out of the house. Crowds of friends kept coming, and it was joyous, their farewell to us, and it was hauntingly sad.

We had to find a home for our horse, Buck, our cow, Bessie, and our dog, Fido. Willie and Taddie wanted to take them all with us on the Presidential train, for there would be room for them all in or around the White House. Surely. They sobbed many tears of frustration when their father told them Buck, Bessie and Fido would be happier in Springfield than in Washington. "Pa," said Taddie, "if they stay here, I must *personally* approve of their new home. "

"I think that is very wise," said my husband, wisely.

And both Willie and Taddie carefully chose the new homes for Buck, Bessie and Fido. They had to be separated, but got to live near each other.

My mind had to grasp that we were moving to the *White House,* that we had to sell our furniture and leave our home of the last eighteen years. My mind grasped the danger my beloved was moving into, and by January of 1861, I had become terribly depressed. I was forty- two and going through what no one talked about then, the menopause. My old hated migraines returned with a vengeance, and I grieved that we were going away and leaving Eddy behind, as if he had not already left us. "Mother," said my husband. "You must try to cheer up." He knew how I loved beautiful clothes and how I loved to actually purchase them again, and not sew them for myself. "Go to New York and buy yourself a nice wardrobe," he said.

And so I did, and the New York clothing shops were glittering kingdoms - I was in awe of them, and people in them seemed to be in awe of me. It was a *very* bad combination. People who were rich and mighty fawned all over me. I was flattered shamelessly. The fearful extravagance for women's clothing, right out of *Godey's Ladies Book,* was all around me - women's bonnets, two hundred dollars, a lace scarf, two hundred dollars - and one costing *one thousand five hundred dollars,* which I promptly bought. Did I want to look like some frump with no culture or breeding? My gentile appearance, in the *right* clothes would not do anything but help my husband. I had to show that his wife was a refined and cultured woman. Wasn't he always proud of my pretty looks? Didn't he like me to look nice in nice clothes? Shouldn't I look nice for the *Northern cause?* And foreign tariffed goods helped the *North* financially. To buy wealthy was patriotic!

It was a time of dreadful ostentation.

My vanity for fine clothing was now becoming an obsession.

My husband had greeted a parade that had stopped in front of our house. I remember he had on a white suit, and he made a short speech and then, having not slept well the night before, lay down in his study for a nap. He slept for a while, and then another parade, another band, woke him up, and before greeting his visitors, he went to the mirror to try to comb down his hair. In the glass he saw himself two ways, his face alive and his face as a corpse. This shook him so much that he told me about it and even told me he knew what it meant.

He told me that he had had a vision that he would never come back from Washington alive.

"Father, we cannot then leave," I said. I was in a total panic. "If they are going to kill you in Washington, we must not go there!"

"I am elected," he said. "I have been chosen by the people and I must serve them as I was elected to do."

"Not with your *life!*"

"With my life if it has to be," he said. "I have said in speech after speech, I am nothing, and democracy is everything. That is what I am. That is what I believe."

"Father," I said, and tears were in my eyes. "You cannot -" What would he 'cannot?' Could he say, *sorry folks, you went and elected me to guide you, but I had this vision I would die in Washington* - "Oh, God," I moaned.

I remembered the words of the leaders of the South about their *peculiar institution.* I recalled how those that opposed it were hated, beaten, silenced, even murdered. And this is what my husband was to face, to try and *reason* with - to keep in the Union. The *Union - the* repository of our new world experiment in democracy. "If dreams cannot die," I said, "a dreamer can."

"When it is my time to go, and if someone is determined to kill me, I cannot stop it. There is a time and a tide for all things -"

"Not *that*," I said. "Those are just *words*. Father, I could not bear it if they killed you."

He looked at me, and then he looked beyond me. "Molly, you will be surprised what you can bear," he said. "Maybe we all are."

I went into his strong arms, and he held me warm and close, just as he did when we were courting. "Father, what will we do?"

"Go to Washington and do the best we can, Molly. The best we can." On December 20 my husband wrote another biography for publication. In it he said he was born of "undistinguished parents." In his eighth year he moved to "a wild region with many bears and other wild animals in the woods." He briefly attended "so-called schools," and the teacher had no more qualifications (Other than being alive) than reading, writing and ciphering up to the rule of three. That was as far as he went. "I have not been to school since. The little advance I now have upon this store of education, I have picked up time from time under the pressure of necessity." He was raised on a farm and did farm work until he was twenty- two. He had lost interest in a political career until the repeal of the Missouri Compromise. He noted he was six foot four, lean, weighing 180 pounds, had dark complexion, coarse black hair and grey eyes —"no other marks or brands recollected." He apologized at times for his photographs saying "this is the best that can be done from the poor subject."

So my husband was elected President of the United States. If I could have turned back time, I would have done it. I would see my husband lose the election and not be the center of so much ridicule, hate and violence. I would have remained at Eighth and Jackson where, after work, he walked home with Willie and Taddie, one, or both, catching a ride on his broad shoulders. And when the black clouds thundered out across the prairie, there he would be - by me - comforting away my terror of being struck by lightning. I would have lived there all my days, to meet my husband at the gate, crooked from so many dear children swinging on it, and we would walk into our home hand in hand, or arm in arm, and the pomp, the glory, even his exalted place in history, would be nothing at all to the sharing of all of my life with him.

Chapter Sixteen

I returned to Springfield on January twenty fifth. We had rented our house, sold our furniture, and would stay at the Chenery House before we left for Washington. My husband made a visit to his beloved stepmother in Coles County, and she said to him, "I fear you will not come back alive. Oh, Lord, I fear it *so!*"

I wonder if he thought the same thing. I wonder when he saw those old places in his mind - when he visited his father's grave - he remembered his mother's, and how he helped put her in it, and how the autumn leaves fell, and how she had loved their bright color, and how he had tried to shelter her grave from the first winter snow. He wrote a poem about light, how it envelopes us, and how it sadly, and still magically, it shimmered in all of his childhood days.

In Chenery House he roped our trunks and labeled them for mailing, *A. Lincoln, White House, Washington, D.C.* He was to leave Springfield on February eleventh, and Taddie, Willie and I were to meet him in Indianapolis the next day. It would be his fifty- second birthday.

That February eleventh was cold, rainy, *dark*. Mud was hub deep, but a huge crowd had come to see my husband leave. He had announced he would make no speech. At the Great Western Depot's waiting room, people filed by him and he shook their hands. People outside were asking to see my husband and Taddie was charging money for strangers to meet his father, and he took the money and directed them to someone else, who was pleasantly surprised at so many enthusiastic *admiring* hand shakes.

Robert stood with his father on the train platform, and the boys and I were in the umbrella-covered audience looking up at them. I have never seen my husband's face sadder. Tears were in his eyes, and he began an impromptu speech. His voice deepened with emotion.

"My friends - No one in my situation can appreciate my feeling of sadness at this parting. To this place, and the kindness of these people, I owe every thing. Here I have lived a quarter of a century, and have passed from a young to an old man. Here my children have been born, and one is buried. I now leave, not knowing when, or whether ever, I may return, with a task before me greater than that which rested upon Washington. Without the assistance of that Divine Being, who ever attended him, I cannot succeed. With that assistance, I cannot fail. Trusting in Him, who can go with me and remain with you and be every where for the good, let us confidently hope that all will yet be well. To His care commending you, as I hope in your prayers you will commend me, I bid you an affectionate farewell."

I may or may not return. The words gathered like poison in my heart. He had seen in the mirror two faces - one alive - one dead. *Molly, it means I will not come back from Washington alive.*

The rain pattered on my umbrella. Such terrible emotion swept through me - the rain when Eddy died - the total *frailty* of life - *father, lover, husband, beloved companion - what are we going into?*

My husband's obvious display of emotion hushed the crowd into a long silence, and I saw there was not a dry eye near me. *He is deeply loved. God will protect a man so deeply loved!*

But he is as deeply hated.

Then Willie and Taddie led the cheering. Willie would have made a speech of his own, but when his father's train left the station, so did the crowd.

The boys and I took a later train that night which *just barely,* at eleven in the morning, met the Presidential train in Indianapolis. Robert was given the task of guarding his father's gripsack. Leaving Harrisburg, we found the speech missing. *Robert had lost it.* He went off with some friends and left it in the hands of a hotel clerk! And where did the clerk put it? He threw it in with *all* of the hotel baggage. "That is my certificate of moral character!" my husband groaned. He took our friend, Ward Hill Lamon, and they went through the piles and piles of the suitcases, and it was my husband who found his gripsack. "Now I am moral again," he sighed in relief.

February 12, 1861, and on the train we had a birthday party for my husband. With our family were our friends, our dearest Elmer Ellsworth, whom we looked upon as our own son, so close he had become to both of us, my husband's secretaries, John Hay, John Nicolay, and our older friends, William Wallace, my brother in law and our physician, Ward Hill Lamon, and my husband's dear friend from his riding the circuit court days, Judge David Davis. The judge and Ward were so comfortably fat I wondered that our train could carry them *both* and still travel its breakneck and dizzying speed *of thirty* miles an hour. My husband teased Davis by saying the judge had to be surveyed before he could buy a new pair of trousers. He loved to hear Mr. Lamon play the banjo and sing along with it in his very fine voice, and Mr. Lamon did that for us many times as the train clattered over the tracks. "Ward, just one more," my husband begged, for he loved the sad sentimental songs now so popular.

My husband's journey to Washington D.C. lasted twelve days. Every half mile a man stood bearing the Union flag. Every town, every village we passed seemed to be having a carnival of celebration, red white and blue buntings, balloons, or flags were everywhere. Thousands lined the track to wave their own flags and cheer for my husband, and he said to us, "They are not cheering for me; they are cheering for the Union." At every state capitol where we stopped and where my husband spoke, they did shake his hands and say with tears in their eyes, "You must save the Union." That was what they saw my husband as - a man who could save the *United* States of America. Indianapolis had given the Presidential train a thirty–four gun salute for each state within it.

When we reached Columbus, Ohio, my husband had a bad cold, and his voice was hoarse. Robert would not speak to the crowds, and did not want to even be seen by the crowds, and when they shouted for him to appear and speak, my husband announced, "My boy, Bob, hasn't got in the way of making speeches." When the crowds yelled for me to appear, I did not want to either, but my husband introduced me to them, anyway, saying, "Here is the long and the short of it." The crowd roared with laughter, but I was *not* amused.

He never dared to try that again.

His clothes were in their usual mess and the newsboys were even hawking how much better he would look in his photos *when his hair was combed.* I sent for some decent clothing, and when it caught up with him, the *New York Times* declared he looked 50% better. I would still try to tame down his hair, but as soon as he started talking to a crowd - up went his hand to rummage it all up all over again. He was *so* indifferent to his clothing. I sincerely believe he would have felt at home speaking to the crowds in his slippers and nightshirt. "Father, why don't you care what you look like?" I would ask him.

"What is to care?" he always replied. "I am too ugly to do anything about it anyway."

"You *always* say that!" I said impatiently.

"Well, it has been *always* true," he replied.

The Presidential car was perfectly *elegant.* It had dark polished furniture and light carpet, the sidewalls under the windows were crimson plush, and between the windows was heavy blue silk with thirty- four stars. Two national flags were crossed at each end of the car, and red white and blue festoons hung from the dark molding.

When the train stopped, Taddie would rush outside to mingle with the crowds, and say, "Would you like to see the President? I'll take you to the

President!" and collect money for a tour to his father, who still turned out to be someone else. "Taddie is going to be what all women dote upon - a good provider," my husband said proudly. "Taddie is going to be spoiled more rotten," Robert said. "And Willie right behind him."

Although Taddie was happy with his newfound capitalism, and was saving his money in a big bag, he did not like people staring at *him* through the train windows. He threw himself on the floor to spoil their view, by not giving them one, and Willie did not like the staring either. "Pa," he asked, "wasn't there ever a President before who had children?"

But soon we all were in high spirits. Gone were my fears that my husband would be murdered. The enthusiasm and the love of the crowds who came to greet us, made my heart sing. I loved the recognition given to my husband. I *doted* on it. It is marvelous to know that what you know to be true, others also see.

The *New York Herald* printed on February 18 that my husband and I "produced a decidedly favorable impression." At Buffalo we lunched with ex President Milliard Fillmore at his home.

At Westfield, New York, my husband insisted on a train stop and asked if a Miss Grace Bedell were in the crowd before him. When he called out her name she shyly came forward and he asked her if she approved of his whisker growing, and she said she did and that he surely would be a better President because of it.

Then on the train went, festoons on it flying even from the train stairs, and from the frozen Hudson ice skaters waved to us. On the nineteenth we dined at the Astor House, and a reporter studied my husband and wrote, "He is not as bad looking as they say, while he is no great beauty . . . he has a *pleasant* face." I was described as plump, (popular then) amiable, modest, pleasant, and as " a round faced agreeable woman with no silly airs."

But oh, terror *did* return. The bubble of enthusiastic and admiring cheers burst. We were told that the Pinkerton detectives had discovered a plot to murder my husband when we entered Baltimore. He was to leave the Presidential train and go secretly through that city. I insisted on being with him in his secret journey and had quite a fit about it. "I will not leave you!" I wept, and my husband took me alone and he held me still, looking down at me with his stubborn *you cannot change this* look. "Mother, you will not go with me. If one of us is to be shot, it will *not* be you."

On February 23, he sent me a telegram from Washington saying he was safe and I met him that very day, and we stayed at the elegant Willard Hotel until his inauguration. My husband greeted those who came to see him by still shaking hands *frontier* style, with both hands like Willie and Taddie, and still using the frontier word, "Howdy!" Stephen Douglas called, so did General Scott, in full uniform and medals. We dined at Seward's home with Vice President Hamlin. A William Dodge told my husband that more slave states must be allowed in the Union or grass would grow in the streets. My husband said he would preserve, protect and defend the Constitution, with the assistance of the people and the help of the Almighty, in *every one* of the United States and let the grass grow where it may.

A man came up to him and said he was for God and him. My husband took his hand and said, "Well friend, at least you are half right."

But the abuse that came to him! A letter filled with hateful insane venom called him a God damned *black nigger,* the Negro to this demented mind being the anti-Christ. Letters poured in carrying death threats, and my husband cheerily told me that General Winfield Scott had had over three hundred of them, and he was not even President.

Washington in 1860 was a sodden town on the left bank of the Potomac, and in the summers, a mosquito filled marsh. Pennsylvania Avenue ran a mile between the unfinished Capitol and the unfinished Treasury building on Fifteenth Street West. Pennsylvania Avenue was paved with cobblestones, the only paved street in the city. The others were seasonal with seas of muck or flying dust. Each house had an open sewerage drain; even the sidewalks *stank.* The city's open canal, a branch of the Chesapeake and Ohio, bred malaria, and the only completed government buildings were the President's house, the dingy State Department, the War and Navy buildings on Seventeenth Street, the Interior building and Post Office. The bridges across the Potomac were seriously crumbling. Washington's population was sixty one thousand, *intensely Southern,* with just over three thousand slaves.

Of course, the Washington "tidewater elite" shunned meeting us, for we were uncouth and uncivilized from the wild, wild west, and might spit tobacco juice all over them. This shunning did not bother my husband at all. I don't even know if he was aware of it. I was. *How I was.* I had the education and breeding to equal any of the snobs, and I now had the wardrobe to go along with both. I vowed I would *always* dress the part of the First Lady.

Fine *clothes* again – a nemesis to be - the *comfort* of buying. It was not even a pleasure as much as it was *security.*

Ninian Edwards, who still hated my husband's liberalism, refused to accompany Lizzie to his inauguration. She brought her two daughters instead. And my cousin, Elizabeth Todd Grimsley, who had been my bridesmaid, would stay at the White House with me for my first six months there.

My husband had asked her to do this, thinking it would help me adjust to public life. He knew how close I was to my family.

The day before his inauguration my husband read his inaugural address to me. I was silent all during the reading, and silent long after it. "Does it serve?" he asked.

"It serves," I replied. Tears were in my eyes. I left the room, and near it, I could hear my husband's voice. He was praying aloud.

Never comfortable with institutionalized religion, there was no man more aware of a higher divinity, and the divinity within the human soul. He did not believe the path to God to be economic or political. He believed it to be as individual as the seeker.

The day of his inauguration was Monday, March 4, 1861. The dawn was somber and came with a high piercing bitterly cold wind. The night before the street cleaners had swept the streets, and they glistened from it. All of the hotels were filled. People were sleeping in halls, market stalls, on piles of lumber in warehouses. Some walked the streets all night, while through the dark, cavalry platoons rode by. The east portico of the Capitol, where my husband would speak, was constantly under watch, one guard under its floor and a battalion of troops forming a semi circle around it. I could see the crowded city was not decorated; house shutters were grimly closed, as if their occupants wanted no sight of their new President. My husband rode in the Presidential carriage with President Buchanan, and it looked as if the carriage were going into battle. Troops were stationed all along its way; green-coated sharp shooters were on all the roofs, and a full battery stood at Pennsylvania Avenue and Twelfth.

Outside of the Capitol's east front a platform had been built that would hold several hundred witnesses to my husband's inauguration. My family and I watched my husband deliver his inaugural from it, and behind us rose the unfinished Capitol dome, and before us, crowding the East Plaza, was a sea of ten thousand faces - black hats - white shirts - I looked out at them, and some faces were filled with hatred and loathing I did not dream possible, and others were filled with almost a loving veneration, and I thought, so this is where my beloved is, standing between the forces of love and hate, union and disunion, and his towering strength between the two will draw the strike of lightning.

But he always sheltered *me* from lightning.

He wore a new black suit, and new black boots, and a new black hat. I saw his white shirt was new and handsome. Riflemen were hidden in each window of the Capitol wings. Chief Justice Tawney, of the *infamous Dred*

Scott Decision, held the Bible for my husband, and he looked like a corpse. He handed the book to my husband with shaking hands, and I heard my husband take the oath to "preserve, protect and defend the Constitution of the United States." Then the artillery boomed thirty four times for the thirty-four states of the Union, and its sixteenth President began to read, slowly, deliberately his address, with *unsurpassed eloquence.*

The stirring of the crowd ceased. In his magnetic way he said he was no threat to the South in the fact he had no intention, and never said he had had, of interfering with slavery already confined to it. Then he addressed the secession of Southern states:

"I hold, that in contemplation of universal law, and of the Constitution, the Union of these States is perpetual. Perpetuity is implied, if not expressed, in the fundamental law of all national governments. It is safe to assert that no government proper, ever had a provision in its organic law for its own termination.... Again, if the United States be not a government proper, but an Association of States in the nature of contract merely, can it, as a contract be peaceably unmade, by less than all the parties who made it? One party to a contract may violate it - break it, so to speak; but does it not require all to lawfully rescind it? ... the Union is perpetual, confirmed by the history of the Union itself. The Union is much older than the Constitution. It was formed in fact, by the Articles of Association of 1774. It was matured and continued by the Declaration of Independence in 1776. It was further matured and the faith of all thirteen States expressly plighted and engaged that it should be perpetual by the Articles of Confederation in 1778. And finally, in 1787, one of the declared objects for ordaining and establishing the Constitution was *'to form a more perfect union.'* ... .It follows from these views that no State, upon its own mere motion, can lawfully get out of the Union, that *resolves* and *ordinances* to that effect are legally void; and that acts of violence, within any State or States, against any authority or the United States are insurrectionary or revolutionary, according to circumstances...

I therefore consider that, in view of the Constitution and the laws, the Union is unbroken; and to the extent of my ability, I shall take care, as the Constitution expressly enjoins upon me, that the laws of the Union be faithfully executed in all of the States.... I trust this will not be regarded as a menace, but only as the declared purpose of the Union that it *will* constitutionally defend and maintain itself.

In doing this there needs to be no bloodshed or violence, and there shall be none, unless it is forced upon the national authority. The power confided in me, will be used to hold, occupy, and possess the property, and places belonging to the government, and to collect the duties and imposts; but beyond what may be necessary for these objects, there will be no invasion-no using of force against, or among the people anywhere."

He hoped for a *peaceful* solution and a return of *fraternal* affections. There were constitutional controversies, for *no* law can be applicable to *all* questions. And from the questions we *do* divide into majorities and minorities. "If the minority will not acquiesce, the majority must, or the government must cease. There is no other alternative; for continuing the government, is acquiescence on one side or the other. If a minority, in such case, will secede rather than acquiesce, they make a perfect precedent which, in turn, will divide and ruin them; for a minority of their own will secede from them, whenever a majority refuses to be controlled by a minority. . . .

Plainly, the central idea of secession, is the essence of anarchy. As a majority, held in restraint by constitutional checks, and limitations, and always changing easily, with deliberate changes of popular opinion and sentiments, is the only true sovereign of a free people. Whoever rejects it, does of necessity, fly to anarchy or to despotism. Unanimity is impossible; the rule of a minority as a permanent arrangement, is wholly inadmissible; so that, rejecting the majority principle, anarchy, or despotism, in some form, is all that is left. . . .

Why should there not be a patient confidence in the ultimate justice of the people? Is there any better, or equal hope, in the world? In our present difference, is either party without faith of being in the right? If the Almighty Ruler of nations, with his eternal truth and justice, be on your side of the North, or on yours of the South, that truth, and that justice, will surely prevail, by the judgment of this great tribunal, the American people. . . .

My countrymen, one and all, think calmly and *well* upon this whole subject. Nothing valuable can be lost by taking time. . . .

In *your* hands, my dissatisfied fellow countrymen, and not in *mine,* is the momentous issue of civil war. The government will not assail *you.* You can have no conflict without being yourselves the aggressors. *You* have no oath registered in Heaven to destroy the government, while I shall have the most solemn one to 'preserve, protect and defend it.'

I am loath to close. We are not enemies but friends. We must not be enemies. Though passion may have strained, it must not break our bonds of affection. The mystic chords of memory, stretching from every battle-field, and patriot grave, to every living heart and hearthstone, all over this broad land, will yet swell the chorus of the Union, when again touched, as surely they will be, by the better angels of our nature."

Again, those words brought tears to my eyes. The faces filled with hate, the faces filled with veneration, faded, and only those words remained. Right after we were married I said my husband had *a kind of* poetry in his soul. I changed that. Right here. Poetry sang within him, as did its genius in expressing the nobility of his being.

And when the Presidential carriage had begun its route to bring my husband to the podium to make this speech, the sun had burst through the clouds, and I thought it an omen, a mystical omen, that my beloved *had* taken into his hands the thistle of disunion, and he would restore once more, in its stead, the Union, the strength and survival of the opening flower of democracy, to grow and to flourish in the *United* States of America.

Chapter Seventeen

After the inaugural ceremony, we were driven in the Presidential carriage to 1600 Pennsylvania Avenue, the grand home of the people.

The grand home of the people was a *mess*. I guess it was because President Buchanan was a bachelor, or if he had a woman around, she was suffering from a severe lack of eyesight. Or consciousness.

Old Edward, the doorkeeper since President Taylor, opened the doors for us. That night we had seventeen friends to dinner, and then we all retired to our rooms to rest before the Inaugural Ball at ten forty five. I entered that ball on the arm of Senator Douglas. It was *against* protocol for me to enter on the arm of my husband, but I soon changed *that* rule. I certainly did *not* want another woman where I was supposed to be. When my husband entered the room, the band struck up *Hail Columbia,* and our party solemnly marched from one end of the ballroom to the other. My husband wore his best suit, and I had his hair slicked down as best I could do it, and told him *not* to run his hands through it and *to keep on* his white kid gloves.

He did neither.

I wore a dress of blue satin. I had wanted to wear lilac, but my husband wanted me to wear the blue that matched my eyes. I even wore a blue feather in my hair. I danced the quadrille with Senator Douglas, and I remembered how we had danced so many times at Lizzie's with our *coterie.* My husband left us at twelve thirty; the others and I stayed to dance a while longer. I *loved* to dance. My husband had earnestly tried to learn, and had in a way, *his* way, but I felt safer with him when we attended the theater.

We were short of money. My husband was using his own funds, and had to borrow money to pay for the first month we stayed in the White House. The day after the inauguration, I interviewed a former slave to be my modiste, Elizabeth Keckley, who had been a seamstress to Mrs. Jefferson Davis. "You know I can pay you *fairly* but not *extravagantly,*" I said. She was a lovely comely mulatto, and I hired her immediately. We became fast friends. I soon saw her as one of my best women friends in the world. When her only child was killed in the war, I shared in her grief, for how bitterly I already knew the loss of a son. I shared in more than her grief. I shared the most intimate part of my life in the White House. I called her Lizzie, and I said to her, *many,*

many times, "Lizzie, *always* respect the privacy my husband and I try to keep for us here."

"Madame, what do you mean?" she asked.

"Our private life here is ours, and does not belong to the press. My husband and I want it this way. We are not on display - as if we were *performing* for the people, rather than *doing* for them."

"Of course, *of course,*" she agreed.

That first night we were in the White House was so sweet, exciting enough to chase away sleep, and we held each other, and how good it always was between us to talk over the day past and the day to come. Finally, he was asleep, quiet breathing next to me, and I admit to exultation and pride that my beloved was *President,* that we were *living* in the White House.

In the morning we all were up early for breakfast, and we women wore our robes, and did not have to drag around those bothersome hoops I could not wait to get into, and once having to wear the things, could not wait to get out of. After breakfast I did dress properly and toured our home for the next four years. The more I saw of it, the more dreadful it became. Crowds had taken souvenir pieces from the wallpaper and the drapes, and had clearly spat upon the carpets. Every single wall needed fresh paint. And on the shabby walls, the shabby drapes listlessly *drooped.* I told my husband the Green Room got its name from the green algae on its walls, the Blue Room for its blue algae, and the Red Room from being so awful it was straight out of hell. The furniture in the family suite was nothing more or less than a disaster. The mahogany French bedstead was split from top to bottom, and it was the *best* furniture in the room! "Will Congress give money to keep the White House standing up?" I asked my husband.

"Yes," he said. "And don't go over it, or we will pay the difference," but I did go over the money barrier. The Congressional appropriation   I had to work with was $20,000. I spent over it by $6,700, and I was in a total panic that I had done this. I got Benjamin French, whom my husband had appointed Commissioner of Public Buildings, to take the run- over bills to him. I heard my husband paced the floor with the bills in his hands saying, *"Flub Dubs* for this damned old house!" He looked at a carpet bill for $2,500, and he said, "I would like to know where a damned carpet costing $2,500 can be put!"

"Oh," I said when I heard the story. "My husband does *not* swear!"

"He swore this time," said Mr. French.

My husband said to me, "Molly, that money should have been used for blankets for our boys who are fighting for what this place stands for."

"Father," I replied with spirit, "if I had not done what I did, it would not be standing at all!"

Finally, Congress picked up the difference, in two different deficiency bills as I recall.

Why shouldn't the house of the people be worthy of our great country? Why should foreign grand ambassadors, all done up in medals, gold cords and braid, scoff at a *shabby* Presidential house?

I was not discreet. I could not be, but I tried. When I wanted my husband to appoint someone, I did beat about the bush. That is, I went to a political friend, like Mr. French, or Judge Davis. I would say how smart my husband thought they were, and could they give him my idea, but claim it as their own? Then I would not be interfering, but, really, my husband did listen to me. He *always* listened to my political opinions. Very carefully. And then he did what he had already decided to do.

That way, I guess, we were both happy.

I now dressed in *perfect* style. *And so would be the White House.* By our first Christmas in it, Christmas of 1861 - it was *grand.*

In my *master* restoration I had created a *modern* Victorian interior with rosewood furniture and velvet wallpaper with purple or gold drapes that were *alive, vibrantly alive* and not limp, blah and blaher. I bought Dorflinger glassware, the finest in the world, and a beautiful set of Haviland - so beautiful I paid for a set of it for us with my initials at its center instéad of the country's coat of arms. Riggs and Company charged my husband $1,106.73 for our set. It had a wide Solferino border of purplish red. I have never seen more beautiful china. My husband thought so, too, and I did not spoil his appreciation of it by including the price.

I had the White House cleaned and painted. I had all of the windows washed. I bought books for the library, books of poetry by Goldsmith, Mrs. Browning, Spenser, Bryant and Longfellow among others. I bought new bedsteads, chairs, sofas and velvet hassocks. I bought new Bell Pull Rosets and Cords, new washstands and I did use costly fabrics for the walls and the drapes. I had even repaired and varnished the portrait of Andrew Jackson, *Democrat,* for $25.50. The new carpet for $2,500, which I had purchased for the East Room, won praise from *all* who saw it. It was sea green as if its sea were tossing pale roses to its border, and the red room, which we chose as our downstairs sitting room and where we received our guests after a state dinner, was now *exquisite.* Its floor was covered with crimson Wilton at the cost of $292.50, and it had gold damask drapes, a grand piano and a full-length portrait of George Washington. I insisted that there *always* be fresh flowers in this room, and there were. The Blue and the Green rooms no longer got their color from algae; or 1812 moulds of varying hue - the redecorating of all of these rooms and the East Room cost $3,549.00. But my heart and soul went into creating a *masterpiece* guest room upstairs with purple velvet drapes with a gold sash. It would please any visitor, or any monarch done up with golden braid and tassels, even the *British* ambassador.

By November the White House had furnaces, gaslights and piped in Potomac water. No one faulted me on my taste.

Just what it cost.

Here was our arrangement in the no longer falling down White House. Its east half was for public and business affairs, and the west half, except for the state dining room, was for our family. When one entered the White House, to the left, was the famous East Room for all public receptions. To its west, behind the corridor facing south, were three small parlors, the Green, Blue and Red rooms.

Our family dining room was toward the front and west side of the house, while the state dining room was at it southern corner. To the west of the White House was the conservatory from which always came out of season flowers. I saw that all of the rooms being used had flowers from it during the winter.

Upstairs, the west wing was for our two family bedrooms, and the three guest bedrooms. In the east wing, directly over the great East Room, was the location of my husband's office, the adjoining cabinet room, and a waiting room outside of the President's office. West of the waiting room was an office for a clerk. Opposite the waiting room, to the north, were the offices of his secretaries. The large library separated the cabinet room from the family bedchambers.

Mr. Nicolay and Mr. Hay were my husband's secretaries, and I soon thought they were both young snobs and filled with themselves far too much. It is nothing like being in your twenties to have absorbed *all* learning of *everything*. They were cold and curt to the crowds always waiting to see my husband and were *most* unpopular young men. They always talked *down* to me. John Hay said dreadful things about the Todd family. I was told he called me the *enemy*. He later referred to me as a *hellcat, the daughter of the devil*, but out of sight and sound of my husband, of course. He sarcastically called my husband the *tycoon*, out of my sight and sound, of course. When Noah Brooks arrived to be my husband's secretary for his second term, it was a great relief to *both* of us.

My husband's office had a large white marble fireplace with a high brass fender, a few chairs, two hair-covered sofas and the large oak table for cabinet meetings. The gas jets were in glass globes, and there were plentiful kerosene lamps for emergencies. His windows looked south to the lawn and the trash pile around the unfinished Washington Monument, the Smithsonian, the Potomac, and Alexandria, a long grass slope covered with white soldier tents, soldiers, cattle and wagons. Between the tall windows were a large chair and a table where my husband liked to do his writing. In the large pigeon hole desk near the south wall my husband kept the United States Statutes, the family Bible and his volume of Shakespeare.

His work schedule was *all of the time,* and it only got worse as the war progressed. Our breakfast was supposed to be at nine, and he was supposed to work in his office from seven until that time, but later and often, he stayed in the office all night, taking naps with his head on the desk. After breakfast, which for him was coffee, an egg and maybe some seasonal fruit, he went to the War Office to see Stanton or Halleck, then back to the White House to answer his mail, then lunch - a biscuit, milk, fruit in season, then he met the throngs of callers who lined the hall from his office to the Reception Room, many sleeping in the White House halls, some staying *weeks* to see him. One office seeker even walked into our bedroom at *two in the morning!* There were *endless* office seekers, officers who wanted to go higher in rank, or all of their relatives with the same idea, and my husband moaned and said to me, "Molly, there are just not enough oats for the horses."

I received floods of letters to answer, and my own secretary was William Stoddard, whom I called "Stod," and we got along very well. He was down to earth, and as warm and genial as Hay and Nicolay were snobbish and cold.

The custom was that there be a Presidential reception on every Friday night and every Saturday afternoon. *Anyone* could come to the White House and meet us, excluding rebels, which my husband always called *those gentlemen of the South.* It was the age of snobbery, believe me, and we *never* accepted a social caste system. *On a one to one* basis, especially to the *non*-elite, my husband would smile, his face glowing, and he would say, "Howdy, stranger, what can I do for you?" These were the people he invited into his office. But at *formal* receptions he shook hands stoically, and I would see his eyes glaze over as his mind left behind the *endless* hand shaking. One guest getting a handshake said, "Sir, (my husband did not like to be called Mr. President) this hand shaking makes you look tired."

My husband said, "Friend, it was a lot easier to split rails." I recall when he was talking to a great English lord, he saw a friend from Illinois. He said, "Excuse me, my lord, but here is an old friend I haven't seen since we made rails together in Sangamon County!" One of our friends visited and asked my husband how it felt to be President. "Have you heard what the man said when he was being tarred and feathered and driven out of town on a rail?" my husband asked.

"No, Sir."

"Well," my husband said, "a man in the crowd yelled at him and asked how he liked being run out of town on a rail, all tarred and feathered, and the exiter said that if it were not for the honor of the thing, he would have just as soon have walked." Then my husband laughed and so did everyone else around. The British ambassador did, almost, and I thought he was like Mrs. Stanton, afraid to smile and when she did it was more of a grimace.

Cabinet meetings were scheduled for every Tuesday and Friday, and my husband closed them by saying, "Boys, I reckon that'll do. We'll shut up shop for the rest of the day." Imagine talking to his cabinet like that when each one, but Welles, thought he was President! His seven man cabinet consisted of Secretary of State, William Seward, Secretary of Treasury, Salmon Chase, Secretary of Interior, Caleb Smith, Secretary of War, Simon Cameron, and then Edwin Stanton, Secretary of the Navy, Gideon Wells, (who always wore a *great* gray wig) Attorney General Edward Bates and Postmaster General Montgomery Blair.

Mrs. Keckley made me a lovely gown for our first Friday evening levee. It was of a bright rose-colored moiré, and I wore roses in my hair to match its color. When my husband saw me, he sat down by me and said, so all could hear, "I declare, you look charming in that dress. Mrs. Keckley has met with *great* success!"

He even had his white kid gloves on - that is, for a while. Now he constantly groaned when he had to put them on. "Molly, I hate the things."

"Father - your position -"

The position of the gloves was always back into his pocket as soon as my back was turned.

It was printed in the Northern papers that I was an "excellent hostess," really "interested in my guests and showing it," that I could make a dull four hour formal dinner "sparkle with intelligent conversation." I do know that for those state dinners *all* of the White House waxed flowers went into the trash and *fresh* flowers adorned the dining table, just as they always did in our own home.

In the Todd home a fresh flower was served right on the dish with *each* change of course.

The costly state dinners gave way to more public receptions, my idea, and my husband agreed, for they were more democratic.

My good education served me well. The Chilean ambassador spoke no

English, but he spoke French, and we spoke French during the rest of his visit. When the prince of France - Prince Napoleon, came to the White House for a formal dinner, we conversed the whole time in French.

My husband was clearly proud of my social graces and said so to more than one visitor. I heard him say to one in the East Room, "My wife is as handsome as when she was a girl, and I, a poor nobody then, fell in love with her, and what is more, I have never fallen out!"

Actually, I heard him say that *many times.* My heart sang with those words. My heart always sang with the tender way my husband looked at me. A friend wrote home of this "pleasing look the President gave to the woman he so loved."

It was written and, *more than once*, that we looked at each other with obvious adoration.

What were the *non- vitriolic* summaries of me in 1861? I loved beautiful clothes, wore them well, was a devoted wife and mother, loved good jokes, had a very merry and frequent laugh, was generous, tender hearted, affectionate, frank, sarcastic, impulsive, and totally uncalculating. Those close to me always said I had a quick temper, and was always contrite for it. I am happy that what was said the most, by those closest to me - was that I was "good of heart."

What was thought, but not said, was also true. About money, I was becoming irrational. The idea that we were really still poor and would certainly be when we returned to Springfield, was taking a firm grip. I felt we were doomed to live those first seven years of poverty over and over. I thought I had adjusted to those hard years. But they had not adjusted to me. It was so *real* - this constant background terror of a future *with no home of my own.* I could not imagine myself rooming and boarding again, as my husband and I had done at the Globe tavern. Going through the menopause I was falling prey to nervous bursts of energy, then exhaustion, and the migraine headaches that made me feel as if hot wires were being drawn through my eyes, were a frequent occurrence. And of course I had the malaria ague I caught from the swamp on which the White House had been constructed.

The virulent hatred that soon poured out at my husband and me made my weakness worse. I was too sensitive to being hated and despised. When a girl who sympathized with the rebels saw my carriage she would open her window and sing (shout) *Dixie* to me. And those Northerners who hated the South called me a spy for the rebels and this lie lasted all of my life. "Father," I would say to my husband. "How can people be so wicked? How can they hate me when I have never met them?"

"Molly, you are my wife. They get at me through you."

"How can you stand the vicious ridicule - the lies - the murderous hatred?"

"It is directed at what I stand for."

"Father, I am terrified they will kill you."

"If some one wants to bad enough he can."

"What will we do?"

"Live, and do the best we can while we are."

"I will try. I surely will!"

But it was he who stood between the lightning and me.

Here is another of my faults. I have said I was vain, and found security in fine clothes. I was *unreasonably* jealous. About my husband - I was what you could *truly* call a jealous woman. I wanted no other woman on my husband's arm, no matter what protocol decreed. I could not stand a woman flirting with him, and flirt they did, surrounding him and glittering like little stars. In the so-called Wild West, where we came from, women did *not* flirt with married men, but here in Washington they did. *I did not like it.* One young woman rushed up and hugged him, and this made me furious. I told him so. My husband always felt more comfortable around men, laughing with them about his own jokes and parables, and I knew he did not like those brazen women any more than I did. Still, he had to deal with them. He teased me about my obvious jealousy; with eyes twinkling, he would say, "Molly, what women *will* we keep in Washington?"

"Those who do not hug another woman's husband," I replied tartly.

"Well, of them, how many are you going to allow into the reception tonight?"

"Those with husbands near and teeth gone."

"All right, mother. I shall so inform the ushers," he said solemnly, and left repeating to himself, "husbands near, teeth not," and Mrs. Keckley giggled at our in - house drama. "Wives with teeth or not." she said, "You two are so devoted to each other."

"I guess that is a private thing we cannot hide," I said happily.

I took instant dislikes to some people, especially those who looked down on my husband, for they could not look down on him in *any* way. I clashed with Nicolay and Hay from the first. I detested - really *detested* - my husband's Secretary of the Treasury, Salmon P. Chase, and his vicious snob daughter, Kate, who gossiped about me *always,* lying *always.* Vicious lies about me were to come out of the Treasury office all during my husband's Presidency. The great Salmon P. thought he would be President, and daughter Kate thought she would be White House hostess, and he wasn't and she wasn't, and so the vendetta against my husband went through me.

Secretary of State William H. Seward had wanted to be President, and still thought he was, being the real brain behind my husband's - far, *far* behind, in actuality. He had even sent my husband a memorandum, dated April 1, 1861, saying more or less, and not less than more, that he was the real thinker for the administration. He consented to my husband's handling of *local* matters, but as for the *important* affairs, he would take care of them *all.* My husband did not tell me of the memorandum. He did not have to. I saw Seward for what he was immediately.

Our first official reception was to be on April 8, and guess who informed me *he* would give it? William H. Seward. I quickly informed William H. that the reception would be given by *us,* the President and his wife, at the White House. And when the French prince arrived, William H. said he would give the state dinner for him, and I told him the state dinner would be at the White House and given by the President and his wife. Our party of thirty did go very well that August third, and I hope I had the Haviland and the Dorflinger crystal by then, but I don't remember whether I did or not.

My *own sisters* in Springfield began to gossip about me, sister Ann Todd Smith said I was trying to run a court of *Queen Victoria,* and the great Edwards on their great aristocratic hill could say nothing good of my husband - *yet.* Mrs. Edwards wrote I was doing the White House up too fine - that is, it might be done up better than her own mansion. Even my dearest Merce was to refer to me as *her royal highness.* I had not snobbishly elevated myself at all, and these little darts hurt. It was bad enough being maligned by people I never met, but by my relatives and friends - it *hurt.*

The boys were ill with the measles for three weeks. Cousin Lizzie Grimsley and I tended them, and staying with us for so long, she could closely study the character of my husband. She wrote to our cousin John Todd Stuart, "Never have I seen a man of such depth, tenderness and purity."

Hadn't I been telling the Todds that from the first?

When Fort Sumter was attacked early on the morning of April 12, my husband called for 75,000 militia to join the army. Virginia, Tennessee, Arkansas and North Carolina had left the Union by May 20.

Congress was called into special session on July 4 when a message to them from my husband was read. *I think it is one of the most important speeches he ever wrote.* He first noted the states that had seceded from the Union. Then he noted the tragedy of the loss of Ft. Sumter that could not have been held without the presence of twenty thousand more men - "It is thus seen that the assault upon, and reduction of Fort Sumter, was, in no sense, a matter of

178

defense on the part of the assailants. They well knew that the garrison in the Fort could, by no possibility, commit aggression upon them. . . . They knew that this Government desired to keep the garrison in the Fort, not to assail them, but merely to maintain visible possession, and thus to preserve the Union from actual and immediate dissolution - trusting, as herein - before stated, to time, discussion, and the ballot box, for final adjustment; and they assailed, and reduced the Fort, for precisely the reverse object - to drive out the visible authority of the Federal Union and thus force it to immediate dissolution. . . . Then, and thereby, the assailants of the Government, began the conflict of arms, without a gun in sight, or in expectancy, to return their fire, save only the few in the Fort, sent to that harbor years before, for their own protection, and still ready to give that protection, in whatever was lawful. In this act, discarding all else, they have forced upon the country the distinct issue: 'immediate dissolution, or blood.' " This did not just involve the fate of the United States. "It presents to the whole family of man, the question, whether a constitutional republic, or a democracy - a government of the people, by the same people - can, or cannot, maintain its territorial integrity, against its own domestic foes. It presents the question, whether discontented individuals, too few in numbers to control administration, according to organic law, in any case, can always, upon pretenses made in this case, or on any other pretenses, or arbitrarily, without any pretence, break up their Government, and thus practically put an end to free government upon the earth. . . . So viewing the issue, no choice was left but to call out the war power of the Government, and so to resist force, employed for its destruction, by force, for its preservation."

He asked Congress for "at least four hundred thousand men and four hundred million dollars" for the task. He attacked the Southern sophism that it could legally and peacefully withdraw from the Union, without the consent of the Union or of any other state. This was rebellion sugar coated, and used to drug the public mind of their section for thirty years - "Our States have neither more, nor less power, than reserved for them, in the Union, by the Constitution. . . . The original ones passed into the Union even *before* they cast off their British colonial dependence; and the new ones each came into the Union directly from a condition of dependence, excepting Texas. And even Texas, in its temporary independence, was never designated a State." The free and independent colonies had never declared their independence of each other, or of the Union. "Having never been States, either in substance, or in name, outside of the Union, whence this magical omnipotence of 'State rights,' asserting a claim of power to lawfully destroy the Union itself? . . . The states have their status in the Union, and they have no other *legal status*. If they break from this, they can only do so against law, and by revolution. The Union, and not themselves separately, procured their independence, and their liberty. ... The Union is older than any of the States, and, in fact, it created them as States." The Constitution did *not* legalize secession. "The principle itself is one of disintegration, and upon which no government can possibly endure. ... It maybe affirmed, without extravagance, that the free institutions we enjoy, have developed the powers, and improved the condition, of our whole people, beyond any example in the world. ... Our popular government has often been called an experiment. Two points in it our people have already settled - the successful *establishing*, and the successful *administering* of it. One still remains - its successful *maintenance* against a formidable attempt to overthrow it. It is now for them to demonstrate to the world, that those who can fairly carry an election, can also suppress a rebellion - that ballots are the rightful, and peaceful successor of bullets; that when ballots have fairly, and constitutionally, decided, there can be no successful appeal back to bullets; that there can be no successful appeal, except to ballots themselves, at succeeding elections. Such will be a great lesson of peace; teaching men that what they cannot take by an election, neither can they take it by a war - teaching all, the folly of being the beginners of a war."

Using his war power in defense of the government was forced upon him -

"As a private citizen, the Executive could not have consented that these institutions shall perish; much less could he, in betrayal of so vast, and so sacred a trust, as these free people have confided to him. He felt that he had no moral right to shrink; nor even to count the chances of his own life, in what might follow."

Washington was barricaded; public buildings were guarded by sentinels, and the night streets were deserted save for the shadows of marching patrols. "Frontier guards" camped in the East Room and *in all* of the corridors of the White House. But Washington really had no formal defense. The rebels could have taken it, us. My husband and I tried to shield each other from the horror of the city under siege, the thought it could fall, whilst piles of violently hateful letters streamed into the White House. My husband was a "goddamned nigger" and I was a "goddamned whore," "harlot, "hussy", "jezebel" and spy for the North or the South - apparently, I was *already* a traitor to *both* the North and the South.

The army for Washington's defense did not arrive until April 24, the Sixth Massachusetts. It had been attacked by a mob in Baltimore, and my husband visited its wounded. The next day the Seventh New York arrived and marched down Pennsylvania Avenue to the White House, where my husband greeted them. My cousin Lizzy and I watched with tears of relief in our eyes.

My husband sank into deep depression, sought out our bedroom where he could take off his shoes, and stretch back for sleep he had not found the night before. First we would read from the Bible, recite our favorite poems, as if their words could find wisdom and truth, when none seemed to be around us. I insisted that we start a custom of taking a carriage ride away from the White House every single afternoon, and, together, see that, outside of the White House, the sun did shine, and the wind could still leave a glorious path of light among the trees.

The Todds were coming apart as was the nation. Some of my brothers joined the Confederacy, two became Confederate officers, and my favorite brother, George, became a Confederate surgeon. It was terrible for us when the husband of our dearest little sister, Emilie Todd Helm, joined the South. My husband had offered Ben Hardin Helm the post of paymaster of the United States Army, and when he refused to stay on our side, I shed bitter tears.

I was on constant display. There was nowhere to hide. "I don't think I can do this," I said to my husband. I felt engulfed by poisonous snakes, deceit and lies, banished untried to torture, to a desert without any well of human kindness. "Father," I wept. "I can do nothing right. I cannot bear what they say about us - about me."

"Don't pay any attention to them," he replied. "We can do nothing about it. Do not read the hate letters, the news - all of the editorials calling us demons - let it go."

"Oh, God, what do we do?"

He touched my face, and brushed away a tear, as gently as when he first touched my face, before his first kiss. "Molly, only the best we can."

Not *everyone* around hated us. A camp named for me was nearby, and when liquor was sent to the White House, and as we did not drink it, or serve it, Taddie and Willie insisted it be sent on to the soldiers of this camp named for me. They soon were delivering the booze, in person, by the *wagon-load*, and in time, Taddie and Willie, and their entourage of booze wagons, were soldier - cheered at first sight. My name was even included in the cheers! I guess in recognition of my having something to do with the presence of Taddie and Willie and their subsequent booze deliveries.

Other soldiers were having *good* things to say about us, too. They noted my husband saluted their officers, but uncovered his hat for them. They noted he could always move behind the officers to shake their hands and say, "Howdy, boys, how are you doing?" as if he really *cared* how they were doing. Or he would *really* join them, sitting down by them and saying, "Howdy! Can you spare a cup of coffee?"

When he and his cabinet visited a group of soldiers and strawberry shortcake was served, he could see there were not enough seats for the soldiers and his cabinet, so he sat on the floor to eat, and seeing him, his cabinet also sat on the floor to eat. I would have loved to see Chase work his way down to do that.

One soldier wrote home that my husband was not as ugly as reported, and if his nose was a little too large, so was he. Another wrote my husband talked to the common folk watching an army review with him, which was not quite respectable, for he should have been looking straight ahead at the troops, but, anyway, he had a *kindly* face. *But* - for the army reviews, maybe he shouldn't bring his boys along, for one of them was always breaking away and marching along with the soldiers. (Taddie, of course) As for both my husband and me, more than one soldier wrote home that we reminded them of their own neighbors, just "plain *down- home folks* comfortable to be around."

"It's like you could drop by their house for dinner," another wrote.

We were trying to adjust to my husband being President, my being First Lady - the terror of it in an imploding nation - and in May, a terrible blow fell on each of us. On the 24, our dearest friend, a *son* to us, Colonel Elmer Ephraim Ellsworth, was killed when he was taking down a Confederate flag in Alexandria. We went to the Navy yard for his body, and we both wept over that young, still, beautiful form. His services were in the East Room, and at the military service for him, I could not control my grief. When I was offered the Confederate flag stained with his blood, I recoiled in horror. I put it away, and never wanted to see it again. He had just visited us. He had even caught the measles from Taddie and Willie. He had been so manly and so proud in his bright Zouave uniform, so light hearted and buoyant in getting to fight for *the Union.* The next week at the mention of his name, my husband burst into tears, and he said, "Excuse me, but I cannot talk," and left the room.

In June the White House was again draped in mourning. Stephen Arnold Douglas had died suddenly in Chicago. I was shocked to learn that he died in poverty and friends gathered money for his family. I grieved for "Doug" as I had called him when he came to call on Lizzie's *mansion* on aristocratic hill, or to call on me, whichever it was. He had accepted my husband's election in good grace, even holding his hat for him while he gave the inaugural. When old friends pass on, they take a part of us with them, a kinder, sweeter past they had so vividly shared.

Then, in the fall of 1861, our dearest friend, Colonel Edward Baker, for whom Eddie had been named, visited. How I remember that day. It was one of those glorious autumn ones that denied any hint of a winter to come, that hummed yet with summer, the buzzing of bees, fat and lazy in late blooming flowers. There was that bright fall sheen in the air, saying the world was *right*. As we joyously visited, I remember that Willie was chasing and catching the falling autumn leaves, and when the Colonel left, he swung Willie high in his arms and gave him a good by kiss. "Willie," he said. "You go on with your politics and all of your speeches, and then, someday, you will be our President, just like your father is now."

Colonel Edward Baker was killed the next day at the Battle of Ball's Bluff. When my husband heard the news, he passed an orderly and did not return his salute, for both of his hands were pressed to his heart.

When he broke the dreadful news to me, we tried to comfort each other as he held me in his arms. We were never to be good at accepting the deaths of cherished ones. We both had grieved for our Eddy to the point of serious illness. Now we were overwhelmed by the deaths so close together of Ellsworth and Baker. "It will be like this all over the land," my husband said, and tears ran down his face. "All beautiful young boys marching off to their deaths - Oh, God, let this ghastly war end as soon as possible!"

The *unfinished* capitol dome - the *unfinished* monument to Washington, rising above trash - the *unfinished* Republic - "Will we be whole again?" I asked my husband.

"That is what this war is all about," he said.

And in the summer Washington stank and was black with flies. I *hated* heat. I *always* hated heat, and I thought I would suffocate to death, and when I could I got out of Washington's heat and seek, for a short while, the sea shore in New Jersey, I took the boys and went there. I feared what our boys would catch in the Washington swamp with no screens in the windows and mosquitoes as bad as the flies. My husband missed us and we missed him, and soon we decided to spend the summers in the Soldiers Home, higher, cooler and cleaner than Washington. It was an oasis of five hundred *glorious* acres of great oaks, chestnut beech, maple, cypress and cedar. It overlooked Washington and the Potomac. I loved the cooling shade, the calling among the trees of the catbirds, wrens, whistling fox sparrow, the starlings and thrushes - singing in the trees all the day long. This would be where we would go *every* summer. It was just three miles away from the White House so my husband could ride back and forth to work.

Now I was criticized for having too many receptions for the public. In between wondering if I were a Confederate spy, the newspapers said I was the best White House hostess since Dolly Madison. (Her first husband was a Todd) It was the *Boston Journal* that was to say on December 1, 1863, I was her equal "by nature and education, grace and goodness of heart." I am quoting from people who saw me in the White House, *met* me there, *talked* to me there -why should I? Why should I *not* when I am put down as frothing at the mouth in a so- called *tempestuous* (lie) marriage! As Emilie saw me there - written by her daughter in a story of my life - "She was sought by people of intellect who were charmed by her animation and originality of thought, her fearlessness in expressing herself. She was still strikingly youthful in appearance; she was 'fair and forty,' but not fat as she never weighed over one hundred and thirty pounds. Her hair, still a lovely chestnut with glints of bronze, had as yet not a gray thread. Her eyes sparkled youthfully with the zest of living, and the fashion of the day favored her mightily (for) her beautiful shoulders and arms ... loved by friends, deeply disliked by many outside of her circle ...more than merely pretty, she was both brilliant and fascinating...her critics never could criticize her, so they criticized her dress...She had exquisite taste for style and dress..." My husband loved to see me in what he called "fine feathers," and I did love to show off my pretty dresses to him. The wife of my husband's attorney general, Mrs. Edward Bates, wrote of me: "As the wife of a man under constant hostile criticism, she received scant courtesy in some quarters. She lived for her husband and children, banishing before a never flagging cheerfulness her husband's cares of office while at home." The man who painted my husband reading the Emancipation Proclamation was Francis Carpenter (To do a portrait of me in April of 1865) and here is what he wrote of me: "She was a very brilliant woman, an excellent linguist, speaking French as easily as her native tongue. There is no denying a quality and quantity of high spiritedness in her temperament." General Sickles wrote (*hello* Billy!) "It was my privilege to know President Lincoln and his consort through all the years they spent in the White House. I have never seen a more devoted couple. He always called her Mother and she always called him Father. In their domestic relations and in their devotion to their children I have never seen a more congeal couple. He'd always looked to her for comfort and consolation in his troubles and cares. Indeed, the only joy he had after reaching the White House were his wife and children. She shared all of his troubles and never recovered from the culminating blow after his assassination."

I appreciated that. With all of the venom, I appreciated *any* kind word about me. The *St. Louis Republican* sent a woman reporter to the White House to study me. Her name was Laura Catherine Redden Searing, and

I approached her in the Blue room, as it was my wont to see that I greeted each guest. I wore a lilac dress, and she thought it rather elaborate - "it was made very *decollete* as to the shoulders and bust, and arms, but she (me) had a certain dimpled chubbiness as to these which justified the style. That portion of her skin visible was of a becoming whiteness ... the charm of her face was not owing to cosmetics. It was a chubby, good- natured face. It was the face of a woman who enjoyed life, a good joke, good eating, fine clothes, and fine horses and carriages, and luxurious surroundings, but it was also the face of a woman whose affectionate nature was predominant ... you might safely take your oath that she would be fussy on occasion, but the clouds would not last long with her, and she would soon be laughing as heartily as ever." I think she summed me up remarkably well. She saw that I was the wife of the *first* Republican President, that "it would have been quite impossible, under any circumstances, for her to have satisfied opposing factions of the day," that I was not having great social success, and it was my fate "from the first to be pilloried by all the viler elements of society" - that it was my misfortune that I did not bear myself "sublimely in the pillory" insisting instead, on enjoying myself "in her own way she could."

That was in 1861, and I *was* enjoying myself, as best I could. My favorite thing she said of me was, "She is a most loyal wife and mother and a good woman." I did wear my dresses somewhat low in the neck, which was the fashion, (also becoming to me) and my husband told me, more than once, that some of the long trains of my gowns would do better up closer to the neck. I would say, "Father, you do not know *a fig* about the world of fashion."

I was *not* Billy's, or John Hay's *hell-cat any more than my husband regarded himself as a tycoon!* I was just a woman who loved her husband and her children, who did the best for them she could do, and who was human in having frailties. I was timid and weak in the face of a crisis. To be equal to the magnificence of my husband would be impossible, for how many people could do that? *But I did not have to be put down for him to reach the heights he did.*

The marine band played for the public in front of the White House on every Wednesday and Saturday evening. Their last song was always *Yankee Doodle*, and that was also the tune that ended our receptions in the White House.

Here, as the President's wife, I did make lasting friendships with the wife of the Secretary of Navy, Mrs. Gideon, Jane Wells, with Mrs. James, Sally Orne, a very, *very* wealthy woman, and a 'Randolph' of Virginia, Mrs. Albert White. They were dear to me in the high *political* point of my life, and Sally at its lowest. They were truly gentile women and had *not* become their social positions.

By the end of 1861 the White House was immaculate and refurbished, I had malaria, a terrible menopause, migraines that were a frequent torture, so that I thought some cancer was growing in my brain, and I grieved with my husband over the terrible war news. It was going to be a long war and I wondered if either of us would live through it.

But as 1861 closed we had much to be thankful for. We had our boys, Robert, home for Christmas from Harvard, so adult, mannerly and good looking, our gentle philosopher Willie, described as "very tall for his age, handsome, studious, intelligent," our rambunctious *troublesome* Taddie. At Christmas we shared the old familial magic of our home at Eighth and Jackson, those cherished days - toffee pulls, strawberry parties, lightening forking the sky and my husband hurrying home to me - and in all days my meeting him at the gate with so much to tell him- laughter between us - because he was *home.*

December, *our* special season of Willie's birthday and mine - Christmas at the White House - extra lights in all of the rooms - Yule logs in the grates, dear children singing carols of wonder and joy, while in the sky the *Christmas* star shone purely, and snow fell softly - the church bells ringing out in a holy reverence - all to make magic and luminous the celebration of the birth of the best in man.

Chapter Eighteen

Shortly after my husband's inauguration, Willie and Taddie met the children of Judge and Mrs. Horatio Taft. Their daughter, Julia, was sixteen, and she became as dear to me as a daughter of my own. I thought the world of those children, and they thought the world of me. Bud was a year older than Willie, and Holly was near Taddie's age. When they played together at the White House, Julia was to see the four boys behaved themselves. She had no trouble with Willie and Bud, and no success with Taddie and Holly.

Willie and Bud did *quiet* things, played on the White House roof, or read, or painted, but they did join Holly and Taddie when all four boys would jump on my husband to wrestle him to the floor. My husband would laugh merrily and allow this, but when all four could not keep him there, they called on Julia to help out by sitting on his stomach. She refused to do this, being a very proper Victorian lady.

It was so good and so rare to hear my husband's hearty laugh again.

He allowed Willie and Taddie to play under his desk while he poured over war maps, and one day they got into a fierce fight and my husband did not even hear the battle raging at his own feet. And after the boys quieted down by falling asleep, he carried them to their rooms, ducking under door sills and low chandeliers, and he tucked each one into bed, and always looked in at them again, no matter how late he came from his office to our room.

The four boys found a veteran of the French army who had served with Napoleon himself. What they loved about the man was whenever Napoleon's name was mentioned, he would stand, take off his hat and salute. The boys adored seeing him do this, and soon had bets to see who could get his hat off the most, and of course, Taddie won, for money was involved in the bet. Taddie still had his bag of money he had earned for misguiding people to his father on our train trip, and with the money, he was also collecting marbles. He never entered a marble game that he did not end up with *all* of its marbles. "Women will dote on Taddie," my husband repeated proudly. "I think he will be as rich as the Todds before he is eighteen."

Then one *terrible* day, Taddie and Holly vanished from the White House! I went into hysteria. John Hay did not like my boys any more than Billy Herndon did, and told everyone he could tell that h*e lived* for the day when their father would spank them good, and realize at last, how *much they deserved it.* Now, if Taddie did show up, the odds were certain he would, *at last,* get the back of a hair brush! How glorious. How wonderful it would be to see - Taddie getting discipline! I think John Hay's smile but increased as he heard Taddie and Holly were still in the vanished state. Dear *Lord on High, at last, do let Taddie get a whipping,* he no doubt prayed. *A good one, too,* I am sure he added.

After our supper, and after the sun had set, a gentleman brought Taddie and Holly to the front doors. "Do these boys *really* live here?" he asked, looking rather dumbfounded. I had rushed to the front doors, and there were Taddie and Holly looking as if they had dug their way out of an underground tunnel. Which, as it turned out, they had.

"Do these rag muffins live *here?*" the man asked again. "Here - in the *White House?*" He did not look as if this idea was very acceptable.

"They certainly do live here!" I said.

"Well, I went and bought them their supper," the good man muttered as he left, shaking his head. When they had met the nice man on the street and had told him they had just dug their way out of the White House basement, he really had doubted their story. It seems that Taddie had decided that China was under the White House, and if he and Holly dug far enough, they would find it. They went to the sub basement and dug away like two moles, and in the rot and rats they got lost and pounded and shouted until some workmen let them outside where they were found by the nice man who fed them and brought them home.

That night Taddie was too tired to set off the White House bell alarm system that he had grown so fond of doing. He loved the excitement of all those little bells ringing in all of the offices at once and, most of all, watching John Hay streak out of his own in terror. "Here comes Jeb!" he would shout as Hay flew by. I rather liked to see that myself.

Cousin Lizzie Grimsley said Taddie and I were so much alike. She wrote we both were "mischievous, gay, gladsome, bubbling over with merry spontaneous laughter and innocent fun," and that "our laughter rang through the house." She said we both were "affectionate, impulsive, restless, mentally quick" and had "*sunny* dispositions."

Well, if Taddie was like me, Willie certainly resembled his father. He had the inner poetry to his soul his father had, and he was always striving to express his ideas as clearly. While Taddie and I had what I called *great bursts of affection,* Willie was more quiet in his sweet nature, more on an even keel with his emotions, and most endearing to me was the way he still imitated his father while making his father's speeches, with the *exact* same gestures and the *exact* same emphasis on words.

One day, in the spring of 1861, when I was buying things for the White House in New York City, my husband could not sign bills as he could not find his spectacles. He sent John Hay scurrying everywhere to find them, and when John Hay found where they were, he came back to my husband *glowing* absolute triumph. "Tad has your spectacles," he said.

"Tad has my spectacles? Why on earth would Tad have my spectacles?" asked my husband.

"He is *trying to wear them.*"

"Why is he doing that?"

"He is going to play you in a circus on the roof of the White House."

"A play?" asked my husband.

"Something about you coming out of the wilderness."

My husband laughed in delight. "What is the admittance?"

What is the matter with you? I am sure John Hay said to himself, but to my husband he said, "Five cents, for colored and white alike."

"Does he have a good audience?"

"The soldiers that are supposed to be guarding us, and the cooks that are supposed to be cooking for us, and lots of people, I don't even know *where* from the streets *they* came from. But there is *worse.*"

"Worse? How could there be worse?" my husband beamed.

"Willie is playing your wife and he is wearing your wife's favorite lilac satin ball gown. And Bud is playing one of her friends and has on one of your wife's finest white silk gowns a*nd* her bonnet to match. And Julie is rouging Willie and Bud up, and can't get the bonnet to set right on Bud."

"Really?"

"Really!" said John Hay, hoping Willie and Taddie had gone totally into a parental brush to the backside land. "Sir, what do you think of all this?"

"Why, the dear little codgers!" my husband said.

"You know how *filthy* the White House roof is - how many years and *years* the birds have been hitting it, and all of the mud and leaves up there."

"The dear little codgers!" my husband smiled.

"What are you going to do? Surely, Sir, you will do *something!*" The John Hay world was going awry.

"Of course, I will. *We will!*" my husband said, getting up from his chair on which he had been sitting, as usual, on his shoulder blades.

"What?" I am sure Mr. Hay was licking his chops.

"We will go right up to the White House roof!"

"*Good!*" said John Hay, wanting to see, in person, the Taddie and the Willie spanking and know again there was a God in Heaven who had not deserted the world he had created. "Why are we going up to the White House roof?" he asked as they did so.

"Do you have ten cents?' my husband asked him.

"Yes - why?"

"So you can see me come out of the wilderness, of course," said my husband. "I expect that is the name of their play. They like to write plays with me coming out of the wilderness."

They paid their ten cents and were handed a program printed by Willie. The show opened with the cast singing *Hail Columbia,* while Taddie and Bill Sanders sang the *Star Spangled Banner*, and Bud and Joe Corkhead sang a duet of *Dixie Land.* The play began and our darling Taddie sang a song about my husband coming our of the wilderness while he wore his spectacles, and while Holly served lemonade, fresh from the White House kitchen, for another five cents per glass. The stage curtains were two sheets and Taddie had Julie blacken him all up for Part 111 when he played a black Statue of Liberty.

The play ended with another duet by Taddie and Willie of *Home* Sweet *Home.* I heard every detail from my proud husband. It must have been a perfectly delightful afternoon, especially, as John Hay was so miserable in it.

Taddie then decided the White House roof had to be fortified against Jeb Stuart and could no longer be a neighborhood theater. Thus, he had to accumulate money without the cash coming in from roof plays. He set up a barrier on the stairs that led to my husband's office, and no one, no office seeker or senator, or *anyone,* not even the British ambassador, could get by without paying a toll of five cents for the Sanitary Fund to help our soldiers. My husband *always* had reams and reams of visitors, endless, *endless* visitors, and Taddie soon had *endless* five-cent coins. He not only was getting our soldiers rich, but he was causing our halls to overflow worse than usual. There were many complaints, from the cleaning staff among others who just could not clean the halls around so many people accumulated in them. "Taddie," my husband said gently. "You had better move your money machine away from the stairs."

"Why Pa?"

"Son, you are blocking traffic, and there may be one of these people who *needs* to see me."

"Pa - where will my money machine go?"

"Son, you will know. You have a natural instinct about that."

And he did. He set up a table where he sold fruit and candy in a less busy

White House corridor - very, very successfully. He got enough money to buy out the stand of a woman who sold gingerbread near the Treasury, and he set that stand up near the portico where he had the same steady customers of ever arriving office seekers. Outside of the building was better, anyway, for he had more room for more customers. To his gingerbread inventory he added cakes, cookies and whatever else he could get from the White House kitchen before we did. Street urchins soon heard about Taddie, and they came for the food leftovers he always gave them. Once he ran out of inventory for them and took several urchins into the White House kitchen for their supper. And it was no big surprise to my husband and me when he brought several along to have a formal dinner with us, as he did for Christmas dinner of 1861. He never kept any of his fortune for himself, and what did not go to the Sanitary Fund went to hospitals, and buying gifts for the soldiers who were guarding the White House. He knew each soldier by name and he and Willie still delighted in taking wagon- loads of White House gift booze to the camp across the way named for me. Its soldiers adored them and their loaded booze wagons, continued cheering them on sight and would probably have fired off cannon in their honor, too, but war supplies had to be husbanded.

As the war progressed, Taddie became very much into the military. To protect the White House, the four boys had completed a grand fort on its roof. Sometimes, the roof was a Union Man of War, and they had a spy- glass in either case, if attack should come by land or by sea. Washington always needed another soldier company and they raised one, but Willie wrote to a friend in Springfield, it was yet "in a *light* state of efficiency and discipline." The four army officers were all Zouaves, and they got their uniforms for themselves, Willie being the colonel, Bud, the major, Holly the captain and Taddie the drum major, for then he could lead the parade. But, unhappily, the rest of their army was not as devoted to the cause. They ate their rations and went home, leaving the soldier company with only its four officers - even when my husband and I reviewed it, and more than once. My husband had even solemnly presented it with a flag.

When my husband reviewed real troops, our four officers, without their own, begged to be in the review. The generals and officers of the real army did not think this a good thing. But anything our sons wanted to do was a good thing, so in one grand review, even when our boys had bad colds, in the middle of the parade of famous soldier dignitaries came a rickety old cart drawn by a mule, driven by a Negro friend of Bud and Holly, "Champ," they called him, and in the wagon our four Zouave officers stood stiffly at attention, their battered swords in formal salute.

Taddie gave to *every* male he met a union badge to pin on his jacket. "I will see that this keeps you safe in Washington," he promised.

One night at dinner, he decided to see if he could eat his peas with his knife.

"Son," my husband said. "Eating peas with a knife is not good manners."

"Well, Pa," replied Taddie, "neither is it good manners for you to stare at someone while he is eating. And I want to join the army."

"You have your own," said my husband, "and you are its drum major."

"You know our men eat and run, and so we have no army," said Taddie impatiently. "I am going to get Stanton to enlist me all up."

My husband forgot all about this, but Taddie did not. He then went to Secretary of War Stanton and told him he was ready to enlist. Stanton said *no*. Taddie went to his father, and his father told Stanton *yes*. So Taddie became a colonel in the real army. Then he decided he could not serve in the real army without a real army uniform, and he told this to Stanton, and Stanton said *no*. Taddie gave his coded secret military knock to get into his father's office, an important ritual for both of them, and told his father that Stanton kept saying this *no* thing. He got the uniform, and posed for a photo in it, looking very very soldier like. Before too long, Taddie wanted a cannon to defend the White House from his roof fort, or Man of War, and, of course, Stanton said *no*, and his father said *yes*, and when he got his little toy cannon, Taddie and Holly were so mad at Stanton, for being so negative, that at the next cabinet meeting they fired it off in his general direction. It took all of the skill of their commander in chief to calm the cabinet. If Taddie had thought to set off the White House alarm bells and fire his little cannon at the same time, John Hay might have run on right out of Washington. That would have been nice.

One night, when it was raining so hard Holly and Bud could not go home, the boys wanted to attend a state dinner with us. I saw that they all had on clean white blouses and let them sit near the foot of the table. What they wanted to see, and did see, was the ambassadors all tied up in *gold cords*, as they said, in contrast to my husband's always plain black suit.

"Pa," Taddie said. "Why don't you shine up in gold cords like all of these princes?"

"Oh," my husband said. "They would not become me."

"Well, Ma is all dressed up shiny."

My husband gave me an affectionate and admiring look that always melted my heart. "You mother looks very pretty all shiny."

"Ma was all dressed up, you bet," Willie wrote to friends in Springfield.

Taddie might even have wired this as a part of the important war messages he always sent to let Springfield know that Washington was still in the Union. But I think Taddie liked to visit the war office, anyway, to see Stanton turn a rather bright red.

Taddie, Willie, Bud and Holly began to place Union flags on the local houses and dig rifle pits around them in case of an invasion. "We will come back to protect you when needed," Taddie promised, and received a lot of thanks, and even cookies, for his thoughtfulness.

Because Taddie had given so much money to the Sanitary Commission, he received in gratitude a Zouave doll, which the boys named Jack. They loved Jack, but he kept doing these bad things, like falling asleep on sentry duty. For this Tad always sentenced him to die at sunrise, and Willie would always beg for mercy. "Jack is just a farm boy," he would say, "and you know Pa stops Stanton from shooting farm boys who fall asleep on picket duty, because that is the time they usually go to sleep on the farm."

"*The Union* is at stake," would reply Taddie, sternly.

"Pa always says shooting a man does him no good," would reply tender -hearted Willie.

"It is for the *Union*," would repeat Taddie, and then he shot Jack whether it was sunrise or not. But Taddie always saw that Jack had a fine military funeral. There was a drawback to this. Jack's burial site was always where Major Watt, the White House gardener, kept his prize roses. This did not make Major Watt happy, and I must say, the "dead marches" for Jack that went by my window, did not make *me* happy either, for when you combine a migraine with music from four boys using a broken fiddle, a dented horn, paper screeching over a comb and Taddie's drum - it was *awful*. And Taddie *kept* shooting Jack, digging him up and shooting him again, *twelve times*. Major Watt stopped what was going to be the thirteenth execution. I think his patience was thinning out with his roses. "Why don't you get poor Jack a pardon?" he asked the broken hearted Willie who wept before each execution. "The President can pardon him, and then Taddie cannot keep on shooting him."

"Pa is going to pardon Jack like all of the farm boys!" shouted Willie, sure that, at last, he could save Jack's life. The four boys ran for my husband's office, and John Hay said *no,* you will *not* bother the President, and my boys made so much fuss at anyone saying *no* to them, my husband heard it from his office and came out to see why the boys were all yelling and jumping on John Hay. "Pa!" cried Willie, cocking his head in earnestness like his father. "You must stop Taddie from shooting Jack again. He has already been shot twelve times!"

"Well, he fell asleep on picket duty twelve times!" retorted Taddie.

My husband nodded gravely and took the boys off of John Hay and into his office. Julia followed, never having leaped on John Hay with the rest. Nor would she participate in the executions.

"Jack has to be pardoned!" wept Willie.

"Well, I cannot grant a pardon without a hearing," my husband said.

"So many burials are ruining Jack's uniform," said Bud.

"And certainly the rose garden," added Julia.

"The Union must be saved!" argued Taddie.

"Well," said my husband. " Jack has been shot enough. No man can be held twice in jeopardy, much less *thirteen* times, for the same offense." He then, on official White House stationery, wrote,

> The doll Jack is pardoned,
> By order of the President.

Unhappily, Jack could not keep awake, or, in less than a week, had turned into a Confederate spy, and Taddie ordered him hanged. Willie got him a change in venue, so Taddie hanged him from a tree in the Taft garden.

By now there was little of Jack to hang or shoot, and so he had his *last* military funeral with my husband and I in solemn attendance, but *not* in the rose garden. When a bugler played taps for Jack, even Taddie cried, for in all of Jack's executions, Taddie had become quite fond of him.

Taddie now went around singing for all who came to the White House,

> Pa, Pa, a rail-splitter was he,
> And that's how he's going to split
> The Confederacy!

Both Taddie and Willie had nice singing voices.

Willie, eleven, read more and more books, curling up in a chair by my sitting room fire, and I would see him gaze from the book into the flames, and I wondered if he saw in them changing kingdoms, magic fire castles I used to imagine. He was such a comforting calming presence, my Willie, so mature for his years, so bright, so *serious* about the world's problems.

Julia remembered Willie as "the most loveable boy I ever knew." Cousin Lizzie Grimsley said Willie "was a perfect counterpart of his father." He was. Sweet tempered, gentle, deeply, deeply spiritual, and he had his father's magnetism, for people who met him said they liked him at once. All said he had his father's warm and friendly personality, with his father's fearless honesty. Even Secretary of State Seward was fond of him, and when he rode by one day with the Prince of France, he gravely took off his hat as he passed Willie on his pony. The prince, seeing Seward take off his hat to Willie, did the same, and Willie stopped his pony and gravely took off his own hat to each of them.

He was writing more political speeches, keeping a memorandum of important historical events and included within it his father's inaugural address. He was writing of the important battles, the death dates of important men, and how their deaths affected the country. I still called Taddie my little *troublesome sunshine,* and still believed Willie would be the comfort of our old age. There was a *special* bond between us, and I guess that was because he did so favor his father.

Willie wrote a lovely poem to the memory of our dear friend, Colonel Edward Baker, and it was published in the *Washington National Republican.* "Dear Sirs," Willie had written, "I enclose my first attempt at poetry." Here it is:

> There was no patriot like Baker,
>> So noble and true,
> He fell as a soldier on the field,
>> His face to the sky of blue.

> His voice is silent in the hall
>> Which oft his presence graced.
> No more he'll hear the loud acclaim
>> Which rang from place to place.

> No squeamish notions filled his breast,
>> *The Union* was his theme;
> "No surrender and no compromise,"
>> His day-thought and night's dream.

> His country has her part to play
>> To'rds those he left behind;
> His widow and his children all,
>> She must always keep in mind.

How that theme was to be echoed in my husband's second inaugural address!

In his stay in the White House, Taddie took to studying the long lines of people who waited to see my husband, and if he found in them a wounded soldier, or a woman weeping that her son was going to be shot at sunrise, Taddie rushed them right by the ushers, and John Hay, right to his father and a pardon or help. "Why don't you let *any* of these boys be shot?" had raged Stanton, thinking of military discipline. When a sentry fell asleep, he should be shot, he insisted. Even *fourteen old* Daniel Winger. My husband sent Stanton a note. "Hadn't we better spank this drummer boy and send him home to Leavenworth?" Lee's two sons were captured and were going to be shot. My husband heard from Lee through Jefferson Davis and wired the commander of Fortress Monroe: "Immediately release the sons of Robert E. Lee and send them back to their father."

The generals were seeing their rule going down the drain if they could not keep discipline among their troops. "Why do you insist on pardoning *every* soldier about to be shot? Why?" mourned Stanton. "Oh - I know - shooting a man does him no good! Or - farm boys have this sleep pattern thing! Why can't you just say - NO?"

My husband discussed this problem of his with General Egbert Viele. "If I have one vice, and I can call it nothing else, it *is* not to be able to say 'No.' Thank God for not making me a woman, but if He had, I suppose He would have made me just as ugly as He did, and no one would ever have tempted me."

And he went on pardoning so the executions had to be speeded up before he heard of them. Or their mothers, who rushed post haste to my husband to save their sons' lives.

Taddie had taken on the care of the Sanitary Commission, the soldiers guarding the White House, the camp of soldiers near the White House, the soldiers or distraught mothers in line to see my husband, and the soldiers I visited every day at nearby hospitals, and he had to keep the rifle trenches deep around local houses, their Union flags flying, and the White House roof on constant alert. "I never have a spare minute," he complained, and saw that he did not.

Willie enjoyed going to church, still thinking he wanted to either be a minister or President like his father. Taddie went along to see what happened when, on closing, the minister always asked the congregation to pray for my husband. That is when all of the "Seceshes", as Taddie called them, rose in one furious unit, and with pew doors slamming, stalked from the church. Until that excitement, Taddie passed the time away by playing with the money stashed in his pocket, or with any money that happened to be in a near by soldier pocket. One time he brought along a pocket -knife to play with, quickly cut himself with it, and Julia had to stop the bleeding with her *best-embroidered* handkerchief. Furious, she hissed, "I will never take you to church again!" and Taddie said, "Well, just watch Willie then, who is always as good as pie."

Taddie had been given carpenter tools for Christmas of 1861, and he made himself sleds, snow skies for the stairs, (he and Willie tried unsuccessfully to ski down them) and tried to carve an elaborate war map on the side of a table. Wanting to sit in a favorite chair more comfortably, he reduced it by sawing the legs down. Locks on the doors inconveniently changed places; he went to work to remodel a White House wagon, without very good results, promised to transform the White House furniture to send to the hospitals, and had begun work on the state chairs in the East Room when without hearing any scolding or fussing from us, his carpenter tools just quietly disappeared.

This also happened to his beloved pet, Nanny Goat, who pulled him around the first floor of the White house while he rode on his sled. The problem was that when Nanny Goat was inside, she left behind a trail that made the floor cleaners unhappy, or anyone who stepped on it first, unhappy, and when she went outside she made the gardeners unhappy because she ate up all their flowers. When I took Taddie for a beach visit, my husband wrote that the last time Nanny Goat was seen she was standing on Taddie's bed, contentedly chewing her cud, and he just had not been able to find her since. The news of her vanishing got out and Taddie was sent a whole herd of Nanny goats and pastured them on the White House lawn. These, he wisely decided to keep out of the White House and the flower garden.

The children could not wait to hear long ago pioneer stories from my husband. He had so little time to spend with us, and spent it when he was bone tired and had to have a change from the endless applicants and the constantly dreadful things that happened to the Grand Army of the Potomac. "I have an ache I cannot touch," he said to me, when he came back from the War Office where the wires clattered out battle after battle lost for us, blood flow endless. Then, he would gather the children to him, as if from their youth and vibrancy he drew strength and even joy, and with Willie on one knee, Bud on the other, Taddie leaning over the back of his chair, Holly on an arm, he would begin his story, and we would hear of the old Kentucky frontier, honey trees, wild bears, coon hunts by moonlight and the miracle of seeing a cake baked out of *white* flour. Our dog, Jip, would be at his feet. Jip always sat on my husband's lap at lunch- time, and got the most of his lunch. Then Julia would come into the room, her proper Victorian curls *just* so, and my husband would reach out and muss them all up, and send her flying away to get them in order again. She wrote later that it pleased him far more than it pleased her.

"We must have a school for the children," I said to my husband. "Taddie cannot read or write."

"Well, if they *want* it," he replied cautiously.

I had a school set up in the end of the State Dining Room, with a large blackboard and desks. Willie and Bud took to it like fish to water, Holly somewhat, and Taddie, not at all. He had a lively quick mind and endless interests, but not in grammar, which he found to be *totally* incompatible with his life. His interests, aside from defending Washington and the White House, aid for the Sanitary Commission, for every solder he met, and helping women in distress waiting to see my husband about it, were - (1) how to make money and what to buy with it - (2) how machines worked and (3) how the wild animals of the country lived. But school wasn't about these things as far as he could tell. He played so many pranks in the classroom its tutors left to teach somewhere else, *anywhere* else, if, indeed, they resumed teaching at all. I told my husband about all the vanishing teachers, wondering if Taddie ever would become literate. "What are we to do?" I asked.

My husband sighed, "Let the little codger run free; there is time enough for him to learn his letters and get poky."

One afternoon, Taddie thought the soldiers guarding the White House looked tired. "Are you poor, poor soldiers tired?" he asked them.

"Very tired," they replied.

"Well as your officer, I hereby give you a furlough so you can get to bed early tonight," he said and gave each of the guards a signed furlough.

When Robert, home from Harvard, left his carriage in front of the White House, he saw with horror it was unguarded. He rushed right to his father, having a strong suspicion that Taddie was to blame, but his father was so unconcerned they had quite a little row. "Anyone could come in here and shoot you!" Robert said.

Taddie must have thought about this on his own, for he sent the cooks from the kitchen to guard the White House. Of course, he drilled them first, as any good colonel would do. It was only after Taddie was in bed that the cooks returned to the kitchen and guards returned to guard the White House. Our supper was rather late. I don't recall we had any.

I *do* recall one night when we were to have strawberry short-cake, Taddie had taken all of the strawberries to the soldiers' camp. I think we were entertaining that night, too. I hope it *was* not, Lord Lyons, *the British ambassador.*

Chapter Nineteen

Robert was doing well at Harvard, and when he was to graduate he would be thirty-second in a class of one hundred. He was a friend of the daughter of my dear friend, Mercy Levering Conkling though they were going to different schools in the East. I had visited Robert at Harvard in November of 1861, and knew that his studies included Greek, Latin, Math, Chemistry, Religious Instruction, Elocution, Rhetoric, Themes and Composition, History and Botony. His dressing was immaculate and he still seemed popular with his fellow classmates. He would not have the height of his father, being five foot ten, as a proper man was then considered to be. He was growing to be very good looking, and I was proud of the way he was turning out. But, like my own father, he was *distant* - still more aloof from my husband and me - from Willie and Taddie.

One thing hurt me. He never kept a letter I wrote to him. I think he destroyed all of them as soon as he read them. "I am just *private*," he said to me when I mentioned it. It was strange. My husband was a shy man and became gregarious before an audience, and Robert was not shy on a two to two basis, but had a horror of speaking to an audience. Robert was not like his father in humor and personality. He was always a proper and reserved young man. And he was not like me either, for he was far more of a Todd than I. There was that bit of a snob in him, a greater Todd respect for money and *cultural elitism* than his father and I had. I never really understood Robert - ever, once he was no longer Bobby - ever since he had been sent to live with the Todds when Eddy was dying. Some cloning went on there, and I mentioned it many times to my husband and he agreed with me. Robert was of *our* family through birth, but not through integration, I decided. I did not love him less, but we never, my husband and I, got the *unqualified, unjudging* love from our first son that we did from our other boys.

At the White House Willie and Taddie had their beloved pets, our dog, Jip, of course, the goat-herd which ever remained outside and away from the flowers, their rabbits and their precious ponies. The boys rode from earliest childhood, their little feet straight out from the horse's sides, and they were both good riders. In early February of 1862, Willie had been given a new pony, and he adored his new friend and rode him every day, even when I protested the weather was too cold for him to be outside at all. "Ma," he said. " I just love my new pony, and we'll just gallop *away* from the cold."

We had sent invitations out for a ball on February the fifth, and it was for my husband a very important reception. We paid for the cost of the ball ourselves. I was planning to wear a white satin gown with black lace, and Mrs. Keckly and I were planning a lace shawl to go with it, or whether I should wear a lace shawl or not, and the proper jewelry- and then in some ghastly way, it made no difference at all.

Willie became ill. The doctors said he had a cold and was recovering and we should go ahead with the reception. The doctors said it was nothing to worry about, that he would soon be fine and back to riding his pony again.

With terror in my heart, I remembered how the doctors had told us how *well* Eddy was doing when he was *dying.*

On the night of the ball, Willie took a turn for the worse. He was burning up with fever. I was shaking so badly that Mrs. Keckley could hardly get me into my dress, and downstairs the marine band had already started to play, and the jewels went on, and into white slippers I put my feet, and my husband came in and said the doctors had decided that Willie had no more than bilious fever. We had moved him away from the room he shared with Taddie and had put him into our beautiful guest room with the purple drapes and gold cord, and Bud came to be with him. Taddie had become ill himself, and I had just been up all night two nights straight tending to my beloved boys. "I miss Taddie," Willie said.

"I miss Willie," Taddie said.

I stroked their hot little foreheads, and kissed their flushed faces. "You will be back together in your bedroom as soon as you are well," I said.

My husband looked gravely down on both boys, touched their faces and smoothed down their rumpled hair. "Mother and I must go downstairs now," he said.

We must. We must. And if our boys are dying, to go on functioning, we must, we must.

Downstairs hoop skirts gleamed in satin, and women glittered in jewels, and the decor was the Union. Fort Sumter was made of sugar, and a steamer, the *Union,* was made of sugar and bore the stars and stripes, and everything seemed to be made of sugar, and the night was *so bitter.* We were receiving over five hundred people in the East Room, and in the corridor the marine band played gay tunes. I remember that, *gay* tunes, for the cabinet members, the justices of the Supreme Court, Senators, Robert home from Harvard, and he took my place in the receiving line when I left to go upstairs to my boys.

They were breathing so hard and fever was burning them up.

Willie had blue eyes and light brown hair, and he looked at me hopefully with those beautiful eyes, as if I could make him well. I caressed his face, and held his hands. "Ma," he said, when he saw my anxiety. "Don't worry. Tomorrow morning I will be fine."

"Of course you will," I said.

"How is Taddie?" he asked.

"He is fine, as you are," I said, and I willed my voice to be steady, and my eyes tearless.

Taddie was tossing in misery, and his hair and eyes looked even darker against his flushed face. "How is Willie?" he asked.

"He is fine, as you are," I said, and I kissed his hot little face, as I had kissed Willie's. "You two must get your army for the defense of Washington started up again."

Taddie brightened. "Tell Willie, he can be drum major if he wants to be."

"I will tell him," I said.

Downstairs my husband was talking to a senator and tears were frankly in his eyes. "My boys are very ill," he said.

"You must pray," said the Senator.

"I do that all of the time," my husband replied.

About the ball we had wanted to cancel, about the ball that was an agony for us to attend, came another vicious attack on my husband *through* me, about the *Lady-President's Ball*. It was written by one Eleanor G. Donelly, and it told of a dying pain- wracked soldier looking through the White House windows at our ball. Here are three stanzas from the wretched thing:

> What matters that I, poor private,
> Lie here on my narrow bed,
> With the fever gripping my vitals,
> And dazing my hapless head!
> What matter the nurses are callous,
> And rations meager and small,
> So long as the *beau monde* revel,
> At the Lady-President's Ball.
>
> Who pities my poor old mother-
> Who comforts my sweet young wife-
> Alone in the distant city,

> With sorrow sapping her life.

> I have no money to send them,
> They cannot come at my call:
> No money? Yet hundreds are wasting,
> At my Lady-President's Ball!

> Hundreds, ay! hundreds of thousands
> In satins, jewels and wine,
> French dishes for dainty stomachs
> (While black broth sickens mine!)
> And jellies, and fruits, and cold ices
> And fountains that flash as they fall,
> O God! For a cup of cold water
> From the Lady - President's Ball!

The *Liberator* printed the ball was worthy of a woman whose sympathies *were with slavery*, and the *New York Herald* noted on March 18, 1862, "*The White House may have its Delilah.*"

On February 12, my husband's birthday, we received the best of news. The doctors said Willie was so much better that he would fully recover. Taddie was also better, and my husband and I wept in joy for such a wonderful birthday present.

But on the seventeenth, Willie took a turn for the worse, and the doctors said he was dying, that there was no hope for him at all. He asked for Bud to stay with him again, and he did, and late at night my husband would go to Willie, and gently stroke his hair, his hot forehead, and he would say to Bud, "You should go to bed."

"No," said Bud. "If he calls for me I want to be here."

Then later, when my husband came to Willie again, Bud would be asleep by his bed, and my husband would pick Bud up, and dodging the top door-sills and chandeliers, carry him gently to bed, and tuck him into it. "Willie?" Bud would murmur.

"Is asleep," my husband said. "Now you sleep, too."

Taddie heard that Willie had taken a turn for the worse. "Ma," he said to me, his eyes streaming. "Tell Willie I am sorry I killed Jack so many times. We can dig him all up and let him live to be very, very old. And remind him he still can be drum major when we start up our army again."

Then I never left Willie's side and became so worn out, that by Thursday, the twentieth, when Willie rallied, I left him for some sleep. That morning Willie was holding Bud's hand and said Taddie wanted to get their army back together for the defense of Washington. "I am going to be drum major," he said.

Dark settled over the city, and when that long night came, in its deepest, darkest shadow, it took away our beloved, beloved Willie.

Taddie became so ill again, the doctors said there was no hope *at all* that he would survive his brother.

The two had been inseparable, and we did not tell him Willie had died, but he knew it. "I will never see Willie again," he sobbed. "Willie has gone away and left me. He was never cruel to me before!"

It was so strange; here I was breathing, seeing, *living* and my Willie was gone. I was here, *but I wasn't.* After we had given Eddy back to God, I became pregnant right away, but now there would be no more children, no Willie, ever again, no serious, gentle Willie, to cock his head to one side, like his father, when he made an earnest point, no Willie, no Willie, *ever again*, and I never again went into the exquisitely decorated guest room where he died, and I could not look at a photo of him, and I could not go to his funeral in the East Room where we had held that damnable ball with the sea green carpet of two thousand five hundred dollar greenbacks - the *Lady President's* ball, which took me downstairs away from him for *hours* -

For just one more minute with him, one more second - if I could have held the sun to the sky – if I could have stopped the falling of that night!

No child is *ever* ours, and what a fool we are to believe it is so. Our children are as gifts from God to grace our lives, and when they return to God, and I am sure it is in the arms of the sweetest and dearest of angels, it is up to us to live in the light that their love left behind for us. Words are cheap and easy now, but then I was not strong enough to heed this truth. I wrote that I had had a *mild* nervous breakdown when Willie died, and that is what I believed it was.

It was not. It was a *major* breakdown, the increasing of irrational terrors; for a part of a heart to be wrenched away - sooth it over with a touch of madness. I was in an abyss of pain. No, *I was the abyss.* Gone from my mind was everything about the White House, *including* the recent visit by that odious little man who had worn out one wife with childbirth and was after another eighteen years younger than he. Billy had wanted my husband to serve as matchmaker! He wanted a government job for his future brother in law, and he borrowed twenty- five dollars from my husband. He even wanted a government job for himself, which, wisely, my husband never gave him. I was cool to him, and he wrote of me the usual - I was *wicked* and made my husband *desolate,* and had been doing that for years and years. Probably before either one of us was born.

Here we are at war. Twenty- three states of the North against eleven states of the South. Some twenty two million of the North against nine million of the South, with three and a half million slaves to feed the Southern armies. Here we are at war. Listen to the telegraph lines go *clickety, click,* spewing sounds out in blood. Our Union army has 13,000 officers and men; Robert Edward Lee is offered its command by my husband, but Lee, who believes neither in slavery nor secession, leaves with his state. Thomas Jonathan Jackson is to earn the name of Stonewall, for that is how he held his men to face ours on July 21, 1861, when our Irvin McDowell loses at the first battle of Bull Run. Our forces met picnickers on the way to see them win an easy victory, became entangled with them and terror and rushed pell mell back to Washington, even tossing aside their muskets. It was so *hot* that day. Then that strutting George McClellan heads the Grand Army of the Potomac, and I said to my husband, here is another man who can strut sitting down, and my husband said, no, he lets his horse do that for him. The war was not going to be a short one. With *Little Mac* (McClellan's nick name) in charge of the army, it does nothing, and the fighting shifts to the West. Why hadn't the rebels taken Washington after Bull Run? Why hadn't they taken it before we got an army to guard it? Listen to the war go on, *clickety, click, clickety click, 1862* - a man named Grant, who fights, takes Fort Henry on the Tennessee River, February 6 - Fort Donelson on the Cumberland, February 16. Willie was alive. He was to live for four more days.

I let my dearest husband down. I was not a pillar of strength to even share the agony of my grieving husband, and on his shoulders rested the nightmare of our Union torn asunder. On his shoulders rested the pain he felt every single day when he walked to the War Office and heard the keys going *clickety click, Hear me drink ; hear me drink up the nation's blood.*

I could share nothing now. I could give nothing, and I could receive nothing. I was nothing but my pain. With it - I admit - I was *self- possessed.* I withdrew from my beloved. I wanted no touch, no caress, no pleasure from love, for that was what had given us Willie and Eddy for God to take from us. Would exultation in physical love again - take Taddie away? Robert? My husband's bedroom was no longer *ours.*

And I began to hemorrhage badly from the female trouble never discussed. My migraines no longer came and went. They *stayed.*

It was my husband who looked down on Willie's still form and choked out the bitter words of so many bereaved parents - *but we loved him so.* When I saw my Willie dead, I went into violent convulsions. I was so ill I could no longer go to Taddie. I cringed into myself, and I waited to hear that Taddie was gone, his father gone, Robert gone. *My life finished.* Curling into agony, like a worm impaled on a knife, I thought, how do I bear the unbearable?

On May 29, 1862, I wrote about Willie to my dear friend, Julia Sprigg, who lived a block south of us in Springfield. It had taken me two weeks to reply to her letter of condolence, and I apologized, citing my sadness and ill health. I wrote, "We have met with so overwhelming an affliction in the death of our beloved Willie a being too precious for earth, that I am so completely unnerved, that I can scarcely command myself to write. . . . when the blow came, it found us so unprepared to meet it. Our home is very beautiful, the grounds are enchanting, the world still smiles & pays homage, yet the charm is dispelled - everything appears a mockery, the idolized one, is not with us, he has fulfilled his mission and we are left desolate. When I think over his short and happy childhood, how much comfort, he always was to me ... when I can bring myself to realize that he has indeed passed away, my question to myself is, 'can life be endured?' "

If sleep came, and some sleep must come to the most tortured of beings, I awakened to the violent reaction of my body to our loss. My religious faith had always been very strong. But now even its sweet solace was gone, as if the beautiful angel who had carried away my Willie, and my Eddy, had taken that from me, too.

My body reacted to my grief.

No, I was not having a *mild* nervous breakdown. I was entering into mental illness, *unreason* that would come and go, without my will or knowledge. My grief shattered me – it shattered my mind and it shattered my body, and I could not seem to do anything about it. It was as if I had been struck by lightning, and was I to say to the skies - will you take that lightning back?

My husband feared I would never recover. I denied the present and enshrined the past - listening again for the earnest speeches of my Willie, picturing him reading or drawing or writing poetry in my sitting room, sharing with such joy again, his dear presence. Of course, I would have to see that he was *not* with me, not in the forsaken and lonely room at all. It was so *hard.* And so I said to the empty room, with its great clock ticking away in its own time, "Whether preacher or politician - Willie, you would have been *the best!*"

I let my beloved husband down.

And it would get worse.

Willie's funeral was on Monday, February 24, and that day a violent windstorm hit Washington and felled carriages, house roofs and church steeples, and blew down the mightiest of trees.

It was nothing to our grief.

When Bud saw Willie in his casket he had to be carried from the room, and was ill for days. Our friends Senator Browning and his wife came and stayed by the body with my husband, and from the day of Willie's death, on Thursday, to his funeral on Monday, I remember nothing but the convulsions and the anguished weeping because all my tears, and all the tears of every mother on this earth, can never bring back to her a lost child.

"This is the most bitter pill I have ever known," I sobbed to Mrs. Keckley. She tried to comfort. My husband, so wracked with the burdens of the war and his own suffering, tried to comfort, and I wanted to go to Taddie, and could not. I wanted to go downstairs to Willie's funeral, and could not. "Molly," my husband said to me, "you must try to accept. He was too good for this earth. He has gone with the angels."

"But away from us!"

"To a better place," my husband said. "To a better place," he repeated. "God knows - to a better place."

"Father, I cannot bear it," I said.

So I didn't.

My husband, accompanied by Robert, Lyman Trumbull and Senator Browning, took Willie's body to be buried in a vault near Georgetown until we could return him to Springfield when we went home. They rode in a carriage drawn by two black horses, following the hearse drawn by two white horses.

"I have to get help for my wife," my husband told Dorothea Dix when she called at the black creped White House. She was superintendent of the women nurses in Washington.

"There is a nurse, Mrs. Rebecca Pomroy, who has given to death those dearest to her and has found solace in God. She can help your wife."

Mrs. Pomroy did not want to leave the sick soldiers, and for the first time, my husband used his authority in a non- political way, and as commander in chief, and as she was a military nurse, he gave her ten minutes to get ready to go to the White House.

She cared for Taddie. He was burning up with fever and suffering because Willie was gone. "He never was mean to me before," he kept repeating. "Didn't Willie love me?"

My husband stroked his hair, touched the tears fresh upon his face. "Of course Willie loved you. There is a time and a tide that takes us from our bodies, and we must heed it; the same tide that gives us a physical life must carry us beyond it. Willie had a short life, son, but it was a happy one. We must give thanks for that."

"I can't!" wept Taddie.

"Try," said my husband. "Try, son, try."

My husband, with tears streaming down his face, continued to go from Taddie to me, and he said to Mrs. Pomroy, "*Thy will be done!* Did you *always* accept those words?"

"Yes," she replied. "I know that in the hands of God, everything is *perfect.*"

"This is the hardest trial of my life," my husband moaned. "Why? Oh, why is it? Why do the *young* have to go on so far ahead of us? The most precious part of what we are? Why do they die, and we live on - with the palsied old - the suffering, the cruelly maimed, the hopelessly mad -"

"*Thy will be done.* It is in God's hands," she said, and her face was as peaceful and as tranquil as if she were already in Paradise with Him.

My husband read more and more passages from the Bible. He could quote the good book endlessly, and now gained a deeper solace from it. With Willie's death, something opened within his soul - a new light - a new strength, and I thought he already had all of the strength a man could ever have. "I have finally gone to God with my sorrows," he told Mrs. Pomroy and me.

But *my* faith was gone, my traditional church-going faith - gone - and I could *not* honestly say to God, *Thy will be done.*

Robert was horrified at my grief, as I was not handling it in a *proper* way. "She is making grief into a fine art," he said. He wrote my older sister, Lizzie Edwards, to come and stay with me, to help me bear what I couldn't. Or at least to keep my pain *properly packaged.* She left to come to the White House the day of Willie's funeral, and she stayed during March and April. I saw that she occupied the finest guest room, which I never would enter again, and she wrote letters home to her daughter, Julia Edwards Baker, and she said in them what was already clear to me. Let us say, her sympathy was *reserved.* She wrote caustic comments as to my *unexampled frivolity* and *excessive indulgence* as shown, I guess, by the purple velvet drapes with their gold sashes in her room. Or by the many gifts I gave her. I guess she saw that as showing off, or of more *frivolity,* when all of my life I pleasured in giving gifts. She did not want to be away from Springfield, and her children, and her grandchild, Lewis. The White House gloom was ghastly to her. My grief and Taddie's were depressing. She wrote, that *as usual,* I was *totally* unable to control my feelings.

I had the idea that this caustic comment was due to my marrying the *wrong* man, even if he had become the President of the United States. I still think Lizzie was more Puritan than Pilgrim.

I *absolutely* could not get out of bed for ten days after Willie's death. Then Lizzie got me up and saw me put on a black dress, and she wrote her daughter that my loss would shadow my (frivolous) pleasures *for awhile,* but - "Such is her nature, that I cannot realize, that she will *forgo them all,* or even *long,* under existing circumstances."

So I would be back to creating Queen Victoria's court, with fine ball gowns and roses in my hair to match them, would I? When Lizzie went back home, Mrs. Pomroy stayed with us, and she brought comfort as Lizzie never could. Outside, venom was poured on us again for the extravagance of that damnable - paid for by us - *Lady-President's* ball. Imagine, saying I, the *Lady-President,* was running my husband's Presidency! *No one* ran my husband. Gentle, loving, kind and always caring he was to me, but *no one ran him,* and certainly not his Presidency. Had I even gotten him to drop that odious little Billy? To the ball, the papers said, we had invited the *wrong* people. We had defied Washington Tidewater high society. We had made merry while men were dying.

We had done everything but join the Confederacy, and the *Liberator* was sure I had.

How we were hated, despised. My husband was an ape, a gorilla, a baboon, the imbecile Kentucky mule. Senator Ben Wade called him poor white trash. William Lloyd Garrison said he was not honest and had the character of a wet rag. The *New York Herald* did not hate my husband as much as the radicals in his own party; it just said he was a joke incarnated; his election a ridiculous joke, that he was termed honest, a "satirical joke. The style in which he winks at frauds . . . is a costly joke." And, of course, they continued to strike at him through me, and this caused him untold pain. I was a spy for the Confederacy, a traitor to the Union - even as *early* as August, 1861, the *Chicago Daily Tribune* felt it had to come to my defense, writing, "HOLD ENOUGH!" If the First Lady were "a prizefighter, a foreign danseuse or a condemned convict on the way to execution, she could not be treated more indecently than she is by a portion of the New York press. . . . No lady in the White House has ever been so maltreated by the public press."

For *all of my life* the charges that I was a traitor to the Union were made. There is the story that Congress had formed a committee on the Conduct of the War *to investigate to see if I was a traitor*, and that my husband appeared alone before it. Here is how that was remembered: He gave his name and his position, and he "spoke slowly, through a depth of sorrow in the tone of voice. 'I appear of my own volition before this Committee of the Senate to say that I, of my own knowledge, know that it is untrue that any of my family hold treasonable communication with the enemy.' " Without another word, my husband left. So did the Congressional investigation of my loyalty to the Union.

Noah Brooks, who knew my husband and me intimately, could say again and again that my "amiable and dignified life" and my character were misrepresented, as was my husband's - that his presidency stilled his critics, and I had no such chance to vindicate who I was. And as a married couple, Brooks wrote that my husband and I "were a model for the married people of the republic of which they are the foremost pair." He, and all of our friends, saw the way "we looked at each other with love," *Billy Herndon not withstanding.*

My personal secretary, Mr. Stoddard saw me day after day, and did he see me as a witch? He recorded me as "a noble -hearted woman who was one of the best friends I ever had." Of me he wrote, "She was a woman much misrepresented and scandalously abused."

The Treasury Department was *always* a source of malicious slander against me. Dr. Henry, who had arranged for us to meet again, and shortly to marry, knew this, and came to my defense in a letter. He said he had known me from "childhood up, and I can truly say that I have never been acquainted with a kinder and more Estimable woman, and I regard it as an outrage upon all propriety and common decency, to continue men in office who use their position and influence continually to depreciate the President and his family." All this came from the *Republicans,* my husband's party. The Democrats just called me *Madame President,* and had me reeling around drunk and cavorting with Russian sailors who were in some New York port, and toasting with them to *"our cousin,* Alexander 11, Czar of Russia." I must not forget all the secret love affairs I was supposed to be having. That gossip *never* stopped.

There was a woman who worked with me in supplying the hospitals. Her name was Mrs. H. C. Ingersoll, and she *had* to pay me a visit at the White House. She did not want to even see me, but it was, after all, for the cause of the Union, so meet me she did. And was she surprised. Of our hour-long chat she wrote, "I came away from that interview feeling that *never* had I found a person more unlike the newspaper reports of her than she seemed to be."

"Don't you think the truth about you should be told to the newspapers?" she asked me. I thought how on earth could that be done, but here is how she recorded my reply, "I do not belong to the public; my character is wholly domestic, the public having nothing to do with it. I know it seems hard that I should be maligned, and I used to shed many bitter tears about it, but since I have known *real sorrow* - since little Willie died, - all these shafts have no power to wound me. If I could lay my head on my pillow at night, and feel that I had wronged no one, that is all I have wished since his death."

"I will write the truth," she said.

"Do not waste your time," I replied. "They who malign me have created a monster and let *them* live with it."

She wrote an article about me, anyway, as she saw I was, and asked my consent for its publication. I read her article. "I appreciate the heart and the time put into this," I said. "But I wish you would not try to publish it."

"Why not?" she asked.

"A defense of me will bring more slanders. I want what privacy I can get, and my husband and I have agreed to be silent when the press attacks us."

Tears were in her eyes, as well as mine. She, too, had lost a child, and we shared our pain. "Now, with the grief I feel, Mrs. Ingersoll, I don't care what the press says, Radical Republican, Democrat, Confederate - the press can never *never* hurt me again."

How wrong I was.

My husband and Mrs. Pomroy finally got me outside for the afternoon carriage ride I had previously insisted my husband take with me every day. "Father," I said. "Let the cavalry come along with us." I was in a panic *always* that some of the hate filled maniacs would kill him. And that vision he had had of himself - a live face and a dead face side by side - I had decided he was dreaming and dreams told gibberish only - but - still - "Father, let the cavalry come along."

"No," he said, as usual. "If they ride by us with sabers and spurs rattling, I can't hear myself think. Who would want to kill me?"

"All of those demented haters. They want to murder you and what you stand for."

"They can't murder what I stand for," he said with quiet certainty.

A slight breeze was moving through the sun- dappled trees, but the heat was still unbearable. "Father, I am sorry I am not as strong a woman as I thought I was."

"Molly, you are all I ever thought you were," he said tenderly.

"I let you down - my health is weak - my mind in a turmoil - oh, why can't I let Willie go?"

"Mother, we cannot make Willie suffer with our grief."

"I cannot stand him gone - to Heaven- to hosts of angels - gone - just *gone -*"

And suddenly - he *wasn't!* His presence was overpowering, his dear sweet being - closer than in my own heart. Tears of joy stung my eyes. The day was magically transformed - with a sudden clarity - with *light*. "Do you know Willie is with us now?" I asked. I could not keep the joy of it from my voice. "Father, Willie is here! Right *here!*"

"I am sure of it," my husband replied. "Let him see that you are strong, much stronger than you think."

"He must still have that smile - just like yours, Father. I can't *see* him, but I *know so clearly* he is with us."

"You two are so sure that Willie's spirit lives on?" asked Mrs. Pomroy, neither agreeing nor disagreeing, for whatever God did about that would be just right.

"I know now there is just a thin veil that separates us from our boys," I told Mrs. Pomroy. "I know now they *can* reach us beyond that veil, as Willie is trying to do - *right* at this moment."

"He is with God," said Mrs.Pomroy.

"And God is with all of us," said my husband softly.

"God's plan is one of perfection," said Mrs. Pomroy, not surprisingly.

"And that would allow the presence of our son," I said. "He wants me to know he is all right."

"You believe the soul is eternal," said Mrs. Pomroy, really, to both of us.

"Yes," my husband replied. "Because love is." He had slipped my hand into his. "We have been cast down, and in pain must come growth, no matter how hard the pruning. Mother, we must accept life as it is for us *now.*"

But Willie's presence had vanished as suddenly as it had come to me, and the joy that had made my heart sing again was gone with him. "He left us, Father. Willie is gone and the *now* is ghastly," I said. My voice had turned bitter. He had come to me like the glancing light of the sun darting among the tree shadows, and now he was gone, gone back to his perfect world of angel song and no more deaths to bear.

"Yes, he is gone," my husband said. "We have the right to our own pain, but it is our loss. Not Willie's."

We passed sweet smelling mown grass, fields of clover and hay, and the horses took us on a road ribboned with light and shadow, and in the shadow we flushed out singing birds that took to the sky as if they were chasing the echoes of their own song. I was between convulsions of grief, and so I could go on speaking of my lost sons. "Willie - and Eddy - They *will* let us *see* both of them through the veil," I said.

"Molly, I am sure they will."

"I know they will do this," I said. "They understand how much we *need* to see them happy -"

"Molly, I have seen them both - so *clearly,*" said my husband. "They have their same sweet smiles -" He paused, and his eyes swam with tears. He had become physically ill at Willie's death, and for the first and second Thursday after Willie died, he had shut himself away from all of us, his cabinet, his secretaries, the office seekers, the long, long line always outside of his office, and he grieved for Willie in private. He had had framed a painting Willie had done of a Springfield memory, and he had placed it over the mantelpiece of his office. "That painting was done by my son, Willie," he said, in pride, to those who noticed its loveliness.

"But they were with me in a dream," my husband said. "And we must awaken from dreams, the bad ones and the good ones."

"They *will* let me see them happy," I said. "I *have* to see that."

My husband put his arm around me, and the rising wind was not as hot, and as the afternoon wore on, the shadows of the road grew longer and cooling. "Molly, every day now mothers give up their sons to this war, and it will get worse and worse -" His voice deepened. "Human pain is a universal thing."

"Bobby must not go into the army!" I said. "He must stay in college and not die!" I was losing control again. I saw Mrs. Pomroy and my husband look at each other. "If he goes into the army I will go *mad*!" I wept. I saw that look between them again.

Later, in the White House, I had another outburst of agony. My gentle husband took me to a window, and he pointed to a home we could see for the insane. "Molly," he said. "Do you see that large white building over yonder? Try and control your grief or it will drive you mad, and we will have to send you there."

My husband knew then of my mental illness, when I did not. It was killing him with anguish, and he expressed it to a friendly physician visitor. The physician said my purchasing *caprices* were the result of partial insanity. My husband paced the floor, his head bent, as if this added burden with the war, Willie's death, did not allow him to straighten up. "Is the malady beyond medical remedy to check before it becomes fully developed?" he asked.

The reply was that he be kind but firm with me.

My husband replied, "It is only about money - her aberration is only about *money* - in all other respects she is very intelligent - as usual - the spending of money *symbolizes* something - assuages grief -"

"Be kind but firm," the mystery doctor friend repeated.

In my grief, I let my husband down. But to scorn someone for being ill is a terrible thing, for would you hate and scorn someone for breaking a leg? For being shot and wounded? A broken mind is no worse, and I am hated and reviled for *small* irrational things *I could not control.* On the big things, I stayed normal; I never hurt anyone, and I never would.

My husband's love was the beacon light that began to guide me from my sea of despair. Through the furnace of affliction, he took my hand and drew me back to him, our marriage, *living.* "Father," I said to him. "Never let me forsake you again."

"Molly, you didn't," he replied. "We can never ever forsake each other."

"Because love is eternal," I whispered. He had said it. I believed it, and I was safe again, sheltered, *tenderly beloved* in those strong arms.

Our life in the White House changed. The merry goings on of my boys, the Taft boys were gone, and neither Taddie nor I could bear to see the Taft children again, and even, two years later, when Taddie saw Julia Taft, he burst into hysteria of grief.

On April 6 came bloody Shiloh, and in it my half brother, Sam Todd, fighting for the Confederacy, was killed. My half brother, Alexander Todd, would be killed at Baton Rouge this August. In all, I had three half-brothers, one brother, and three brothers-in-law fighting for the Confederacy. I loved them all, and I had kissed my younger brothers with such love when I returned to Kentucky before this dreadful war tore us asunder, and brother did fight brother, and father fought son. "Hey, Bud," one young Kentuckian had shouted at Shiloh. "Don't shoot that sniper in the tree! It's Pa!"

We had no more formal receptions that year. As I had been castigated and hated for our having them, I was now castigated and hated for our not having them. I wore black, and was criticized by the fashion *beau a la mode* for this. I wore less jewelry, and this made the northern part of the United States shabby. Or I had shipped all of my jewels off to the Confederacy, while the Confederacy noted I had shipped them all to the devil along with my soul. The concerts on the White House lawn were canceled. The next year, my husband quietly ordered them resumed, but across the street at Lafayette Square.

On March 2 Taddie was said to be out of danger. He still could not sit up, and he still had to take his medicine, which he decided not to take as he did not like its taste.

On March 8 came the news that an iron clad Confederate ship, called the *Merrimac* was on the James River, and our shot bounced from her sides like rubber balls. She had sunk our *Cumberland,* tore the *Congress* to pieces, and the next day would return to finish off our frigate, the *Minnesota,* which had been driven aground and was helpless. It was a day of despair and deepest gloom for us. If our blockade failed, so well might our cause.

Sunday, March 9, my husband stayed at the war office. We had our own iron clad, the *Monitor*, and when the *Merrimac* came to finish off the *Minnesota* at dawn, there she was. They engaged; neither was sunk, but the *Merrimac* withdrew, and steamed back to Norfolk. There was applause around my husband at the good news, and he said, "I am glad for all of our sakes," and walked back to the White House.

On March 10, Eddy's birthday, my husband was in a grave war discussion with grave men, and Hay entered and told him that his nurse could not get Taddie to take his medicine. "Gentlemen," my husband asked. "Would you excuse me?"

His office and the cabinet room were on the second floor to the east and the family bedrooms were on the second floor to the west, and my husband walked the short walk to Taddie and fixed things all up with him. He made out a check to Taddie for five dollars and Taddie took his medicine. "Pa," said Taddie after he had swallowed the bitter stuff. "I won't charge a dime if, from now on, *you* give me the medicine," so that is what my husband did.

On March 12 Taddie began to walk again, a few feeble steps at a time, and he came to see me. We held each other. "Ma, is Willie all right?" he asked.

"Of course he is," I said.

"Is he with us - now?"

"I am sure he is, for we want that so much."

"Why can't we see him? Talk to him?"

"A veil of *our* blindness keeps us from seeing him," I said.

"I see him in my dreams."

"So do your father and I."

He began to sob in my arms. "I wish I had not killed Jack so many times!" he wept. "Willie didn't even want him killed once."

I *had* to have Willie and Eddy appear to me, when I was *awake*. I went to séances to find them, and had one in the Red Room, with my husband present. All the séances were fakes.

And then I did not need them anyway! Something happened that I did not speak of to anyone but my husband, and he understood and was happy for my deep solace. "Father," I said to him one morning, "I am deeply, deeply comforted."

"Your face shows joy," he said tenderly. "Your eyes show life again."

"Yes," I said. "*They* broke through the veil of my blindness."

He put down the newspaper he had been reading. "Willie and Eddy," he said.

My eyes were swimming with tears of joy. "Yes. Last night, when I was *awake,* after long prayer, *but I was awake,* Willie and Eddy stood at the foot of my bed. Father, they *are* so happy. They still have their beautiful smiles - as you saw in your dreams - and we cannot wish them back. We must *not* wish them back."

"No," he said gently.

"We grieve only for ourselves."

"Yes," he agreed. "And we have two living sons."

Taddie, once he was able to walk again, checked constantly upon his father and me. He was in a terror that one of us would leave him as Willie had done. He now called his father Pappa - dear, that with his lisp, came out *Papa - day.* He never called him *Pa* again.

He checked every morning to see that I was all right, but he spent most of his time with his father in his office. For a while, he even slept with his father, as he could not bear to be in the room he had shared with Willie. Or he would fall asleep under his father's desk, or in front of the office fire, and when my husband went to bed, he would carry Taddie from the office, dodging the same chandeliers and door tops as when he had carried Bud from Willie's room.

Taddie was no longer collecting his fortune and concentrated wholly on watching for distressed women in the line waiting to see his father. If they were crying, or dressed poorly or shabbily with grief on their features, they were taken by him to his father who saw that their boys were not shot, or if they were ill, that they came right home, or if the mother was desperately ill, they also came right home. If his father happened to be at a cabinet meeting when a waiting woman needed his help, Taddie entered the meeting and got his father right out of it. "Papa-day, this poor lady is going to lose her boy!"

"How, son?"

"The army is going to shoot him! He fell asleep, like Jack used to, and I should *never* have shot Jack for that! Even once!"

"No, son," said his father who left the meeting, met the mother and gave a written pardon for her son.

The cabinet did not like this very much. The generals did not like this at all. John Hay thought it was deplorable that Taddie could stomp into a cabinet meeting, ruin it, and called Taddie the terror of the White House.

I was still the hell- cat. Taddie was the terror.

To take pressure from his father, Taddie began to interview the men waiting in line to see him. "Now, why do *you* want to see Papa-day?" he would ask.

215

"Oh, I want a government office," a man would reply.

Taddie would look gravely up at the man and say, "Papa-day is too busy for that. You should go home and split rails like he did."

It was only in June that I regained the pleasure of daily visits to the hospitals to take fruit, candy, flowers, and White House delicacies to our wounded soldiers. In every anguished face I saw my lost sons, and I tenderly held gangrened hands, and from my private purse I sent money home to the mothers of these beautiful boys who had given to the Union with their own blood and such suffering. My daily visits were *never* mentioned in the papers. In fact, a Cleveland newspaper printed, two years *after* I had left the White House, "Just *two* calls each week, with a bouquet of flowers, upon any one of the hospitals that filled Washington, would have made her name immortal."

"Father, they still attack you through me," I said.

"It is all right," he repeated. "I never read the hate letters. I never read the hate editorials. I can do nothing about them."

He worked so hard. He hardly slept. He hardly ate. If it were not for our afternoon carriage rides into the country, he would have hardly healed. "I want the Army of the Potomac to move, to defeat Lee, and not go forward to *stay put*. There is a sore spot in my heart I cannot sustain," he said to me, again and again. "*Nothing* reaches my tired spot. I think I am the most tired man alive."

"Father, you must eat and sleep like other men in the world."

"Other men in the world aren't where I am," he would sigh wearily, and go back to his office.

He had deep circles under his eyes and he was constantly losing weight, taking catnaps for sleep. More often, he would sleep all night in his office, his head on the cabinet table. Or he would work in his office, without *any* sleep, until dawn. Except for a few brief moments when we were still family, my husband devoted all of his energy, all of his heart and soul to see the ghastly war to a close. At the war office when he heard of another battle lost, more young brief lives gone, he would press his hand to his heart and say to Stanton, "My God! I cannot bear it! I cannot bear it!" He hardly did. His photographers, his painters, said the same thing. The painter, Francis Bicknell Carpenter, wrote, "In repose he has the saddest face I ever knew. There were days when I could scarcely look into it without crying." No man could show by facial expression his real feelings as did my husband. No man could go deeper into the depths of despair, and still will himself out of them, than my husband. One night, before friends in the Red Room, he gloomily recited some lines from Shakespeare's *Macbeth*.

> To-morrow, and to-morrow, and to-morrow
> Creeps in this petty pace from day to day
> To the last syllable of recorded time;
> And all our yesterdays have lighted fools
> The way to dusty death. Out, out, brief candle!
> Life's but a walking shadow, a poor player
> That struts and frets his hour upon the stage
> And then is heard no more. It is a tale
> Told by an idiot, full of sound and fury,
> Signifying nothing.

"Do you believe that?" asked our dear friend, Senator Charles Sumner.

My husband did not take his eyes from the fire that he had gotten up to stir. The silence was long. My husband was always so quick to reply to a question, and I wondered if he was going to answer this one. "Rarely," he said, finally, but his voice was tortured.

And yet, I heard him talk to a Quaker woman, a Mrs. Gurney, and she asked him what he thought God's plan for man was.

"Perfect," he replied.

"Perfect?" she asked.

"Yes. The purposes of the Almighty are perfect, and must prevail, though we do not often see them in advance. It is not a question of God being on our side. It is the other way around. It is a question of our being on God's side."

My husband's sense of humor was also his lifeline. It was the line that brought him up from the depths of his suffering. He said to another office seeker, "Come in and tell me what you know. It can't take long." A stranger came and wanted to be ambassador to Spain. "Do you know Spanish?" my husband asked.

"No, Sir, I do not."

"Well, go home and learn the language, and then I will have something for you."

The man went home and studied Spanish, and when he had learned it, he returned to my husband. "I now know Spanish!" he said, beaming in triumph.

"Good for you!"

"Now, Sir, what do you have for me?"

My husband smiled. "This," he said and handed him the Spanish volume of *Don Quixote.*

He teased his Secretary of the Navy as looking for Noah's Ark so he could put it into the Union navy. He was told this about a famous Greek historian, "No man in our generation has plunged more deeply into the sacred fount of learning." My husband instantly replied, "Or come up dryer."

He was touring a hospital in Washington when a young lady attached herself along and became interested in a wounded soldier. "Where were you wounded?" she asked.

"At Antietam, " he replied.

"I mean - where - on *you* - were you wounded?"

"At Antietam," the soldier responded stubbornly.

She asked my husband to solve the puzzle as to where the soldier was wounded. He did, soon rejoined her and said, "My dear girl, the ball that hit him would not have injured you."

At the Patent Office Hospital I was visiting wounded soldiers with my husband. I saw my husband linger by a sick patient who weakly held a religious tract just given to him by a well-dressed lady full of religion and good cheer. He looked at the tract and then up at her and began to laugh. "Son," my husband said kindly. "This lady gave you a gift. It is hardly fair for you to laugh at her gift."

"I think it is," the soldier replied. "She has given me a tract on the sin of dancing, and both of my legs were shot off."

"You see, Molly," my husband grimly said to me later, "It never pays to lose your sense of humor."

On a windy freezing night my husband was walking out of the telegraph office. He noted the guard outside had a terrible cold. "Son, go inside and get warm," my husband said.

"Oh, no, sir, my orders are for me to remain *right* where I am."

"But you can still guard what you are guarding where it is not freezing."

"No, Sir. "

"You will not oblige me by going inside and out of the cold?"

"Oh, no Sir!" He then walked his beat, shivering and teeth chattering.

"Do you know who I am?"

"The President, Sir."

"Am I not your commander in chief?"

The soldier stopped walking and blew his nose.

"When you get that completed, I *order* you inside!"

The soldier went and told that story of my husband many times.

He loved to tell what two Quaker women told about him and the President

218

of the Confederacy.

"I think Mr. Davis will succeed."

"Why does thee think so?"

"Because he is a praying man."

"But so is our President."

"But God will think *he* is joking."

And then my husband would laugh, and no man still had a more hearty laugh. It was so infectious, as I had heard so long ago at Speed's store. He would just *effervesce,* and if you did not understand one word he had said, you would laugh along with him. I read what a Pennsylvania editor, Alexander McClure, said on meeting my husband, "I have often known him in the space of a few minutes to be transformed from the saddest face I have ever looked upon to one of the brightest and most mirthful." Another man wrote of his dusty shabby black suits, and he said to another that my husband's face was one part grotesque, and the other man interrupted, saying, "and three parts sublime."

Many people saw my husband in many ways.

Mary Livermore wrote his face was haggard, and bore "hues of midnight." Noah Brooks recorded of my husband, "his simple hearted manners made a strong impression on those who saw him for the first time. I have known impressionable women, touched by his sad face and gentle bearing, to go away in tears." Walt Whitman said he had the face of a Hoosier Michael Angelo, "so awfully ugly it becomes beautiful." Whitman said his face had deep cut lines but he was captain of the ship of state, keeping it afloat with almost supernatural tact - head steady, flag flying as high as ever. "I say never yet captain, never ruler, had such a perplexing dangerous task as his the past two years. I more and more rely upon his idiomatic western genius careless of court dress or court decorum."

One man said he was an athlete of the first order, lean, lithe and agile. One of his generals, Egbert L Viele, recorded, "Few are aware of his physical strength. In muscular power, he's one in a thousand." Viele wrote of a trip with my husband on the cutter *Miami.* "One morning, while we were sitting on deck, he saw an ax in a socket on the bulwarks, and taking it up, held it at arms' length at the extremity of the helfe with his thumb and forefinger, continuing to hold it there for a number of minutes. " All of the sailors on board tried to do this and none could. "I could do that since I was eighteen," my husband proudly told them.

He met a rarity - a man taller! He had so much fun with that, and said all of the things to this man he had heard said to him most of his life. "Do you ever have to *swim* a river - don't you just *wade* through them all? How long does it take your head to know where your feet are going? How does the rest of you know when your feet get cold? How long does it take a fever to travel all through your body?"

"Enough! Enough!" said the tall soldier.

"My words reached up to your ears?" my husband laughed. "That must be because we are so near the same height."

A man told my husband books were not important. My husband replied. "Not because I am an educated man, but it is a loss to a man not to have grown up among books."

"Sir, men of force get on pretty well without books. They do their own thinking instead of adopting what other men think."

"Yes," my husband said frostily. "But books serve to show a man that those original thoughts aren't very new after all."

"Well - I won't want to be thought a fool -"

"It is far better to be thought a fool than to open your mouth and remove all doubt," replied my husband.

One day he took Taddie to Fort Monroe. "Will you be good?" my husband asked him.

"Papa-day, that is what I am - always good!"

But he wasn't during the trip. He bothered everyone. "Tad," my husband said, "if you stop being so troublesome and not disturb me any more until we get to fortress Monroe, I will give you a dollar." Taddie brightened but never stopped bothering his father. When they reached the fort he said,"Papa-day, I will take my dollar now."

"Tad, do you think you have earned it?" my husband asked soberly.

"Yes."

My husband sighed sadly, opened his billfold and handed him a dollar. "Well, my son, at any rate, I will keep *my* part of the bargain."

Taddie was stung and *almost* gave the dollar back.

My husband loved to tell true soldier stories that scoffed rank and pretension. "A picket challenged a tug going up a river. "Who goes there?"

"The Secretary of War and Major General Foster."

"Aw! We got generals enough up here. Now why don't you just bring us some hardtack?"

A man pressed my husband to answer his critics. Here is his recorded reply, "Oh, no, at least not for now. If I were to try to read, much less answer, all of the attacks made on me, this shop might as well be closed for any other business. I do the very best I know how; the very best I can; and I mean to keep doing so until the end. If the end brings me out all right, what is said of me won't amount to anything. If the end brings me out wrong, ten angels swearing I was right would make no difference."

To another anxious visitor about the scorn heaped upon him, my husband said, "It is true you may fool all of the people some of the time, and some of the people all of the time, but you can't fool all of the people all of the time."

His cabinet could not believe he always blacked his own shoes. Mr. Chase said, "Sir, true gentlemen do *not* black their own boots."

My husband looked at the good job he was doing on his own and asked, "Well, then, *Sir,* whose boots do they black?"

Reporters were still fascinated at how my husband could run his hands through his hair and make it such a mess. Some called it his wild *republican* hair, but the English gentlemen who called were truly shocked, not only by his large rugged hands, which held theirs in a vice that made their bones and sense of life squeak, but by his hair - *totally* uncombed, they said. Not only was it marching off in every direction at once, it was *totally untamable* they said. Yet with all of these negatives, they had to write that the President of the United States had "an air of strength, physical as well as moral, and a strange dignity coupled with all of this grotesqueness."

Carolyn Kirkland met him and said, "He is the handsomest man I have ever seen." A child looked up at my husband and said, "Oh, Pa! He isn't ugly at all! He's just beautiful!" And when Senator Tad Stevens brought a mother to thank him for saving her son from execution, she looked up at my husband and said, "I knew it all the time! It was just a copper head lie!"

"What was?" asked Stevens.

"Why, they told me he was an ugly looking man. He is the handsomest man I ever saw in my whole life!"

Most agreed he looked younger and better looking than his pictures. He was seen as dark and swarthy, gentle looking, having a fine smile, *perfect* teeth, but his hair, *all agreed,* was a serious detraction. His attire was described as "mussed, careless and befuddled," but not as bad as his hair. Nothing could be *that* bad, continued the consensus. They should have seen him the way he *liked* to go around in our rooms upstairs, *no* slicking up by me of his hair, no oil on it *at all,* wearing an old ragged robe and worn out slippers down at the heel - I was firm that he could *not* meet the people in his old robe and ragged slippers. But he might even have thought of this himself.

Another man said that for all of his *physical grotesqueness,* "there was an air of strength, physical as well as mental, and a strange look of great dignity." This was from another *Englishman,* Edward Dicey, who considered my husband a great political failure. "Still," he continued, "if you would never say he was a gentleman, you still could less say he was not one . . . there is about him a complete absence of pretension, which is in essence, if not the outward form, of high breeding. There is softness in his smile, making his plain features good looking, a sparkle of dry humor in his eye, but still he has this *sad* face. He is in terms of total equality with his guests." But Dicey and his fellow Englishmen were in a horror that my husband's western words might seep across the Atlantic to pollute their English - *Howdy,* his own made up words - *by jenks, skedaddle, bogus, deadhead, come-up-pence - interruptious.* Truthfully, it was thought that his whole style of writing was too plain, for it could be so easily understood. They said that Sumner should have written the *Emancipation Proclamation.*

Nathaniel Hawthorne, our leading novelist, came all the way from Massachusetts to look over my husband for the *Atlantic Monthly.* He asked my husband how tall he was. "When I get the kinks out, I reckon six foot four," my husband replied. In this July, of 1862, Hawthorne wrote of my husband as "a tall loose jointed man" - "the homeliest man I ever saw, yet by no means repulsive or disagreeable" - "there was no describing his lengthy awkwardness . . . and yet it served as if I had been in the habit of seeing him daily, and had shaken hands with him a thousand times in some village- street. . . . He was dressed in a rusty black frock coat and pantaloons, unbrushed and worn so faithfully that the suit had adapted itself to the curves and angularities of his figure. . . . He had shabby slippers on his feet. His hair was black, still unmixed with gray, . . . and apparently been acquainted with neither brush nor comb that morning. (He had gotten by me) . . . he has thick black eyebrows and an impending brow; his nose is large, and the laugh lines about his mouth are very strongly defined." His *coarse* appearance was "redeemed, illuminated, softened, and brightened by a kindly though serious look out of his eyes . . ." Mr. Hawthorne liked my husband's appearance on the whole, "with the homely human sympathies that warmed it." His manner was "wholly without pretense, and he yet had a kind of natural dignity." In conclusion my husband was seen by Mr. Hawthorne as a man of "keen facilities," one of "powerful character and integrity", a man "teachable by events" with a "flexible mind capable of much expansion," and if he had been a mere backwoods humorist, "he had transformed himself into a great statesman."

Senator Sumner brought Ralph Waldo Emerson to meet my husband in early February of 1862. It must have been before Willie took ill, for he remembered my husband's "boyish cheerfulness" and his perfect white teeth when he laughed. He had expected to meet a coarse man, and "the President impressed me more favorably than I had hoped - frank, sincere, well meaning" - and " he was not vulgar as (his enemies) described."

How did a famous black man see my husband? Frederick Douglass was asked how he was received at the White House. "I will tell you how he received me," said Douglass. "Just as you have seen one gentleman receive another, with a hand and voice well balanced between a kind cordiality and a respectful reserve. I tell you - I felt big there." In the crowds waiting to see the President, "I was the only dark spot among them." He had expected a wait of days, even weeks, "but in two minutes after I had sent in my card, the messenger came out, and respectfully invited 'Mr. Douglass' in." He passed whites muttering, " 'Damn it, I knew they would let the nigger through.' When I went in, the President was sitting in his usual position, I was told, with his feet in different parts of the room. . . . as I came in . . . the President began to rise, and he continued rising until he stood over me, and reaching out a hand, he said, 'Mr. Douglass, I know you; I have read all about you'. . . putting me at ease at once. . . He impressed me. . as being an honest man. I never met with a man, who, on the first blush, impressed me more entirely with his sincerity, with his devotion to his country, and with his determination to save it at all hazards." My husband had read that Douglass had accused him of vacillating, and he replied to this accusation. "Mr. Douglass, I do not think that charge can be sustained; I think it cannot be shown that when I have taken a position, I have ever retreated from it." What was the Douglass' conclusion regarding my husband? *He would be recognized as the equal of George Washington.*

My husband was out riding with some aides. On the road they met a shabby old Negro who looked up at my husband, took off his ragged hat and bowed. My husband stopped his horse, took of his hat and as gravely bowed back. "Now, why would you do that?" asked an astonished aide as they rode on.

"I allow no man to be a greater gentleman that I am," replied my husband.

One day a handsome man was in his office and two officers from the Spanish navy thought he was the President and addressed him accordingly. My husband signed for the handsome one to play President, and when the Spanish officers left, he said to the handsome one, "I want to thank you for making the President of the United States so good looking and not expecting an office for your trouble!"

Robert had problems, from the first, with his father's lack of self - importance. He was with his father one day when some troops marched by, and his father did not know what troops they were, or even what state they were from, and he asked two nearby pedestrians, "What is that, boys?"

One of the pedestrians looked up at him and growled, "It is a regiment of soldiers marching down the street, you damned old fool!" Apparently this set my husband off into gales of laughter, and when Robert told me of the incident, the *mortifying* incident, my husband was consumed with laughter again. "Bob," he said, "remember, it does a man good sometimes to hear the truth."

He loved to tease. An aide told him he was going to bring him a special rabbit's foot for good luck. My husband said, fine - do it. When the aide arrived with the rabbit's foot, my husband took out a potato from his own pocket.

"Sir, is that for good luck?"

"No. It is for rheumatism."

"Does it work?"

"Most certainly. I haven't had a twinge of rheumatism since I began carrying it."

"That is truly wonderful!"

"Still more wonderful is the fact that it is retroactive too. I never had a twinge before I began carrying it, either."

My husband never dictated messages to his secretaries. "I have to write them," he said. "Apparently, I can never think except with my fingers."

My husband saw the open contempt that Nicolay and Hay showed to me, and decided to have Noah Brooks, correspondent for the Sacramento *Daily Union,* become his secretary. He had become a good friend to *both of us.* Nicolay and Hay were good friends to *neither of us.*

In July, after we had moved to the Old Soldiers Home on the first, I took a short trip to Boston and New York City. It was that month, while my husband rode the three miles to the White House, someone tried to kill him, shooting his hat right off of his head. He told me *nothing* about it, but lamented to others, " I just lost my best eight dollar plug hat." I heard his horse reared, and he also said he did not know which was worse, being killed by some rabbit hunter or by a government horse.

In October, I took Taddie to New York City with me where Mrs. Keckley joined us. She was working on a magnificent cause, help for the freed men, with money, education and moral support. On September 22, after our victory at Antietam, my husband had proclaimed that his Emancipation Proclamation would be issued January 1, 1863. Mrs. Keckley *frequently* said to us, "I know what liberty *is* because I knew what slavery *was.*"

When free, the Negroes would have to have help to survive, and I thought the Contraband Relief Association, formed in the summer of 1862 for this purpose, was wonderful. I supported it every way I could. I saw it received money from those I knew in the North who hated slavery as much as I did, and I gave the first contribution of $200 and continued to give money. On that trip Taddie lost a tooth, I had a severe hemorrhage, and no letter from my busy husband. I wrote a letter on November 2, to "My Dear Husband," and said, "I have waited in vain to hear from you, yet as you are not *given* to letter writing, will be charitable enough to impute your silence to the right cause. Strangers come up from W - & tell me you are well - which satisfies me very much - Your name is on every lip and many prayers and good wishes are hourly sent up, for your welfare - and McClellan & his slowness are as vehemently discussed. Allowing this beautiful weather, to pass away, is disheartening to the North - (After Antietam, Little Mac was sitting on the army and doing *nothing* with it - allowing Lee's escape into Virginia - anyway, my husband was about to fire him) Dear little Taddie is well and enjoying himself very much - General and Mrs. Anderson (Anderson was the defender of Fort Sumter) & myself called on yesterday to see Gen. Scott . . . A day or two since, I had one of my severe attacks, if it had not been for Lizzie Keckley, I do not know what I should have *done* - Some *of these periods* will launch me away -" I told him again how McClellan should be replaced by a man who would fight - "Many say, they would almost worship you, if you would put a fighting general in place of McClellan. This would be splendid weather for an engagement. I have had two suits of clothes made for Taddie which will come to twenty six dollars . . . I must send you Taddie's tooth -" Then I lamented no letter from him, closing my own with "One line, to say that we are occasionally remembered will be gratefully received by yours very truly -"

The next day I wrote him of the Contraband Relief Association. (contraband was the slang word used in the South for their escaped or freed slaves) and how Mrs. Keckley had been unsuccessful in raising enough money to help - "She says the immense number of Contrabands in W - are suffering intensely, many without bed or covering & having to use any bit of carpeting to cover themselves - Many dying of want -" I suggested $200 be given to help from a General Corcoran $1,000 army fund, for "the soldiers are well supplied with comfort." The $200 was donated for Contraband relief, and my husband continued contributions out of his own pocket, too.

We were to leave for Washington on December 21, but on that day my husband sent me a wire, "Do not come home on the night train. It is too cold. Come in the morning."

December 21. Willie's birthday. He would have been twelve.

I had constantly wondered if I did something wrong. If I had done this, or had not done that, perhaps Eddy and Willie would be sharing this coming Christmas with us. Now, as the trees went up again and bore their lighted candles - what did they mean? What did the lights put by man on a tree signify? There was no answer. The season had lost its magic, for surely, time engulfed by your child's death is not magic. The candles glowed like those Macbeth saw, as we march on to dusty death in a tale told by an idiot.

But on that Christmas Day of 1862, with the windows frosting up against the cold outside, with the sweet voices of children singing old Christmas carols, I gave thanks that I had my husband by my side, Taddie well again, and Robert, filled with Harvard learning and dignity, home for Christmas. I would try so hard to meet life on its own terms.

I had sent a box to Lizzie in April packed with toys her little grandson, Lewis Baker, might enjoy. Among them was Willie's train set that Taddie could not bear to look at again.

As Christmas night came, and from the outside the White House lights became shuttered with falling snow, I gave thanks in my heart that another little boy could lie on the floor, and before a warm Christmas fire exclaim in joy over beautiful toy trains, and keep them running, like Willie, just on schedule.

Chapter Twenty

We gave our first public reception after Willie's death on New Year's Day of 1863. This was the date the *Emancipation Proclamation* was issued freeing Confederate slaves. Two weeks before, we had lost the bloody battle of Fredericksburg. My husband was in such pain and I was in such pain, but there we stood in the receiving line, and he stayed. I did not. I could not. I went upstairs and allowed my grief its full devastation. The date of Willie's death was coming up. And then I remembered how he came to me again, standing at the very foot of the bed where I lay, how he had brought Eddy one time, and their little dear faces were so joyous, so filled with *light* - and I wiped my eyes. Both of them were with God - in Heaven - cherished by hosts of heavenly angels, *and I still wanted them with me.*

"Robert must not leave Harvard to fight," I told my husband again. "Father, I am *very* firm about this. He must not!"

"Molly, he wants to," my husband said.

"Father, we can *not* give in to him."

My husband sighed and looked out of the window at the dark and gloomy day. "Mother, he has always been interested in joining the military."

I rose and went to him, and for once was looking down on him, for he had remained sitting. "Hear me. Listen to me. I have lost two sons, and I cannot lose another and live."

Mrs. Keckley was with me, and I saw her exchange a look with my husband. That look. That *Mary is on the brink* look. I hated it and was to see it until my death.

Robert, who was such a help to me when he was home on vacation, did not let the matter of his entering the military rest. He nagged at my husband, and even told him it was a political liability that he was not in the army. "That is very true," my husband said. "But your mother is very ill, and your going to war right now might kill her."

I heard this from Mrs. Keckley. "His loyalty is always to you," she said.

"I know, " I replied.

But gently, my husband repeated to me that other mothers were sending their sons off to war every day. "Molly," he said, "the services of every man who loves his country are required in this war. It is for the survival of the Union. You must not take a selfish view of this."

"I am. l will," I wept. I *would* meet life on its own terms, but *not this one.* "Father, I fear we will lose him, too!"

"And so feels every mother," my husband said, and his eyes were as wet as mine. "Mother, you are placing me in a terrible position."

Robert will be going off to die. I knew God would take him back, too. I cringed around my terror. My ague was back, and I was shaking so sometimes I could hardly sit in a chair. I had terrible malaria from living in Washington - *had malaria killed Willie?* The usual migraine was drawing burning wires from my brain through my eyes. "There are many young men at Harvard, and they are not in the army," I said to my husband. For a while he let the matter rest.

Don't think my husband was not capable of great anger, and its expression. Congressmen brought papers of vile gossip against our dear friend, Senator Baker. My husband read them and his face grew wrathful. "Gentlemen," he said. "are these papers mine to do with as I will?"

"Most certainly, Sir. They are yours to keep."

"Thank you," said my husband and threw them all into the fire. "Good *day*, gentlemen. Now we have seen the last of this. And of *you*," he added, and he looked so towering, so menacing in his rage, I do not believe those gentlemen *ever did* return to his office.

It was not as easy to defend me.

The famous singer of our time was Adelina Patti, and after Willie's death, my husband invited her to the White House. Here is what she recorded of me. "The President's wife was a handsome woman, almost regal in her deep black and expansive crinoline, only an outline of white at throat and wrists. Her manner was most gracious without a particle of reserve or stiffness. 'My dear, it is very kind of you to come to see us,' she said. Taking both my hands in hers and smiling in my face, she added, 'I have wanted to see you-to see the young girl who has done so much, who has set the whole world talking of her wonderful singing.'" She recorded when she sang for my husband and me - *The Last Rose of Summer* - that I went to a window, turned my back and wept for Willie - and she remembered that my husband asked her to sing *Home Sweet Home,* and that when she left the "Bereaved parents," she was weeping herself.

My little brother Sammy I used to rock when he was a baby - killed at Shiloh, on the Confederate side, and for all of them I had to keep my tears private. Sammy had been so full of fun and life - well - that cannot end for them, if our seeing it has. Not all the newsmen hated me. Not *quite* all. In this dreadful dark time - *I was not hated by everybody!* In one paper a Dr. Russell wrote of me, "Her manners would adorn a court." This also was printed in the news media: "The lady who presides as the wife of the Chief Magistrate brought with her from the West a reputation for refinement and love of the beautiful that has admirably been realized. The stamp of her exquisite taste has been left on the furnishings of the Presidential mansion that never has looked so well as now ...She possesses that calm and conscious dignity, that is unruffled by envy and unsullied by detraction, though malice hides itself in the tongues of the Secessionists. She was celebrated for her conversationalist powers in the society in which she moved in St. Louis and Chicago, and her kindness and cordiality has acted like oil poured on troubled waters here. In youth she must have been very beautiful...her whole features illuminate with their joyous sparkle of a cultivated intellect."

As a correspondent, Noah Brooks wrote to *Sacramento Union,* "It is not a gracious task to refute these things, but the tales that are told of the First Lady's vanity, pride, vulgarity and meanness ought to put any decent man or woman to the blush, when they remember they do not *know* one particle of that which they repeat, and that they would resent as an insult to their wives, sisters or mothers that which they so glibly repeat concerning the first lady of the land. Shame upon these he-gossips and envious retailers of small slanders." He wrote he found me a "true American woman, and when we have said that we have said enough in praise of the best and truest lady in our beloved land."

"If you cannot get at the man," Noah Brooks bitterly told us, *"get him through his wife."*

I remembered those words well when I saw *myself* as a symbol for all my husband had done in his life, what his very life had stood for. I would *always* hear him saying, "It is the Union, the *Union* that safeguards *liberty,* the Union, controlled by the people, make it and liberty, one and inseparable. The heart and the soul of the American Revolution was the right of man to have the inalienable God given right to life, liberty and the pursuit of happiness. In this respect, we hold these truths to be self evident - that all men are created equal - as they are equal before their God, so must they be before their government. Let this divine truth be the beacon star of liberty for every man, for every age to come. Let this be the North Star of hope for every nation." My husband said it and knew it. The boys fighting to preserve the Union believed it, wrote home of it, and it was a question of *free* labor against *slave* labor, and that my husband made so clear, he was able to issue and sign the *Emancipation*

Proclamation. "With the people you can do anything," he always said. "Without them you can do nothing."

Certainly, the temperament of the times was not for black equality, but it was the political genius of my husband, not only to gain the acceptance of the ending of slavery in the Confederacy, but also to gain the acceptance of blacks into the Union Army.

Black soldiers did magnificently. An ignorant man called on my husband to say that making blacks soldiers was a grave error. They never would fight, were too dumb to fight and too lazy to fight, and would not fight for the Union anyway, hating *all* white men. My husband replied that he had heard nothing but praise of the black soldier who was fighting for all our freedom as well as his own. If the Union flag had fallen, a black soldier went to get it, and delivered it on his own death. "A black color bearer," my husband said, "was told by his colonel of the regimental flag, 'Defend it; protect it; die for it if need be, but never surrender it.' " My husband looked at the man seated in his office. "Do you know what the black color bearer said?"

"No, I do not."

"He said, 'Colonel, I will return this flag with honor, or *I will report to God the reason why.*' Do you know what happened?"

"No, I do not."

"He died defending the flag. Do not tell me the black soldier will not fight."

The grand Army of the Potomac just could not get a general that deserved it; every time it almost had a decisive victory, its commander backed off. I did not like General George McClellan at all. In fact, I *despised* his arrogant treatment of my husband who was his President and his commander. His nickname *Little Mac,* had everything to do with the size of his common sense and nothing to do with the size of his ego. After our disaster of Bull Run in July of 1861, he was given command of the army. What did he do with it? He marched it around in one grand review after another, but the salutes and the cheering were all for himself. He marched *his* army in glory in front of *his* house, not the White House. He had foreign dukes and counts and princes in his camp, and I do not know who called whom - your *excellency* - or - your *royal highness.* He sat, *and his army sat* as he drew up magnificent war plans to take all of the east and the west and probably their sunrises and the sunsets, too. He sent directions to my husband on how to be President. He had the President call on *him* - and when my husband did, he kept him waiting, and once, *knowing* he was *waiting downstairs,* went on upstairs to bed *without seeing him!*

"Father," I said. "How can you tolerate such a man?"

"Molly," he replied. "I will curry his horse every day if he wins a battle."

"You probably would have to be pushing his horse into it," I said.

Little Mac would not break his soldier rest camp. He rode through it under panoplies, with his own *cavalry* guard, *his* own *infantry* guard, and with his blue blood orderlies, all of them bowing to all the huzzas. "He is huzza happy," I said to my husband.

"He just has a case of the *slows*," my husband replied.

My husband asked Little Mac if he ever intended to use the army, and if not, could he not borrow it for a while?

Little Mac had no sense of humor, seeing himself divine and not needing one. He did not reply. Could you at least *point* the army toward Richmond? my husband asked.

No reply. "Little Mac is marching it around his house instead," I said. "Maybe his wife likes to see that he still *is* in the army."

Finally, my husband *ordered* Little Mac to march and to let him know *every single day* what he was doing with the army. Little Mac went sarcastic and sent my husband in impudent wire. "Today I have captured two cows. What should I do with them?"

My husband wired back immediately, "Milk 'em, George."

One day, as my husband was running down the stairs, he met a soldier bearing a message running up them. He collided with my husband, hitting him right in the stomach. When the soldier saw he had made the President breathless, he said, "A thousand pardons, Sir!"

My husband said, "Not one needed. I am pleased that at least a part of the army *can* charge. You do not know what that does for my peace of mind."

A man came to him for a pass to Richmond. "My friend," my husband said. "I have already given Richmond passes to the 250,000 men of our army and they have not reached it yet. How could another from me ever help you?"

In January of 1862 my husband had given Little Mac the *order* for him to attack Richmond. Little Mac said he could not do this because he needed more men, more supplies and more balloons. "He never has enough men," my husband said. "Sending him men is like shoveling fleas across a barn yard floor; they never go where you want them to."

The month of Willie's death and Willie's funeral, on February 22, my husband issued for Little Mac THE PRESIDENT'S WAR ORDER NUMBER 1. He was to take the army and use it against Confederate General Joseph Johnston who was guarding Richmond from Manasses. Little Mac had three men to Johnston's one, and my husband knew this very well. "My horses are too worn out. They're too tired," moaned Little Mac. "How can they be tired?" my husband asked. "They have been resting since *July of 1861.*" February moved on, but not Little Mac. WAR ORDER NUMBER 2 came on March 7, and with no reply, my husband issued WAR ORDER NUMBER 3 on March 8. But by the ninth Johnston had broken his winter-camp, with no encouragement from Little Mac, who could then count coup over its deserted grounds and the Quaker (dummy) cannon left behind. But he and his army and all of his blue blood friends marched back to Washington as if they had actually met and defeated a rebel general! In the meantime, he had wasted one million dollars in engineering, *himself,* a boat bridge to Harper's Ferry. His boats were six inches too wide for the locks there. Little Mac's brain sought space only for the huzzas that kept his heart beating. He hated me, and called me *Mrs. President,* for when he was about to execute a boy for falling asleep on picket duty, Taddie could not reach my husband to save him. I could, and did.

I cannot advance without more men, Little Mac said. Where will I get them? my husband asked, for men in the Union Army could not clone themselves twenty fold as they apparently were doing for the Confederacy. *From McDowell's men guarding Washington, of course,* said Little Mac. But we must also guard *our* capitol, said my husband. Now use your army to advance on *theirs.*

Of course, if they took our capitol, Britain, and thus France, would recognize the Confederacy as a separate country and attack our blockade. I thought the friendly Russian ships in our ports helped keep the British ships there as friendly.

In April - *Little Mac decided to move!* His plan was to leave Washington by water and attack General Johnston at Yorktown. He needed and received 113 steamers, 188 schooners, 88 barges and 121,500 men, all of which he got to the peninsula between the York and James Rivers, with 14,592 animals, 1,150 wagons, seventy four ambulances and forty four batteries. When he established himself at Fort Monroe, he *immediately requested more men.* Johnston had 55, 633 men and Little Mac still had his 121, 500, if they had not melted away in the rain. He complained to my husband about the rain, and my husband told him it was likely falling on Johnston, too. But Johnston had slipped away from Yorktown, and when Little Mac took it on May 4, all he found was more Quaker (dummy) cannon.

Congress was erupting. *How many generations of soldiers would pass under Little Mac's command before his army engaged the rebels? No general but Little Mac could take longer to find the enemy army and stop faster when he found it.* Yorktown would have immediately fallen, but he besieged it for a month anyway.

"He reminds me of a mean dog," my husband said. "He runs along a fence, snapping and foaming at the dog at the other side, and when the fence disappears at its end, so does his."

Defeat the army defending Richmond, my husband urged. *If it falls to us their hope of recognition by Britain and France is gone.*

Battle found Little Mac, and his men were glorious. From May 31 to June 1 came the battle of Seven Pines, Johnston's 60,000 Confederates against 121,000 Federals. Jefferson Davis and Robert Edward Lee were present, just *seven miles* from Richmond. Johnston was wounded; the South lost 5, 700 men, the North, 4, 300. Joy swept Washington; gloom swept Richmond. Then, on June 2, Lee was given command of the Army of Northern Virginia, and he would work with Stonewall Jackson, one the right hand of the other; never had such mutual military genius been joined. Lee knew Little Mac. He would *never* have enough men to attack; he was waiting for McDowell's men who were defending Washington, the 40,000 *more* men my husband was going to send to him. Lee prevented this. He sent Jackson with 17,000 men to the Shenandoah as a threat to Washington to keep McDowell where he was. This left Lee with *66,000* men against Little Mac's *121,000*. Little Mac told my husband he had too few men to fight, that he was facing Lee who had *at least* 200,000 men. Thus he had to have *immediate* reinforcements.

Jackson marched his men 170 miles in 14 days. He took 3,000 prisoners, whose shoes his men delighted in wearing; he took $200,000 in supplies, and 9,000 rifles. John C. Fremont was supposed to keep Jackson from rejoining Lee, but he took the wrong road, and Lee had Jackson and his men back in his army. On June 12-15, J.E.B. (James Ewell Brown) Stuart rode his cavalry around the *whole* Union army, *unopposed*. There was a bloody seven-day battle of the peninsula, from June 26, to July 1, and in it the Confederates were fighting barefoot and took shoes from our dead. Little Mac actually won this battle, but he refused to believe it. He just had *not* had enough men to do that.

"It can't be!" cried my husband.

It could be and was. Instead of ordering an *advance* on Richmond, Little Mac ordered a *retreat* back to Washington. Lee began chasing Little Mac! The Confederates had had 8,062 killed, and the Union dead numbered 1,734. Wounded, the Confederates had 15,909 and the Union 8,062. Little Mac still saw himself drowning in Confederates. "We did not have a chance," he lamented, leaving for Lee almost all of his supplies, including 35,000 needed small firearms. Yet, he told Congress if he had only had the army in March, he would be, by now, into New Orleans!

"I guess Lee would love another advance by Little Mac," I said. "He would drop off enough supplies for him to do the rebellion into the next century."

"I am as desolate and as nearly inconsolable as I can be and still live," my husband said. Little Mac's penchant for wanting someone else to get him out of what he had gotten himself into reminded him of a man who was visiting the Illinois State Penitentiary. He got lost and went up to an inmate's cell and angrily asked, "*Will* you show me the way out of here?"

Little Mac also reminded him of another story. A farmer had a prize vicious hog and told his two boys never to let it out of its pen. Of course the boys did, and of course the hog seriously went on the attack. One boy got up a tree and the other got a hold on the hog and was going around and around with it. He yelled up to his brother, "Come right down here and stop me from holding on to this thing!"

My husband was asked if he knew how many soldiers were in the Confederacy. "Oh," he said. "It is as simple as Arithmetic!"

"Sir - how so?"

"Well, they have 1,600,000 men."

"One *million, six hundred* thousand?"

"Oh, yes."

"Sir - how do you know that? How do you know the exact number?"

"It is not hard. Whenever one of our generals is licked, he *always* says he was outnumbered four to one, and, under arms, we have 400,000 men."

Little Mac now wanted more men to join in his retreat. "If I filled his camp with more men," my husband moaned, "they all would have to sleep standing up." He went to visit Little Mac at Harrison's Landing where Little Mac solemnly presented him with *detailed written* instructions as how to win the war, govern as President, and, above all, he instructed, the Confederate slaves must not be freed. My husband had the wrong stand on slavery, and if slaves were freed by Presidential proclamation, the Army of the Potomac would melt away. "I thought it was already doing that," my husband sighed wearily.

"What are you going to do about McClellan telling you how to run your office?" Senator Sumner asked.

"Nothing," my husband said. "But he reminds me of a man whose horse kicked up and stuck his foot through the stirrup. The man said to his horse, 'Well, if you are going to get on, I will get off.' "

Little Mac thought he was in direct communication with God, or perhaps, it was the other way around. He acted more and more lofty, patronizing and contemptuous of my husband. It was common Washington gossip, and of course we heard it, that he scoffed about him to all of the blue bloods of his high class entourage, that he wrote that he was serving *fools* and *dolts* in Washington, and that my husband was aptly named a *gorilla*. Now that *his* - *the Little Mac* army was back in Washington, all of its former small shop owners, farmers, clerks, store hands and ditch diggers, Little Mac rode among them for his huzzah high. Trumped up with feeding on it, he said to a friend, "How these brave boys love me! What power they place in my hands! What is to prevent me from taking the government into my own hands?"

I would have said, "Being hanged for treason."

"Leading the Army of the Potomac has worn me out," Little Mac said, and my husband gave him a rest. He fired him.

That summer of 1862 my husband, on July 1, signed the Pacific Railroad Act. The Central Pacific would build east from Sacramento, and the Union Pacific would build west from Omaha. The next day he signed the Morill Land Grant College Act, giving 30,000 acres of government land to each state to establish a college devoted to agriculture, engineering and military science. My husband always considered free education an integral part of free labor. When he was asked what came first in his mind, capital or labor, I heard him say, "Labor, for without labor there would be no capital." He always supported the right of labor to organize and work in a *clean* and *safe* workplace for *living* wages. Like Jefferson, he believed capital was beholden to the community it was using. For the use of the community it was obligated to make it a better place. That, he said, was the real basis for a charter that a state gives to a corporation.

Free public education -*Free* labor-*Freedom* to choose the government, and a *free* press to see it remained so-these were my husband's four pillars of democracy, and like Jefferson, his hero, he thought the free press the most important of them all, for without it, like Jefferson, he said, "With a free press, you will have a free government, and without it, you will not." How can the people govern when they do not know what their government is doing? How can they *be* the government if they are kept in the dark about it?

General John Pope was brought from the West to be in command of Fremont, Banks and McDowell. General Henry Halleck was made head of the Union armies. Little Mac was to guard Washington, stationed at Acquia Creek on the Potomac, fully retreated now from the peninsula between the York and James Rivers.

Once more the genius of Lee and Jackson was a disaster to us. The Battle of the Second Bull Run, or the Second Manasses, raged on August 29-30, and

Pope was soundly defeated. The bells tolled for us and rang out jubilantly in the South. Before Jackson and Lee joined we were just seven miles from Richmond, even had an observer in a balloon (the most shot at man in the war) looking down on it; we had western Virginia and three armies in the Shenandoah. Now we had been driven from the peninsula, from western Virginia and the Confederates were saying the only Yankees on their land were under its soil or in its prisons.

It was sad to hear that Lee's house on the Chickahominy had been burned down. It was called the "White House" and here George Washington had proposed to Martha.

But we were now in a horror. Lee could have taken Washington if he had known he could. My husband restored Little Mac to command. He had no one better; if Little Mac failed this time, my husband said, *they both would be in a rough row of stumps*. Or, *the hog would be too heavy to carry*. Or, *the bottom would be out of the tub.* He always used farm expressions.

In September Lee crossed the Potomac into Maryland, and on the seventeenth and eighteenth McClellan really defeated him at Antietam, not knowing it, as usual, even when he had been handed a copy of Lee's whole battle plan! He rested and pined for more men, and my husband said, "If he doesn't stop Lee from escaping to Virginia, I will fire him." He didn't; Lee did, and Little Mac was fired. Ambrose Burnside was given command, and on December 15 came our ghastly disaster of Fredericksburg. As far as our generals were concerned, I wondered if the tub *had* a bottom. In January of 1863, the command of the Army of the Potomac was given to "Fighting" Joe Hooker.

On February 21, 1863, I wrote a thank you note to my dear friend, Mary Jane Wells, wife of Gideon, our Secretary of the Navy. She had *lost* a *sixth* child the preceding November.

"Allow me to thank you for your sympathizing & kindly remembrance, of *yesterday,* when I felt so broken hearted. (The anniversary of Willie's death) Only those who have passed through such bereavements, can realize, how the heart bleeds at the return, of these anniversaries, - I have never been able, to express to you, how I grieved over your troubles, our precious lambs, if we could only realize, how far happier they now are than when on earth!"

Enough said of that letter. In February we had a reception for Tom Thumb and his bride who had been Miss Lavina Warren and both were Barnum dwarfs. My husband *really* had to bend over to shake their tiny little hands.

By this time our Saturday receptions were *crushers,* and I was *appalled* to see people come into the White House, cut away souvenirs from rugs, furniture and drapes, and Brooks even caught one man skinning off the damask cover of one of our finest sofas!

The White House belonged to all of the people - not just to visiting looters. Of this Brooks wrote back to his paper,"Mine Gott, vat a Peoples!"

In early April my husband visited the army opposite Fredericksburg at Falmouth Heights. He took Taddie and me, and Attorney General Bates, Noah Brooks and our dear Dr. Anson Henry. We had floored wide hospital tents and camp beds, and the reviews of Hooker's men were magnificent. There was a strong gusty wind, at first, very cold, but later it warmed some. I enjoyed the cavalry, reviewed on April 6, for in it, Taddie solemnly rode, his military gray coat flying almost parallel in the wind, and I saw my husband touch his hat to the officers, and take it off for the enlisted men. He rode by General Hooker, "riding just like a veteran" I heard men say. He was an *excellent* horseback rider. That pleased me, but it did *not* please me when I heard a young lady had flung herself on my husband and given him a kiss. "Father!" I said. "Why did you allow such a *wicked* thing?"

"Mother," he replied. "I had *not* put that on my schedule."

It was magnificent to see so many lovely young men fighting for their country. The ground was soft with melting snow, and the prancing horses kicked it up, the martial music loud enough to make the horses skittish, banners whipping in the wind, columns to be reviewed by my husband stretching far beyond my sight. The men of Meade, Sickles, Sedgewick - marching by, bayonets glinting in the sun, the shining guns of the artillery, and then the reserve artillery - endless - endless. My husband visited the hospital tents, shook the hands of each of the boys there, and I heard, he left not one dry eye behind his departure.

In our tent, my husband stretched out and he said, as he often said, "Molly, *nothing* reaches this tired spot." He enjoyed the martial music, always had, especially the fife, drums and trumpet. His favorite band was that of the Eleventh Corps of General Oliver O. Howard. "Schurz's men are the best drilled," he said. Suddenly, he added, "Hooker is too confident. I even think he thwarted Burnside at Fredericksburg." He had written this to Hooker. And Hooker said, "He wrote like a father to a son, and if the letter was hard on me, I will say I love the man that wrote it." That was the way and warm personality of my husband. Any man that did not see this was like Little Mac, too puffed up to see beyond the mess puffed up to the top of his head.

My husband always was keenly aware of all of the battles, keeping track of them on maps with markers. Now Hooker decided to attack Lee from the direction of Chancellorsville, west of Fredericksburg, dividing his army into two wings. Lee divided his own army and sent Stonewall Jackson to strike Hooker's detached right under General Oliver O. Howard. He succeeded brilliantly, rolling up Howard on an attack from front, side and rear. Howard's men were caught, with arms stacked, cooking supper. Lee kept Hooker too busy to send help to Howard. The battle of Chancellorsville raged from May 1 to 5, and on the second, Jackson by accident, was shot by his own men. By May 6, Lee had won the battle, an indecisive one, for our army was still formidable, and he would have to engage it again. Without Stonewall, who died on May 10.

My husband and I heard we had lost the battle on May 6, and he held the telegram behind him in clasped hands, and never had I seen him so broken since Willie's death. "My God! My God!" he said. "Will this slaughter ever, *ever* end?"

Every battle saw him haunting the war office, and every loss sent him into deeper despair. I think he saw in the deaths of *all* of the young men, North, South, as if they were the deaths of our own two sons again - all those dear boys - fife, bugle and drum sounding - flags flying - marching to an early grave for them and undying grief for their parents.

Now Lee had to decide if he should send troops west to relieve Pemberton and Bragg to save Vicksburg from Grant's tightening vise.

Aside from the rebels, personal attacks on Grant began. Men flooded my husband's office with them. True, he *was* winning the battles of the West, but he was a *drunkard*. "He is?" my husband asked.

"Sir - he *is*." This was from a doctor of divinity from New York, heading a whole *divine* delegation.

My husband looked at them all, and then he looked at the good doctor of divinity. "Can you tell me where he gets his liquor?"

"Sir?"

"Doctor, could you tell me where he gets his liquor?"

"No, Sir, I can not." He looked at his companions, and they couldn't either. "Why, Sir, do you want to know that - if I may be so bold to inquire."

"I would direct my chief quartermaster of the army to lay in a stock of it and give it to all of my other generals."

"*Sir?*"

"Grant *wins* battles - they *lose* them," my husband said.

When Grant defeated Pemberton at Vicksburg, on July 4, and paroled his army, delegations swarmed all over my husband again. My husband had his feet on his desk, or a chair - I heard both — but he listened to them and said soberly, "Gentlemen, have you ever heard of Syke's dog?"

The men looked puzzled.

"Syke's *yellow* dog?"

The question was not made clearer. "Well, I will tell you of Syke's yellow dog. He was an extraordinarily *mean* dog. He was unpopular with the little boys around as he kept taking greater and greater chunks out of them. Even Sykes could see that his dog was getting unpopular; the prejudice growing up against his dog threatened to wreck his own popularity. The boys finally fixed up a cartridge, with a long fuse, in a piece of meat and they dropped the meat in front of Syke's door, and perched themselves on a fence a good distance off, with the end of the fuse in their hands. Then they whistled at the dog, and he came out to eat at them. He saw the meat and went at it instead, bolting it down cartridge and all. The boys touched off the fuse with a cigar and there was a noise from the dog like a small clap of thunder. Sykes came bounding out of the house, and yelled, 'What's up? Anything busted?' He looked up and saw the air filled with falling pieces of yellow dog. He caught the biggest piece he could find and turning it all around, looking at it all over, he said, 'Well, I guess he'll never be much account again - *as a dog!* ' "

My husband stretched and said, "Gentlemen, I guess Pemberton's forces will never be much account again - *as an army!*"

On May 16 of 1863 there was a meeting in Albany of support for the Union cause but of censure for my husband's policy of military arrests and detention without benefit of a trial. On June 12, my husband wrote to Erastus Corning, and others, about this. He wrote that he was not using unconstitutional means in suppressing the rebellion, now a civil war, which was an effort to destroy the Union, the Constitution, the law, under cover of liberty of speech, press and Habeas Corpus to help the rebel cause. Civil courts are unfit to handle a rebellion and the Constitution states that in the case of an invasion or a rebellion, applying to the present case, that civil crime and rebellion are not the same, that a small percentage of criminals is not the same as an extensive uprising against the government. It was all about public safety now in suppressing a civil war with temporary measures due to the crisis that will not be permanent. "The Constitution itself makes the distinction; and I cannot be persuaded that the government can constitutionally take no strong measure in time of a rebellion, because it can be shown that the same could not be lawfully taken in time of peace, than I can be persuaded that a particular drug is not good medicine for a sick man because it can be shown to not be good for a well one." He also wrote that while a limb (of Habeas Corpus) could be sacrificed to save the body, the body cannot be sacrificed to save the limb.

In June Lee had moved north to engage the Army of the Potomac with his three great corps under James Longstreet, Richard Ewell and Ambrose Powell Hill. The prize could be victory and the recognition of the Confederacy by Britain and France. The Army of the Potomac, *finally* under George Meade, went north, too, to protect Washington, and to engage Lee and destroy his army.

It was not a matter really of our "swapping queens," Richmond for Washington. It was a matter of the *Army of the Potomac* destroying the *Army of North Virginia.*

In June I took Taddie on a short trip to Philadelphia. We were worried sick about his frail health, and wanted him where the air was cool and clean. My husband and I communicated *every day* by wire. We had to know, all of the time we were parted, how the other one was. He was well. My husband had seen to new tires on the carriage wheels. Perhaps he would be taking a ride in the carriage soon. He didn't.

We moved to the Soldier's Home. I think it was the *hottest* June I had ever seen. It was the *hottest summer* I had ever seen. *In the shade* it was over one hundred degrees - forever - and, of course, Washington *stank* and crawled with flies and mosquitoes to see which would be king killer of the city. News came there was a great battle between Lee and Meade at a little farm town in Pennsylvania called Gettysburg. The first word was bad - on the first of July our men had been driven from the town on to some hill. The two armies were still gathering more men. My husband stayed with the telegraph wires. News *had* to come that we had taken Lee and his army.

On July 2, I had to go to the White House. Someone had planned to kill or injure my husband by dismantling the Presidential carriage. They took the screws from the driver's seat. I was the only passenger, and as the carriage moved briskly toward the White House I was praying that this battle would prove decisive enough to end the rebellion. Suddenly, there was a wild lurching of the carriage. The driver was thrown from it and the horses went careening down the road in terror. I screamed and tried to hold on to something, but was thrown violently outside and hit my head on a sharp rock. I remember thinking, oh, *not my head!* I had so much pain from my head already. Blood was pouring over my bodice, and I do not remember being carried to the hospital where my deep wound was dressed. Then I remember being taken to the Soldier's Home. My husband and Mrs. Pomroy were with me. "It is all right, Molly," my husband said. "This is not a serious wound."

But it was. The wound became infected, and for three weeks Mrs. Pomroy attended me night and day, and for three weeks I slipped in and out of consciousness. "Father?" I asked one morning.

"I am right here, Molly."

"Gettysburg - did we win?"

"Yes. More - or less. The more is we won, and the less is that Meade let Lee get away."

"What? *How?*"

"Lee retreated without pursuit. Even the flood of the river detained him, and Meade had twenty thousand veteran troops with him, and more in supporting distance, as well as those who fought with him at Gettysburg - and Lee could not have received any more men - not a single recruit - and Meade stood still while the flood ran down and Lee built bridges and moved back into Virginia *at his leisure.* I wrote all of this to Meade on the fourteenth, but did not send the letter."

"This is terrible!"

My husband sighed. "I told Hay that Meade has the same dreadful idea of McClellan, who said, after he *failed* to take Lee at Antietam - well, I *saved* Maryland! And so Meade says he *saved* Pennsylvania - when will our generals learn? *The whole country* is our soil!"

I worked to hide my pain. I saw Taddie looking at me with his father's anxiety filled eyes. "Where is Robert?" I asked.

"Ignoring my telegrams for him to come here."

Robert never came, nor replied.

"You must get yourself and Taddie out of this heat," my husband said. When I could, I did.

When Vicksburg fell to Grant, my husband wrote, "The Father of Waters again goes unvexed to the sea."

On the fifteenth my husband wrote a proclamation of thanksgiving, for all of us to go to the church of our choice on August 6 and pray that the needless and cruel rebellion cease - "to guide the counsels of the government with wisdom adequate to so great a national emergency, and to visit with tender care and consolation throughout the length and breadth of our land all those who . . . have been brought to suffer in mind, body or estate, and finally to lead the whole nation, through the paths of repentance and submission to the Divine Will, back to the enjoyment of Union and fraternal peace."

Robert joined Taddie and me in the White Mountains, and on Mount Washington my spirits improved. Our side was doing better. My head wound was healing, and beauty of the mountains was a soothing balm to my body and my spirit. I was *always* be sustained by being in the mountains. "I want your father here," I told my sons. Whenever something was lovely, I always yearned to share it with him.

August in Washington continued the heat wave - one hundred and four in the shade. We were gone from stink fly mosquito town for two months, and my husband and I wired back and forth, and sent letters back and forth. We saved our letters, and, as I said, Robert burned them all up. Was he ashamed that we revealed our love so frankly? That we were parents - *and* lovers? Now he was moping about a girl he liked - loved? - who had just married someone else. In September we were in New York at a hotel on Fifth Avenue, and there a telegram reached us from my husband. And then came another on September 22:

"Did you receive my dispatch of yesterday? Mrs. Cuthbert (seamstress and later chief housekeeper of the White House) did not correctly understand me. I directed her to tell you to use your own pleasure whether to stay or come; and I did not say it is sickly and that you should in no account come. So far as I see or know, it was never healthier and I really wish to see you. Answer this on receipt."

I wired back that I wanted a railroad car ready for me at the "earliest possible moment. I have a bad cold and am anxious to return home as you may suppose. Taddie is well."

While the armies on the East were quiet, they were not in the West. The Union army there under the command of William Rosecrans lost the Battle of Chickamauga, September 19-20, to Braxton Bragg. It was a slaughterhouse, comparable to Antietam and Gettysburg. We had 1, 600 killed and they had 2, 300 killed. My husband wired me a list of the dead officers, and included was the name of my brother in law - Little Sister's husband, Ben Hardin.

When I returned to him, my husband and I shared that grief together -Little Sister Emilie was the daughter we never had had. "Father," I sobbed. "Do we live but to march hopelessly on to dusty death? Is that where all of our yesterdays and all of our tomorrows have already gone?"

"Molly, did you not see Eddy - and Willie - *in the light?*"

"But, father, we are not with them."

"Maybe we all are in the same light all the time and they are showing us this."

"I can never reconcile to our loss," I said. "Father, I could never reconcile to death for Taddie, for Robert - for you! I could not!" I was weeping as if it had already happened and I was bearing it not.

"Molly, when our mortal tasks and lessons are done, think of us here as in a dark, confined cocoon, our mortal blindness - and when the time is right we reach the light - we emerge to a sun and find that was sustaining us

242

all of the time."

"No more deaths!" I wept.

He got that half dreamy and half melancholy look I knew so well, and he looked away into the years and years ahead. "A faded photo - a dried up flower of remembrance pressed and long forgotten in an old family Bible," he said softly. "Who put that flower there? Why? Then the flower gone to dust, as if it had never lived to bloom at all - and look at the eyes in that old photo - yours, Molly, - mine - did they look on that day with joy-sorrow? Who is to say? The dead rest in no grave, Molly. We will rest in no grave. We will go toward the light of some magical shore, and we spread our wings - like a butterfly from a cocoon- to the sky, and leave behind in the spent cocoon death, and all the grief of those we thought lost to it."

"Father, do not do what Ben did to Emilie - *die before I do!* Promise me!" I went to him and I held him, clung to him, as if that touch could keep my wish true.

He stroked the hair back from my tear streaked face, and he looked so old, so very, very old, as if he had lived long enough in this world to absorb all of its pain. "Molly, dearest Molly. You cannot make that promise to me, and I cannot make it to you."

"Make it anyway."

"What I *am* - will never leave you."

"Always stand between me and the lightning."

He held me against his strong beating heart. "Maybe, if I cannot, Molly, you will just meet and absorb the lightning."

"How?"

"As no more than *light*."

He never explained that, and I did not ask him to.

In September of 1863, Professor Mahan of West Point wrote that my husband was a man of the people, not of a class, and his words reached the popular heart. Jefferson Davis, on the other hand, was respected but not loved. None of his generals loved him. "Not one. Not one. ... and more than one of these it is said, hate him bitterly."

Kate Chase married New Jersey Governor William Sprague who was very wealthy, and I am sure she and her father expected her bridegroom to replace my husband when the election of 1864 rolled around. Her marriage was magnificent - she wore a tiara of pearls and diamonds, white velvet for her gown, a real point lace veil, and gifts to bride and groom were over $100,000, I was told, before they both whirled off in the bridal barouche. My husband attended and stayed for about an hour and a half. I did not attend, saying I had a cold, which I still had, and sent Kate a gift of a small exquisite fan to cool down her Presidential ambitions.

By November, Taddie was very ill again. There was going to be a dedication of a cemetery where the battle of Gettysburg had been fought. It would take place on Cemetery Hill, where our boys had stood firm on July 2 and 3, and how well my husband knew that whole battlefield! The ceremony was planned around the keynote speaker, Dr. Edward Everett, who had taught Greek at Harvard and had been its president. He was sixty- nine, had been in every other important office, and was considered the greatest speech-writer and orator in the country. He was given *six weeks* notice. Then, as an afterthought, my husband was invited to also speak, and in his *six-day* notice, he was told he was *not* the keynote speaker, so his speech *must be brief,* and <u>note,</u> this was to be a *solemn* occasion! No jokes from the wild untamed west, you see.

Tad Stevens was going around saying my husband was a "dead card" politically, and when he went to Gettysburg, " it was a case of the dead going to eulogize the dead." My husband heard and repeated this to his cabinet, and I am sure that Mr. Chase agreed. On Sunday, November 8, my husband went to get his photo taken by Alexander Gardner, and Noah Brooks walked along. "I have Everett's speech," my husband said.

"It looks like a long one if it fills up that envelope."

"It does. I'll read it while at Gardner's."

"Have you written yours?"

"I have sketched out some ideas. My speech is going to be short, short, *short.*"

Everett's speech is seen on the table by him in the two Gardner photos, but he never got a chance to read it then. When he was walking with Lamon later he took his own speech out of his hat and read it to him. "I just don't have the time to write a proper speech. And this one does not satisfy me very much."

I didn't get to hear it. Taddie was so ill I could think of nothing else. I was in a horror that he would die. The doctors did not know what was making him ill. "Papa-day?" asked Taddie. "Do you have to leave?"

"Yes, son. I must. I will be gone only a little while."

"Is it *very* important for the cause?"

"Yes. I want to be there to show my respect for the cause."

"Then, Papa-day, you must go and do that."

He boarded the train to Gettysburg on November 18. It was a four car special carrying red white and blue bunting. The train reached Gettysburg at sunset, and my husband was driven to the residence of Judge David Wills.

I believe Dr Everett stayed there that night, too. The town was mobbed; over 3,400 came to see the ceremony, and people were sleeping on the floors of hotels or in private homes. The weather that night was unexpectedly warm, and the moon full. Military bands were playing and serenaders went to the Wills' house to hear my husband make a speech. He appeared before them, a tall shadow against the lights of the house. "In my position it is sometimes important that I should not say foolish things," he said.

"If you can help it!" a man shouted to him.

The crowd laughed. "Yes. Yes," my husband said. "It very often happens that the only way to help it is to say nothing at all. I have the best excuse in the world for not making a speech. I have not written one. Being that is my present condition this evening, I must beg of you to excuse me from addressing you further."

The crowd did not like this too much and went off with the bands to rouse up speeches from someone. Seward came out and mumbled a lot of words, and so did five other men, and I do not know whom they were.

On November 19 the weather had turned very cold. The dedication was scheduled to begin at ten and that is the hour my husband came out of the Wills' house and mounted a spirited chestnut, the largest horse they could find for him. He wore his best black suit, his best silk hat, and *he even allowed his hands into white kid gloves.* Crowds mobbed him and the rider procession to Cemetery Hill did not begin until an hour later. A lieutenant Cocrane rode behind my husband and his horse wanted to bite off the tail of my husband's horse, and the two horses fussed and reared about it all the way to the ceremony. Crowds standing along the way cheered, and my husband gravely bowed right, left, and Seward's pants rode up on the stirrups and revealed his home made gray socks.

Cannon fired as they rode down Baltimore Street to the famed Emmetsburg Road, then to Taneytown Road, and on to the cemetery. In the fifteen minute ride I can imagine the thoughts going through my husband's head - how the now peaceful ground - the stubbled gold of wheat fields - the orchards with blossoms and leaves fled before autumn winds - how they had been rent with cannon and bullet fire, and the agony, terror, courage, as the men in butternut gray fought the men in Yankee blue. All of that blood so silently seeping into the earth - he must have seen vividly in his mind. He probably heard the moans of the wounded, too, and he probably felt the suffering all of those dying boys he had come to commemorate. The cannon firing along his way, echoing a more vivid picture of sound and fire on the second and third of this last July, the wind touching his face and saying to him, *this ground has been already hallowed by their blood and their pain.*

He had heard from Stanton that Grant was engaging at Chattanooga, that Meade was threatened at Knoxville, and my telegram said, "The Dr. has just left. We hope dear Taddie is slightly better. Will send you a telegraph in the morning."

At the ceremony platform, the speaker of the day had not arrived. Bands played until noon, awaiting him. When he did arrive, after a prayer offered by Reverend of the House, Thomas Stocktown, to thousands of bowed and uncovered heads, Benjamin French introduced the Honorable Dr. Edward Everett. He spoke, some said, a little over two hours, and some said, for a little less than two hours, his voice strong and clear, his white hair disturbed by the breeze, his head flung back at his most dramatic points. He concluded to great clapping and cheering. Then the Baltimore Glee club sang a song written by Mr. French - really a prayer - and at its conclusion, Ward Hill Lamon introduced my husband.

When he spoke, they said his face was sober - *hauntingly* sad. They said his voice *clearly* carried to the thousands before him. He held two sheets of paper and "occasionally" glanced at them. His words were slow and deliberate, and when he finished, the clapping was very, *very* sparse. A photographer had readied to take his photo as he gave the speech, but the speech was over before the photographer could even get his head under the hood for an exposure. I think few really knew he had completed his speech when he did. I can see those standing near him, perhaps a restless baby crying, so the mother did not hear him, and when the baby was stilled, there was no longer a speech to be heard. There was *no* enthusiasm shown for it, and my husband said to Lamon, "Well that fell flat. My speech just did not scour." *Scour* is an old farm expression meaning when the mud sticks to the mold-board of a plow it cannot do its job and cannot *scour*. "I wish I had taken more time - had taken greater care with this speech," my husband said gloomily to Lamon. "Well, I wasn't down on the program for an address, anyway."

The media went into a frenzy - *our* media. *The Patriot and Union* of *Harrisburg*: "We pass over the silly remarks of the President; for the credit of the nation we are willing that the veil of oblivion shall be dropped over them and they shall no more be repeated or thought of." The *Chicago Times* foamed at the mouth at my husband's address - *our* town - *our* state - not the *Richmond Times* - but the *Chicago Times*. My husband "did most foully traduce the motives of the men who were slain at Gettysburg." In his saying we would lose our democracy unless we had *a new birth of freedom,* the paper vehemently disagreed - "They gave their lives to maintain the old government, and the only

Constitution and Union." My husband had insulted the dead with "ignorant rudeness" in his *perversion* of history, misstated the cause for which they died, insulted the memory of the dead and used such bad taste that - "The cheek of every American must tingle with shame as he reads that silly, flat, dish-watery utterance of the man who has to be pointed out to intelligent foreigners as the President of the United States." He was like a foreign despot because he had a bodyguard of soldiers - to a funeral sermon he had taken "boorishness and vulgarity" and - was he "less refined than a savage?" Obviously, he was. The rebel *Richmond Examiner,* which had called my husband an arch fiend from hell, contented itself this time to say that at Gettysburg he had "acted the clown." The *Chicago Times* printed all of that diatribe, too, to go along with its own; the *London Times* saw the whole ceremony made "ludicrous" by the "sallies" of the American President - "Anything more dull or commonplace it would not be easy to produce."

Here are the words - the so-called *boorish, vulgar, ludicrous, silly, flat, ignorant, shameful*, insulting to the soldiers of Gettysburg - proof of author savagery - words - the make you *tingle with shame* words - in short - the words of immortal grandeur my husband thought just did not *scour*.

"Four score and seven years ago our fathers brought forth upon this continent, a new nation, conceived in Liberty, and dedicated to the proposition that all men are created equal.

Now we are engaged in a great civil war, testing whether that nation, or any nation so conceived and so dedicated, can long endure. We are met on a great battlefield of that war. We have come to dedicate a portion of that field as a final resting place for those who here gave their lives that that nation might live. It is altogether fitting and proper that we should do this.

But, in a larger sense, we cannot dedicate - we cannot consecrate - we cannot hallow - this ground. The brave men, living and dead, who struggled here, have consecrated it, far above our poor power to add or detract. The world will little note, nor long remember what we say here, but it can never forget what they did here. It is for us the living rather, to be dedicated here to the unfinished work which they who fought here have thus far so nobly advanced. It is rather for us to be here dedicated to the great task remaining before us - that from these honored dead we take increased devotion to that cause for which they gave the last full measure of devotion - that we here highly resolve that these dead shall not have died in vain - that this nation, under God, shall have a new birth of freedom - and that government of the people, by the people, for the people, shall not perish from the earth."

Dr. Everett wrote to my husband the next day, "I should be glad if I could flatter myself that I came as near to the central idea of the occasion in two hours as you did in two minutes." My husband replied on November 20, saying, "I am pleased to know, that in your judgment, the little I did say was not entirely a failure."

A reporter for the *Springfield Republican* wrote of my husband's Gettysburg address, "Turn back and read it over, it will repay study as a model speech. . . . His little speech is a perfect gem; deep in feeling, compact in thought and expression, and tasteful and elegant in every word and comma. Then it has the merit of unexpectedness in its verbal perfection and beauty."

"*Back at Gettysburg the blue haze of the Cumberland Mountains had dimmed till it was a blur in nocturne. The moon was up and fell with a bland golden benevolence on the new made graves of soldiers . . . In many a cottage over the land, a tall old clock in a quiet corner told time in a tick-tock of deliberation. Whether the orchard branches hung with pink-spray blossoms or icicles of sleet* - Do you know these magnificent lines? A poet wrote them about my husband in one of his six volumes on my husband's· life - And a little boy grew up and learned to read the hours and the minutes of the clock, and went away to die at the Battle of Gettysburg. Among the unidentified he slept, and then came the consolation of a man *of solemn authority* who stood at those graves and said, "*We cannot consecrate - we cannot hallow this ground -*"

The ground is hallowed now, and many more snows fell and many more springs came, and more of the usual talk of *seed time, harvest, rain or drought*, but the ground was also consecrated, as that great man of *solemn authority* stood on it and said what was in the purity of his being.

If his words were hardly understood then; if the restless breeze carried them away among the new graves and the old graves of Cemetery Hill; if the little baby cried and the new mother could not hear these words at all, they went from his heart into the heart and the soul of America, and I know, forever, they will there remain.

Chapter Twenty-one

My husband's train reached Washington at midnight. During the trip he was exhausted and lay down on one of the side seats of the train, holding a wet towel over his forehead. "It is that tired spot I cannot reach," he said. His doctor found that he had a mild case of smallpox, Varioloid, and my husband brightened, saying, "Show in the office seekers - At last I have something I can give to *everybody*."

From November 23-25 there were the battles of Lookout Mountain and Missionary Ridge. William Rosecrans, after his defeat at Chattanooga, seemed to just sit and mope there until his army died of hunger, I guess. Thankfully, he was replaced by George Thomas, and Grant was elevated as commander of our Western army. We were besieged at Chattanooga, and the rebels, under Braxton Bragg, had the main heights of Lookout Mountain and Missionary Ridge. We had to clear the Tennessee River for supplies, which Grant did at Brown's Ferry, and got his army "cracker line" open. William T. Sherman worked eastward from Memphis, repairing railroads at top speed, and as the Army of the Potomac was not engaged with Lee, Hooker was sent west to aid in the Chattanooga campaign against Bragg. Luckily for us, Bragg went stupid. While we were *concentrating* our forces, he sent Longstreet *away*, with 15,000 men, to attack Burnside at Knoxville! I guess he was going to regain eastern Tennessee while he was losing its west? Grant now had 60,000 troops to Braxton's 40,000. Sherman attacked the rebels at the north end of Missionary Ridge, while Hooker struck at them on Lookout Mountain and took it in a *battle above the clouds*, as it is said. Bragg's main army on Missionary Ridge stubbornly held on, and by 3:30 on November 25, had not fallen. Two of Thomas's divisions were ordered to take the rifle pits at the *foot* of the ridge. Instead, to the astonishment of their generals, they went up the mountain and took *the whole thing*. One of the generals, Granger, who must have been a real fool, was so incensed that his orders were not followed, he rode among his men saying, "I am going to have you all court-martialed! You were ordered to take the works at the foot of the hill, and you have taken those on top - you have disobeyed orders, all of you!" My husband *loved* that story of general idiocy.

Bragg's army fled, those that could, and Tennessee was generally in our hands.

When my husband was better, I went to New York in December to appear at public functions for the cause. I arrived on the fourth with a vicious headache and without Taddie. My husband sent me a telegram that day, "All going well," and the fifth and sixth, he wired, "All doing well," but on the seventh I heard nothing! Was he ill again - Taddie ill again? I sent a wire to my husband, "Do let me know immediately how Taddie and yourself are. I will be home by Tuesday without fail; sooner if needed." I sent another wire to Edward McManus, of the White House staff, right after the first one to my husband. He was to let me know *immediately* and *exactly* how Taddie and my husband were. My husband wired back on the seventh, "All doing well. Tad confidently expects you tonight. When will you come?" I wired back, "Will leave positively at 8 a.m. Tuesday morning. Have carriage waiting at depot in Washington at 6 p.m. Did Tad receive his book. Please answer."

Taddie had received it with a card enclosed "from his loving mother." My husband wired, "Tad has received his book. The carriage will be ready at 6 p.m. tomorrow." *Three* telegrams back and forth between us on the seventh, while my husband was so busy - increasing the size of that tired spot nothing could reach.

It was so good, *so safe,* to be home, to hug my Taddie, and be held by my husband. He told me about little sister. She had attended Ben's funeral at Atlanta and was attempting to reach her mother's house in Lexington. She was stopped at Fortress Monroe, Virginia. An officer told her she could not enter Union territory unless she took the Oath of Allegiance. Of course, she would not do this, and the officer wired his problem to my husband. "Send her to me," my husband wired back.

And so, we saw Little Sister. She was pregnant with her third child, and had brought along her eldest, Katherine. (Who was to write a book about me in an attempt to correct that odious little man, but who listened?) What could we say to each other, my little sister and I? Her husband had just died in a war against the fact that my husband had been elected President. And her husband was a rebel to me, for the cause of my husband was as much a part of my own heart as his. Emilie was pale and she looked as drained and as tired as did my husband. "Little Sister," I said, and hugged her, tears streaming down my face. My husband then hugged her, and said nothing - his own tears said it all.

Emilie and I dined alone. "Molly," she said. "I am impoverished. I have to take my children and go home to mother. I have no other recourse."

"You could stay with me," I said gently.

"Here? At the *White House?*" she shuddered. "No. *Never.*"

And that was all of politics we discussed.

We both wore black. We both were in deep grief, and I wanted to assuage hers - mine. "Dearest Emilie, I have words that can comfort. Both of us. If we will *heed* them."

She put down her teacup and looked away. Her tears went unchecked. "I have given up my husband to die, Molly."

"And I - two sons."

We were silent, and we listened to the crackling of the fire in the grate, and I looked into the fire for those magic kingdoms of disappearing fire castles. "Emilie," I said. "Ben is not dead."

"What? Molly, what are you telling me?"

"Only his *body* is dead - that little frail outer shell -"

"Molly - *what* are you saying?"

"You know - *we* live beyond our bodies."

"My husband is *dead.*"

"No. Not his *real* self - as you sit here, with tears on your face, I think he is right here to comfort and to help you -"

"Molly! Aren't I suffering enough?"

"There is a thin veil of *our* blindness that *seems* to say they are gone. But," and I clasped her shaking hands, "they are *not.* Love is what makes eternity - love binds the beloved to us - *forever!*"

"Oh, Molly - dear sister -"

"Hush! *Listen* to me! Just last night I awoke from my sleep and there were Willie and Eddy at the foot of my bed! They are so happy - and they wanted me to see it! They have allowed me to see them many, *many* times!"

Emilie looked at me in horror.

"Little Sister, don't look at me like that. I am *not* mad."

But - later, in a whisper, I heard her tell my husband I was. "If anything happened to Robert - to Taddie - to you - she would die. You must not allow Robert into the army! Molly is very *very* ill!"

Meaning, mostly in the head.

Emilie kept a diary of what it was like in those days she spent with my husband and me in the White House. "Allusion to the present is like tearing open a fresh and bleeding wound, and the pain is too great for self control," she wrote. "The frightful war comes between us like a barrier of granite, closing our lips, but not our hearts, for though our tongues are tied, we weep over our dead together and express through clasped hands the sympathy we feel for each other in our mutual grief." She noted how my husband, without words, tried to comfort her, that he was the most tender and loving of husbands, and how our eyes followed each other with "*adoration.*"

She also recorded that that November was very cold, the fires comfortable, and that "Sister has always a cheerful word and a smile for her husband who seems thin and careworn, seeing her sorrowful would add to his care."

She was put in our beautiful guest room with the velvet purple drapes and golden sash, the room where my dearest Willie died, and the room I swore I would not enter again. But I did, and Emilie recorded it. I knocked on her door after we all had gone to bed. I told her again that after Willie's death I had fallen so deep into despair, there was no ray of light anywhere. If I had not felt the necessity to cheer my husband, whose grief was as great as my own, I would never have smiled again. But Willie had broken through the veil of death, or my blindness, he *had*, and he had brought Eddy - and tonight, they were with their Uncle Alec! He told me they love their Uncle Alec, and are with him most of the time. "Sister's eye were wide and shining and I had a feeling of awe as if I were in the presence of the supernatural," recorded Emilie.

I did not convince Emilie that this was *natural,* that the loved and the lost long to comfort us in our sorrow at their departure. She said, "Mary - Mary! This is unnatural and abnormal!"

I hugged her, and we both wept together, and I know Ben was with her, but she would never know it. I went back to my sleeping husband and I gave thanks with every fiber of my being that I could lie down beside him and hear his quiet breathing.

Emilie had lost her husband, I two sons, both of us, three beloved brothers. "Let's take the carriage and ride out to the county!" I said one day. And we did. I should have been cautious of carriage rides, since my last one, but I was not. We had a terrible accident. A precious little boy jumped off a streetcar right into our path, and our carriage could not stop. It broke his leg and I jumped from the carriage and went to him. "My poor baby! Where does he live? I will take him to his mother!" I said. A doctor took charge and did that. Emily and I followed. "I will do everything I can do to help," I said to the distraught mother. I looked down at the suffering little angel and touched his face. "You will have more toys tomorrow than you ever dreamed of! And fruits - and flowers!"

"Mary mothers all children," Emily recorded, saying,"He is a brave little fellow, his eyes glisten when he sees us coming and he forgets he has a broken leg in his pleasure over his toys."

Of course I kept my word, and visited him again just to see the joy the gifts had brought to him. If Willie and Taddie still had their army, this little boy would have been another major officer in it.

Emilie read of the vicious attacks on me in our papers. "These are worse than ours!" she said in amazement. "And from your own party!"

"I am the scape goat for both North and South," I said. "Emilie, tell me you love me! You are like a daughter to us; stay with us, please!"

She did stay with us - for a while. Taddie liked his little cousin Kate. He told her of all his busy valiant military service and one night, in front of the fire, he brought out family pictures to share. "This is the President!" he said proudly. "This is Papa-day, the President of the United States of America!"

Kate looked shocked. "The President is *Jeff Davis!*"

Taddie was furious. "The President is *Papa-day!*"

"The President is *Jeff Davis!*" shouted Kate.

Taddie went for his father and told him his problem. My husband joined us before the fire and put each child on a knee. "Tad," he said, "I am your father, and I am Miss Kate's uncle, and there can be *no* argument about that."

Robert argued to go into the army. He kept at it, and at it, and at it. "Father," I said. "You must *not* let Robert go into the military."

"Molly, he wants to."

"You must not allow it!"

"Mother - other mothers have to let their sons go."

"I will not lose all of mine!" I wept.

"It will kill Molly, if he goes," said Emilie. "It will just kill her."

Mrs. Keckley said the same. "Sir, you will be signing her death warrant."

My husband looked so ashen, so bone tired. But I knew his concern was for me, and at least, for a while longer, Robert was safe.

The next day when my husband was ill again from varioloid and lying down in his office, Senator Ira Harris, of New York, our friend, I thought, and General Sickles called. I received them, and by my side was Little Sister. I could feel disapproval because my sister, a widow of a Confederate officer, was standing by the First Lady of the White House. "Why isn't Robert in the army?" asked the Senator. "He is old enough and strong enough to serve his country. He should have gone to the front some time ago."

I felt the color drain from my face, but I kept my voice soft, as I usually did. "Robert is making his preparations now to enter the army, Senator Harris; he is not a shirker as you seem to imply, for he has been anxious to go for a long time. If fault there be, it is mine; I have insisted that he should stay in college a little longer as I think an educated man can serve his country with more intelligent purpose than an ignoramus."

Senator Harris was raging. "I have only one son," he said, "and he is fighting for his country." He turned to Emilie, his face redder, and he made a sarcastic bow to her, "Madame, if I had twenty sons, they should *all* be fighting the rebels."

Emilie straightened. "And Sir, if I had twenty sons, they *all* should be opposing yours!"

Sickles went running upstairs to tattle this to my husband. Here were *two* female rebels under the public roof, one a first lady, so she could not be kicked out, but surely Emilie could. When he heard what we had said, my husband smiled and Sickles lost it and pounded on the table. "You should *not* have that rebel in your house!"

My husband asserted that "strange dignity" noted so many times. "Excuse me, General Sickles, my wife and I are in the habit of choosing our own guests. We do not need from our friends either advice or assistance in the matter. Besides, that little 'rebel' came because I ordered her to come; it was not of her own volition."

On December 14 Emilie was given a pass by my husband to return home. I gave dear little Kate a fancy china inkwell of mine she so admired, and I tried again to bring solace to Little Sister. "They came to me again, last night," I said. "And they still had with them our dear brother Alec - you cannot imagine the comfort this brings to me-"

"Oh, Molly! Molly!" wept Emilie. She looked up at my haggard husband. "Will this dreadful, dreadful war ever end?"

"Little Sister," he said. "I tried to have Ben come with me. I hope you do not feel any bitterness or that I am in any way to blame for all of this sorrow." She went into his arms and they both wept. "I feel as though I shall never be glad any more," he said.

As 1863 closed, we had taken rebel ships worth thirteen million dollars; we had seventy five iron clad ships and our entire naval force had doubled, the post office was self sustaining, the new Homestead Law had brought almost one and a half million acres under settlement. "The Indian tribes must be protected," said my husband.

"How?" I asked.

"The Federal government must make and *keep* treaties with them. There is room for the settlers without taking from the tribes."

My husband proclaimed as a day of Thanksgiving the last Thursday in November.

Sherman marched on Knoxville and relieved Longstreet's siege of Burnside there. Now Sherman could go on to Atlanta and cut the Confederacy in two again - and my husband declared the Emancipation Proclamation would never be revoked, to abandon the negroes would be, he wrote, "a cruel and astounding breach of faith." In the Confederate Congress Representative Foote of Tennessee said of my husband that he was the "imbecile and unprincipled usurper who now sits enthroned upon the ruins of Constitutional liberty in Washington City . . . a miserable and contemptible despot." The *Richmond Examiner* called him a "Yankee Monster of inhumanity and falsehood." Not even an *arch-fiend from hell* this time.

But something dear to me was being written and was soon to be published in Charles Eliot Norton's *North American Review*. The author was James Russell Lowell, poet and Harvard Professor, following Longfellow, in the chair of modern languages and *belles-lettres*. Here are excerpts:

"Never did a President enter upon office with less means at his command, outside of his own strength of heart and steadiness of understanding, for conspiring confidence in the people, and so winning it for himself . . . chosen by a party with whose more extreme opinions he was not in sympathy . . . he was to carry on a truly colossal war. . . disengage the country from diplomatic entanglements . . . and to win. . . in the confidence of the people, the means of his safety and their own . . . perhaps none of our Presidents since Washington has stood so firm in the confidence of the people . . . his kingship as conspicuous by its workday homespun. Never a ruler so absolute as he, nor so little conscious of it, for he was the incarnate common sense of the people." With all of his sweet sadness, the tenderness of his nature that touched those who saw him with its own pathos, "there was no trace of sentimentalism in his speech or action." His one rule of conduct was "to let himself be guided by events, when they were sure to bring him out where he wished to go . . . No higher compliment was ever paid to a nation than the simple confidence, the fireside plainness" to which he addressed the American people. "This was, indeed, a true democrat, who grounded himself on the assumption that a democracy can think . . . To us, that simple confidence of his in the right-mindedness of his fellow-men is very touching, and its success is as strong an argument as we have ever seen in favor of the theory that men can govern themselves . . . Homely, dispassionate, showing all the rough-edged process of his thought as it goes along, yet arriving at his conclusion with an honest kind of every-day logic, he is so eminently our representative man, that, when he speaks, it seems as if the people were listening to their own thinking aloud."

I saved those lines. They were help in the pain of my grief for my sons, for my brothers, for all of the abuse and scorn born by the man I so loved.

And so there came another Christmas season with us at the White House. Again, as it had been done in the past, and as it would be done in the future, the yuletide sweets were baked, the yuletide logs cut for the fires, Christmas carols sung, and the snow fell softly and purely, as if it and the season, could mask the grief fallen over the suffering land.

Chapter Twenty-two

1864 began with our usual New Year's reception. It was mobbed, and I stood by my husband and shook hands, and more and more receptions followed. At every one, it snowed, or poured rain. 1864. This was the year my husband would stand for re-election, and I would do everything I could to see him win if I stood in reception lines until I dropped. He said, "Molly, do not expect me to be President much longer."

"Father, you have to be re-elected."

"Unless a military miracle occurs, I rather doubt it."

Taddie wanted a little theater of his own, for he had so enjoyed going to the theater with us, or just his father, if I had a migraine. He loved the National Theater, for its manager, Leonard Grover, had a son named Bobby, and he and Taddie became fast friends. Taddie got to know all of the carpenters who built the sets at the National, all of the actors who acted at the National, and on two occasions, had even joined them on stage, singing, marching, waving the flag, much to the utter delight of my husband.

For his own little theater Taddie had the props from the National, any costumes he desired, and for his own actors he had the Buck Eye soldiers guarding the White House, and there were plenty left over for his audience. Along with my husband and me, of course. His stage had at its center the bust of our dear Edward Ellsworth, for whom our dearest little Eddie had been named, and at his death, the object of a poem by Willie, and the stage had flowers just where needed, gas lights at the edge of the stage and a little picket fence separating the stage from the audience. Taddie *loved* his theater. It was his own magic kingdom where he was in total control, even more so than in his officer headquarters opposite the laundry room in the White House basement where he wrote out his numerous passes for the White House soldiers.

In February Francis Carpenter came for a six-month visit to paint a picture of my husband holding the Emancipation Proclamation, with his cabinet placed around him. Brady came to take pictures of the cabinet so Carpenter could paint them, and he needed a dark room for his chemical what-nots to get the pictures done. He used Taddie's theater for this, as it was good and dark, but he did *not ask Taddie if he could do this*. Taddie was enraged, and just locked his theater and all of the chemical whatnots up tight and would not give away the key to anyone, not Carpenter, not to anyone else on the White House staff who tried, and so they went to my husband who got the key and the photos were saved for the painting.

"How did Papa-day get the key?" I asked Taddie.

"He told me I was causing him trouble," Taddie said, his eyes welling with tears. "I would *never* cause Papa-day trouble!"

We were going to proclaim a Fast Day, and when Taddie heard about it, food began to disappear from the White House kitchen. Then the coachmen of the Presidential carriage began to smell something in it that was not at all pleasant to be around. Their noses led them to a box under a seat, and when they were fishing out its contents, Taddie appeared and said, "Give that up, I say! That is my Fast Day picnic!"

He knew *how* to prepare for the fast, but not exactly *how long* before to prepare for it. He came rushing to me. "Ma, this is my food for Fast Day! The coachmen tried to take it away!"

I cringed at his cache and tried not to gag. "Taddie, the meat is spoiled." In truth it was alive again with wiggling crawling things.

"Ma - it is better than nothing."

"Not really, Taddie," I said, and I did gag.

"I will *not* be put into starvation at Fast Day," he said stubbornly.

"Taddie, if you give up your - picnic, (gagging gain) I will see that on Fast Day, you do not starve."

"Your solemn word?"

"My solemn word."

"Shouldn't Papa-day put that into his Proclamation on Fast Day?"

"He is too busy to add it, Taddie. Just take my word." And he did.

On the night of February 10 the White House stables caught fire and the firemen saw a tall figure rushing to put the fire out. They recognized my husband and restrained him, fearing an assassination attempt. "Sir, you cannot save the horses," they said.

My husband sat down on the grass. "Willie's pony was in there," he wept.

When I had to tell Taddie, he could not be comforted. He cried more for Willie's pony than for his own. Then Julia Taft visited and when Taddie saw her his grief was inconsolable.

She never came to the White House again - Julia, Bud, Holly, all of their laughter gone with Willie, and laughter was so alien to us all now. "Life is so hard with Willie gone," he cried. "You and Papa-day must never leave me."

258

I held him and kissed his precious little face. "Not for a long, long, while," I promised.

My husband was eating less and less; I had some fricasseed chicken made, my style, with dumplings and gravy, and had it served in our private dining room with no servants around. My husband entered, smelled the delicious smells and beamed. "You would think Evil Eva was here!" he said, and he ate *three* helpings of food.

On March 10 my husband made Grant commander of all the Union Armies. He had arrived to meet my husband on the evening of the eighth, and when he was presented to me in the East Room by Seward, I never saw such a little scruffy unimposing little man, chewing on a cigar, pitching along forward - for *a kind of walk* - he just looked *scrubby*. "He will win for us," my husband said. "He does not *sit* on a victory to smother it. He will not defeat Lee to watch him walk away. He will hammer and hammer at him - until this dreadful war is done."

"Well, he certainly does not strut sitting down like Little Mac."

"I was never afraid of Little Mac," said my husband. "Of my generals - who would be dangerous? Little Mac is too vacillating to seize power; Grant is too sound to try it, Fremont too lazy - and I would say that Butler would be the dangerous one, but like Jim Jett's brother - the damndest scoundrel that ever lived, but in the infinite mercy of Providence, also the damndest fool!"

"Father, you swore."

"Molly, that is part of the joke. I did not swear."

"Then, what did you do?"

"I *quoted*."

Since the fall of Vicksburg and our victory at Gettysburg volunteers were building up our army. In the spring of 1864 our hope was for Grant to take Richmond and Lee's army defending it; Sherman was to engage Joseph Johnston defending northwest Georgia, and Phil Sheridan would take the Shenandoah Valley. Grant and the Army of the Potomac, under Meade and inactive since Gettysburg, crossed the Rapidan May 4, and before they were out of the wilderness Lee attacked. Grant had wanted the confrontation to be in the open plain, but on May 5 and 6, a fierce battle was fought between our boys and theirs in the wilderness thickets. It was ghastly, and we got the worst of it, 18,000 wounded, and of them, 2,000 dead. They had 10,000 lost, and I don't know their dead. Then Grant did not do what our other generals had done, and what Lee expected to be done. When we were licked, *or even if we had won*, our army retired, another commander was tried, and Lee would have time to gather up another offensive. But marching through corpses,

Grant launched another forward attack, moving by his own left flank, and in mostly hand-to-hand fighting, we lost over 26,000 in killed and wounded. "The little man is a butcher," I told my husband. My husband looked near death himself. He had great black rings under his eyes, his face ghastly in its lack of color. "Grant will have to go on," he said. "This war *has* to end, and it will end only with the defeat of Lee."

To Carpenter he said, "My God! My God! Over twenty thousand men killed and wounded in a few days fighting, and I cannot bear it! I cannot bear it!"

Of his Presidency my husband said, "If to be head of hell is as hard as what I have to undergo here, I could find it in my heart to pity Satan himself." Carpenter asked him if the North would win. My husband got that sad far away look in his eyes and said victory would come, "but I may never live to see it. I feel a presentment that I shall not outlast the rebellion. When it is over, my work will be done."

My husband was getting more and more gaunt, his face furrowed with lines of care, his deep set grey eyes "sunk to hollows of sadness" it was said. He bent with weariness and he said over and over, "I fear I will never be glad anymore." I worked so hard to be cheerful, to give him some joy within all of this despair.

The *worst* came when Grant, on June 3, attacked Lee in a strongly entrenched position, allowing enfilading fire against us. It was our greatest slaughter of the war. Our three corps flung at Lee's entrenchments lost 12,000 killed and wounded in *eight minutes* of fighting. A shudder of horror went through us, all of the North. "Father," I said. "You must eat - you must sleep - I don't think you will live through another term."

"Molly, I don't think that will be a worry for us at all. There will be no second term."

Our papers started calling Grant *blood and guts* - a *butcher,* and our losses from the Wilderness battles through Cold Harbor were equal to the size of Lee's *whole* army.

Lee's men were hungry. He had a starving army, and he could get no more recruits, or war equipment as we could. But he presented an impregnable barrier to Grant's march *on to Richmond.* Then, as he could not take Richmond from the north, in forty days of bloody fighting, Grant decided to take it from south of the James. There were no bridges or guides for him, but he got his men across the Chickahominy and the James from the 12th to the 16th of June. This involved brilliant engineering, and it took Lee completely by surprise, as none of our commanders had ever done that before. On June 17th the siege of Petersburg began, for Petersburg was the gateway to Richmond. If that idiot Butler had done what he was supposed to have done against Beauregard and not snoozed away at Bermuda Hundred, shut off from joining Grant, Petersburg might well have fallen before the arrival of Lee and his army. So the siege would be a long one, the spade replacing the rifle as it were, with Richmond in Confederate possession and our generals Smith, Burnside, Warren and Hooker, with Grant, seemingly wasting the lives of the 55,000 men they had led to be killed or wounded.

While Grant had moved south from the Rapidan in May, William Tecumseh Sherman moved against Joseph Johnston, replaced by John Hood, and Atlanta fell to us on September 2. After the Battle of Cedar Creek on October 19, Sheridan had defeated Jubal Early in the Shenandoah Valley. He now could help Grant against Lee, and we thought there would be no more Washington raids against us by Jubal Early.

Our military victories won my husband his second term.

During the interim, the New York Workingman's Democratic Republican Association called on my husband and asked him to be an honorary member. He gratefully accepted, and he told them that the present rebellion by the South was no more than "a war upon the rights of all working people." Then he said working people should *never* be against other working people, and he was quoted on this, too. "The strongest bond of human sympathy, outside of the family relation, should be one uniting all working people of all nations, and tongues and kindreds." What did he think of the wealthy? They were fine as long as they allowed others to be the same way - "That some should be rich shows that others may become rich, and hence is just encouragement to industry and enterprise." They discussed more on slavery, and he told them what he was to write the next day, "I never knew a man who wished to be himself a slave. Consider if you know any *good* thing, that no man desires for himself."

In April I had dreadful migraines and could not keep any food down because of them. "Go to New York and take Taddie," my husband said. "Get out of this place - do a little shopping in New York."

I did that and Taddie worried about his goatherd while he was gone from it. I wired my husband on the 28th. "We reached here in safety. Hope you are well. Please send me by mail to-day a check for $50 directed to me, care of Mr. Waren Leland, Metropolitan Hotel, Tad says are the goats well?"

My husband wired back the same day, "The draft will go to you. Tell Tad the goats and father are very well - especially the goats."

Then in April a ghastly story, one of total horror reached us.

It involved Major General Nathan Bedford Forrest, former slave trader who had made a fortune from this heinous pursuit. He was born for war, apparently, really loving to kill, solving everything he wanted to by force - as he did, *quote*, "in my *nigger* yard in Memphis." He said this of the South's so-called war for independence, "If we aint fighting fer slavery then I'd like to know what we are fightin' fer." Forrest took several Union garrisons, and of them, one was Fort Pillow on the Mississippi, some forty miles north of Memphis. On April 12 (remember the firing on Sumter on April 12 that began this hideous war?) he had 6,000 troops against the fort, and when the white flag of truce was flying in the fort he attacked it. In fact, *during the truce negotiations* he moved to attack from a better position. He took the fort and in a frenzy of racial hatred murdered over half of its garrison. Of the 262 negro soldiers, they killed *all* of them, burned some alive, after nailing them to the floor of a tent set on fire, or nailing them to a side of a building set on fire - this bestiality does shame to the most savage animal - kill the *nigger*, women, children in the fort - kill them all - bash in their brains as mothers plead, their children cry for mercy - kill the *niggers, kill the niggers* - so you thought you were free, did you, die, die, burn the hospital tents, and if men escape the fire, shoot them down - *no quarter, no quarter* - kill the god damned *white nigger lovers* fighting along side *our slaves* - shoot them - rob them - take their filthy green backs first, *hand me your money, you damned son of a bitch* - Forrest relishing the slaughter - *they were in my nigger yards,* he yells, *shoot the god damned nigggers* - bury a wounded one alive, or burn them alive, *and show the world how we treat a man who would be free.* And lie, and say to men of character like Lee - *they would not surrender - this is just a part of war* - and to think my own treasured brothers fought and died in their army! You *cannot* deny this massacre. There were too many witnesses who survived and talked before Congress - *this was no battle.* This was *wholesale lynching,* and you dare to call us savage Yankees when there was *no* record by *any* Southerner of murder or rape by Sherman's men as they marched to the sea. The savagery and the horror of Fort Pillow filled our papers all spring and summer. The *so- called* savage Negro followed the rules of war; my Southern kin did not.

"Molly," said my husband. "You are making yourself ill over this."

"What are you going to do about it?"

"What can I do? Aren't we already at war?"

"You are so placid about this! *All* of the survivors cannot be lying! Those burned corpses -"

"I believe it is true. What would you do, Molly, if you could? Kill the same number of their men we have prisoner?"

"Of course not!"

"Then - what, Molly, *what?*"

He spoke in Baltimore, April 18, six days after the *massacre.* He noted that three years ago our men could not even pass through the city without being attacked. He noted that neither side had expected such a long war, nor that slavery would be affected, "So true is it that man proposes and God disposes." What *was* liberty? It was a different thing to the American people. "With some the word liberty may mean for each man to do as he pleases with himself, and the product of his labor; while with others the same word may mean for some men to do as they please with other men, and the product of the other men's labor." The two forms of liberty are "called by two incompatible names - liberty and tyranny.

The shepherd drives the wolf from the sheep's throat, for which the sheep thanks the shepherd as a *liberator,* while the wolf denounces him for the same act as the destroyer of liberty, especially as the sheep was a black one.... Hence we behold the processes by which thousands are daily passing from under the yoke of bondage, hailed by some as the advance of liberty, and bewailed by others as the destruction of liberty."

He talked of Fort Pillow - a painful rumor - true, he feared - and he told how *he* had allowed the use of colored troops. "I am responsible for it to the American people, to the Christian world, to history, and on my final account, to God." He would not have murdered prisoners on the assumption they murdered ours - that would be too cruel a mistake. The Fort Pillow affair was being investigated - and if the charges were true, there would be retribution - "it must come."

It never did. More battles - more bloodshed - and it sank away but its stain would ever, in my opinion, remain. Man's bestial (pardon to the beasts) *inhumanity to man.*

On April 30, 1864, my husband wrote a pardon for twenty-six Sioux Indians to be hanged at Fort McClellan. They were ordered sent home to their families or relatives.

In May the statue of armed freedom on the Capitol dome was unveiled, and a white dove lighted on it, and the crowds watching were moved, and said, "It is a sign of peace." In June, I went to Boston without Taddie, for Taddie wanted to be with his father when he visited Grant. My husband wired me on the 24, "All well, and very warm. Tad and I have been to Gen. Grant's army. Returned yesterday, safe and sound."

On July 8 my husband, in a proclamation concerning reconstruction for restoring the states in rebellion, said he was not "inflexibly committed to any single plan of restoration," but he hoped for and expected "that a constitutional amendment, abolishing slavery throughout the nation, may be adopted, nevertheless."

In the second week in July the rebels under Jubal Early got so close to Washington the canon from our Fort Stevens could be clearly heard from inside of the White House. Fort Stevens was poorly manned, and for three days, July 10, 11, and 12, we did not know whether it would hold until Grant sent help. And there my husband went, and I went right along, too. When he stood on the parapet with his doctor and me, we were exposed to enemy sharp shooters. The doctor was shot in the leg, and, as he was the last to leave, soldiers screamed for my husband to get down, Oliver Wendell Holmes yelling, "Get *down,* you fool."

Finally we got help and the rebels fled.

From the Soldiers Home my husband rode to work, passed a poet named Walt Whitman every day, and the two began to exchange courteous bows. "He has the saddest eyes," the poet said. "Our captain has the *saddest* eyes."

John Hay had read some of Whitman's poems and *hated* them. I found some and *loved* them and took them to the hospitals and read them to the wounded, along with Elizabeth Barrett Browning. Both, in my mind, wrote of the joy and the power of human love.

I was at our hospitals so many times; the rebels called me *the Yankee nurse.* When I left Washington, on my return, *the Chronicle* noted "the sick and wounded soldiers in our hospitals will hail her return with joy." I was always giving our own money - there is the telegram my husband sent about it to Hiram Barney, that I had $1,000 for the benefit of the hospitals and I would send it if I could get $200 worth of good lemons and $100 worth of good oranges!

On August 10 I was in Campbell Hospital in Washington and wrote a letter to a mother of a soldier who had almost died of fever. I had taken him flowers on my first visit, and on my second wrote his letter. He did not know who I was, and I never told him. He never found out until he returned home, and his mother showed him my signature. My note read as follows:

"My dear Mrs. Agen-

I am sitting by the side of your soldier boy. He has been quite sick, but is getting well. He tells me to say to you that he is all right. With respect for the mother of the young soldier -"

Taddie often got my husband to go to the toy store of Joseph Stuntz on New York Avenue near the White House. They would walk down the street, hand in hand, and watch, for a while, while Stuntz hand carved the little wood soldiers. "I am a soldier of France," Stuntz said. "And these are the little French soldiers that were killed in my sight but never in my memory."

I do not recall if this was the *same* toy-shop Taddie rode his pony into because it was raining, and he did not want his pony to get wet.

We had trouble with my husband's Cole County relatives, and more from mine. His wanted money for his step-mother who never seemed to get it, and mine wanted much more. They wanted my husband *to commit treason.* My half sister, Martha Todd White, of Selma, Alabama, wrote my husband in the end of 1863 and wanted permission to come north and get new clothes for herself. My husband wrote her the pass and she stayed until after March of 1864. The story of this broke in the papers, and our enemies said she was taking home clothes with gold buttons, worth from four thousand to forty thousand dollars for the Rebel cause. Her three trunks grew in size as did their contents, and of course I was to blame, too, being her half sister. The *truth* was I did *not* like her, and did not receive her at the White House, although she sent me a number of pleading notes. My husband simply gave her a pass to return home, and she sent him a sassy note saying he must put in the pass that her trunks did not have to be searched! This my husband refused to do, and she began terrible talk against him, our cause, showing her signed pass by him while she did it. My husband got a message to her. If she did not leave immediately, she could room and board the rest of the war out at the Old Capitol Prison. She left and then my drunken brother, Levi Todd, demanded money - $200 – that we did not send. He had left his wife and children to fend for themselves while he boozed it up until he died from it. I do not consider myself, or my husband responsible for this, but, heart–breaking enough, Little Sister did! Then she came to the White House in the summer of 1864 and begged for my husband to do what he couldn't legally or morally do. She wanted her cotton out of the South so she could sell it. My husband said this was only possible if she signed the loyalty oath, and she refused to do this. "Then, Little Sister," my husband said, " by law, I cannot get your cotton out of the South." When she got back to Lexington, she heard Levi had died and she wrote a bitter letter to my husband. Levi was just "another sad victim to the powers of more favored relatives," and she begged again to get her cotton and sell it, with no loyalty oath, which my husband could not allow. She had used the last of her money for her visit to him; he knew her plight, for she had told him all about it and she requested only what was right, "which humanity and justice always gives to widows and orphan. I also would remind you that *your minnie bullets* have made us what we are . . ."

Those words sent me into tears, and her half apology of being a woman crazed with misfortune did not assuage.

"Father, what is the extent of human suffering?" I asked my husband.

"I think we have about found out," he replied.

We heard a story of a fiddler for our army who had to have his leg amputated. He said, "Do not strap me down while you do it. Get a violin for me," and while the forty minutes passed it took to cut off his leg, he played the violin and never missed a note.

My husband, on June 7, had been nominated in Baltimore *unanimously,* to run again for the Republican National Union Party. Andrew Johnson of Tennessee would be his Vice-President. Here is what my husband wrote about it. "I do not allow myself to suppose that either the convention or the League have concluded to decide that I am either the greatest or the best man in America, but rather they have concluded it is not best to swap horses while crossing a river." At the Chicago Wigwam, where my husband had been nominated in June 1860, on August 29, the Democrats chose Little Mac and Senator George Pendleton of Ohio to run against him

In August the war was going badly for us. Here is a memorandum my husband wrote on August 23. "This morning, as for some days past, it seems exceedingly probable that this administration will not be re-elected. Then it will be my duty to so co-operate with the President elect, as to save the Union between the election and the inauguration; as he will have secured his election on such ground that he can not possibly save it afterwards."

On August 31 he spoke to the 148 Ohio Regiment on its way home from the war - he wanted to thank them in this struggle for the life of the nation, for the very survival of its national existence. "We are striving to maintain the government and institutions of our fathers, to enjoy them ourselves, and transmit them to our children and our children's children forever . . . It is worthy of your every effort. Nowhere in the world is presented a government of so much liberty and equality. To the humblest and poorest amongst us are held out the highest privileges and positions. The present moment finds me at the White House, yet there is as good a chance for your children as there was for my father's."

Always this was the message about the land he called the home of his *life, his liberty and his love.*

Torchlight Democratic parades snaked across our streets - cries of, *Hang the President, Swap horses on November 8 - no emancipation, miscegenation, confiscation, subjugation and no more vulgar jokes!* My husband heard that a soldier was refused a pass through the lines as he was going to vote for Little Mac. My husband sent for the soldier, gave him a handwritten pass, a handshake and said, "God bless you, my boy! Show them that; it'll take you home." Another soldier ran into trouble for supporting Little Mac. My husband said, "Tell this officer to return to his post. Supporting General McClellan for the Presidency is no violation of army regulations, and as to the question of taste in choosing between him and me - well, I am the longest, but he is better looking!"

August came - before the fall of Atlanta. Before our army victories saved my husband from defeat - I was in a constant state of hysteria. I had done things my husband never dreamed I did, and never knew I did. On my trips to New York, I had long gone on buying binges. I was deeply, deeply in debt. I had bought jewelry, furs, dresses, bonnets, and gloves - oh, how I bought the gloves! And I did not know how I would pay for them all. My husband knew that I had gone irrational on the spending of money, and he knew it as associated with the death of Willie, or my need to ease pain by *buying something for myself* - by getting - *something* - *to keep!* It was more complicated. I know I have said this before. I rationalized - first, I must look elegant for I was the President's wife, wasn't I? Then, I had to buy all of these fine clothes because - if we were poor again, I could sell them to put us back on our feet! Then in such a pickle, in terror that my husband would know of my irrational behavior, I became worse.

As the men he had appointed to office prospered in their jobs, I thought they should all share in my debts, just like my husband's devious Johnstons of Coles County thought they should share in his money. I knew how he hated that, but I went to Isaac Newton, his Commissioner of Agriculture, who seemed such a charming friend to me, and begged him to help pay my debts and not tell my husband. "What if the other side finds out what I have done?' I wept. "It could cost my husband the election!" *(and you your job)*

I asked the charming Abram Wakeman for help, for my husband had appointed him to the *lucrative* position of surveyor of the port of New York - why *couldn't* he give me help? If *enough* of them did - my husband had done *so* much for them - and he wouldn't be concerned, for he wouldn't know about it - and the other side would not either - and November 8 came, and I was sick with dread. My husband would know. What was my debt? Sixty thousand? Eighty thousand? Twenty thousand? Did my husband have that much in the bonds he kept buying with his salary?

Election day was dark and stormy and portended *horrors* to me. I went to bed with a migraine. Noah Brooks came and spent the afternoon with my husband. At seven that evening my husband splashed through the rain and the mud to the War Department to find by telegraph the election returns. He did not return to my room until after midnight. "Molly," he said. "I think we won."

By the lamplight I could see how weary he looked, and yet there was a peace on his face. "I can see the war end, and those gentlemen of the South back into the Union."

"Father, I am so happy." *Could* I pay off my own National debt in four more years?

At two in the morning it was clear he had won, for a message came from the telegraph office saying so. Then a crowd came to serenade him, and from a window he made a short speech. He inferred his election would serve the best interests of the country. "I earnestly believe that the consequences of this day's work . . . will be to the lasting advantage, if not the very salvation, of the country . . . I am thankful to God for this approval of the people. But while deeply grateful for this mark of their confidence in me, I know in my heart, my gratitude is free from any personal triumph. I do not impugn the motives of any one opposed to me. It is no pleasure to triumph over any one; but I give thanks to the Almighty for this evidence of the people's resolution to stand by free government and the rights of humanity."

On October 20 he had set aside the last Thursday of November as a day of Thanksgiving, as a *permanent* national holiday.

On November 21 he wrote a letter to Mrs. Lydia Bixby.

"Dear Madame - I have been shown in the files of the War Department a statement of the Adjutant General of Massachusetts, that you are the mother of five sons who have died gloriously on the field of battle.

I feel how weak and fruitless must be any words of mine which should attempt to beguile you from the grief of a loss so over-whelming. But I cannot refrain from tendering to you the consolation that may be found in the thanks of the Republic they died to save.

I pray that our Heavenly Father may assuage the anguish of your bereavement, and leave you only the cherished memory of the loved and lost, and the solemn pride that must be yours, to have laid so costly a sacrifice upon the altar of freedom. Yours, very sincerely and respectfully."

Another American treasure, from the light of his being.

I had heard terrible news from Hannah Shearer, my dear neighbor in Springfield. She had lost her eldest son, and on November 20th I wrote her a letter. I told her that I had not written old friends for they recalled the old days when Willie was alive and we all lived in our home on Eighth and Jackson, and it was torture. "Now," I wrote, "in this, the hour of *your* deep grief; with all of my *own wounds* bleeding afresh, I find myself, writing to you, to express my deepest sympathy, *well knowing* how unavailing *words* are, when we are so broken hearted." I said we cannot understand why they are taken from us, and that I was glad that she had a devoted husband and two more children for comfort. I told her that in my sorrow I had not even written to my own sister, Lizzie Grimsley, and that since Hannah and I met last, "I have sometimes feared, that the deep waters, through which we have passed would overwhelm me.

Willie, darling Boy! was always, the idolized child, of the household. So gentle, so meek, for a more Heavenly home. We were having so much bliss. Doubtless, ere this, our Angel boys, are reunited, for they loved each other so much on Earth . . . I had become so wrapped up in the world, so devoted to our own political advancement that I thought of little else besides. Our Heavenly Father sees fit, oftentimes to visit us, at such times for our worldliness, how small and insignificant all worldly honors are, when we are *thus* so severely tried. Please remember to your family & accept so much love for yourself, from your truly attached friend."

The lines of supplicants waiting to see my husband seemed to grow as time went on. One day he met with some ladies from Tennessee who asked that their husbands be released because they were so religious. He released the men and said to one wife, "You say your husband is a religious man; tell him when you meet him, that I say I am not much of a judge of religion, but that, in my opinion, the religion that sets men to rebel and fight against their government because, as they think, that government does not sufficiently help *some* men to eat their bread on the sweat of *other* men's faces, is not the sort of religion upon which people can get to heaven!"

Before the Christmas season my husband returned to the Stuntz toy store by himself, and he bought so many toys for Taddie, Mr.Stuntz asked how one little boy could play with so many toys. He remembered my husband's eyes filled with tears, and he said, "Perhaps I am buying for Tad what Willie cannot have - Willie, my boy - who went away."

And so the Christmas decorations went up again, and the sweet carols were sung, and Taddie brought to our Christmas dinner again his urchin friends from the street. We had been sent a turkey for Thanksgiving dinner, but Taddie had immediately made a pet of the turkey, named him Jack, and was as determined to keep this one alive as he had been to shoot the other one. Jack and he adored each other, and every where Taddie went, there Jack followed. Even to the soldier camp across the way, and they dared not eat Jack either. Nor did we for Christmas dinner.

New Years came and Jack Turkey still had the run of the White House. I knew Taddie was telling Willie again, in his way, that he should not have shot the Jack doll so many times, and I took his earnest precious face in my hands and kissed it. "Ma, do you think we are licking the seceshes?" he asked.

My husband looked up from his papers. "Papa-day - are we licking them at last?"

"Yes, son. I believe we are."

"Will next year be good?"

My husband sighed, and put his glasses down.

"It will be very good," I said quickly. "The war will end, and then papa-day will have more time for us."

1864 - gone - *thank God* - gone. 1865 - I would find some way to pay off my own national debt. I would be alluring and filled with joy again, for life's thunder-storms were vanishing with 1864. My beloved husband would never have to stand between me and lightning again.

Chapter Twenty-three

On New Year's Day, in the great East Room, we held another reception for the year to come. As the glittering crowd passed in all pomp and circumstance, my mind went fleetingly back to the New Year's Day of 1841, when how bereft and lost I was because our engagement had been broken by my husband, and I still blamed Ninian, in a way, for that long period of misery when we were apart. My husband shook hands automatically, his face worn, sad, and I guess I, too, more or less greeted the endless automatically. Why are you here? I asked to myself, as some ladies even curtsied to me. To see if I am a Rebel spy, the demon witch of both North and South? To see if I am a snob? Or, an uncouth woman from the West, with no history of a wood floor, candles, lamps, or bed sheets? Then, I saw something *wonderful!* Brown faces were timidly appearing among the whites - the silks and velvets, pearls and diamonds - and more - and more - so shyly - and my husband smiled and greeted them into the reception line, his face alive, younger, *beaming.* "Howdy!" he said, clasping brown hands in both of his. I showed my appreciation of these beautiful people, and I eagerly gave them my hand, and when I saw tears of love for my husband in those soft dark eyes, my heart sang.

Robert was quarrelling with his father about not being able to enlist. "I cannot stand for him to go," I wept to my husband. "Father, if you want me to live, you cannot let him go and get killed!"

"She will not live through it," said Mrs. Keckley. "Your wife is very, very ill." She kept saying that. And she was very, very right.

My husband came to me when I was sick in bed with another migraine and could not hold down food. He sat on the bed and he took my hands in his. His eyes were wet. "Molly, Robert has graduated from Harvard. He insists on serving in the army."

"Stop him! You are President!"

"I am also a father."

"And a husband!"

"Molly, I have said he could."

"Could - what?"

"Could join the army."

"My God!" I wept, and hid my face away from him.

What he did not tell me is the letter he had written to General Grant. Here it is:

"Please read and answer this letter as though I was not President, but only a friend. My son, now in his twenty- second year, having graduated from Harvard, wishes to see something of the war before it ends. I do not wish him put in the ranks, nor yet to give him a commission, to which those who have served long are better entitled and better qualified to hold. Could he, without embarrassment to you, or detriment to the service, go into your Military family with some nominal rank, I, and not the public, furnishing his necessary means? If no, say so without the least hesitation, because I am as anxious, and as deeply interested, that you shall not be encumbered, as you can be yourself."

General Grant appointed Robert to his staff as captain and assistant adjutant general of volunteers, February 11. Robert would resign June 10, 1865.

By January my husband told two jokes I had not heard before. A governor friend of his visited the state prison where every man in it told him he was innocent. Then another spoke up and said, "Sir I done it, and I am *guilty*." The governor said, "Then, sir, I must release you immediately, for I cannot have you in here corrupting all of these good men." Then the governor visited a nearby insane asylum. A handsome man came up to him and said, "Sir, why aren't you saluting me?"

"Why should I do that?" asked the governor.

"Because I am Julius Caesar!"

The governor gave the Caesar salute and passed the man again, and the man said, "Sir! You must salute me!"

"I just did," said the governor.

"You did not. I am Napoleon Bonaparte, and you did *not* salute me."

"But just a minute ago you said you were Julius Caesar."

"Certainly, but that was by another mother!"

A little garnered laughter – strangely new to the White House. My husband was looking so ill it gave me nightmares. He had probably lost forty pounds, could not sleep, and I heard that he told Harriet Beecher Stowe he would not live to see the peace.

"Father, why would you say such a terrible thing!" I scolded.

"Molly, the war is killing me."

"I cannot bear for you to even *think* that!" But deep in my heart, I had a horror that he would be killed suddenly and violently, and told of it to Mrs.

Keckley. "I could not live without him," I said.

"Madame, he is such a good man. God will protect him."

I wiped my eyes. "Were Eddy and Willie *bad?* Was your own son - *bad?*"

Mrs. Keckley made no reply. There seemed not to be one.

My husband visited the James River to look toward Richmond, "the Promised Land," as he called it. On a stroll in the rain, he came across some men building cabins for the wet weather. He visited with them and then asked for an ax. "Sir, be careful, that is *very* fine-edged."

My husband took it, saying, "It is all right. I used to be good on the chop," and using the ax as a broad-ax, he quickly shaped the rough-hewn sides of a big log until it was a perfect slab. He handed back the ax and left with the men cheering behind him.

By the beginning of 1865 the main contest was between Lee and Grant around Petersburg and between Sherman and Johnston in the Carolinas. In the midst of this my husband agreed to meet with Confederates at Hampton Roads. A letter had come from Jefferson Davis on January 12 in which he said he was willing to discuss peace between our *two* countries. My husband wrote back that he was ready to bring peace "to the people of our *one* common country." The conference was held on our transport, *River Queen* on February 3, between my husband and Seward, and for the Confederacy, its Vice President, Alexander H. Stephens, R.M.T. Hunter, and Judge John A. Campbell. Stephens, "Aleck," had been a friend of my husband, and he was always a frail sickly little man. It was chillingly cold, and he was well wrapped up against it. When the four-hour conference began, he took off coat after coat, mufflers, comforter after comforter, and my husband sighed and said when Stephens finally got down to his self, "Was there ever such a little nubbin after so much shucking? I have never seen so small a one come out of so much husk!"

My husband had written before the conference that he was firm on three things, reunion, no receding from the Emancipation Proclamation, and no cessation of hostilities until the forces hostile to the government were disbanded. Mr. Hunter told my husband he should deal with Jefferson Davis, *as head of state,* as did Charles the First with his Parliament. My husband replied that it was his recollection that Charles the First *had lost his head.* He also said that the rebel leaders had lost all right to immunity from punishment, for they had committed the highest crime known to the law. Mr. Hunter gasped and said, "Then, Mr. President, if we understand you correctly, you think we of the Confederacy have committed treason; that we are traitors to your government; that we have forfeited our rights, and are proper subjects for the hangman! Is not that about what your words imply?"

"Yes," my husband said. "You have stated the proposition better than I did. That is about the size of it!"

Mr. Hunter tried a smile, a pleasant one, I heard, and said, "Not as long as you are President if we behave ourselves."

He then said the South would be ruined if the slaves were freed, for they would not work, and whites and blacks would both starve to death.

My husband said this reminded him of an Illinois farmer who had to feed his hogs until butchering time in December, and hit on the idea of letting them eat his potato crop. Then he would not have to dig the potatoes himself. A neighbor said the ground would freeze before December and asked, "How would the hogs then dig at your potatoes?" The owner of the hogs said, "Well, it may be pretty hard on their snouts, but it will be root hog or die!"

My husband said he would be lenient to the returned South, and he, himself, believed in compensation for the freed slaves. The conference ended with no agreement reached, but with friendly handshakes. My husband said he would get Stephens' nephew out of our military prison at Johnson's Island, and after the Confederates had rowed back to their own boat, Seward sent them a bottle of wine, yelling, "Keep the champagne, but return the Negro delivering it!"

Dear Dr. Anson Henry visited us in February, and never was I glad to see again such a devoted friend. He was also a friend of Noah Brooks and helped arrange for Nicolay and Hay to give up their secretary jobs and take new positions in France. Brooks became my husband's secretary and I thought, this year will be good to both of us. Surely, in it, this dreadful war will end.

My husband's second inaugural was on March 4, and at noon the Senate was to swear in new members and the new Vice-President, Andrew Johnson. Then my husband was to take his oath of office outside on a platform at the east front of the Capitol. It was raining a light drizzle, but there was a strong gusty *cold* wind. A mix up occurred. My husband was already in the Senate wing, signing bills, and I was to leave the White House at nine in the Presidential carriage, accompanied by Robert and Senator Harlan. (Robert had fallen in love with the Senator's daughter, Mary) Our carriage could not move. There was a parade on Pennsylvania Avenue between the Capitol and the White House, and there we were, stuck at the west gate. The White House guard, ready for escort duty, sat their horses, rain pouring on their white gloves, spic and span uniforms, and ahead of us was a tangled mess of fire engines, parade marchers, troops, and I said for us to *move.* We did. At a gallop until the Capitol was reached. There the crowd was huge; ladies stood with rain drizzling off their bonnets, their crinoline dresses marred at the skirt by street mud. I took my place in the Diplomatic Gallery and saw a little minister from a little country fall over his braid and medals and almost into the Senate pit below. At twelve Andrew Johnson came in and shocked us all with his drunkenness. I think the Supreme Court members all dropped their jaws below their polished shoes as Johnson could not remember the name of Wells, beat his *being* a *mere plebeian* to death, staggered, thundered, and Hamlin kept pulling on his coat tails for him to shut up and sit down; a clerk of the Senate, who had shared his booze the night before, tried to flag him down with a loud whisper; Sumner covered his face with his hands, and finally bowed his face on his desk; several Republican Senators bent their heads over to look down at the floor, and my husband just looked more weary. Johnson repeated the oath of office so no one could understand him, kissed the Bible, rambling, "I kiss this Book in the face of my nation of the United States." I heard that he took the booze to alleviate a recent illness, but I always heard that one before from my brother, Levi.

When we moved to the inaugural platform, my husband gave orders that Johnson was not to make another speech. Outside, I looked down on the crowds of people who waited to hear my husband's second inaugural. When he rose from his seat after being introduced, a roar of approval greeted him, and then almost mystically, the sun burst forth in what Brooks described as "unclouded splendor." There was a hush as if peace was divinely portended, and those that looked skyward could clearly see Venus in the noon- day sky. "I never saw that before," I heard a man say - *in wonder.*

My husband read his speech, slowly, clearly, and I think all, except those in the outer fringes of the crowd, heard it. He addressed his *fellow countrymen,* and he said this inaugural address did not have to be as long as the first one. The war had come. "Both parties deprecated war; but one of them would *make* war rather than let the nation survive; and the other would *accept* war rather than let it perish." About slaves, one eighth of the whole population - "These slaves constituted a peculiar and powerful interest. All knew that this interest was, somehow, the cause of the war. To strengthen, perpetuate, and extend this interest was the object for which the insurgents would rend the Union, even by war; while the government claimed no right to do more than restrict the territorial enlargement of it. . . . Neither anticipated that the cause of the conflict might cease with, or even before, the conflict itself would cease. . . Both read the same Bible, and pray to the same God; and each invokes His aid against the other. It may seem strange that any men should dare to ask a just God's assistance in wringing their bread from the sweat of other men's faces;

but let us judge not that we be not judged . . . Fondly we do hope - fervently do we pray - that this mighty scourge of war may speedily pass away. Yet, if God wills that it continue, until all the wealth piled by the bond-man's two hundred and fifty years of unrequited toil shall be sunk, and until every drop of blood drawn from the lash, shall be paid by another drawn with the sword, as was said three thousand years ago, so still it must be said, 'the judgments of the Lord, are true and righteous altogether.'

With malice toward none; with charity for all; with firmness in the right, as God gives us to see the right, let us strive on to finish the work we are in; to bind up the nation's wounds; to care for him who shall have born the battle, and for his widow, and his orphan - to do all which may achieve and cherish a just, and a lasting peace, among ourselves, and with all nations."

Reporters wrote that after his final paragraph was read, they saw tears coursing down faces, with no attempt to wipe them away. There was a great prolonged cheer at the speech conclusion and then Chief Justice Chase swore in my husband and cheers began again, and cannon boomed.

What did the vampyre press say about his Second Inaugural? About the same as of his Gettysburg Address. But E. L. Godkin, writing from here to his readers in the London *Daily News,* rebuked the London papers and praised my husband, saying, perhaps, he was the only man in the North "who has never wavered, or doubted, or abated one jot of heart or hope. He has always been calm, confident, determined, the type and embodiment of national will."

What did my husband think of his Second Inaugural Address? In a letter to Thurlew Weed, he wrote, "I expect the address to wear as well - perhaps, better - than anything I have produced; but I believe it is not immediately popular. Men are not flattered by being shown that there is a difference between the Almighty and them."

We had a reception at the White House that night. Frederick Douglass decided to attend, but the policemen at the White House entrance told him he could not enter. He bolted right by them and inside, was seized by two other policemen who were ready to throw him out on a window plank. He told them the President had even sent a carriage for him just a few months ago, that he had had tea with the President, that they were *friends.* Someone told my husband of Douglass's predicament, and a message immediately came to the guards that Douglass was to be escorted into the East Room. There, when my husband saw him, he beamed, took his hands and said, "I saw you in the crowd to-day listening to my inaugural address. What did you think of it? There is no man's opinion I value more than yours."

Douglass said, "Sir, it was a *sacred* effort," and before my husband shook more hands, he said, "Mr. Douglass, I am glad you liked it." But in all of the crowd, for it was a *huge* reception, Mr. Douglass was not presented *to me*, and my husband heard about it, too. "Father, I so wanted to meet him!" Changing the subject, my husband said, "Tonight I split out two pairs of kid gloves. Molly, you will have to admit, sooner than later, that my hands and kid gloves were not created for each other."

The newspapers were still interested in my clothes, describing a dress of "heavy brocade and purple silk," they said, "all trimmed with rich black velvet," they said, or a dress of *exquisite* lilac with a shawl of white lace - I think the white lace was exquisite, too, and they liked a "rich dress of pearl color, heavily trimmed with the richest black lace, with a neat head-dress composed of a coronet of exquisite flowers." I still did like a flower in my headdress to match my dresses if possible. And of course my shoes must match, too. And these articles about my clothes made me more vain about them, and to want more and more of them. Still, my national debt hung over my head, and I would need the full next four years of my husband's salary to pay it off.

How I was going to do this without his knowledge, I had no idea. I had a terror that my debt was *more* than his next four years of salary. Surely, someone in his party that he had appointed to a rich office would help me out? *Secretly?*

While we were shaking hands at another reception, I heard my husband say to Judge David Davis, whom he had appointed to the Supreme Court, "Judge, I finally learned how to spell the word *maintenance*." Syllable by syllable he spelled it correctly for the judge as he continued shaking hands - *without his kid gloves*.

Grant wanted to start a major offensive against Lee and he wanted to meet my husband at his headquarters in City Point, Virginia, to discuss the details. I wanted to go along, for Robert was there, and surely the change of scene would help my husband who was having head aches of his own, and each visit to the wounded in the Washington hospitals left him so drained, so exhausted, and more so did the endless, *endless* lines in the White House - he *had* to get away.

On Thursday, March 23, the *River Queen* took Taddie, my husband, my husband's bodyguard, William Crook, and me, to City Point. The Potomac was filled with boats, gunboats, material transports, and Taddie looked at each one and told me its life history and what it would do in the future. My husband was *so* proud of him! When we anchored at the James River, we slept on board, Crook sharing a stateroom with Taddie, and I got up in the night to see that Taddie was covered warmly enough. Taddie and Crook, whom Taddie called *Took,* became fast friends, but no one was around Taddie for long who did not become his fast friend. That included the whole crew of the *River Queen,* and in no time, Taddie had been shown and had learned, as Crook said, "every screw of the engines." When morning came, Saturday, March 25, we could see the harbor where we were anchored - more and more boats, sail boats, fishing boats, transports for supplies and troops, and it all breathed *excitement.* There would be no Presidential review here, for Lee's army was too close, and its tents could be clearly seen from the bluff of the river.

Early that day Robert called, and Taddie inspected his captain's uniform, and wondered if it was an improvement over his own.

Robert asked to speak to me privately. "Mother, could you return to Washington and bring back -"

"Mary Harlan!" I said joyfully. "Of course I can - and will! I am so happy you two are in love!"

Robert flushed, his face almost as dark as his father's. "*Mother,*" he said with Todd dignity.

"What is wrong with being in love?" I chided to my secretive son. "Why do you have to keep the most wonderful experience on earth to yourself?"

"Moth - *er,*" sighed Robert again.

"In spite of your *lofty* attitude, I will do it," I promised.

He said nothing. "That is only because I want that dear girl for a daughter in law and the mother of my grandchildren," I said, and I thought Robert would reel away at my saying exactly what I thought. "Robert, you are *so proper,*" I said in disgust.

My husband joined us, and caught the drift of our conversation. "When are we going to have our daughter - at last?" he asked Robert, his face beaming.

"You *two,*" said Robert, rushing back to Grant - to where there was only a war to face.

We ate our meals on board unless we were guests of the general whose quarters were on the bluff above us. My husband conferred with Generals Grant, Sheridan and Sherman (who had temporarily left his army) on how to defeat Lee in Virginia and take Johnston in the Carolinas - I of course, did not hear the details. Another killer migraine was drawing red-hot wires from my brain through my eyes. The 26th came, and my husband rode from City Point to review the troops of Major General O. C. Ord, and Mrs. Grant and I were to join our husbands on the review grounds. We rode there in an ambulance over rough *log* roads and we went at a crawl, and I was afraid we would be late and miss the review. "Can't you move faster?" I asked impatiently of the driver. Mrs. Grant was talking, my head was *killing* me, and I did not know if it was from her endless chattering or the jolting of the ambulance and then we hit a contrary log and our heads were battered against the top of the wagon, and I was in a hysteria of agony. "I am getting out of this thing!" I cried, but even I could see that the mud around us was over hub deep.

I had injured my head again. I know it. Two days later I still was obviously ill. I wonder if I had a slow growing cancer in my brain.

When we reached the review field I was shocked and enraged to see that the general's *lovely looking* wife, and a *superb* rider, was leading the review - riding *side by side* with *my* husband! "Is that the First Lady?" asked a soldier in admiration. That did *not* make my mood improve. *My* husband was riding side by side with *another woman,* and one who looked *very* happy about it, too!

My head was killing me. We were late for the review. I was crazy with pain, frustration *and - jealously.* That I must admit. I was jealous of any other woman getting too friendly with my husband, too close to him, flirting with him, and if the woman was as attractive and flirty as this one - well, I wanted to jump out of the wagon and right into the mud, and pull her right off of her prancing horse on which she pranced and flirted and looked like she *belonged* by the side of *my* husband. "You must not jump out into the mud!" said Mrs. Grant.

"I will jump into what I want to jump into!" I snapped, and might even have snarled. Maybe not. Probably not. I don't think so. I usually kept my Southern charm and grace - my soft melodious voice -

A young officer cheerily rode up to us and said how *smart* my husband's *horse* was to *choose* to ride by Mrs. Ord. He took one look at my face, and saw what he had done for himself, and without another word, galloped off as if cannonballs were snapping at his horse's tail. Mrs. Grant swallowed and turned white as Mrs. Ord rode to our wagon to pay her respects, and I paid my own, and I do not really know all of them yet, but they brought tears to the eyes of Mrs. Ord. What was *she* doing there in an *army* review - by *my* husband? She should not be in the review at all, and if she were, what was the matter with riding by her *own* husband? Did she think *she* was the First Lady? See, the Southern charm and grace did not stand up to jealousy!

To be honest, I remained in a frenzy all day long, and when my husband later rode up to me, I gave him a tongue lashing, too, and I did not care if every officer and every man in the army heard it. I would not have cared if it were heard by the man on the moon.

My husband looked down at me with his gentle, gentle eyes, and he showed no other reaction at all.

In our stateroom that night I made my apologies. I had had no outburst against him - like this - *ever* before. And this one was not even private. "Father, I was terrible. I was jealous. I was in such pain -"

He held me tenderly, and he held me lovingly, "It is all right, Molly," he said. "I understand."

"Father, I do *not*," I wept.

He held me all night long. It was as if he was holding Eddy in his illness and torture, or Willie - I was never so self-shamed, and never so completely loved. Just before sleep I went back to the way I had spoken to this man I did no more than idolize. "Father, I fault you for nothing, and if a *whole cavalry* of Mrs. Ords chooses to review with you - I will accept that -"

"I don't think so, Molly. I don't think so," he smiled, brushing the curls from my face. When I went to sleep in his arms, I thought, I am so unworthy of this man.

The next day I could not raise my head from my pillow. Generals Grant and Sherman called, but I could not see them, that day, or the next day. "My wife is not well," my husband said. I was sick of soul for my jealous temper and compared to that my hot wires in my eyes felt good. In my deep shame for the embarrassment I caused my husband, all the old horrors came back. Eddy dying. Willie dying. I was in a terror that Robert would now die. I was in a terror that my husband would now die - *any crazed man could kill him.* "Why am I so unworthy of you?" I sobbed.

"Don't say that. Molly never say or think it!"

Why am I so quick tempered? Why am I so jealous of women who cling to him when I know he does not like them to do it? Why did I let Eddy and Willie slip away? What did I do wrong? Surely I could have done something to save them!

I wept in pain. I wept in terror. I saw myself without them all, Eddy, Willie, Taddie, Robert and my husband – and I was alone on a ship without purpose or compass, *and it was so real!*

And there was my national debt to buy all of those silly clothes - why did I do it?

Has Willie's death driven me mad? Worry over Bobby – worry over my husband being killed – I hear my husband quietly talking to his generals - see water reflected on the walls of our cabin – and I am so ill – what is the port of call left for us?

"Molly, Molly!" scolded my husband. "It is over and done with! You lost your temper -"

"Father, it is worse."

"Only if *you* allow it, Molly."

On Wednesday, the twenty- ninth of March, Robert had a part in the fall of Petersburg. "Father, if he is killed -"

"Molly, he will not be killed."

All of that rainy night we saw the lights in the sky of our cannonade and its flashings reflected in the water around us.

I went to Washington, without Taddie or my husband, on Sunday, April 2, and on that day my husband wired me that Grant told him, "All now looks highly favorable . . . Robert yesterday wrote a cheerful little note to Captain Penrose, which is all I have heard from him since you left." Petersburg was completely surrounded from the river below to the river above, my husband said in another wire that day. On April 3 he wired Stanton that Grant reported Petersburg evacuated with Richmond sure to follow.

I returned to City Point on Wednesday, April the fifth. I brought with me Mrs. Keckley, Senator Sumner, his guest, the Marquis de Chambrun, and the Harlans, *including* their lovely daughter, Mary, to see Robert. The two, so in love, met and walked alone near the *River Queen,* her rails alight with the colored lamps that reflected like jewels in the rippling water. They must have said what lovers always have said and always will - in the miracle of a world new again within the boundlessness of mutual love.

And - *the war was really ending!* My heart was singing with the joy of it, with relief. It would not kill my husband. We would share our grandchildren together - grow old together - have all those sweet unhurried years ahead to share - to relish.

But I had missed connecting with my husband and Taddie. Richmond had fallen and he had taken Taddie along on his first visit there. It was on April the fourth, Taddie's twelfth birthday. They had taken the *River Queen* up the James to meet Admiral Porter's fleet, met an obstruction in the river, had to go ashore on the captain's gig, and went into Richmond with *no guard* except Crook, Captain Penrose, and the few sailors. If I had been along, that never would have happened. For him to take Taddie and walk those dusty miles under silent and open windows, with those who hated him staring out - *never* - could I have stood for such a dangerous thing! Negroes were the only ones who came to greet him, and they wept at his feet. This was very embarrassing for my husband and he said, "Good people, do not do that."

My husband took some refreshment at the Davis mansion, left very clean by Mrs. Davis, and then when cavalry escort finally arrived, toured the city. Fires had been set by the rebels in their warehouses, and flames had spread to near by homes under a stiff wind. My husband, Taddie, and Crook spent the night on Porter's flagship the *Malvern*, on which my husband got up in the middle of the night to be sure Taddie was covered warmly. We both worried constantly about his weak lungs.

They were at City Point on the Fifth, and that is when I joined them. We had heard that Seward had had a terrible carriage accident that day, but was expected to recover. My husband took Taddie and me to Richmond, and to Petersburg, where he visited the wounded of *both* sides, the reporters wrote, with *"infinite tenderness."*

We took the train back to City Point. On the way, my husband told me how the colored came to him when he and Taddie entered Richmond. "They were weeping with joy. One said, 'Bless de Lord, dere is the great Messiah. I knowed him as soon as I seen him. He's been in my heart fo long yeahs, Glory hallelujah!' He then fell to his knees, and others came to kneel at my feet. I told them not to do that. They should kneel only to God, and thank God for their freedom - not me."

He looked so tired, my husband, so very tired. He sighed wearily, and closed his eyes as if this would bring him some rest. "I am so glad that I was a *scrub*," he said, finally.

"Your husband never thinks he might be shot," Crook told me. "It was too dangerous for him to have walked in Richmond like that."

"Thank God the war is almost over," I replied. "When it is over, there will be no reason for anyone to kill him."

My husband and I were being driven along the James River when we passed a quiet country cemetery. My husband had the carriage stopped. "Why, Father?" I asked.

"I would like to take a little walk and look at old graves," he said.

And so we did. The sun was bright, the grass a tender green, and brilliant flowers bloomed among the moss covered head stones. The air was warm, fragrant with the damp smells of a recent rain, and birds sang over us in a joyous greeting to spring.

"Father, everything seems *right* again."

"This is a beautiful place," my husband said. He picked a flower and smelled it. "Molly, you are ten years younger than I, and when I have shuffled off this *mortal coil* of Hamlet, and gone on into the light - will you see that what I leave behind is put away in a place like this?"

"Father - what are you saying?" The soft beauty of the day went away. It was as if it had never been at all. I shivered. Cold from the graves at our feet, from the dead at our feet, crept all through me, and I was shaking from it. "Father - why are you saying this now?"

He smiled, looking so thin and tired, and looked up at the sunlight darting with the wind among the tree shadows. "Because, Molly, when it needs to be said to you, I will not be able to say it."

He took my hand, and I clung to it as we walked back to the carriage - to our duties - to his Presidency. His hand was so large - so warm. The day became beautiful again. Those under the moss covered grave stones were gone, their past lives done, completed or not, and I thought of John Keats' nightingale singing in another spring *among shadows numberless in full throated ease*, and everything was *right*. Peace was coming. Soon. No longer the *clickety clack* of the wires bleeding with young mens' blood. No longer my husband's anguished all night vigils to hear them. He was so strong. He would see the nation one again. He would see democracy triumph in this land of his life, his liberty and his love - to show that if self-government could be here, it could be everywhere.

It was a race now between Lee and Grant to keep Lee from going south to join the army of Johnston. Grant had to surround Lee with what he called a ring of men and steel. By early April Lee had lost 19, 000 men to us as prisoners, and I am sure they were thankful for at least having food to eat. Lee's men were starving while plenty of food for them had been holed up in Richmond - food we discovered. Davis and his cabinet had fled, though Davis was insisting the war go on. Grant pushed his army so Lee was surrounded, and notes were exchanged between the two regarding the surrender of Lee's army. On April the Seventh, Lee said he wanted to avoid any more bloodshed and asked for terms. On Palm Sunday, April the Ninth, Lee and Grant met at the McLean house in the village of Appomattox Courthouse.

They met and Grant said, "I met you once before, General Lee, while we were serving in Mexico. . . . I think I would have recognized you anywhere."

"I tried to recollect how *you* looked," replied Lee, "and could not recall a single feature."

The two talked in a friendly way of their days when they had both served the same government.

Robert was standing on the front porch and did not hear one word of this meeting, for the two men spoke to each other so quietly.

And Lee could have said what he thought - my surrender is worse than dying a thousand deaths. He was nobly handsome, immaculate in dress, while Grant was unshaven; sloppy, mud spattered, he would be taken as any private except for his shoulder-straps. Lee was not asked to surrender his sword. His men could keep their horses and mules, "to work their little farms," Grant said; officers and men were released on parole. That day Lee surrendered

26,000 men, and when Lee bade his army farewell, he rode off to his home in Richmond. The tears, the cries and the sobs of his men must have echoed in his ears - *we wanted to serve with you forever - now I am ready to die - I wanted to see all of the damned Yankees sunk into hell - General Lee - I would have followed you anywhere!*

The news of Lee's surrender reached Stanton at 4:30 in the afternoon of that April the Ninth.

The Presidential carriage reached the *River Queen* at the wharf, and as we were driven back to the White House, there were bonfires in the streets, and people were shouting in joy. "Lee surrendered! Lee surrendered!"

For all purposes, with that surrender, *the war was over.* Newsmen reported it and went out and got drunk. Cannon was booming by daylight the next day, and all Washington was mad with ecstasy. People marched together through the muddy streets, shouting, singing; red white and blue flags, or bunting, appeared everywhere, and my husband told Stanton to find some flags for Taddie. The government gave clerks the day off, and they stayed and sang in office corridors. The Treasury employees sang together, *Praise God from whom all blessings flow -* " and then they marched across to the White House. We were eating breakfast when they did, and they sang, beautifully, oh, *so* beautifully, *The Star Spangled Banner.* Taddie found a flag and waved it from the window, keeping time with the notes. "Papa-day, oh Papa-day, look what you did for us!" he said, chewing on a muffin and waving the flag. "If Willie could be holding a flag, too!"

Tears of joy were already in my eyes, and now I thought of my Willie. "Taddie," I said, "I am sure he is. He would not miss an historical occasion like this."

April the Tenth wore on, and more and more noise in the city with it. Crowds began to gather in front of the White House. "The streets are all filled with brass bands," said Brooks. "Howitzers from the ships are dragged up from the Navy yard and are firing everywhere in the city; down Pennsylvania Avenue steam fire engines blow their whistles and are covered with flags, riders among them swinging cowbells, and boys and men blowing tin horns, and there is a life and death contest in this city to see who can make the most noise!"

That was obvious enough. *Huge* bells appeared from everywhere, and parades appeared from everywhere, brass bands, endless fife and drum corps, everyone wanting to be in a parade and forming one, marching and singing between the colors of the red, white and blue. Six and eight horse wagons, loaded with anything that could make noise, did, and brewery wagons, hauled by giant horses and driven by giant men, stopped and drew free beer for the marching crowds.

At Willard's Hotel an elderly gentleman had drunk enough booze to leap to the bar top where he led his fellow imbibers in patriotic tunes, ending with *John Brown's Body*.

"The whole city is dancing," I said to my husband, "and my heart, right along with it."

Church bells began tolling, one - two, then in every church built within the city, joined by the whistles of the factory and all the riverboats.

During the tumult my husband took Taddie to Alexander Gardner's studio to pose for several photos. There was one taken of my husband and Taddie together, and one of my husband, with a gentle smile upon his face, the only one ever taken of him with a smile.

That morning a procession started up Pennsylvania Avenue, and in spite of the rain and the deepening mud, there were three thousand marching time with a band. At the War Department they could not smoke out Stanton, so they marched on to the White House. There, they filled the portico, the carriageway, the pavements to either side, and then more came and they just stood in the rain and looked up for my husband to appear. Bands played, howitzers joined in, and the crowd began to yell for my husband to speak. Taddie appeared, right away and gladly, and orchestrated the crowd's swaying back and forth as they yelled for my husband. Finally, he did appear, or the crowd never would have gone home to eat lunch or gone on with life. A reporter from *Harper's Monthly* thought my husband looked younger than he had imagined and was looking happy because everyone else was.

"Fellow Citizens," my husband began. He told them he was to make a speech the next night, "and I shall have nothing to say if you dribble it all out of me before." There was great laughter and applause. He noted the three bands. He wanted to close the interview with the bands playing. "I have always thought 'Dixie' one of the best tunes I have ever heard. Our adversaries over the way attempted to appropriate it, but I insisted yesterday that we have fairly captured it. (laughter and applause) I presented the question to the Attorney General, and he gave it as his legal opinion that it is our lawful prize. (Laughter and applause) I now request that you favor me with its performance."

We heard *Dixie*, and the band closed with *Yankee Doodle Dandy*, and when my husband left the window, the crowd left, and tried to smoke out Stanton again, with no luck.

At five thirty they came back to the White House. My husband made a longer speech saying he was not going to make one until the next night.

On that day my husband again told Stanton to get Taddie more flags and told Wells to get him a Navy sword. He wrote out a pass for Ward Hill Lamon to go to Richmond when he chose to.

That day my husband *still* had the long lines of supplicants, and among them were some women who wanted their sons freed for being deserters. My husband freed them all. One mother wept and told him they would meet again in heaven, and my husband said if he got there, she surely would be. Then his old friend Joshua Speed came to see him, dear Joshua, who had brought him to the cotillion to be *formerly* presented to me. That meeting made my husband so happy, and when Joshua asked him how he wanted to be remembered as President, my husband used the thistle and the flower analogy I had heard him say before. Being so Southern in his view and in his support of slavery, I do not think that Joshua understood what my husband was talking about.

On the evening of April 11 all the public buildings of Washington were to be illuminated and decorated. It would be a gala and *magnificent* sight, and I wrote a note to Sumner and the Marquis, the Marquis in French, to call at the White House about eight thirty, and to share a half hour carriage drive to see the beautiful city lights. My husband's Friday tour of the hospitals, "though a labor of love, fatigued him very much," I wrote. He was to make a short speech, which they could attend, and then the ride - "It does not appear to me, that this *womanly* curiosity will be undignified or indiscreet, *qu'en pensez-vous?*"

Sumner did not attend my husband's speech. I think it was because he was of the radical wing of the Republican Party and my husband was not.

As night fell, Pennsylvania Avenue gleamed with bonfires and the newly completed dome of the Capitol shone above the mist in its own light. Across the Potomac Lee's Arlington mansion was illuminated from within and without, fireworks blazed on its lawns to arch to the sky, and under them, ex-slaves, by the thousands, sang, *The Year of Jubilee.* The White House was as brilliantly lighted as we could make it, and soon all the crowds came to it. In front a battery from the Navy Yard appeared and fired victory salutes. More and more brass bands gathered and played; fireworks hissed their way into the air and exploded into gorgeous colors. I was getting ready for our guests and the carriage ride; my husband was eating his dinner and glancing at his speech while he drank his coffee.

Taddie had disappeared. When my husband and Noah Brooks went upstairs for my husband to deliver his speech, they heard a tremendous roaring of laughter from the crowd. Taddie had found my Confederate flag, that Ellsworth had died taking, and he was waving it before the crowd, almost falling out of the front window to the right of the staircase. Old Edward, the doorkeeper, was trying to drag him inside, and not having too much luck with it, and the more he was pulled by the seat of his breeches, the more stubbornly Taddie waved the flag. He loved the attention he was getting, the roaring of laughter, and tried to bow to his audience while he was waving the flag, and managed to do both.

In the window facing Lafayette Square my husband appeared and a roar of approval went up in the air, along with hats, *anyone's* hat.

He began his speech, and that constant charisma wove its spell once again.

"We meet this evening, not in sorrow, but in gladness of heart. The evacuation of Petersburg and Richmond, and the surrender of the principal insurgent army, give hope of a righteous and speedy peace whose joyous expression can not be restrained." There was the problem of reconstruction. "Unlike the case of war between independent nations, there is no authorized organ for us to treat with. No man has authority to give up the rebellion for any other man. We simply must begin with and mould from, disorganized and discordant elements. Nor is it a small additional embarrassment that we, the loyal people, differ among ourselves as to the mode, manner, and means of reconstruction."

I knew how true that was. My husband's plan was one of the Presidency rebuilding the Union as the war progressed. In his proclamation of December 8, 1863, he offered pardon, with certain exceptions, to any Confederates who would take an oath of loyalty in support of the Constitution and the "Union of the states they're under." When, in any state, a loyal nucleus of 10% of those who had voted in 1860 did this, and established a state government abolishing slavery, there would be executive recognition of such government. The radicals in Congress introduced the Wade-Davis bill, July 2, 1864, which my husband allowed to die with a pocket veto. This bill would allow reconstruction of a state, not based upon *minority future* loyalty, but on *majority past disloyalty* to the Union. No one who had served the Confederacy, in a state or Confederate office, or who had born arms against the Union, could vote or serve as delegates in a state convention. No Southern state chose to re-enter the Union under the Wade-Davis bill, and Tennessee, Louisiana, Arkansas and Virginia were trying to enter under my husband's plan. Louisiana had been under our military occupation since early 1862, and had formed a government abolishing slavery in April of 1864. My husband supported this new government, and now he reviewed the subject of the new state government of Louisiana as regarding all the seceded states.

"I distinctly stated that this was not the only plan which might possibly be acceptable . . . the Executive claimed no right to say when, or whether members should be admitted to seats in Congress from such States . . . whether the seceded States, so called, or in the Union or out of it . . . that question has not been, nor yet is, a practically material one . . . As yet, whatever it may hereafter become, that question is bad, as the basis for a controversy, and good for nothing at all - a merely pernicious abstraction . . . Finding themselves safely at home, it would be utterly immaterial whether they had ever been abroad. Let us all join in doing the acts necessary to restoring the proper practical relations between these states and the Union . . ." About the new government of Louisiana - "It is also unsatisfactory to some that the elective franchise is not given to the colored man. I would prefer myself that it were now conferred on the very intelligent, and on those who served our cause as soldiers." So - if the Louisiana government is not perfect - "The question is 'Will it be wiser to take it as it is, and help to improve it; or to reject, and disperse it?' Can Louisiana be brought into proper practical relation with the Union *sooner* by sustaining, or by *discarding* her new State Government?" The new government had elected a free-state constitution, "giving the benefit of public schools equally to black and white, and empowering the Legislature to confer the elective franchise upon the colored man." Would it not be better to allow this to "ripen to a complete success? The colored man too, in seeing all united for him, is inspired with vigilance, and energy, and daring to the same end. Grant that he desires the elective franchise, will he not attain it sooner by saving the already advanced steps toward it, than by running backward over them? Concede that the new government of Louisiana is only to what it should be as the egg is to the fowl, we shall sooner have the fowl by hatching the egg rather than smashing it?" Of course, he said, every state would have its own unique problems, "that no exclusive, and inflexible plan can be safely prescribed as to details and collaterals. Such an exclusive and inflexible plan, would surely become a new entanglement." BUT, "Important principles may, and must, be *inflexible*."

He would make new announcements to the people of the South, "and shall not fail to act, when satisfied that action will be proper."

As he spoke, Taddie was impatiently catching the falling pages my husband discarded, piling them neatly on a nearby table and saying, "Papa-day, *hurry up* with the rest of the pages!"

When my husband had finished, Senator Harlan asked the crowd, "What shall we do with the rebels?"

And the crowd shouted, in unison, "Hang them!" and Taddie looked at his father and said, "Papa-day, don't *hang* them - hang *on* to them!"

And my husband told that to the crowd, "Tad has got it right! We must not *hang* them, but hang *on* to them!"

And the crowd cheered that idea, too.

Here you have it. I think my husband would have made all of the difference in reconstruction. He would have gotten the people behind him - the very people that made war because of his election. He wanted the colored to be educated, and he wanted them to have the vote, and he would have stood firm on their *inalienable* rights as human beings - but he would have to see that the Southern majority accepted this, too. Remember? With the people behind you, you can do *anything*. Without it, you can do *nothing*.

I believe he could have created the support he needed.

I believe his political genius, moral strength and charisma - would have done this, just as it had served to save the Union.

I believe here was a man unique, and could have contributed, more than any other man, to justice acceptable in the South.

Chapter Twenty-four

On April 12, in spite of being swamped with work, my husband sat down and wrote me a love letter. In it, he invited me to take a carriage ride - *just us* - on the fourteenth. We would plan our future, and with his work done and our being free of the White House, we would do with our lives just what *we* wanted to do. When the note was delivered to me, I thought - I have given my boys to God, and I will *accept* their departure and not just *say I have*. I have my living sons. And I have my husband. You are my completion, I thought again, as I put the note away, and clasped pearls at my throat, and put on my pearl earrings, and the scent of lavender at my temples.

My thoughts went to what my husband had written me. Things were so good with the war ended. The Union of the United States of America was saved. Surely, we all would reconcile. Surely, the blacks would be seen as the equal human beings they were.

I looked in the mirror. I had lost weight but my face looked more serene than it had since we lost Willie. *What is haunting me now?*

It is his dream! That damnable, damnable dream that keeps repeating to him!

He had told it to Lamon and me "I keep having this dream," he said. "I dream it over and over, and when I wake myself out of it, I go back to sleep and dream it again!"

"What dream?" Lamon asked.

"Of a death in the White House."

I shuddered and wrapped my lace shawl more tightly around my shoulders. There was silence except for the crackling sounds made by the fire. "Not Willie's again?" I choked.

"No. I am alone, and walking upstairs - going toward my office, I think - and there is the sound of sobbing, but I cannot see those sobbing, for room after room I go through is empty. Then the crying leads me downstairs, and to the East Room, and it is shrouded in black - black crepe over the chandeliers, the mirrors, and I see a catafalque holding a corpse."

"Father!"

"There are soldiers guarding it - four soldiers, I think, and I say to one,

'Who is there?' indicating the catafalque."

" 'The President,' the soldier replies. 'He was killed by an assassin!' "

"I don't believe in dreams!" I said in horror. "*Thank God,* I don't believe in dreams!"

"What ends the dream is this wild sobbing, *hysterical* sobbing that always wakes me up. It is so painful hearing it - so *painful!*"

"Why haven't you told me of this before?" I asked. "Dreams aren't true - but, Father, you must never have this nightmare again!"

He smiled, and I noticed he had lost his tired as death look. In the firelight and the lamplight, he looked serenely *radiant.* "Father," I repeated. "If I believed in dreams, you would never leave the White House for any reason!"

Of course we did. In the celebration that never ceased in the city, my husband and I took the Presidential carriage and went on a long drive with the Harlans. We had become fast friends and they were Robert's future *in laws.* We were driven across the Potomac into Virginia toward Richmond, my husband's *promised land.* "Your husband looks so different now," Mr. Harlan said to me. "That sad look is gone!"

My husband smiled. "So is the war," he said.

Senator James Harlan wrote of that day later. He said of my husband that his whole being had marvelously changed. "He was in fact transfigured. That indescribable sadness which had previously seemed to me an adamantine element of his very being, had suddenly changed for an equally indescribable expression of serene joy! - as if conscious that the great purpose of his life had been achieved. His countenance had become radiant, - emitting spiritual light something like a halo. Yet there was no manifestation of exaltation or ecstasy. He seemed the very personification of supreme satisfaction. His conversation was, of course, correspondingly exhilarating."

Some of that joy was captured in the Gardner photo of April the Tenth.

Thursday night, April 13, my husband had another dream, and it was powerfully vivid. "Don't tell me of it, if it is bad," I had said.

"Molly, this just means something important is going to happen."

"What do you mean?"

"In the past, I have had it before we win important battles. It means - a *victory.*"

"How - with the war all but over? Is it of Johnston's surrender?"

"It is a *victory.*"

"How?"

"I am in a boat and it is going rapidly to an unknown - very, very misty shore - it is an unknown vessel going to an unknown shore - all shrouded in

291

blinding fog - but the shore is *desired - good -*"

"How is it good?"

"Because through the mist I see that it is a shore of light."

"I do not believe in dreams, and never have," I repeated.

"But Eddy and Willie and Alec - came to you in dreams -"

"No! They were with me, and I was *not* dreaming! Father, I was *awake.*"

My husband took my hand, and he gently kissed it, as he had gently kissed me that night after we had loved and the fire had drifted away into coals that lingered on into the dawning. I remember that so vividly. When I woke up, and he was still resting by me, the fire coals casting a faint light on the ceiling and the walls, I said to Eddy and Willie, *Godspeed, dearest sons, be with the sweet angels your grandmother Nancy heard singing to her - so close to the earth.*

April the Fourteenth dawned cold and deep in fog. My husband did not go to his office until seven that morning, one hour later than usual. As the Washington business day began at seven thirty, people began to walk in the fog, horse cars clanged their way through it, and drays passed loudly on the cobbled streets, their horses steaming as they pulled produce to the markets. Through the thick mist the Capitol dome and the Washington Monument poked their heights, as if to say something to those half hidden below. No one knew what it was, and do you know now - in your day?

In our days when *whilst* was used for *while,* when *veard* was used for *near,* *yesty* for *yesterday,* *ere* for *before,* *veriest* for *very most,* and walking on foot was called using the *shank's mare,* the word *yonder,* used then for *far away,* could you, on this April the Fourteenth, now join us? Would you walk this day along the one sidewalk of Pennsylvania Avenue, its *west* side - on the east side were the open markets and the drainage ditch - you can hear someone still singing the popular tune, *When This Cruel War Is Over.* You can hear it behind medicinal doors that read, *All cancers cured for $2.00* - or *teeth pulled, each $2.00 and with gas, $2.50.* More people are walking with you in the mist, scurrying, busy, breathless people, late for their jobs, having had breakfast, or not having had breakfast, and the smells of burning wood and smoke rise around you, and near you are squealing pigs, rooting in the mud or wallowing in the bountiful street puddles. Ducks and pecking chickens might be walking by your feet, and to your south and east you see the Freedmen shanties, and see women from them begging for work to feed their children.

It is not an ordinary day, for the bloodiest war in American history is drawing to a close. You probably love the man in the White House, have heard bad things about his wife, and have seen Taddie's goats still grazing on the White House south lawn. You might have heard that ten thousand troops still sleep in the White House basement, with tons and tons of flour gathered there for a siege, and you might later be taking a horse car to the Navy Yard, or be going to the Baltimore and Ohio railroad terminal. There, a train can get you to Baltimore, forty miles away, in one and three quarters hour! Or, you can go to New York City in nine hours!

The finest hotels are having *indoor* toilets, along with their polished spittoons. *Willards* is still the finest at Fourteenth and E, but there is also the *National, Brown's,* and *Kirkwood's.* Breakfast is served from eight to eleven, the menu being steaks, oysters, ham and eggs, hominy and grits, and, of course, whiskey - *all of this in one meal!* Dinner is at *noon,* with seven courses. Supper is between four and five, (eight courses) with teas at seven thirty and often a cold supper entree served from nine to ten. Needless to say, stout people are admired, for they are the ones who can afford all of this.

April the Fourteenth is Good Friday and the churches fill. It is a time of joy and deep reverence among men, for the cruel war is really over. God is ever merciful. Six hundred thousand Americans have been killed in battle. Twenty nine million Americans are left. War casualties are over one million. The debt is $2,366,000,000, but the northern economy is a sound one.

Stay with me!

At seven thirty my husband is reading in his office. I am not to forget our afternoon *romantic* carriage ride together. He sends me another note telling me so. He is in such lilting good humor - as if he were a little boy having to drag stones up a steep, steep hill, and has just finished hurling them all over to the other side. He is *radiant,* as the Harlans had noticed, and in his expressive eyes, there is a peace - a serene kind of *remote* peace - that I had never seen before. We were to all have breakfast together, for Robert was home, though tired from traveling the bad roads getting here. My husband's favorite desert is fresh home baked apple pie, and for a surprise, I have that for him at breakfast. The coffee is fragrant, and the other smells are of apples and cinnamon, cloves and nutmeg, and he eats *two* pieces of the pie. "I think, Molly, that you have smuggled in Evil Eva," he smiles.

Robert showed him a photo of General Robert Edward Lee. My husband studies it after wiping his glasses on a napkin. "It is a good face; it is the face of a noble, noble brave man. I am glad the war is over at last," he says.

"I am, too," says Robert.

"Now, Bob, it is time for you to get on with your law studies," says my husband. "You must finish them."

"So soon?" asked Robert.

My husband smiles. "Marriage and books *can* go together."

"Fath-er," says Robert uncomfortably.

"Fath-er," I repeat mockingly. "We are not supposed to know that Robert is in love with Mary Harlan, and that Mary Harlan is in love with Robert?"

Robert frowns. "I *adore* your Mary," I say to him. "I schemed and plotted to get you two acquainted and for you to -"

"Moth- *er*," Robert scolds.

"Get married," finishes Taddie, ten years younger, and in so many ways, so much more into living.

We continue our visit in my favorite sitting room, the Red Room, with the painting of George Washington on the wall, the painting that Dolly Madison had saved from the British - Dolly Madison whose first husband had been a Todd! (with one more D than God) By ten that morning the mist vanishes, and the Washington monument and the capital dome rise unimpeded to the sun.

Upstairs, at eleven, my husband begins his Friday cabinet meeting . News has come that the Union flag is again flying over Fort Sumter. There, the Reverend Henry Ward Beecher spoke and said the war had been started by the small ruling class of the South, and now the common people of both North and South would see to their own reconciliation. When General Grant enters for a brief visit, my husband shakes his hand, with both of his, frontier style, and the cabinet breaks into applause. Frederick Seward, acting as Secretary of State for his father, reports his father is improving, and the cabinet settles down, Gideon Wells, Secretary of the Navy, John Usher, Secretary of the Interior, the new Secretary of Treasury, Hugh McCulloch, Postmaster -General, William Dennison, and James Speed, (Brother of Joshua Speed) Attorney General. Edwin Stanton, Secretary of War, is always late for cabinet meetings, and this day is no exception. While they wait for Stanton, my husband tells of his dream of going rapidly to an indefinite lighted shore.

"What does that mean?" asks Wells.

"What does *any* dream mean?" asks McCulloch.

"I know what this one says," replies my husband. "I had the same dream before Sumter, Bull Run, Antietam, Stone River, Gettysburg, Vicksburg and Wilmington. It always comes before a great battle - or a great victory - I expect we will soon hear from Sherman - *good* news - and the war will be completely closed out."

When Stanton arrives, it is decided the draft should cease, the army cut, and army contracts ended. My husband knew reconstruction of the South might not follow his plan, for the Wade-Davis Bill represented opposition from Congress. What he had said on the eleventh, and what he said now, was that he wanted a generous and *speedy* restoration to the Union of the South, and generosity extended to their leaders - his executive power he hoped to replace by complete home rule, and *as soon as possible.*

"What about the leaders of the *rebellion?*" he is asked. He replies, "I should not be sorry for them to go out of the country, but I should be for following them pretty close to make sure they did." He is happy the Thirty -Ninth Congress had just adjourned and would not meet again until December, for, by then, he hoped to get the South back into the Union, a functioning *skeleton* of Southern reconstruction, with order there maintained.

"What if the rebel leaders do not leave the country?" Stanton asks.

"I hope that there will be no persecution, no bloody work after the war is ended. No one can expect me to take any part in the hanging or killing of these men - even the worst of them," my husband replies.

By the noon hour smoke haze is thick over Washington. The church bells cease ringing, and in the produce markets oysters are shucked and slabs of beef are turned in the brine barrels. James R. Ford has a buggy full of flags when he meets famous actor John Wilkes Booth who asks him what all of the flags are for. "The President's box - he and Grant will attend tonight's performance - it will be a sell out! Will you be there?"

"I can't promise," Booth says and rides away.

Sir Frederick Bruce, the new British ambassador replacing Lord Lyons, is waiting in town to be presented to my husband tomorrow. His appointment is at two in the Blue Room.

At 2:20 my husband has lunch with me and finishes the apple pie - *all of it!* I tell him that he is beaming - *glowing* with happiness.

"Molly, I *am* very happy. I have done my best."

"You will be in time for our carriage ride?"

He nibbles on some more cheese that was served with his pie. "Molly, I made that engagement."

At three he returns to his office where Vice President Andrew Johnson is waiting to be shown in. My husband chews on an apple and more cheese and calls Johnson *Andy,* and discusses his ideas of Southern reconstruction.

A desperate black woman is pleading to see my husband. She and her children are starving because her husband's soldier pay had suddenly stopped. The guards at the front gate finally let her through, telling her she would only be stopped at the White House porch. She is. She darts under the soldier's arms and runs upstairs toward my husband's office, where she is stopped again by the Presidential guard. "What are you doing here? How did you get up here? You cannot see the President!" he says. In despair the woman breaks into sobbing, which my husband hears and appears by her side. He scolds the guard. "There has always been time for people who need me," he says. "Let the good woman in."

He seats her by his desk and listens to her story. "Madame, you are certainly entitled to your husband's pay. Come by this time tomorrow and the papers will be signed and ready for you."

She bursts into tears again, and she later writes, "He escorted me to the door, and there, he bowed to me like I as a natural born lady."

At four the sun is brighter, and the day turns very warm. It is the supper hour and the restaurants are crowded and the streets fill with buggies, surreys and gigs, and on the wooden walks women stroll in pairs, and it is a relief that the passing riders and buggies do not splatter mud up onto their clean skirts.

I am getting ready for our carriage ride, and I have chosen a lilac dress and an exquisite lace shawl, and my pearls - for my throat and my ears. I am through wearing black. I love dresses of color, of my new life, of my life to-be now after the war. I am thinking that my husband and I will be cheered up at Ford's by the English comedy, *My American Cousin*, with Laura Keene, a fine comedienne. It will be so good to hear that hearty laugh of my husband again - to have him with me at the theater again - opera, drama, even a silly comedy - we *always* loved the theater. We had seen the play once before, but that did not matter. It was light hearted and fun.

Taddie comes by. "Are you going to the theater with your father and me?" I ask.

"Ma, I am going to the National to see *Alladin or The Wonderful Lamp*. If you and papa-day come, they might even let me act on the stage again!"

"It is announced, Taddie, that we will be at Ford's with General Grant. We must not disappoint the people who come to see us."

"All right," agrees Taddie. "I can get on the stage and act for you another time."

"Who is taking you?"

"My tutor."

"He is *still* around?" I ask in surprise. Really in amazement, for Taddie and tutors were not very reconcilable.

Later, Robert comes by. "Why don't you go to the theater with your father and me?" I ask. "General Grant and his wife will be with us, and you could bring *your* Mary-"

"Moth -er," says Robert flushing again.

"I love to see your face turn color at the mention of her name!"

That is too much for Robert who goes off to change colors by himself.

Through with his office work, my husband 'closes shop,' as he calls it, and walks to the War Department. His body guard, Crook, is by his side, and Crook says to him, "You could still be in danger, right now. Even if the war is all but over -"

My husband looks around at a lovely spring day. His face still has that new look of serenity. "I reckon there are people who would have me killed," he says. "Crook, I have no doubt they will do it."

"*Sir?*"

"Yes."

"What? You have no doubt - *they will do it?*"

" I don't think about it. If it is to be done, it is impossible to prevent."

Crook shudders. "Who are the - *they?*"

"Those that can pay someone else to do it. I am sure they will have someone else do it - probably someone so well known the *they* will be completely in the dark - probably forever, too-"

Crook is stunned. "This is terrible! Who?"

"Oh, an assassin driven into *so-called* madness - *some crazed fanatic* - over the war - I think, Crook, it will be really over what I might do *after* the war."

Crook stops and looks up at my husband. "Do you know - have you been told something I have not?"

"No -not at all. But at least, Crook, they can only kill me once!"

"This is no joke," said Crook.

"This is no joke," repeated my husband. Crook recalled to me his face was sober, but its new luminous look remained. "He might as well have been talking about spring flowers ready to be picked - it was so *strange* -"

At the War office my husband asks for Major Thomas Eckert to be his bodyguard for the evening and Stanton says no, he had something else for him to do - and he leaves without telling Eckert what it is! But in many ways, Stanton never seemed to realize that my husband *did* outrank him. I thought Stanton had cruel eyes, and, of course, Taddie did not like him at all. The only nice thing about Stanton I can recall was the pleasant smell of the perfume he put on his whiskers, and that you could smell them from clear across the room.

At five, exactly at five, my husband and I take the barouche for a carriage ride to the Navy yard. Our coachman is Francis Burns, and two cavalrymen follow us at a respectful distance. A cooling breeze has risen, and my husband tucks a blanket around both of us. "Father," I say.

"What Molly?"

"I am so happy. I never thought I would be this happy - ever again!"

"I am happy, too, Molly," he replies, and takes my hand and holds it warmly within his own.

I think of Eddy and Willie, and remember their sweet smiles when they visited me beyond the veil of death. "They are happy, too, father," I say, my eyes filling with tears.

"Of course they are," my husband says gently.

"I did see them, father. And it was not in a dream!"

"I am glad you did."

I remember the horses were two fine matched blacks, and that as we went down *the* Avenue, people shouted and waved, and my husband tipped his tall silk hat. Down G street - down New Jersey Avenue - "Father, what do you want to do after you leave office?"

"Practice law - maybe with Bobby!"

I hadn't thought of that. "And maybe Taddie, too."

"If Taddie ever learns to read!"

The growing breeze is ruffling the treetops, and flattening the grass along the road. The air is filled with the scent of spring. The warm sun shining on the meadows makes them luminous with light - bird song in the air - it is a *glorious* day!

"But first, Molly, let's travel - see all the places we have read so much about - Britain, Scotland, Germany, France and Italy -" His face is so joyous, I say, "Dear husband, you almost startle me with such great cheerfulness!"

"I don't think I want to go back to live in Springfield. The memories there of Eddy and Willie - we'll sell our house and move on."

"I will never go back to that house, Father. It would kill me. I would always be waiting for them, see them swinging at the gate, coming home - pushing and pulling *you* home - first Eddy and Bobbie, and then Willie and Taddie - oh, Father, I suddenly feel as if we are *ghosts* of ourselves!"

A fleeting cloud has darkened the sky.

"We'll never live in that house again, I promise you, Molly. We can cross the Rockies and take a look at California, where our young lads are digging gold to pay off the debt -"

"California?"

"After I have taken you to Europe!"

"Father, I would *love* that!"

"Robert will be married, and Tad loves to travel - he might even go to school in Europe - if he chooses -"

298

"Father, you are creating a wonderful future!"

The cloud has passed, and all is sunny again, sunny and bright and *safe*.

"Molly, what about California? Or - Chicago?"

"Wherever you are - wherever you are - I will be," I say. We are silent, and I dream of a future without being hated, blamed for living - *and he still has that amazing luminous look - as if with his mother he hears angels singing so close to the earth.*

We reach the ocean, its wheeling gulls and all of the sea salty smells. I watch the gulls. They dive into the water to sweep up to the sky again in a sheer joy of living.

"Molly?"

"Yes?"

"Never have I felt closer to you."

I lean back in content, as much as my bonnet will allow. I hear his laughter about the greedy farmer. I hear the rain on our wedding night, and the livery bell ringing out for the shelter of new coaches, and I am back at Lizzie's ball and he is telling me he wants to dance with me the *worst* way. I remember my worry over his not ever dancing before, and over his great Conestoga boots - then I remember - I looked up into his eyes and was worried no more.

At the Navy Yard my husband *has* to explore the deck of the monitor, *Montauk.* I watch him talk to its sailors. I remember when the *U.S.S. Monitor* was fighting the *Merrimac* - Willy had just died and Taddy was so ill - and I wonder as I had for so many times - if I had kept Willie off of his new pony on that cold day - if I had kept Eddy inside - away from whatever killed him, and my husband is in the carriage again, and he reads my face, and as usual, he knows my thoughts. "Molly, you are the best of mothers."

"I am not the best of wives."

"Molly - promise me - no regrets. Have no regrets -"

"City Point -"

"No regrets. I fell deeply in love with you, and I have never fallen out."

"I love it when you tell people that."

"I am not the best of husbands." He tells Coachman Burns to take us back to the city.

"You are the best of husbands," I contradict.

"I would still forget to stash the coals for morning. I always mess up my hair. I love to sit on my shoulder blades with my feet up on a desk - I answer the door in my shirt sleeves - I love old worn out slippers and would send all my kid gloves to hell if I could - Molly - you buy them and I wreck them - split them right down the middle."

We laugh in companionship, and the day is yet sunny and bright that Good Friday, and all is calm in the land, the bitter war stilled at last, and I give to death my sons, and my brothers. Beside me, holding my hand warmly again, is my lover, best friend and husband. I revel in the look of serenity still upon his face, the relief of a job so well done, and even my favorite flower, the lilac, is in bloom.

Chapter Twenty-five

On the drive back to the White House I noticed the breeze had died and the flags and bunting on the shops and houses hung limply. The city was half celebrating, and half moving on into its old familiar routine. Farmers were driving into the city to sell their produce to the stalls, and hay to the stables. I thought, *how permanent all of this looks,* and some day, when it is not, the generations after us will wonder what we were like, as the generations ahead of them, will wonder what they were like.

"Molly, you look so pensive. Are you thinking of our European tour?"

I smiled and took his hand. "I am thinking of all of this - this city, this year, this month and this day - and how all that matters in it, is that we have each other and our two sons."

He smiled in return. "I reckon that about says it. And I reckon, Molly, I might have done what I was elected to do."

It was six when we were driven up the gravel drive of the White House. "All of a sudden I have a head ache," my husband said.

"I feel one of my own. I have a terror of it getting worse. Should we not go to the theater?"

"We promised to attend, and there will be people there to see us. The Grants have declined and are leaving the city - we have to be there - or I do."

I smiled, for my husband still looked so *radiant.* "Wither thou goest-" I teased, and we walked to the front door, hand in hand, as we always did to the front door at Eighth and Jackson. Inside were two dear friends of my husband, the new governor of Illinois, Richard Oglesby, and General Isham Haymes. "You must come to my office for a visit," my husband said.

"Father, not for too long," I said. "We are going to have supper in a half hour. Gentlemen, would you join us?"

They declined and my husband took them upstairs to his office. There he read to them the latest sally against him by the humorist, David Locke, known as *Petroleum Vesuvias Nasby*, in which he was called an ape and a *gerilla,* and he laughed at it until tears rolled down his face. "I always say I am going to write a letter to Petroleum and tell him to communicate his talents to me, and I will swap places with him."

My husband then discussed dreams, but did not tell his own. "Dreams are very important," he said. "They are symbols - surely a part of the workmanship of the Almighty."

"Why don't we understand them? Why do they always seem so *strange?*" asked Hays.

"The symbols await to be deciphered," my husband replied.

"You do not believe they *literally* tell what is going to happen?" asked Oglesby.

My husband's face sobered. "Symbolic - they are *all* symbolic, awaiting for us to find the meaning." He probably wondered what the four soldiers at the dream catafalque stood for.

Sunset was at six forty five. Fire smells and smoke still permeated the city. The morning mist returned and thickened into fog. Now the opaque gas globe in front of the main entrance at the Ford Theater was lighted, and inside the theater the ushers were dusting the gas globes on the walls. This night would be Laura Keene's last performance of *My American Cousin*. The audience draw would be the presence of my husband.

On the streets the lamplighters climbed their ladders to bring at least small pools of streetlight within the falling dark. Houses were still illuminated more than usual; taverns were full and boisterous with rented carriages waiting outside, both doing good business with the continuing of victory celebrations.

The thick fog made the coming night chilly. Women in carriages passed wearing muffs and coats, the wealthier ones, furs.

At our supper of cold cuts, our family was together and my husband asked Robert if he did not want to go to the theater with us - the play was supposed to be silly, but funny.

"I am too tired, " said Robert. He would just stay in and visit with John Hay.

"Papa-day, why don't you come with me to see Aladdin?" asked Taddie. "We *always* go to Grover's."

"Tonight I am expected at Ford's."

"I told you, Taddie -" I said.

Taddie was torn between pushing for his own way, or allowing us ours. "All right," he said, finally, after sober reflection on it. "I guess it *is* better for you to go to Ford's."

House Speaker Schuyler Colfax called on my husband and asked if he was going to call a special session of Congress, and my husband said, no, he was not. George Ashmun called and said he had a cotton claim against the government, and my husband told him to come back the next morning at nine.

Be with me!

I decide to change into a white dress and am seeking a nice bonnet to go with it. I settle on one with tiny pink flowers. I look in the mirror and see it is becoming. I wish I had not lost so much weight. I did not look pleasingly plump as I used to.

William Crook is waiting to be relieved of guard duty for the night, and he has been waiting three hours. The new guard is John Parker, who has been a Washington Metropolitan police officer. I am the one who signed for him to be a guard, assuming he had been an efficient police officer, or his name would never have come up for the position. When he finally arrives, Crook tells him to meet us at the theater. We stand at the front porch awaiting the carriage, and with us are Noah Brooks, Colfax, Ashmun, and Crook still waited with us. I am chilled and when the Presidential carriage finally pulls up, I am happy to see that it is closed against the growing night cold. The time is around 8:10, and I am worried that we will miss the opening of the play. "Father, we have to go to Senator Harris's to pick up our guests," I say to hurry him along.

When Charles Forbes, the Presidential valet and footman, helps me into the carriage and my husband follows, our friend, Isaac Arnold, who had stumped for my husband's election in Illinois, runs toward us waving his arms. My husband leaves the carriage and hears what Arnold whispers, replying, "Molly and I are on the way to the theater. Excuse me now - come and see me in the morning." Two cavalrymen come up behind the carriage and will accompany us on our journey. My husband gives his heavy shawl to Forbes, nods to coachman Francis Burns, and we are on our way at last. He waves goodbye to his friends watching us leave.

They all remembered he had never looked happier.

"Father, I heard you say, "Goodbye, Crook."

"Yes, I did."

"Why good*bye* - and not good *night*?"

He leans back, smiling. "Whatever I said, Molly, everything is *all right*." Then he takes off his silk hat, and runs his hand through his hair, making it a mess as usual.

"Father, what are you doing?' I ask.

"Taming down my hair," he smiles. He looks at me affectionately. "Since *you* did not take the time to slick me all up."

The words bring back how I used to do that every day in Springfield before he left for the office, those *dear* sweet days, when we were no more than a close family. Of course, in the theater he would have to remove his hat, but it would be dark, and in the loge were drapes that would hide his mixed up hair - "Father, where *are* your gloves?' I ask, making mine smooth.

"Molly, they jumped right into my pocket and refuse to come out!"

"Father - remember the big black crow that tattles on fibbers -" I smile, for my headache is gone, and we are on the way to the theatre. It would be good for us to join in laughter.

The fog is thicker. The lights on the avenue are blurred, two paths of zig-zagging gas lamps that gleam enough to look mysteriously enchanting. The newly finished capitol dome is shining above the fog, and its light seems a beacon of hope for a nation united once more.

The Presidential carriage turns north at fifteenth, and then east on H Street and stops at the front of Senator Ira Harris's home. The lamps are lighted on its porch, and as Forbes leaves the carriage to ring the front house bell, I think, *how strangely mysterious seems this night!* The fog is so eerie, and it is so *blinding*. Caught in it, I remember another carriage ride to Ford's with Mrs. Mary Clay. It was last winter - an iron hoop caught under the carriage and we were stalled until it was fixed. *My husband is going to be shot!* I had thought. *This is a deliberate assassination attempt!* But it wasn't. The carriage was fixed and soon on the way to the theater. I thought of Mrs. Clay asking my husband if he thought the mounted men behind us protected him. "Not much," he had replied. "When my time comes nothing can prevent my going."

Why was I thinking of that dreadful scare? It was the fog, the eerie mist that made everything seem suddenly - so *menacing.* John Wilkes Booth had been in the play that night - he was playing the part of a villain, and he shook his finger at my husband - *three* times - so my husband noted it and smiled, "He does look at me pretty sharp doesn't he?" *But I cannot think of such a silly thing.* Didn't his brother, Edwin Booth, save Bobby's life in 1863 or 64 - when Bobby had fallen into the slot between the platform and an oncoming train? Booth jerked him from the slot back on the platform in the nick of time. *Think of this - and the war is over and the menace of my husband's murder gone with it - tonight the theater, comedy, laughter -* I adjust my bonnet as Major Henry Rathbone and his fiancee, Clara Harris, enter the carriage. I had learned that they were step-brother and sister, and when they sit opposite us, facing the back of the carriage. I say, "Miss Harris, how becoming is your outfit!"

We women do all of the talking as the carriage goes down Fourteenth, over to F, where there has just been another victory parade. We are on to

Tenth when I notice that the major is not in uniform and he is not armed. And I notice his huge walrus moustache and the mutton chop whiskers, and I cannot decide if they are becoming or not.

Close to 8:30 we arrive at Ford's Theater, and I see a wooden ramp in front of it, a consideration that protected women's skirts and men's boots from the street mud. There are many soldiers on leave in front of us, and they all turn and stare at my husband as he, and not the footman, helps me from the carriage. Their faces are friendly, and they also smile warmly at me, but, of course, there are no *tidewater aristocrats* among *them*. We are late; I know the play has already started. More late-comers are still in line buying tickets at the box office, and across the street I can see people leaning out of windows to see my husband. A policeman in front of the theater keeps pedestrians moving along. "Don't *dawdle* here," he says. "Move along - no *dawdling*!" and I marvel at the word, never having heard it before. Our two cavalrymen leave to return at the end of the play, and I *finally* see John Parker, leaning casually against the wall of the main theater entrance. I do not like his attitude, and resolve, in the future, to see him away from guarding my husband again. He must have been a very inactive and inattentive police officer. A sudden gust of wind blows back my bonnet, and this apparently also stirs up Parker who then leads us into the theatre and up the stairs to our loge.

The audience, 1,675 persons, knows we have come into the theater, and so does Miss Keene. In the middle of stage lines she ad-libs, "Anybody can see *that*." The band strikes up "Hail to the Chief," and the audience gives my husband a standing ovation. He acknowledges the applause, and in what had been boxes seven and eight, we settle down to enjoy the play. My husband has an overstuffed rocking chair for his comfort, and I sit by him. The two boxes made into one have comfortable furniture, even a sofa. Miss Harris and Major Rathbone are in view of the audience, I partially, and my husband not at all. Forbes stays with us. "Sir, would you like to wear your shawl?" he asks my husband.

My husband says he does not want it.

I see General Burnside come down the lower aisle and seat himself, but, of course, I can*not* see our loge guard, John Parker, *leave his station*. He, I heard, went to a nearby booze house, *Taltavul's, meets Booth*, and they drink ale together. Later, Parker joins the audience *downstairs*. He *does not* stay and guard our door as he is supposed to do.

This, of course, caused the death of my husband, and for his gross negligence, and I wonder, *treason*, Stanton never gave him a cross word or any punishment whatsoever! He didn't even lose his job! *Think on this*. Stanton went to great pains to show that Charles Forbes was not in our loge when we all agreed he was, though both Clara Harris and Major Rathbone changed their original recollection. Now why would this be? Was it to protect John Parker because Forbes said that he *saw* that Parker was not guarding us?

But now my husband is so happy - eating and sleeping again, and my heart sings for the ending to war's horror. I look at him and smile, and he gives me his beautiful smile in return. "Father - your gloves -"

"Won't leave my pocket, Molly! That is where they say, for they have a mind of their own!"

His hair is a fright, and he makes it worse, running his hands through it. "Father, I should comb down that hair - you have it going in all directions!"

I have a comb in my purse, but I have no grease of course, and then I decide no one can see him, and when they did, he would have his hat on, so I should let the matter - the mess - rest.

At intermission, with the increased light, the audience looks up at our box with its silken flags festooned over the painting of George Washington. After 9:30 a message comes to my husband from the War Department, and when Hanscom enters our box with it, I see Miss Harris suddenly start with fear. My husband thanks the messenger, gets up and puts on a coat. "I felt a chill," he says.

"Was the message important?" I ask.

"Not really," he says, sitting back down.

"Why did Stanton bother you?"

My husband shrugs. "Maybe he wants to know where I am."

I am pleased with my dress and my bonnet, and I can see my husband is too. "You have not forgotten our world travels?" I ask.

"I have not," he smiled. "And there is no city I desire to see so much as Jerusalem."

During the third act I snuggle against him. Miss Harris and the major are holding hands, and my husband takes my hand in his. It was always wonderful, feeling that strong hand holding my own. I look up at him, into those sweet, so expressive eyes, and I say, "What will Miss Harris think of my hanging on to you so?"

He gives me the smile I had treasured ever since our first meeting, and he says, "Molly, I don't think she will think a thing about it."

These are the last words he ever will utter. These are the last sweet moments of my life when my heart was whole.

The audience is so noisy. This was supposed to be one of the funniest parts of the play, but I did not like all of the noise from it. We would not have been here but for the audience expecting to see Grant. My husband shrugged off our headaches and said, "Well, they can see me instead – you don't have to go, Molly."

And I had said, I remembered now, "It is sort of amusing and it might do us good." But the noise – it was not that amusing!

Then I feel my husband's clasp loosen on my hand, and I see him suddenly slump backward in his chair. I don't know what is the matter. Had I heard a gun shot? I still don't know if I did. I think I did not, for all the noise at the time. A frenzied young man is slashing at Rathbone with a knife, cutting his arm to the bare bone. Blood is all over Rathbone, and I scream in horror. Who is this madman in the loge with us? Why is he trying to kill Major Rathbone? The frenzied man jumps on the stage, and as he does his right boot catches on a regiment flag. I look at my husband. He is so strong. Why didn't he help the poor major?

But my husband's eyes are closed. He looks peacefully asleep. "Father! Wake up! Wake up!" I am screaming, for he will not open his eyes. He will not wake up.

The frenzied man has broken his leg and he hobbles across the stage. "Stop that man!" someone in the audience yells.

"Water! Water!" Miss Harris yells to someone below.

"Father," I weep. "Why don't you hear me? My God, why don't you hear me?"

The gas jets of the stage are turned up; people pass a young doctor up to the loge, for its door is locked from the inside - "I am Dr. Charles Leale," he says. I press my head against my husband's chest. "Father, father - *wake up!* You must tell me you are all right!"

There is no response. *I know now.* My God, I know now! I hear myself moaning, as if I am detached from that awful sound, and I see him already gone to that island of light, and he will never stand between me and the lightening again; he can never tell me everything is all right again, for it will never, never be all right again.

"Help me, doctor!" moans Rathbone.

The doctor is placing my husband on the floor, very, very gently. "Be careful," I sob. "Be careful!" Some soldiers appear through the open door now, and help him. The doctor seeks a wound, finds it in the thick matted hair I did not slick down that night, and another doctor is lifted into the box, Dr. Charles Taft, he says - artificial respiration is begun on my husband, and I cry, "Is he dead? Will he recover? Oh, my dear husband! Oh, my dear husband!"

The doctors see he has been shot in the brain - behind the left ear and the lead ball has moved to lodge behind his right eye. I am told he is dying, that for him there is *no* hope. He will hardly last the night.

The ship rapidly taking him through the mist into light - the dream - the dream of victory! *Did he say it was always before a victory?* I feel a great rushing of darkness, and I am in a shrinking circle of light, and then no light.

When I awaken, Miss Harris is patting my hands, and another doctor is with us, Dr. Albert King, and Leale is still working on my husband. "He is breathing better," he says. He gives my husband a small sip of brandy, and my husband keeps it down. "Tell me he will live!" I plead.

All of the doctors turn to me and their faces say he cannot.

I sit on the sofa and Miss Harris tries to comfort, and Laura Keene is suddenly there, holding my husband's head on her lap. I have to rock back and forth on the sofa to keep in balance with it.

They talk of taking him to the White House to die. Then they decide on a place near by, and I say, "But he has made appointments to keep at the White House," or maybe - I thought it, and did not say a word.

And we have the rest of our lives to finish together, and we will not go back to our home, for neither of us can bear to look at Willie's empty room - Eddy's -

And it is after ten, and outside the fog has drifted all away and a large moon shines high in the sky, two days from being full. Farmers report that they saw blood on the moon that night, and they knew a horror had happened to them, to the country.

Then I am following the men who are carrying him down F Street, and the theater casts such a dark shadow, for the moon is so bright. Crowds are pressing against us from everywhere; they are gathering on Tenth as far as the eye can see. Men around us begin to weep openly. Soldiers clear a path for us. I hear a *roaring* from the crowd. It is a roaring of pain. Miss Harris and Laura Keene are suddenly with me in a strange little place, the William Peterson House, 453 Tenth Street, and we are in a sitting room. Both pat my hands as if I have not already opened them to give my heart away.

My husband is placed diagonally on the bed in a room rented the night before by Private William Clark of the 3rd Massachusetts Infantry. I remember the wallpaper as a drab oatmeal color, and that the room had two little windows facing a courtyard, and in the courtyard moon shadows played tag with the wind in the trees. I kneel by my husband and I kiss his face. "Dearest - take me with you! Father - take me with you! You have never refused me - don't leave me here alone!"

Oh, if here on earth, our earthly pleas could be met! If love could stay death, a kiss awaken the loved one - if time could turn backwards - but, it cannot, and here the past is in memories that stab the heart and in dreams that haunt the long nights.

And in the dawn that says over and over – *he is gone.*

Doctors are talking around my husband in whispers. I can hear clanking spurs of military men outside. "Father - you never have refused me! Squeeze my hand!" How could a man so strong, so in love with me, not hear a word? He gives no sign. He looks peacefully asleep and so he gives not one sign of a goodbye, and on his face the worn look is gone - the tired spot he never could reach - that must be gone, too – *and the horror of you dying is killing me!*

"Get that woman out of here!" snarls Stanton. I am led back to the front sitting room, and then I am back by my beloved, and Robert is standing at the head of the bed. "Get Taddie!" I tell him. "He will wake up for Taddie!"

Then our physician, Dr. Robert Stone, and our pastor, Dr. Phineas Gurley, are with him, and I groan in more loss than I could even *nightmare* possible. Eddy, Willie, my husband - it was altogether – each loss – one, and the one more than my strength could stand.

"He was shot at ten fifteen," I hear a man say.

Major Rathbone faints from lack of blood and is taken home. A stove is across from me, and I can see coals in it, coals that burn, and I wonder how - and for how much longer. I rock back and forth on the sofa, and I hear that roar of pain outside again, that roar of total grief, and I hear cavalrymen cursing outside to clear the crowds, and more jangling spurs - military boots - *tramping* - tramping on the wound of my heart - *up* and *down* - somewhere. "Mother, you must control your grief!" It is Robert, who blushed at the mention of love, and I say to him, "Robert, I *am* my grief."

The next time by his bed, two men hold me up, and I do not know who they were. "Live, dearest live!" I sob. I do not see the blood behind his head, for they change the napkins under it constantly. "Father - beloved husband - you must take me with you!"

On his face an expression of even more tranquility begins to form while the area around his right eye darkens.

"I must go with you!" I cry.

"Get that woman out of here!" Stanton shouts.

Then I am back in the miserable sitting room with the coals living, my husband dying, and Robert weeping and saying, "How can it be so? Oh, God, how can it be so?"

I look up at him in surprise. He had shown no emotion since he had become a Todd. "Mother," he said, wiping his eyes, "put your trust in God, and all will be well."

In the other room again, I see Senator Sumner standing at the head of my husband's bed, and he is weeping. Robert takes my husband's left hand in his, and breaks down, terribly. I want to go to Robert, now and in the long, long ago - when he was Bobbie, finding stray kittens for his little brother - and I want to say - because you have a little brother, does not make us love you less, Bobbie - stop running away! Don't you know you keep running away from showing your feelings?

And the night wears on, and, somehow, the fire I watch in the stove keeps on burning.

This is all a nightmare. This is a dream that will end with the sunrise, and my husband will say, Wake up Molly! We will have breakfast - was there some apple pie left? The cheese I love to nibble on?

Now there is no noise from Tenth Street. Two soldiers are patrolling in front of Peterson House. Andrew Johnson is told to get ready to take the oath of office. When I see Johnson come into the room, I take his hand, and try to speak, but cannot.

At five the doctors say my husband is having another brain hemorrhage. Feeble light begins to show in the windows; Gideon Wells is in the room. One doctor, one named Barnes, is trying to monitor my husband's pulse at the carotid artery, and Beale holds his wrist to do the same thing. Robert stands grimly at the head of the bed, his face drained of all color. I am taken back to the sitting room. Clara Harris and Laura Keene still sit with me in front of the fire, and it is burning as strongly and as stubbornly as ever.

He will go right to our boys. He will pick up Eddy and Willie - he might even be walking back to our home now - with one of them balanced on his great shoulders. And other little boys will rush forth to look into his gentle eyes, and he will look gravely on those who were too young to die, in fire, shot and shell, and he will say, Boys, I think we all did what we were supposed to do.

Outside the colored people silently gather. Now most who gather in the dawn are of dark skin, and their eyes express their pain, and their tears assuage it not. Rain begins to fall around six, a heavy pelting *beating* rain, and they stay right where they are. Drenched, cold, shivering, they stay right where they are.

I watch the rain drumming against the glass. *Rain against the windows on our wedding night – Can't we go back to that November 4, 1842? Can't I take back every cross word I ever said to you? Father, lover, beloved – how can I live without you?*

"It is time," a doctor tells me. My husband's right eye is black. I can hardly stand, and when I see him, I faint. When I am conscious again, Robert is sobbing, and I am helped away from them both - father and son, to that damnable fire *that is still burning.*

My husband died at seven twenty two, and ten seconds. Robert told me this. Dr. Gurley knelt on the floor, and the cabinet was there, and prayed with bowed heads.

I did not pray. I cast myself on him, and I covered his lips with kisses, those tender gentle lips. A white sheet was then placed over his head, and I was carried from the room. I could not walk. I could not get my legs to do my bidding, or will my body to be strong and to heroically bear the loss of its heart.

I heard the tolling of bells over the sound of the beating rain.

I heard that on the morning horse trolleys the grieving drivers took the bells from their horses, and inside the trolleys, men heard why, and their tears fell on the straw covered floor. Something of rare magnificence and compassion had come into their lives and now it was gone.

It was nine in the morning when I returned to the White House.

The bells tolled all that day, in every church in the North.

A little girl was playing on her front porch when she heard the bells toll, and then her father rushed right by her weeping. She had never seen him weep, or any man weep, and it was strange and it was awful. She went into the house and found her parents in the kitchen where her mother had been preparing lunch. "What is it?" she asked in panic. What could make *both* parents cry?

"They killed the President," her father wept. "They killed the President!"

Her mother began to weep, too, and her mother and her father clung to each other and her mother cried, "He was such a good man!"

That night the little girl walked to the telegraph office with her father, and through the scurrying clouds, she saw stars, and she wondered how that could be, that the stars were still there, shining as usual, when their President had been murdered.

Chapter Twenty-six

Rain and wind continued to beat against the White House portico. Noah Brooks wrote that my husband's death had left me "more dead than alive, shattered and broken by the horrors of that dreadful night, as well as worn down by bodily sickness." My niece wrote in her book that my collapse was "utter and complete; she couldn't lift her head from the pillow without fainting." That was true.

Mrs. Keckley was sent for and stayed by me, in my "darkened chamber" as it was described. The pain in my head was killing me. Hot wires were drawn from my brain out of my eyes. I was in bed for five weeks. I could not will myself out of bed for very long, for my legs would not stand the rest of me up. Robert stayed by me those first days, and he was kind and affectionate. I did not want to see anyone but my sons, and then Mrs. Gideon Welles called, and we clasped each other, pain-to-pain, sorrow-to-sorrow, and we said not one word.

When Mr. Welles called that April 15, shaking the water from his hat, Taddie walked down the stairs, and he said, with great dignity, "Mr. Welles, who killed my father?"

"A very, very bad man," replied Mr. Welles.

Taddie looked out at the rain and the crowd of colored people mourning in front of the White House. "What will happen to them?" he asked. "Will they still be free?"

"Yes, Tad. They will still be free. Your father saw to that."

When the sun rose in such splendor on Sunday morning, Taddie was in my room and he opened the drapes. "The sunshine means papa-day has awakened in heaven," he said. "He is with Willie, and little Eddy I never knew - but he is still papa-day."

"Yes," I said. "Of course, Taddie, of course."

He came to me and looked at me so tenderly, it was as if he were his father. "Mama, I am *Tad* now. Papa-day called me Tad, so I am *Tad* now."

"All right. Tad." But in my letters and in my thoughts, he was still Taddie.

He looked out of the window, and so much desolation was on his little face, I thought it would kill me. "I am not the President's son now. I am just an ordinary little boy," he said.

I reached for his hand and pressed it to my lips. "*Tad* - but never ordinary."

"I am not the President's son now. I won't have all those presents any more. Well, I will try to be good. I will make Papa-day proud of my life."

"He already is, " I said. "He already is."

That night, in the deepest, deepest dark, when cannons were still booming for the death of my husband, and my head was my mortal enemy, and I had physical pain to match the grief of my heart, I cried out in agony, and Taddie came and stayed at the foot of my bed. "Don't cry, Mama. Don't cry. Papa-day is in Heaven with Willie and Little Eddy - he is happy with them. He is with God. When you are in Heaven, you are happy. Mama, don't cry, for you are breaking my heart!"

I clasped him, tenderhearted beloved son, and tried to calm myself.

Funeral services for my husband were held in the great East Room of the sea green carpet, green from the $2,500 greenbacks I overspent, where we had attended the services for Ellsworth, and where he had attended the services for Willie, and I could not be there by his side.

On that April 19, I was not at his funeral service. Neither Tad nor I attended. We were both too ill. Robert attended with our friends, and there was a lying-in-state at the Capitol, and on the morning of April 21, my husband's remains were placed in a black draped car of a funeral train that would take its long circuitous journey back to Illinois. From the Oak Hill Cemetery of Georgetown, Willie's coffin was also placed in the car, and the train moved out of Washington - keeping right on schedule - which both of them would have appreciated, especially Willie.

Across our land the news was realized, and not realized. He was one of us, some people said. He was one of us who met a challenge and triumphed over it, and his words to Mrs. Bixby, his words to us at Gettysburg, and in his inaugurals - they are a part of what we hope to be - from what we are - those who loved him said, *He was one of us.* He was of the common people and never tried to hide it. Didn't he say that God must love the common man, for he made so many of them?

He believed in government *of* the people, *by* the people and *for* the people. He cast such a long shadow, for he was a man who stood so tall in the light. He defined human rights and property rights and gave a new definition to property rights in saying, "If slavery is right, nothing is wrong." He had created an expectation again within the words of Thomas Jefferson, words he so revered, *we hold these truths to be self evident, that all men are created equal* - the words - the light of freedom so vital within the sanctity of the human soul.

Those who loved him said this. Those who love him say it still.

The lonesome funeral train followed the tracks for seventeen hundred miles. By the tracks people waited to see the funeral train pass, and some put flowers on the tracks before it passed and some after it passed. For twelve days the lonesome funeral train bore him and his son, and bore the grief of the nation he had served so well. There were services in Baltimore, Harrisburg, Philadelphia, New York, Albany, Utica, Syracuse, and on then, the funeral train, into the night, with bonfires lit by the tracks and its train whistle lonely and lost in the darkness between the burning fires. Cleveland, Columbus, Indianapolis, Chicago, and home to Springfield, the Sangamon flowing sweetly by, and the lilacs still in bloom, and many, in grief, picked lilacs and pressed them between book pages to keep as a flower of that time, that year, that month, when it bloomed and he was still alive.

David Locke saw my husband, and wrote, "The face was the same as in life. Death had not changed the kindly countenance in any line. There was upon it the same sad look that it had worn always, though not so intensely sad as it had been in life. It was as if the spirit had come back to the poor clay, reshaped the wonderfully sweet face, and given it an expression of gladness . . . .The face had an expression of absolute content, of relief at throwing off a burden such as few men have been called upon to bear - a burden which few men could have born." Of course, I saw that look on him the last days we were together. I should have been celebrating in my heart that he was free at last, with no more mortal pain - but, Oh, God, *I yearned for him so*, and my posthumous life without him was just in its beginning.

To Walt Whitman my husband was the glorification of the ideal of democracy, and he had seen my husband close enough for them to exchange many grave bows when my husband rode from the Soldiers Home on his way to the White House.

> O Captain! my Captain! rise up and hear the bells . . .
> It is some dream that on the deck,
> *You've fallen cold and dead.*

> When lilacs last in the dooryard bloom'd,
> And the great star early droop'd in the western sky in the night,
> I mourned and yet shall mourn with the ever-returning spring . . .

Here, coffin that slowly passes, I give you a sprig of lilac.

If I could be a poet, too, if I could have crowned him with a halo of stars, I would have. If I could have stopped the sun in the sky to have that last day with him forever, I would have. If I could hear him say - just *once* more, "Miss Todd, I would like to dance with you the worst way -"

But my words are poor, and that poet - author of volumes on my husband said what I love, Chapter SEVENTY TWO - THE CALENDAR SAYS GOOD FRIDAY - do you know it? *The purple lilacs bloomed the April the Fourteenth of the year Eighteen Sixty Five. And the shining air held a balance of miracles good and evil. . . .*

Do you recall? Here are my favorite lines:

"Did any poet or genius of imagination picture the ancient crowded Hall of Valhalla alive with tumult of a new come arrival who would stand before them only a trifle abashed drawling, 'Well, this reminds me . . . ?'"

Black crepe was hung over all the festive red, white and blue; newsboys hawked the latest about his murder, wiping tears away with grubby hands, and inside of the grieving houses black crepe was hung in the doorways. Why? What good did it do? No one knew why. They just did it within that great wave of agony that swept over the North - *The captain had weathered every reef, his fearful trip* was *done.*

Not ours. Not mine.

Negroes moaned, "O Lawd! O Lawd! Marse Sam is dead! Uncle Sam is dead!"

That kind sad face, those tender eyes, the way they lit in joy to see their dark faces, and shake their dark hands, while he said, "Howdy! You know - I shake hands frontier style like my boys -"

And where he had been raised as a boy, with the peculiar light of the wilderness he wrote about in a poem, Sarah Bush Johnston was told he was dead, and her face bore tears, that coursed unheeded down a weathered face. "I knowed when he went away, he would never come back," she wept, and she thought of how he had made children shoe prints on her ceiling, and ate her corn dodgers while he sat on a snake rail fence to read a coveted book, and she said something so gentle and so loving was gone from the earth, she would never see its likes again.

He was the last casualty of the Civil War. He had joined the long march of the boys he grieved over who no longer could reply *here* to the calling out of their names.

"With the tolling, tolling bells' perpetual clang.

Here, coffin that slowly passes,
I give you my sprig of lilac."
Grieve, America grieve, but remember - *remember.*

And live my broken heart, for my two sons, and to see that *no one dare sully his name!*

Dear Doctor Henry came to stay with me and remained until I left the White House. But I do not remember the last days there at all. Judge David Davis came to handle my husband's affairs. Robert sent for him, and he came immediately from Chicago. They say I kept saying that my husband's wishes had to be carried out. He had intended to make an appointment, and on May 3, I saw that that appointment was made. I wrote to President Johnson from "your obliged friend." Albert Pike was an applicant for West Point and my husband had decided to give him this appointment. "And if any word or entreaty of mine at this time, can expedite this matter, I heartily trust it will avail in this young man's behalf - for I am deeply, not to say personally, interested in his success." I also wrote the new President a note about our dear doorkeeper Tad always called *Tom Pen.* "You will confer a personal favor upon me by retaining as principal doorkeeper, Thomas F. Pendel. He has been a sober, faithful, and obliging servant."

I saw that the poor colored woman got her husband's pay.

I received a letter of condolence from Queen Victoria. It read,

"Dear Madam, though a stranger to you I cannot remain silent when so terrible a calamity has fallen upon you & your country, & must personally express my *deep & heartfelt* sympathy with you under the shocking circumstances of your present dreadful misfortune.

No one can better appreciate than I can who am myself *utterly broken hearted* by the loss of my own beloved Husband, who was the *light* of my Life - my stay - *my all,* - what your suffering must be; and I earnestly pray that you may be supported by Him to whom Alone sorely stricken can look for comfort in this hour of heavy affliction.

With the renewed expression of true sympathy, I remain, dear Madam,
                    Your sincere friend Victoria."

I replied on May 21 from the White House.

"Madame:

I have received the letter, which Your Majesty has had the kindness to write, & am deeply grateful of its expressions of tender sympathy, coming as they do, from a heart which from its own sorrow, can appreciate the *intense grief* I now endure. Accept, Madam, the assurance of my heartfelt thanks & believe me in the deepest sorrow, your Majesty's sincere and grateful friend."

Dr. Henry assured me my husband was with me, that he never would leave me, for, as he had put into my wedding ring, *Love is Eternal.* "Mary, you, yourself, told me that you were with Eddy and Willie - that they both came to you to show you they are alive - always alive."

"You - accept I saw them?"

"Yes."

"If I see my husband again, I will go with him! I will!"

"Then, Mary, I imagine you will not see him," said Dr. Anson Henry. "You have to live for your boys and to keep his name untarnished."

"His name never could be tarnished, *never*," I said.

When they gave me his kid gloves from his coat pockets, I said, "I just cannot bear it." *How can I live when you were the balance of my life, when I was always so beautiful in your eyes? How can I live without the sound of your laughter? How can I live and say – I must tell him this – and you are gone? How can I live when you stole my heart away and took it with you?*

I had to distribute mementos from him to his friends. I wanted the doorkeepers, the guards, the valets and waiters to have something of his, something they could treasure for all of the rest of their lives. I wanted dear Sumner to have something, and wrote to him on May 9th.

"Your unwavering kindness to my idolized Husband, and the great regard, he entertained for you, prompts me to offer for your acceptance this simple relic, (my husband's cane) which being connected to his blessed memory, I am sure you will prize. I am endeavoring to regain my strength sufficiently to be enabled to leave here in a few days. I go hence, broken hearted, with every hope almost in life - crushed. Notwithstanding my utter desolation, through life, the memory of the cherished friends of my Husband & myself, will always be most gratefully remembered."

On the 14th I wrote to him again, sending along a likeness of Mr. Bright, such a friend to my husband he had had the likeness above his mantel in his White House office. Bright was "so noble & so good a friend of our cause, in this unholy rebellion. The news of the capture of Davis (May 10) almost over powers me! - In my crushing sorrow, I have found myself almost doubting the goodness of the Almighty!"

Mary Jane Welles continued to call and give solace and so did dear Sally Orne.

I had to leave. The new President never sent me a line of condolence. He never paid one call on me at the White House. I detested him and believed he was in on my husband's murder. I *never* believed it was over the fall of the Confederacy. I always believed traitors in his own government paid Booth to murder my husband. Why? Because they did not like what my husband stood for - *democracy?* Or was it because his plan for reconstructing the South differed from what they wanted? Or was it reconstructing the *whole* country for *whose* benefit? There goes crazy Mary again – but think on these things. Parker by not doing his duty caused my husband's murder. Stanton, who was so eager for shooting farm boys who fell asleep on picket duty, did nothing to John Parker. *He even kept his job!* My husband walked to the War Department on his last afternoon, and he asked that Major Thomas Eckert be his guard, and both Stanton and Eckert refused this! Eckert was too busy! My husband did not insist – but to refuse the commander in chief – and Eckert had no pressing duties at all. And why did Stanton deny this visit and say the visit to the War Department was on the thirteenth? My husband had invited General Grant and his wife to go with us to the Ford theater. Stanton talked him out of it that afternoon, according to Grant's cipher operator, Sam Beckwith, and Grant was sent out of town - or went out of town – *for an early visit to his children!* Why was the presence in our loge of our footman, Charles Forbes, denied and kept hidden in official accounts of that night? Why was Hanscom's delivery of Ord's telegram kept hidden? (Nothing important at all – why did it go to my husband in the first place?) Forbes saw that Parker was *not* doing his job. Hanscom saw that Parker was *not* doing his job. I think Stanton cut them from his story to protect Parker. The Washington papers got their war news from Stanton. For two hours after my husband was shot – he said nothing. It was three hours before Stanton disclosed the name of Booth as my husband's assassin. Most Americans did not know he was until the afternoon papers of the fifteenth. Fifteen minutes after my husband was shot all the telegraph lines from Washington to the outside world were cut. Maybe they all succumbed to a sudden sneezing spell, but Stanton controlled the one line left open. The other lines were in limbo for two hours, so the news got out when Stanton wanted it out. This was never noted in the official story of that night, but it was noted in print by one George Alfred Townsend, a reporter for the *New York World,* in that paper and later in his book, *Life, Crime and Capture of John Wilkes Booth,* published in 1865.

Every avenue of escape from Washington was blocked by Stanton except one, and that is the one that Booth and David Herold took. This cat was let out of the bag by hostler James Fletcher who worked for the Nailor livery stable. Herold had one of their unreturned bays and when Harold was riding away on it, Fletcher followed him all the way to the Anacostia bridge over the east branch of the Potomac into Maryland. There he met Sergeant Silas D. Cobb and learned that Booth has passed over the bridge, giving his proper name, and that Herold had followed. Rumor was that Booth had shot my husband and this caused Fletcher to go to the police with his story. The chief of police requested from General Augur horses for a police chase and Augur, in constant touch with Stanton, refused. Fletcher then goes to Augur and tells his story, and the general does nothing. A Captain Gleason arrives and tells the general that he knew Booth and knew he would be taking the road to Port Tobacco and begged for a mounted squad to follow him and he is refused. Booth's route to Virginia was unobstructed and when a Captain Beckwith got on his trail he was recalled. Booth kept a diary and what happened to it? Where was it finally found? It was locked up for two years in Stanton's war office. Eighteen pages were missing, and pages were written over. But what was not written over was Booth writing, "I almost have a mind to return to Washington and ... clear my name which I feel I can do."

Booth shot my husband during loud laughter, and, I, holding my husband's hand, *did not know he was shot.* Why did not Booth slip away undetected? Why did he jump on the stage for a stage appearance as if to say, *look at me, I did it!* Stanton had charge of the trial of the murderers - what did they have a chance to say? This gross injustice and distortion of the American Constitution - having the trial of my husband's murderers before a military commission, a secret trial with the court closed with Stanton controlling what of the trial would be made public! The *New York Times* said, "It would have been far better every way if these trials could have been held before the ordinary civil tribunals of the land and in the presence of the people. How can such a trial be reconciled with the plain provisions of the Constitution?" The excuse was that my husband was commander in chief of the military. My husband was president to all the people! Why was not Booth taken alive – twenty- eight armed men could not take one wounded man alive? And what about his talking on and on when he was shot in the *neck?* (Tell my beloved mother I died for the beloved Confederacy, etc. and etc., and maybe he threw in his latest weight gains and losses, too.) Why did Stanton keep the body of Booth buried in nameless places - *places* - it seems, when Booth's own Doctor Frederick May, said the body Stanton showed him *was not Booth?* What was it doing with a left boot on when Booth had a fracture of his left leg, and wore no boot on it after being treated by Dr. Mudd? *And the left boot was what implicated Mudd when it was produced at his house.* The people who knew Booth before the murder were hanged or imprisoned for life, but the people who helped him escape were released or became a government witness!

Did the Republican Party remain faithful to the freed slave - or even - the common man? Did it back free government with a free press? Did it back free labor - free public education for ALL?

Did it celebrate my husband but ignore what he stood for?

I believed, and I said that powerful people *in Washington* had something to do with my husband's murder, and I think that contributed to my being so demonized before and long after my death.

In this now of 1865 I had clothes to pack. I never had thrown a piece of clothing away since our first seven years together, those hard times, so I had crate after crate of my own things to have packed. I had decided to move to Chicago. I would never return to our home at Eighth and Jackson, never, never, never, and I would visit my beloved's grave in a quiet *country* cemetery, but never in Springfield.

In all, I would take sixty crates of my things, and my husband's things, from the White House. And while I was secluded in all of my pain, while I was struggling to live through it, crowds came into the White House and pillaged it. They took figurines, china, silver, candlesticks, whatever large furniture they could carry out, and what they could not carry out, such as the drapes and carpets, they slashed and carried off in great hunks. So, of course, when I left with my belongings, *I was accused of doing this,* marching off with the White House treasures, and if the very columns of the portico had been stolen, I would have been accused of carrying them off, too.

Robert went back for his father's burial on May 4, and Tad and I did not. It was Robert who visited our old home and saw it hung in black crepe, and the apple tree in the backyard in full bloom, the tree under which all of the boys had played, and the tree they picked clean for their father's apple pies. It was Robert who visited my sisters in Springfield, but I do not recall any visits of condolence for me from them, or letters, either.

I guess, if you were running the court of Queen Victoria, you do not need such things.

I would wear black the rest of my life. I never wanted to see lilac on me again, or white, or *any* color. I never would step inside of any opera or any theater again. I, who loved and admired actors, never intended to see another one, or read about another one.

I was forty-six years of age. I lived for two things, my sons, and to cherish the memory of my husband in all ways, as long as I drew a breath.

Chapter Twenty-seven

On May 22 I could hardly walk down the stairs of the White House to be driven to the depot for my journey to Chicago. I had with me my sons, Mrs.Keckley, Dr. Henry, William Crook and another White House guard, Thomas Cross. At six in the evening, at the Washington depot, we boarded a private car for the fifty-four hour journey to Chicago. They say I spoke to no one during that time. They say I wept or sat stonily in a daze.

I was still in the carriage going into the thick fog that shrouded the evening of April 14 - my husband waves goodbye - so happily - to his friends still standing on the White House steps - no - I was back in that lilac dress when we drove to the naval yard - and we talk of our sweet life to come - a new home - traveling to Europe *—Beloved, I have not your great core of strength - I never had your balance - and I failed you at City Point - I turned from you when Willie died, and you had the burden of those telegraph wires pouring out the blood from battle after battle - and there were always those lights of love for me in your eyes - father, father, husband and lover - my dearest friend in the world — won't you let me see you again?*

"Mama," said Taddie. "We must be strong."

"Mother," said Robert, "we must go on - with *dignity.*"

And the train clattered on into its endless miles, and house lights shone through the night, and I saw within them man and wife and dear children, and I thought my heart would stop in its futile beating. I heard the train whistle, a lonely calling back to the tracks it had long passed, also lost to the night.

The White House carpenters would be tearing down Taddie's little theater, and removing the desk from his office quarters in the basement where he used to write out his soldier passes. Or they might be gathering the Stuntz toys Taddie left behind, the *too, too many* toys his father had bought for him, because he no longer could buy any for Willie. Taddie didn't want those toys any more. He could not bear to look at them, any more than he had born looking at Willie's trains when Willie had died and had left them packed away ever so neatly in his toy box.

In Chicago William Crook and Dr. Henry saw us settled in a fine apartment at the popular Tremont House. One week there was all we could afford, and

I sent Robert out to find cheap rooms for us. The best we could do was the resort community of Hyde Park, seven miles south of Chicago on the lakeshore. I *tried* to like our new three rooms. I *hated* the three rooms, and so did Robert, and so did Taddie.

Then, through the stupor of my grief, my worst life long nightmare was realized. WE HAD NO MONEY. My husband's salary was gone. He had left no will, and since June 16, as my husband's executor, Judge Davis, was trying to disentangle all of that heir and money complex. And - what *did* I owe for those *damnable* clothes?

My national debt?

How much?

Robert, of course, did not have the funds to go on and study law at Harvard. He had to study law in the Chicago firm of Scammon, a friend of my husband, McCagg and Fuller. Now he could not marry Miss Harlan, and after the long commute into Chicago, he returned to Tad and me, and the miserable hated three little rooms - it was all gone - all gone - for him, the glory days of the Todd wealth and his father's presidency.

Mrs. Keckley left us, for she had to go on with her own life. I still heard not one line from my wealthy relatives in Springfield. *Not one line.* Not one visit. Destitute, in a horror that we would not even have a roof over our heads, I never asked any of them for financial help, and none of them offered it.

But I did have news from Springfield, bitter, ghastly news. Right after my husband was murdered, some of our friends, and some prominent men who were not, decided where my husband would be buried. Without one word to me, they formed some kind of a burial association and bought six acres of the Mather grounds, for $5,300, *in the middle of Springfield.* When I heard of this, the vault for my husband's body was all but completed! I wired them and said he would *not* be buried in their vault in the middle of the city. He wanted to be buried in a quiet country cemetery, and I had selected Oak Ridge as such a place. When my husband was buried there, the same men formed a monument association and were going to place a monument to my husband on their acres, and on June the Fifth, I wrote to Richard Oglesby, Governor of Illinois - who had been our friend, I thought, and who had visited my husband in the last night of his life.

"I learn from Newspapers & other sources, that your association has it in contemplation to erect a Monument to my husband's memory, on the Mather Block in the City of Springfield, instead of over his remains in the Oak Ridge Cemetery.

I feel that it is due to candor and fairness that I should notify your

Monument Association, that unless I receive within the next ten days, an Official assurance that the Monument will be erected over the Tomb in the Oak Ridge Cemetery, in accordance with my oft expressed wishes, I shall yield my consent to the request of the National Monument Association in Washington & that of numerous other friends in the Eastern States & have the sacred remains deposited, in the vault, prepared in Washington, under the Dome of the National Capitol, at as early a period as practicable."

I got my way, but made many enemies in Springfield. The vault for my husband would also bear the remains of his wife and sons.

I became a recluse. My eyes were blinded and almost swollen shut from weeping; the malaria chills and migraines never left me. Robert and Judge Davis pressured me to return to our Springfield home, and I said my suffering would only be increased if I did. I could not bear to *ever* look at that house again, go into its gate, into the rooms we all had shared, and where Willie had learned to speak just like his father. My sisters in Springfield were hostile, my best friends gone, and my moving back would be more than I could stand. *Every day* I would be waiting for him to return from the office, damper down Evil Eva, chop the wood for the fires - or come right home when thunder rolled out across the prairie -

No. No. No. I could not fit back into that. Together we had not wanted to go back and live in that house. Without him - *I could not.*

My only contact outside of my sons was through letters, and I wrote and wrote and *wrote* letters, black- bordered letters, and they said, in one way or another - It would be so much easier if I had only had *one* farewell glance from him! There was some poem - *it was not like your great and gracious ways - to leave me without even a backward glance* - or maybe it hadn't been written yet, or written only in my own heart.

And with this grief was my worry over money, and it widened the scar from our first lean seven years - but then, I had him. Then I knew with him I was safe, that we *would* get out of debt. And I knew now that if he had lived we would have a fine home wherever he chose for it to be, and we would pass our last years in joy and comfort, but he was struck down in the damnable war. He gave his life for the Union as did all of those boys he so cherished and spoke over at Gettysburg. I was bitter. Grant had had $110,000 raised for him, and *three* mansions given to him, and here, the family of his commander in chief, the President - *the last war casualty* - was discarded without a whim of remorse or conscience. When we were treated so cruelly, I knew how my husband would have suffered because of it. They could build marble monuments for him, and weep crocodile tears for him, but the family he so loved eked out a mere existence in cheap rooms.

I saw this as an insult to him and to his memory.

I saw this as a betrayal of him by his friends he had placed on high and made wealthy.

There was no money.

There was no money.

The words pounded in my aching head all of the days and through all of my sleepless nights. For three years, from April of 1865 to October of 1868, when my husband's estate was *finally totally* settled, it was a horror to me, another horror upon horror. The newspapers immediately carried the sum of my husband's estate, $75,000 in bonds and $10,000 in Iowa land, *and people said I was rich,* and the creditors, who were patient while I was the First Lady, now clamored for their money. I did not have it. We were each to be given a pittance from the estate to live on, each of our share doled out by the judge, and when the estate was released, Judge Davis had increased it, through wise investment, to $110,000. This was to be divided equally between my boys and me, Tad not getting his money until he was of age. The thirty seven thousand to each of us would have to earn interest for our support, as the principal would not be touched. These were times of dreadful inflation, after the war, and I was to support Tad and myself on an *annual* $1,500 - $1,800.

I did not see this as allowing me the livelihood of being the widow of a President of the United States. And there was the debt for the clothes, and I was determined it would *not* come out of my husband's estate. That was my debt, not his, nor Taddie's, nor Robert's. So I begged, directly and indirectly, from those who had become rich from my husband's appointments. This was wrong. This was mad. But I was mad, and it would get worse - this madness of fearing *abject* poverty.

There was the problem of Taddie who had to be taught to read and write. He now decided he wanted to learn, and I began to teach him. He, as usual, was cheerful and loving, and learned very, very rapidly, although we had quite a fuss over why *a-p-e* did not spell *monkey*. I gave him three long lessons a day, and in September, he was ready for public school.

We all still *hated* our miserable rooms at Hyde Park, and in November, finally moved into the better Clifton House in Chicago. There, Robert took his own two rooms. It was my passion for all of us to have our own home in that city. If my husband had not decided to settle in California, we would have moved here, in a *home worthy of an ex-President.*

In July of 1865, another blow had come. Dearest Dr. Henry, my friend all of my life, the man who arranged the renewed engagement for my husband and me, who came and comforted me after my husband's murder, who had seen us settled in Chicago, drowned. He was on his way to Olympia, Washington, and he was lost at sea. I wrote to his widow, Eliza, on August 31.

"Bowed down and broken hearted and feeling so deeply for you, in your agonizing bereavement, I feel justified in approaching you at this time when, we all feel alike crushed. We have both been called upon to resign to our Heavenly Father, two of the best men & and devoted husbands, that two unhappy women ever possessed . . . In this great trial, it is difficult, to be taught resignation, the only comfort that remains for us, is the blessed consolation, that our beloved are rejoicing in their Heavenly home, free from all earthly trials & in the holy presence of God and his Angels . . . Without my idolized husband, I do not wish to remain on earth . . . The world without my beloved husband & our best friend - is a sad and lonely place . . ." I had tried to find a cane and a family Bible for the doctor, but had not had the time to do it. When I could, I would send them to her. I also sold some stocks, when I had them, to help her in her widowhood. In our time, when our husbands died, so did our financial security.

On the same day I wrote to my wealthy friend, Sally Orne, and tried to hawk some of my clothes. Did she know anyone who would purchase them? They were worth $4,000, but I would sell them, *hardly worn at all,* for $2,500. The double lace shawl I wore *only for two hours* at the second inaugural ball - and I had some material I would sell - some 16 yards of white moire antique purchased at $11.00 a yard - for $125.00. "If any of your friends would desire such articles, please advise me - they are rich and beautiful ."

She knew no one who wanted them.

I had written to Elizabeth Blair Lee on the 25th, and I told her what I thought of General Grant becoming President. "I think, he had better let 'Well' alone. He makes a good general, but I should think, a very poor President - all of this is *entre nous* . . ."

I used *entre nous* a lot, for I wanted privacy as much as did Robert, but my mania over money *was* making me more and more irrational. It was a *mania,* and I was to be worse - over the fear of losing my money.

My mother prided in my looking beautifully dressed. When she died, I wanted beautiful dresses to continue. When I was to feel new losses - buying at least gave *something* to me!

Molly, your spending is attached to your grief over Willie. And your grief is driving you mad - Molly, look over yonder at that insane asylum - your grief can drive you into one -

Thank God my husband never knew how much I did spend. (really,

$20,000) It was my debt, and it had to be cleared, for he never left a debt unpaid in his entire life. I got Alexander Williamson, the boys' former tutor, involved. He could contact those made rich by my husband's appointment and get *them* to pay off my debt! They owed my husband, and so they should aid his widow. Or they could get Congress to do it, or get a subscription started for my husband's destitute family. Look what they did for Grant. I would see he was well paid out of what I got. We both would help each other.

I sent Mr. Williamson my husband's shawl, dressing gown and slippers, and I wrote on September 9, "They were given to you quietly & in the belief, that no parade, would be made over them, only your grateful appreciation of them, as having been worn, by the best man, the world ever saw."

I was pressing that Congress pay the *entire* four-year salary my husband did not live to earn. Hadn't Grant been given $110,000, along with his *three* mansions? And Grant had not given his life for his country, as had my husband. If we were to receive $100,000, I could buy a home, have the money to keep it up, and live in dignity, *privacy*, without my pain on exhibition with having to *board*, and security as befitting a *President's* widow and the widow *of the last casualty of the Civil War.*

And certainly one of the greatest Presidents this county had ever known.

All of my treasures from my life, all of my husband's things were in storage, and a fire had burned down a warehouse just two miles away - what if my things were next? I had no place to put them.

I sold our carriage at auction, and it was the first time in twelve years we had no family carriage. I was hounded more by my creditors, and was afraid Judge Davis would find out about my clothes debt, and Robert. My God - *Robert.*

Thanksgiving of 1865 was a torment. I wrote to Mary Jane Welles, "If I could close my eyes & not awaken until the day has passed, if possible, I would be less miserable. These anniversaries are so terrible, to the deeply bereaved!" To Francis Bicknell Carpenter I wrote, "The saddest of all my very sad days, has passed, *Thanksgiving* day, and by way, of diverting my mind & memory, from the recollection of yesterday, I have concluded to reply to your very kind note. . . Only those, who have suffered & lost, what made life so well worth living for, can fully understand the return of anniversaries, that recall the past so vividly to the mind & make the day of general praise & and rejoicing so painful . . ."

December of 1865 found Taddie very, very ill; he seemed to have one cold after another. When he was well, Robert and I had to go to Springfield. My husband's body was to be taken from the receiving vault at Oak Ridge and placed in a temporary tomb while the monument to him was constructed.

It was a bitter, bitter winter wind that blew that Christmas season, our *own magic season,* we had called it, and I saw where my own body would lie, and seeing his grave-site made me collapse. I arrived back to my rooms to the full realization that Congress had voted me only my husband's salary for his last year, as they had done for the widows of Harrison, a very, very wealthy man, and the widow of Taylor, also a very wealthy man. With deductions I would get $22,000, *and no possibility of a home.* It would mean public rooming and boarding, with the shame of no privacy and the vampyre press viewing me trapped in a glass cage.

I was bitter. I was frantic. Judge Davis had heard something of my debts, and I had written him on the thirteenth a lie -"any indebtedness I have easily settled." A ghastly, ghastly lie for a ghastly situation, *and then Robert found out!* I don't remember how. I might have told him about my terrors myself. "I will pay back every cent," I sobbed. I could see that look on his face - the *Mary is mad look* I hated so much.

On Christmas Eve of 1865 I wrote to Sally Orne, and in the letter I said, "Dear little Taddie, often says, 'dear Mother, three of us here, three in Heaven!' . . .Think of the sorrowful memories this Christmas brings me! I dare not pause to think -'"

But I did. How I did. In Springfield there was our house, rented out, filled with ghosts of the past and the ghost of my self, and I could picture other lamps lit in it by other people who would sit in our rooms, in the library across from the company parlor where my husband had liked to lie on the floor near the fire and dangle a child on his knee while he read. And before the fires that had burned for us, other children played, laughed, and were warm and cozy against the winter night. May God grant them life and joy, I said to myself, and pictured their sweet little faces and hoped their father would put on a great apron and make Saturday night toffee for them and for all their little friends on the block.

I sent Williamson to secretly go to creditors and see if they would take my things back - if there was *anything* on my bill I could *quietly* return -and when I got the money from Congress, of course I would settle.

On the twenty-ninth I wrote to Mary Jane Welles, and my letter was so bitter, I asked that she burn it. Congress had given the three of us each an income of $1,800 - how was that to get us a house? My migraines were keeping me in bed three days a week.

On the thirtieth I wrote to Sally Orne in reply to her letter just received. Some idea of my grief and anger - the family of the martyred President to be homeless wanderers forever - Grant's services were certainly not superior to his, and within the last eighteen months Grant was presented with three mansions - a general's salary was $25,000 a year, and on New Year's Day, he is to be presented with the $100,000 more, raised in New York - "Life is certainly, *coleur de rose* to him . . . all *darkness* & *gloom* to the unhappy family of his fallen chief ."

And I awaited those who put me where I was, and his sons where they were, to deliver their *mock turtle* eulogies on the 12th of February!

Jeweler Galt allowed me to return the jewels at the price I had purchased them - he was a very kind man - and I made a list of every single piece and its price - for a total of $2,146.

That was $2,146 off of my back.

Taddie had adjusted to school in the city. He made friends of everybody, as he had done with all of the soldiers he loved to write passes for at the White House. He had his pony. He always had to have his pony, and I saw that he had stabling money for him, and my husband's last gift to Robert was a horse, and he was stabled, too. Robert had purchased a 'near ' covered buggy, and we could get out a little.

But Taddie yearned for our own place. He hated to room and board as much as I did, and he did not want to go back to our home in Springfield, either. "I could never live there without papa-day," he said, using that old expression, when he had mostly lost his speech impediment.

Then, on May 22, 1866, I bought us a house! It was a beautiful, *beautiful* stately house on 375 West Washington Street with a magnificent stone front. It was on the pleasant West Side and near Union Park, a park with a lovely lagoon and bridges over it, flowers everywhere blooming, trees dappling the sunlight and bearing the bird song I had loved so much at our Soldier Home summers. There was the nearby Third Presbyterian Church to attend, and a fine school for Taddie, the Brown School on Warren Avenue between Page and Wood Streets. There Taddie was in a class of thirty boys and girls, and he began to really notice the girls, settled on one to join him in ice skating and walks in the park, and walks to and from school. He was not interested in learning how to dance, but he became editor of the school paper, the *Brown School Holiday Budget*, a four page illustrated paper with the motto of *Excelsior*, in honor of Longfellow. Taddie had his father's humor, as well as growing into his height, and he wrote a mock serious article on the veracity of there being a Santa Claus. How could he get down a chimney if he was so fat and carrying all of those presents? How could he keep from tripping on all of those steep house roofs? Get all of his presents into his little cutter? The article concluded that Mammas had *very much* to do with Santa Clauses.

I heard from Simon Cameron that a collection was being taken up for my boys and me. His affluent friends were doing it, and he expected to raise at least $20,000. We could live on that, and surely more help would come to us from those who had loved my husband and knew we were now destitute. With the $22,000 given to me by Congress, I could buy a home, and so I had. A builder gave me terms on the twenty thousand dollar home - $12,000 down and $8,000 due in July. But by mid-June, none of the Cameron bounty had arrived, and when I wrote about it, there was no reply. I was frantic. The builder came down to a total price of $17,000, but where was I going to get another $5,000 and live? Furnish the house? Heat the house? Finally, Cameron answered me. There was no savior fund. Jay Cook, the wealthy banker, where most of it was to come from, refused to help.

And Judge Davis was still hounding me to return to Springfield, and I had written to Cameron on April 6 about that. I was angry with Davis, saying he was honest but cold, that he had been appointed to the Supreme Court by my husband, with an office *for life,* and he said I should live on the $1800 a year in interest from my husband's estate, and move right back into our old house. "After the many years of happiness there with my idolized husband," I wrote, "to place me in the home, deprived of *his* presence and the darling boy, we lost in Washington, it would not require a day, for me to lose my entire reason - I am distracted enough, as it is, with remembrances, but I will spare myself & my poor sons, this additional grief. After the death of my little Willie, my loving and indulgent husband told me, that he would never carry me back, to a place, which would remind us both of so great a loss .. . Judge D- He would like to force us back to S- but I would eat the *bread* of *poverty* first here -"

It seems that was what I had to do.

I wrote to Charles Sumner on April 10. People in England were just beginning to comprehend the greatness of my husband - "and the nobility, of the great, good man, who had accomplished his work, and before *his Judge,* it was pronounced complete."

I disliked Andrew Johnson. He was going to undo all my husband had done for the colored if he could. Slavery was the great evil that had been so long allowed to curse the land. Johnson had vetoed their civil rights bill, but Sumner and his friends overrode that veto. "Johnson," I wrote, "and his unprincipled artisans cannot eradicate, the seal, that has been placed on the Emancipation Proclamation. It is a rich and a precious legacy, for my sons & one for which I am sure, and believe they will always bless God and their father . . . how it must try your soul to see a man, placed in *his* high office, to protect the Nation from its wrongs, to take these rebellious traitors so kindly, by the hand, and willingly place them in places & positions, that should only be claimed, by those who had 'fought the good fight' - and rejoiced with us, in victory." Never, never was Johnson carrying out my husband's policies. He would not have allowed the old ruling class of the South to do the old shameful things to the colored. *Never.*

In August of 1866 *that* man decided to go on a good personality tour to fight the likes of Sumner in Congress, and he took along, for props, Generals Grant and Custer, Admiral and Mrs. David Farragut, Secretary of the Navy, Gideon Welles and his wife, (my dear friend - *how could she?*) and his daughter, and Seward would also join them, as if Johnson were touring around as my husband. They were all to come to Chicago for Johnson to lay a wreath on the grave of Stephen Douglas, and planned to do the same on the grave of my husband. I did not intend to be present in my home to see the man who was on his *royal progress,* or, *more likely,* to be snubbed by his party, and so I went to Springfield to visit again the tomb of my husband. While there I hoped to see Billy Herndon. I had heard from Robert that Billy was going to write a book about my husband, and he had wanted to interview me. Robert and I agreed that we would help Billy write an *accurate* book, and because my husband had liked Billy, I tried to drop my own distaste for him. I wrote him on August 28, and among the things I wrote - "The recollection of my beloved husband's truly affectionate regard for you, and the knowledge of your great love and reverence for the best man who ever lived, would of itself cause you to be cherished with the sincerest regard by my sons & myself . . . those who loved my idolized husband aside from disinterested motives [sic] are very precious to me and mine." I told him I would visit the tomb "which contains my All in life - my husband."

We would meet where I would stay, the St. Nicolas Hotel, on Wednesday, September 5, at ten in the morning, if that satisfied him.

It did. That meeting was one of the biggest mistakes of my life.

Chapter Twenty-eight

I smelled booze all over him. He looked blurry eyed and disgusting, but he was my husband's junior partner, and we both had loved the same man. "Billy, you did not know him as President," I began. "You do not know how he grew and grew into that job, and the men around him soon learned he was above them all. I never saw a man's mind develop and soar to the heights his did. His writings - He had a kind of poetry in his soul. I always said it. I always knew it - his words will always be remembered -"

Billy was not writing anything down.

"He was my All. He was the other part of myself. We had twenty three years of a wonderful marriage, but I know, a love such as ours, is started first -"

His rheumy eyes were cold. He would not understand about souls meeting first among the angels, of souls separated in the night to unite again in the light. He did not even believe there was a God, or a soul, or life after death, or the possibility a love such as I had known and so treasured.

"Did your husband join a church?"

"No. He joined no church for he was uncomfortable with political, *institutionalized* religions. He used to say that when he was a boy, he was asked his religion."

"What was his reply?"

"My religion is - 'when I do good, I feel good, and when I do bad, I feel bad.'"

"You say he was not a *technical* Christian." He was writing this down.

"My husband was not spiritually *orthodox*, but no man was closer to God. No man felt more love for God."

"Were your husband's parents married?"

I was shocked and began to shake, but my malaria gave me chills and the shakes all of the time, and this noxious little man was worse than malaria, or typhoid, or cholera. All at once. "*Of course* they were married!"

"Do you have proof?"

"*What?*"

"I heard they were *not* married."

"My name is not *Hanks!* My children were not and are not named

Hanks!"

"Do you have proof of the marriage?"

"His family Bible! The marriage was recorded in the family Bible. How can you sit there and ask such a *dreadful* thing?"

"Were there *witnesses?*"

"From - 1806?" I was trying to remember the year *when* my husband's parents *were* married.

The interview finally ended, and I returned to our home in Chicago and my scheming how to keep it. I dreaded the winter to come. How would I pay for coal to heat our house - pay for the taxes on my pittance in interest? I hoped Davis and my husband's friend, Leonard Swett, a rich lawyer now practicing in Chicago, would help me out. I wrote them both hardship letters. I was skipping meals, and living as frugally as I could. *I had to keep our home.*

Then on November 16 Billy Herndon gave his first Ann Rutledge lying lecture. It seems he was going all over the place being an authority on my husband whose death was the most important thing in his miserable life. Now he would be rich and famous by the fact he was my husband's junior law partner, and so he made up what he felt like saying, and he was to use *my interview* with him for saying my husband was an *atheist!* And *illegitimate!* And he said my husband never loved me, his wife - the mother of his sons. He loved a girl I had never heard of before, Ann Rutledge, and he had never stopped loving her for one minute, and was miserable with me and ran away from our wedding and married *me only because I married him for revenge* - these were all of the twisted tales of that odious little man. This man who knew all about our home life, *never* having *once* entered our home!

Robert was furious. He called on Herndon in Springfield and got nowhere, and Billy said terrible things about him, too. Meanwhile, Billy stole all of my husband's books left in the law office, and I said to all I could say it to, we know Billy is a drunk, an outrageous liar, and we can safely now say he is also a *thief.*

Robert told Judge Davis that Billy was making an ass out of himself, *in writing*, and Billy went on in his merry way, and said that when Ann died my husband went mad and had to be placed under a suicide watch - he was getting this mixed up with my husband's despair over *our* separation.

The news made headlines and spread *and spread,* and it broke my heart. My husband never lied about anything, and he told me, and it was music to my ears- I was the first and *only* woman he had ever loved.

As this ghastly lie first made me into a witch - and worse - let us now examine the evidence. *There isn't any.*

Ann was engaged to John McNamar, who also used the name of McNeil, and my husband and he were good friends, and my husband affectionately called him "Mack." Mack went to New York to seek his fortune, and when he returned to New Salem, Ann had died, and my husband grieved that she died so young.

That was it.

Can you believe a man with the integrity of my husband, would court his *best friend's* fiancee? Do you think a man with my husband's integrity would court a woman, tell her he adored her, had never loved another woman, that his love for her was eternal, marry her, constantly repeating his love - and not mean it? *Lie about it?* My husband never told a lie in his life. He never did a dishonorable act in his life. Billy was making him out to be a cad - and the cad throne was already occupied by Billy.

With Billy lying and embellishing the romance that never was, denials came forth from those who then knew Ann and my husband. James Short was one of my husband's close friends then; my husband stayed at his house when he was out that way, and Short said he knew of *no* "engagement or tender passages" between my husband and Ann Rutledge. Short wrote this to Billy on July 7, 1865.

McNamar wrote a letter to Billy on December 1, 1866, that he knew of no romance between the two, and he did not know *of all New Salem encouraging the romance,* and he did not know of any *crazy grief spell* of my husband at Ann's death. Ann's brother, R. B. Rutledge, knew of no romance and wrote this to Billy on October 22 and 30 of 1866, assuming Billy knew things about the romance he did not. Ann's aunt said Ann loved Mack until her death and the two had never stopped corresponding.

Billy could not say that my husband told *him* of the romance; he had to admit my husband never discussed *anything* of a private nature with him. The only intimate my husband might have discussed this with, was his best friend, Joshua Speed, who formally had introduced us, and Speed wrote to Billy on November 30, 1866, saying he *knew of no such romance.*

My husband's half-hearted courtship of Mary Owen was going on when Ann was alive, and not even ill. Billy even dredged up a witness to the Ann Rutledge romance who placed Ann in *Iowa* while it was happening!

Then the noxious little man had the nerve to write our dear friend and former pastor, Reverend James Smith, in Scotland. His letter was insulting and insolent. Billy wanted *proof* that my husband was as much an infidel as Billy was, and demanded *written evidence* that my husband was a Christian - the *exact words* as proof - and he was to answer as a *gentleman* and not as a

Christian minister. And, of course, he was to verify the fact that my husband never loved me, that after the death of his beloved Ann, he never used the word *affectionately* for another woman, nor told another woman he loved her, or - ever again even used the word *love!*

Thank God. Smith replied in an open letter published in the Chicago *Tribune,* and with it, he included Billy's shameful letter to him. Would my husband had solemnly promised to God to be a faithful loving and affectionate husband and lie about it? asked the pastor. That would make him worse than a dishonest man. Perhaps Billy did not have too much of an idea of my husband's home life in his view *from a law office* - it was within the family circle "the man exhibits himself as he really is," and the pastor was at our house many, many times, and saw my husband's "heart overflowing with love and affection" to his wife.

Billy had launched his attack on *me* from the first, and Robert, who hated *any* kind of publicity, tried to stop it. On December 13, 1866, Robert wrote this to the noxious little man: "All I ask is that nothing be published by you, which after careful consideration will seem to cause pain to my father's family, which I am sure you do not wish to do."

In a letter to Judge Davis written March 6, 1867 I called that noxious little man a *dirty dog.* I would have called him worse, but why blame his *mother* for what *he* became? How he maligned me. How he maligned my husband. He could never take the glory of my life - the love between my husband and me - away.

But you have believed this lie - all of these years. For me to be bad, Ann had to be the angel love, and believe me, that little man *hated* me as I grew to *hate* him. His book with Jesse Weik was published in 1889, seven years after my death, and I was not here to refute it. Robert would not, as he wanted no publicity about his parents, especially about me, and Edgar Lee Masters even made Billy's lie into poetry - remember the last lines?

I am Ann Rutledge, who sleep beneath these weeds -
Beloved of my husband,
Wedded to him, not through union
But through separation.
    Bloom forever, O Republic
    From the dust of my bosom.

No. *From the lying pen of the odious little man whose brain or character never rose above the seat of his pants.*

In 1942 his papers were opened, and in them Billy writes to his writer (literary collaborator) about these Ann Rutledge love facts. "*Draw on your imagination and fill up* - it will please the people." Billy was bothered - some - that Ann *was* engaged to another man - so what did he write about *that*? "Again, the more I think of the Ann Rutledge story the more do I think that the girl had two engagements... I shall change my opinion of events & things on the coming of new facts and on more mature *reflection* in all cases -"

So Ann was engaged in Billy's addle pated mind - to my husband *and* John McNamar - as for Billy's *mature* reflection - he never got there.

Robert had his law degree in early 1867, and on February 25, he was admitted to the Illinois bar. He formed a partnership with Charles Scammon, son of Jonathan, where he had studied law. Charles caused trouble with his drinking but then "dried out" in treatment, and the partnership was to last for several years.

I had begged for help to keep our home I bought on May 22, 1866. I had economized on everything, and in every way I could. My income of $1,700 a year did not suffice. I wrote to Davis on April 6 of 1867: "As it is utterly impossible with my small, contracted means to keep house - in order to meet even ordinary expenses - I shall have to dispose of my furniture which you may be assured will be a fresh trial to me." For the best price I was told I had to sell the furniture from the house and not at auction, and it must be done by the 20th of this April. I had to do it. I could not go another year "being compelled to count every *cent* I must spend" ... "Of course having an auction sale, at the house - will be as great a trial to Robert as well as myself - But I *find* that *pride* does not give us bread & meat -" And I could not resist my bitterness. "A poor return *all this is,* for the immortal services rendered by my beloved husband, to his Country!"

Then I had an idea about saving myself. About *surviving.* I had written to Mrs. Keckley in March. "... I have not the means, to meet the expenses of even a first-class boarding house, and must sell out and secure cheap rooms at some place in the country. It will not be startling news to you, my dear Lizzie, to learn I must sell a portion of my wardrobe to add to my resources to live decently ... I cannot live on $1,700 a year, and as I have many costly things which I shall never wear, I might as well turn them into money, and thus add to my income, and make my circumstances easier. It is humiliating to be placed in such a position, but, as I am in the position, I must extricate myself as best I can ..." I asked her to meet me in New York to assist me in selling my clothes.

Was this idea against flag and country? What was I expected to do? Beg in the streets? Join a freak show at Barnum's? I would never wear again those furs, those jewels, those shawls and those elaborate gowns and bonnets - they were costly - they were *valuable*, and that was the only way I could see to pay my debts and to shelter, feed and cloth myself and Taddie.

I had to sell my furniture. Then I had to rent my home. I had it barely a year. So in two years, we had had four resident changes. In late June Taddie, Robert and I were summoned to Washington to testify in the trial of John Surratt. I was to ill to go, and seeing Washington again would be ghastly. John Surratt was a possible accomplice to my husband's murder, and Taddie thought he was the man who had tried to get to my husband on the *River Queen*, but nothing came of it. When he was in Washington Robert became engaged to Mary Harlan, and I could not have been happier. I thought her incredibly lovely in looks and character and she would be like my own darling daughter.

When my sons returned to Chicago, in August, I took *temporary* rooms at the Clifton House again, and enrolled Taddie in the Chicago Academy for the school year of 1867-68.

Now I was determined to get my house back from renters by selling my clothes in New York, *very* secretly of course, under the name of Mrs. Clarke. I wrote again and asked Mrs. Keckley, my dearest friend in the world, to meet me in New York and help me through the ordeal. I would have enough money from my clothes to reward her as well.

But in New York, because she was colored, we could not rent decent rooms, so we shared a tiny ghastly attic room, and when we were to be served meals at the hotel, she could not be even served there.

"Lizzie," I said, "we can eat at a public restaurant."

"I won't have you do that," she said. "You - the widow of the President of the United States!"

"But no one knows who I am." I was heavily veiled, for the last thing I wanted was for anyone to know who I was.

I was served a meal and took part of it to Lizzie in our attic rat suite. The next morning, *both* of us, heavily veiled, discussed what we should do while we sat on a bench in Union Square Park. "Lizzie, I want to give the clothes to W.H. Brady and Company."

"But you said they were rude to you -"

"Well, they discovered who I am and became all smiles and promises. They said when it is known *whose* clothes they are, I will get at least *one hundred thousand dollars* for them."

W. H. Brady and his partner, S. C. Keyes, at 609 Broadway, received us as if I were royalty, and told me I was to leave everything in their hands along with the clothes, for they were keen business men of New York City, and I would have my hundred thousand in a few weeks. How thrilling that was to hear! Money for our home again! No more begging letters to write!

Mrs. Keckley saw to their getting the clothes, furs, jewelry, but then Brady and Keyes told me to write to local politicians to let them know about the clothes - men who were in my husband's administration. "Why?" I asked.

"They will make heavy advances to keep it from being known that you have to sell your clothes, *worn at the White House,* to live."

"They will buy the clothes?"

"They should, and they surely will."

This was along my own line of thinking, and I agreed.

But it got worse. Brady decided to let the wealthy politicians know if they did *not* buy anything, he would publish my pleading letters to them in the newspapers. That was a form of blackmail, but then it did not seem so to me. Surely, the letters would *not* have to be published.

One example: I told Brady to contact Abram Wakeman, my friend, my husband's friend, and my husband had made him wealthy when he appointed him Surveyor of the Port of New York. I wrote Brady on September 14, about Wakeman, "He was largely indebted to me for obtaining the lucrative office which he has held for several years, and from which he has amassed a very large fortune . . . Mr. Wakeman many times excited my sympathies in his urgent appeals for office, as well for himself and others. Therefore he will be only to happy to relieve me by purchasing one or more of the articles you will please place before him."

He didn't.

I was stunned. I was mad with worry. *Mad* is the definitive word. My husband knew I was irrational about spending money, but he did not know *how* irrational! Thank God he did not know! After Willie died, and I went into my first breakdown over grief, he wanted me to cheer myself up some way - buy something pretty, he would say. I had overspent in decorating the White House; I had overspent when I first shopped s First Lady - one my husband knew, the other he did not.

Brady had the clothes go on public exhibition for sale and my pleading letters published in the *World.*

I did not expect those pleading letters to be published!

On October 18 I wrote to Rhoda White, who had just lost her own husband. "Our sorrows must certainly draw us *very near* to the loved ones, who have only 'gone before.' " About the clothes scandal I wrote, "Having no further use for the articles purposed to be sold - and really requiring the proceeds - I deposited them with an agent & presumed no publicity would result from it - I was more astonished than you must have been to see my letters, in print . . . every act (of mine) is seized upon & distorted."

Even with the damnable printing, the clothes did not sell. Brady was not daunted. All we had to do, for my hundred thousand, was to get a circular letter about my clothes' plight signed by *notables,* and then the *public* would buy.

Neither happened.

Then *Brady* decided to send my clothes off on a curiosity tour, where admission would be charged to see them, including the white dress I had worn on the night of my husband's murder!

I was horrified and, in early 1868, got all of my clothes back.

And on March 4, 1868, paid Brady and Keyes their fee of $824.

And had the vampyre press down on me in venomous editorials about that *dreadful* woman hawking her *useless* finery, forcing her *repugnant* personality *upon the world-* the intensely *vulgar* woman - all her relatives *secessionist - her sympathies were always with the rebellion* - and the *worst* from the radicals in Congress I had always supported in their fight with Johnson! And *they* said I was *hawking off my husband's clothes,* with my own - most of these lies from the *World* and the *Springfield Republican.*

On October 6, 1867 I wrote to Mrs. Keckley, *my dear Lizzie,*

"I am writing this morning with a broken heart after a sleepless night of great mental suffering. R (obert) came up last evening like a maniac, and almost threatening his life, looking like death, because the letters of the *World* were published in yesterday's paper. I could not refrain from weeping when I saw him so miserable. But yet, my dear good Lizzie, was it not to protect myself and help others - and was not my motive and action of the purest kind?. . . I pray for death this morning. Only my darling Taddie prevents me from taking my own life. I shall have to endure a round of newspaper abuse from the Republicans because I dared venture to relieve a few of my wants . . . I am nearly losing my reason." And on the 8th - to Lizzie about the Republicans, "They will *howl on* to prevent my disposing of my things. What a *vile vile* set they are! . . . I suppose I would be *mobbed* if I ventured out . . . The glass shows me a pale, wretched, haggard face, and my dresses are like bags on me. And all because I was doing what I felt to be my duty . . . The politicians, knowing they have deprived me of my just rights, would prefer to see me starve, rather than dispose of my things." And the next day, the ninth, I wrote to *My dear Lizzie* again. "It appears as if the fiends had let loose, for the Republican papers are tearing me to pieces in this border ruffian West.

If I had committed murder in every city in this *blessed Union*, I could not be more traduced. And you know how innocent I have been of the intention of doing wrong. A piece in the morning *Tribune,* signed "B," 'Pretending to be a lady, there is no doubt Mrs. L- is deranged and has been for years past and will end her life in a lunatic asylum.' They would doubtless like me to begin it *now*."

I did not hear from Lizzie and I wrote to her again on Sunday, October 13. I said the people in this ungrateful country are like dogs in the manger who will not help me and will not allow me to help myself. And the *Springfield Journal* was editorializing I had been *deranged* for years, and should be *pitied* for my strange acts.

I know why some members of Congress had this great crusade against me, declaring me insane. Someone started a rumor that I was writing a book about my White House years, including *their* business transactions during the war. They must have done crooked things to so fear exposure. The press printed *again*, I had stolen the White House furnishings, that I pretended to be pregnant so I could stay longer and steal more silver spoons. *(Pittsburgh Commercial,* October 29, 1867) The *Southern Opinion* of Richmond wrote on October 12 that I was about to marry again, and on November 30, that what I was trying to sell, I had received as bribes! They included a precious little poem about it, using the pseudonym I had first used of Mrs. Clarke.

> What cabinet member (now hid in the dark.)
> Bought his seat by his gifts to you, fair Mrs. Clarke?
> What opulent presents were made in advance?
> By seekers of missions to Russia and France?

This poem was *disrespectfully* dedicated to me.

To me - bearing my beloved husband's name, the man I now idolized as a true savior of his country, and every morning this vile *garbage* was thrown at my doorstep.

Do you see how this vileness fitted in with Billy's lies about my husband hating me, my hating him, and the Ann Rutledge travesty?

I wrote Lizzie my new address. Taddie and I wanted to go back to the Union Park neighborhood of our *rented-out* home, and we roomed and boarded there on 460 West Washington Street. On October 24 I concluded in a letter to Lizzie, "If man is not merciful, God will be in his own time."

There were friends who did not dessert me. Charles Sumner, Mrs. White, Mrs. Orne, and colored fiends, like Lizzie, and that fine man, Frederick

Douglass, and Reverend Henry Highland Garnet, and these two dear men wanted to lecture on my behalf. They wanted to tell the truth about me, how I was always more radical for their freedom and citizenship rights than even my husband. How could they help me - the *despised* defending the *despised?* Through Lizzie, I expressed my gratitude and told them not to bother.

On November 12, Robert went to Davis to settle my husband's estate, and toward me he, I wrote Lizzie, "is very spiteful at present, and I think hurries up the division to *cross* my purposes."

The vampyre press was now saying, while First Lady, I stole, by giving state dinners so I could pad the expenses and steal the money! And, of course, there were my political bribes as First Lady, all along with my giving military secrets to *both* sides of the war -

Another February 12, and more crocodile tears shed - Oh, my darling, how he suffered at the calumny thrown at me! How he would hate it now.

When the estate of my husband was settled, I learned nothing of it from Robert; the first I knew of it was from the press. Then Robert did call on me and gave a complete report, and I wrote Davis and thanked him for managing the money so well, for building up $85,000 to $110,000. My annual income would fluctuate in annual interest from $1,600 to $1,800. I got the rent from the Union Park house and shared with my sons the rent from the Springfield house. Each of us got $50.00 a year from the latter. My sister Fannie was in trouble herself, for her husband, Dr. William Wallace, died in the summer. I suggested to Robert, and he suggested to her that she take our Springfield home, but she thought it too large. Robert and I would give Fannie money when we could do it - which we did.

I wrote to my friend, Rhoda White, who had just lost her daughter, and I said what I believe yet, "It is the lot of humanity to suffer - otherwise we would cling too fondly to earth and its *transitory* enjoyment."

December - 1867 - the closing of another ghastly year without my husband. I was cringing at the *old clothes scandal,* as they called it, for I felt I had shamed his name. If the papers would just *drop* it.

I sent some gifts to my husband's dear step mother he so loved, and I sent her a note with them on December 19 - "In memory of the dearly loved one, who always remembered you with so much affection, will you not do me the favor of accepting these few trifles? . . . In my great agony of mind that I cannot trust myself to write about, what so entirely fills my - mind - thoughts - my darling husband; knowing how you loved him also, is a grateful satisfaction to me. Believe me, dear Madam, if I can ever be of service to you, in *any respect,* I am entirely at your service . . ."

Another Christmas - celebrations with lights and songs and new fires and old memories. I was being demonized for the old clothes scandal and because I was not Ann Rutledge. And so hard, *so hard,* I willed my husband to let me see him once more, to bring Eddy and Willie with him, but that did not happen. Somehow, I had to live out my days without this joy, too.

By January 15 I was back at the Clifton House. If we went anywhere, Taddie and I went by streetcar. One time I did not take my money with me and found it stolen when we returned. I lost $82.00 and a new pocket book.

In the spring of 1868 the vampyre press *finally* let the old clothes be. Then came another shock, another blow - I was betrayed by Lizzie Keckley! She and a ghostwriter, or writers, wrote her life as a slave and her life in the White House with my husband and me. She named it *Behind the Scenes,* and she should have called it, *My Knife in Mary's Back.*

My best friend in the world had betrayed me. She knew how my husband and I always wanted our private life private, and I told her when I hired her, it would be under these conditions. In her book she told of my irrationality after Willie's death, and how my husband had mentioned that if I could not control my grief I would go mad. In her book she printed what Robert and I wanted secret, how we were going to pay off my debt, which I did, *in full.* But to print my agony because of my buying sprees, and about the old clothes' scandal, she included the negative things I wrote to her then about Robert - *being spiteful* - *raving distracted* - my thinking when Robert was younger, he thought himself a *lofty* soul - and in her wrong to me she included my *private* soul-revealing letters to her, twenty four to be exact. Her book dredged up no scandal about me, and she did not lie and assassinate my character, but she exposed my private life and my husband's, and she betrayed his trust and mine.

This was a blow, as bad as noxious *little-man-Billy* hauling around Ann Rutledge. I expected the worst from *him,* but from Lizzie? That ended my friendship with her, and Mary Jane Welles' adoration and support of the miserable *colored-hating Johnson* ended that friendship, too.

Robert now had more to be ashamed of about me. His future father in law, James Harlan, now considered me mad, and Robert laid all of this out for him - you see, sir, I love your lovely daughter but I have this problem - *a mad mother -*

Robert was all Todd. With one more D than God.

When my husband's estate was settled, Judge Davis assumed legal guardianship of Tad, allowing him $100 a month, for Robert soon would be married, and I was sure that I would not live very long. That June of 1868

Taddie and I returned to Springfield, and Taddie formerly presented one of his father's canes to Jesse K. Dubois, my husband's close friend. I remembered when Taddie and Willie had smoked cigars with the Dubois boys, and how all of them had become so ill from it.

I saw the monument being built for my husband's tomb, and visited with my favorite cousin, John Todd Stuart. The visit to Springfield was hard, and I seemed to be another person there, already gone from it in body and soul, half between the old world there I had so cherished and the barren world I now had to bear *because it was without him.* Oh, Father, I thought. Monuments and ceremonies are like pressed flowers placed in the family bible you spoke about, really lifeless, so silent of the sun that had nourished them - *why can't I see my boys again? Why can't you bring Eddy and Willie to me, and stand at the foot of my bed with them - Father - lover - husband – don't you remember I said my heaven is where you are?*

Taddie, fifteen, now thin and tall, and with his father's dark hair and swarthy complexion, looked more and more like him. He had his father's gentle affectionate nature, and the bond between Taddie and me was now my strongest tie to life. In Springfield, he walked the old familiar streets, met his childhood friends who had taken turns seeing parades from my husband's shoulders, all of them who came to our taffy pulls, who cheered all of Willie's speeches for the election of his father. I think he went back to the house on Jackson, but I certainly did not. He visited aunts and uncles. I do not recall that I was invited.

Taddie and I spent that summer in the Allegheny Mountains at the health resort of Cresson Springs, and I met a lovely woman, Eliza Slataper, and her son, Danie. She became a dear friend, and Danie became one to Taddie. How I *loved* the mountains. Taddie and I both felt such calm and such peace when we were in the mountains. I walked beautiful mountain paths and waited for a sign my husband was with me - but - as usual - he was gone - and so totally now, were Eddy and Willie. Did I see those angels at the foot of my bed at the White House when I was *awake?* My husband accepted my seeing them, and it had brought him joy. A breeze moved the trees, ruffled my hair, caressed my skin - but in it - not a word from my lost treasures. "Mother," Taddie said. "Papa-day," he smiled, "Papa-day and Willie - and your precious little Eddy - I am sure they are here with us."

"Why can't I see them?"

"You always told me, why."

"What did I say?"

"That if we are blind here in this finite and limited world of the senses,

they are in another world where blindness is gone with all separations."

"I said that?"

"Both you and father said that."

"Do you feel the presence of your father?"

"Whenever I think of him."

"Why can't I? Why can't I?" I choked.

"You will."

"I try so hard!"

"Mother, I don't think that is something you can *try* for."

Robert was going to marry Mary Eunice Harlan in the home of her father, in Washington, that *horror filled* hateful city. I had to go to the wedding, and not act *too* mad now and scare Mr. Harlan right out of his mansion.

Robert, twenty-five, and his Mary were married on the evening of September 24, 1868, and the bride looked beautiful, *truly* beautiful. She wore white silk trimmed with satin folds, and a crown of orange blossoms held her veil. The house was decorated with exquisite taste, flowers everywhere, and Taddie had bought himself a white vest, which he wore with great pride. He adored his older brother and wanted to look grand for his wedding. I wore black and no jewelry except for my wedding ring.

Tad stayed in Washington for a week after the wedding, but I fled the city for Baltimore as fast as I could. I had made up my mind to live in Europe, away from the vampyre press that would never stop maligning me, going abroad as my husband and I had planned - away from this land and home of my deepest sorrows.

Taddie did not want to leave his brother and his new sister in law, but when the doctors told him that only a change of scene would keep me alive, he agreed living in Europe would be better for both of us.

We sailed for Europe on the steamer, *City of Baltimore,* on October 1, 1868.

I knew Robert had made a good marriage and would be a good husband. Robert, after his stay with the Todd's at Eddy's sickness and death, was never as close to my husband and me. I thought him noble, intelligent, and honorable. He was just a social recluse, (his wife worse) and the exposure of my mental state in the old clothes scandal scarred our relationship the rest of my life. I know he never got over his embarrassment because I tried to sell my clothes. That is why he burned every tender letter between his father and me, as if that love were not a good one, and should never have been.

No, it was Taddie who made me cling yet to this frail body of such ill health, the mind that could not resign itself to deaths that took my heart away with them - until the time that would come, and it *would* come - as God is ever merciful - and I would be at the *coterie* ball again, my favorite waltz playing, the chandeliers all alight, and I would be on the *wing's of life's expectation!* Then a tall, tall man with the kindest eyes in the world would look down at me, and in his eyes would be lights of love for me that I saw there the rest of our lives, and he would say, *Miss Todd, I want to dance with you the worst way.*

And we would be in the beginning again, rain against the windows while we made love, boys in the apple tree picking them for his pies, smells of cinnamon, nutmeg and cloves as the apple pies bake in the oven of Evil Eva, all the walks to the gate to meet him, our gate so crooked because the children loved to swing on it — watching him put on his great apron to make Saturday night toffee, and the thunder clouds could rumble, and lightning could fork down to the earth from them, and what would I care? He had come home to me. My home was where he was. My heaven will be where he is.

Chapter Twenty-nine

Our ship docked at Bremen, Germany, and in two weeks we were in Frankfurt, which in my letters I spelled Frank*fort*, Kentucky style. We were charmed with the city, and decided to stay there. It was a city of beauty, history, a medical and educational center. It had an English-speaking colony and nearby watering places for one's health. I enrolled Taddie in the fine, fine boarding school of Dr Hohagen, attended by both English and German boys. Taddie was to have *special* instruction in English, German and French. In this school, he lost all trace of his lisp, and even developed in his English, a German accent!

I stayed at the Hotel *d'Angleterre,* rented only one room and took most of my meals in it, as I did not want to be stared at in Germany any more than I had enjoyed it in America. My expenses were about four dollars a day, the *lowest* rate I could find. Of course, I was known as the widow of an American President and thought to have a great pension and was charged accordingly.

I was in a land of strangers, and glad of it. At last I was free of the Puritan public-press pillory. Robert had a flourishing law practice, that wonderful, wonderful dear sweet girl for a wife, and I had my Taddie in a fine school and anything he wanted. I scrimped, but Taddie did not. I saw to that, and always would, until he probably would become a successful lawyer like his father, like his brother. How wonderful it would have been if my husband had been able to have lawyer sons for partners! I don't think his father would have even out debated Willie.

And how wonderful it would have been if Taddie and I had walked to the sites drenched in history with my husband, as he so had wanted. He enjoyed history more than anyone I knew. My grief was more subdued now, as if all of that anguish had mainly become physical. Physician fees were eating away at my small income, and I had to move to cheaper quarters - on the *fourth* floor - no carpet - and cutting down on heat. My migraines had company - pain up and down my spine and constant colds. And, of course, I had the money worry; *that* haunted me day and night.

Robert had wanted me to loan him money by allowing him to cash in my

1881 bonds purchased by my husband in 1865. Robert would use them, I wrote to Judge Davis on December 15, 1868, "-in connection with John Forsythe of C (Chicago) in building 28 homes on the North Side - thereby of course increasing his money & offering me 10 percent on the money, for four years." At first, I wrote, I told Robert that I would do that, but now I was afraid to and sent Robert a telegram saying so. "With my great love for my good son, the necessity of refusing his request, has made me quite ill," I continued. It would have worked out well, I know now; for Robert was to become very, very wealthy, and was an excellent shrewd businessman. The bonds were then worth $55,000, and from them I would have had a yearly income of $5,500, better than the $1,800 interest from my share of my husband's estate. Then, I did not know if I would lose it all and have *nothing*.

The Frankfurt weather was icy harsh and my physicians told me I had to go to Italy for the winter, but I had no money for it. I added to Judge Davis, "I cannot but believe if Congress knew the circumstances of the case, they would allow me a pension of say $3,000 - a year - to help me out of my difficulties. With my certain knowledge of your great goodness of heart, dear Judge - I am sure if *it is* brought up before Congress, *you* will aid, than oppose it."

I had heard that Sumner was going to introduce such a pension bill for me. Other war widows got pensions - why couldn't I? That money would change my life; allow me decent meals and *heat*, and even a *carpeted* room.

In December of 1868 I wrote a begging letter to the Honorable Vice-President and Members of the Senate:

"I herewith most respectfully present to the Honorable Senate of the United States an application for a pension. I am a widow of a President of the United States whose life was sacrificed to his country's service. That sad calamity has greatly impaired my health; and on the advice of my physician I have come over to Germany to try the mineral waters and during the winters to go to Italy. But my financial means do not permit me to take advantage of the advice given me, nor can I live in a style becoming to the widow of the Chief Magistrate of a great nation, although I live as economically as I can. In consideration of the great service my deeply lamented husband has rendered to the United States, and of the fearful loss I have sustained by his untimely death- his martyrdom, I may say - I respectfully submit to your honorable body this petition, hoping that a yearly pension may be granted me so that I may have less pecuniary care."

On January 14, 1869, Oliver Moton of Indiana introduced into the Senate a joint resolution for my financial relief - my husband had been commander in chief, had been killed in wartime, and surely I was entitled to a pension "upon the same principles and for the like reasons with any other officer who fell in the war." Charles Sumner had really formed this resolution, but the amount of the pension was not stated in it. He suggested it be $5,000 a year, which would be the interest on the rest of my husband's salary if he had served out his term. The resolution was referred to the Committee on Pensions, and after ten days of study, they recommended it be *turned down*. There followed an acrimonious Senate debate over a pension to me, and the vampyre press got into it, and all of the dirt cast at me was dredged up again, *every* detail of my finances, and on March 3, the Fortieth Congress *rejected my pension,* 23 for, 27 against, and 16 Senators not voting. I didn't need the money, I guess, and I didn't deserve it anyway. I could live on my fortune garnered from all the White House stolen spoons.

Sumner would not be stopped. On the 5th he introduced a second pension bill, of $5,000, to the Forty-First Congress and he expected an immediate vote on it. Instead it was sent back to the Pensions Committee that sat on it for a year.

Hoping to suffocate it to death.

In January of 1869 the bitter cold of Frankfurt was killing me, and my physicians said again I had to go to a warm climate or perish. On February 17, I wrote to Eliza Slataper from Nice, *France.* I was at home with the language and wrote, "I find the weather as sunny & balmy as June is with us. Flowers growing in the gardens, oranges in the trees, my windows open all day, looking out upon the calm, blue Mediterranean." I stayed outside all I could, marveling at a slow sweet way of living - tranquil, calm, amongst old historical places, while in America the vampyre press was demanding I die in misery. I told Eliza of the charmed castles I had visited on my way to Nice, castles haunted by the past presence of Napoleon and one haunted by the *white lady* ghost. And then - of some joy that had come to my heart, as a lovely warm day can bring - "Was there ever such a climate, such a sunshine, such air? - You cannot turn for flowers, beautiful bouquets, thrust into your very face. I never return from my walks without my hands being filled - and yet to me, they bring sad, deeply painful memories. I often wonder, how I could have touched them. Time brings to me, no healing on its wing, and I shall be only too glad when my mission which I know, to be my precious child Taddie, is completed, to be rejoined by my loved ones, who have only 'gone before.' Such a dream as I had of my idolized Willie last night. Some day, I will tell you *all.*"

I never had the chance. It was *not* a dream of Willie. It *was* Willie, but he was alone. Where is your father? I asked. Where is our little Eddy? And when Willie started to explain something in his old serious and sober way, I lost the contact.

Those contacts were *not* a dream. They were *not* daydreams. Did Willie come to me, or did I go to him? As he was so surrounded by radiant energy, more in reality than any found here in the world, I decided it was I who went to him. Then - why did I not see all of them? Eddy? *Why did I not see my husband?* Why did I see Willie so clearly, but not my husband? What had the doctor said? "Only when it is your time to go, Mary. Only when it is your time to go, will you see him."

"Don't I decide that?" I asked.

"Not for now," the doctor had replied, so - *certainly.*

And shortly, he went to sea and died, finding his own shore of light.

After three days of travel, on March 22, I returned from Nice to Frankfurt. That day, I wrote a long loving letter to Robert's wife. I told her that Taddie had grown even taller, it seemed to me, and he still had his "bright complexion," but his face was thinner, as if he had not been eating properly. I would see that he ate his dinner with me, a *proper* dinner for "His presence has become so necessary even to my life." About her - my own sweet daughter, Mary - "Do oblige me by considering me as a mother, for you are very dear to me as a daughter. *Anything,* and *everything* is yours. If you will consider them worth an acceptance" . . . of my *non sold* finery - "It will be such a relief to me to know that articles can be used and enjoyed by you . . . I never see anything particularly pretty - that I do not wish it was yours. My spirit is willing, but my purse not very extensive." Some one had told my daughter in law that housekeeping and babies "were," I wrote, "an uncomfortable state of existence for a young married lady. I think her experience was different from most mothers who consider that in the outset in life - a nice home - loving husband and precious child are the happiest stages of life."

Later, after her child had arrived on October 15, 1869, *Mary,* named for me, and her own mother! I wrote to my daughter in law just what I wanted her to do. "You should go out *every day* and enjoy yourself - you are so very young and should be as gay as a lark. Trouble comes soon enough, my dear child, and you must enjoy life, whenever you can. We all love you so very much - and you are blessed with a devoted husband and darling child - *so do go out* and enjoy the sunshine." I wanted her to go through my things and take something which would *just* suit her - "the double India shawl, with a red center, which I never wore, and make faithful use of it."

The summer of 1869 was a beautiful one for Taddie and me. I was determined it be so, *and it was.* During Taddie's vacation we toured Scotland *for seven weeks!* Beautiful, beautiful Scotland, land of my ancestors, haunted by mists and myths of kings and their great stone castles looking out over unquiet seas and clouds making moving shadows on all the emerald hills – loch and streams and rivers with the magic of fairy rings in the nearby wood, and long rays of the sun that set *so* late to take the day *on* into so much of the night.

We had stopped in Paris and London on our trip, by way of Brussels, but Scotland was what captivated us, and we went from one end to the other of that country of Scottish Chiefs, Highland clans and poets. Edinburgh and Glasgow charmed us; the Scots delighted us, as Lock Lomand, Lock Catherine all - all of them - abbeys, the birth place of Robert Burns, the poet of the people so loved by my husband – deeply, deeply pleasured us both. Glamis Castle, King Duncan's ever restless ghost, the prison home of Mary Queen of Scots, *Lochleven,* the grave of poor Highland Mary- Rob Roy Country- Abbotsford - down into the deep of Fingal's cave - and I wrote to Rhoda White about it. "It is only in visiting such a spot, that we can fully realize the greatness & power of the Creator."

And *more wonderfully,* in Scotland we were met by our dear former pastor, Dr. James Smith, who had baptized Taddie. And had publicly refuted the Billy lies about my husband and me.

"Mary, you look - almost serene," said the Reverend.

I smiled. "Well, no one here knows who I am and so does not hate me."

"Those lying wicked tongues. It will all come back to them some day."

"I don't think there is any of it left to go anywhere. It has all been used up on me. It was a horror when my husband was alive, but now - without him -"

Taddie looked at me tenderly, so much like his father. "I think Papa-day has enjoyed our vacation with us. He must be drawn by that smile of yours he loved so much."

I sighed, and the smile vanished.

"Tad," said the Reverend. "I think you will look more and more like your father - even with your dark eyes -"

"Taddie -"

"Tad," corrected my son.

"Tad - is what makes me want to stay alive."

The Reverend looked old, frail, tired, and I was glad we had seen him once more. "Mary," he said, "I have known you forever, so I can graciously tell you that life is not conditional. It is based only on *you.*"

"God," I corrected. "And God."

"And God is found through *you.*"

I got Taddie back late for the school term, not reaching Frankfurt until

349

mid August. I was alone again, and the only cheer I had was from the hope I would be granted a pension, but when I went through my mail, there was a letter from dearest Sally Orne. She, her two daughters, a maid and a valet were touring Europe, and she was on her way to Frankfurt to see me!

She did not reach me at the fine *Hotel d'Angleterre* as she expected, but at the cheap *Hotel de Holland,* and she wrote about this to Charles Sumner, September 12, 1869, from Baden Baden. She found me on the fourth floor, and to the back, too, "in a small cheerless desolate looking room with but one window - two chairs and a wooden table with a solitary candle . . ." This, for the "petted indulged wife" of the murdered President - "My very blood boiled in my veins and I almost *cried out - shame on my countrymen . . .* if her tormentors and slanderers could see her - they surely *might be satisfied."*

Sally and I had such a marvelous visit. For three days and nights we spent every waking moment talking of the past, and she said she would use her influence to see that I did get a pension - she would never stop trying, and she and her wealthy husband had powerful friends everywhere - even Grant was among them. Her brother, Charles O'Neill, was a Philadelphia Republican Congressman, and as we talked through the night about new hope for me, my near-by roomer neighbor came to my door and said, "Ladies, I would like to sleep *some,"* and we said, "Well, go ahead and do it," and went on talking more quietly, we thought, but then the house waiter rapped on our door at 2:30 and asked if we could not complete our conversation *later* in the morning.

Now the *pension to surely be* - became my obsession. I thought of Taddie, and I thought of the pension, and war clouds were forming over Prussia and France, and I did not notice. From Paris Sally sent me the news she had received from home. Her brother heard *I was to get my pension before winter,* and Grant told her husband that when Congress reassembled, his first duty would be to see to my getting my pension.

The weather in town was hot, so I went to Kronber, a near by village in the mountains, and stayed there until cold weather came in October. My headaches resumed, now called neuralgic headaches, and I became so ill that Taddie had to take care of me. I wrote Sally, "that my very affectionate young son, is almost continually by my bedside. In his loving and tender treatment of me at all times, & very especially when I am indisposed - he reminds me so strongly of his father - for *he* was never himself - when I was not perfectly well -"

Edwin Stanton died in December, and over $100,000 was quickly raised for his *wealthy* survivors. General John Rawlins died, and $100,000 was raised for *his* family. And I - struggling, *a part of my beloved husband's memory* - to survive in a dark, back, upstairs room, of a cheap lodging, without carpet or heat.

A stamp came out with my husband's face on it, and Sally sent it to Taddie. I wrote her and thanked her for it. "Taddie was very grateful for the stamp. The beloved face of his father!" On November 28 I wrote to her of "the rain beating against my window & my heart filled with dreariness," But I had present, "my bright little comforter Taddie," and although "The darkness is very great - we can only pray - that dawn is at hand." Yet, back to reality, Sally, write me, write me, write me - "The loneliness of this Winter words could not express nor pen write its terrors!" Those cold sleepless wintry nights, the cold gray days - trembling fearful days - I felt I had lived for centuries of terror that I could get *even poorer.*

I lied dreadfully about my age now. I said I was fourteen years and ten months younger than my husband, instead of nine years ten months. December 13, 1869, I was fifty-one. I wrote to Sally on the twelfth about how hard it was not to make idols out of admirable men - "My husband was so richly blessed with all of these noble attributes that each day makes me worship his memory - *more & more.* . . Always - lover - husband - father & all to me - Truly my all."

The vampyre press coiled its snake tongue across the Atlantic and the London press reported I was about to marry some German Baden count, who wanted me because he wanted a *rich heiress* for a wife!

The day before Christmas I became very, very ill again, fever, burning up and down my spine, no one near me to hand me a glass of water. Taddie came and called a physician, and on the 29th I was able to write to Sally. "Taddie, is like some *old woman* with regards to his care of me - and two or three days since - when I was so very sick - his dark loving eyes - watching over me reminded me so much of his dearly beloved father's - so filled with deep love." I was remembering his being with me during Taddie's birth, when I had the *worst* child birth - and the suffering on his face for my pain.

By February of 1870 the doctors said a cold had settled in my spine, and I could not sit up. Or I had a spinal disease that arose from an agitated mind. Whatever it was, I had it and no pension. My beloved's birthday passed - how silent is the grave - and how freezing was the winter - how damp, cold, *miserable* - Stanton's family was given $111,466. 23 - I added the twenty - three cents - why skimp for *his* family? Mrs. Grant was involved in some money scandal with that crook robber baron Jim Fisk or Jay Gould - probably both - they had tried to corner the gold market, and Mrs. Grant's sister was married to their lobbyist, Abel Rathbone Corbin - and her share was said to be $500,000

- and she already had received $25,000. All this from the vampyre press, and whether this was true or not, Grant *was* surrounded by crooks who knew just what they wanted. *My, my.* With all of *my* misdeeds, and dire Delilah wicked ways, I never speculated in a familial cornering of gold.

In my illness, I slipped in and out of delirium. At the end of March I could sit up in bed and wrote of my spiritual experience to Sally. I know Taddie was with me, *but so were they.* Eddy and Willie. And I was at home on Jackson Street, and I could see our apple tree loaded with fruit for his favorite apple pies, and I was waiting - *we* were waiting - for *him,* and it was so hauntingly *ordinary.* I wrote to Sally my lost boys were with me, and I ached to join them - "would that I *could* have joined them . . . Burn this shocking letter -" Taddie held me here. *My troublesome little sunshine* I used to call him. Now he was just my *sunshine.*

By this time Mrs. Stanton had $150,000 from our grateful nation, along with her $75,000 mansion, and from the grateful nation Grant had the nation.

On April 26 I wrote to Sally's brother, Charles O'Neill, about my pension, closing with, "If I have acted injudiciously in writing & urging my claims upon you & friends of our country, pray pardon the error."

Then on May 2, 1870 the House passed my pension bill, $3,000 a year, without debate! (80 to 65, 77 not voting) It went to the slumbering Senate where Lyman Trumbull read it aloud and asked that it pass "unanimously and graciously."

But the Pensions Committee was still sitting on the first pension bill of $5,000, and had to make a verdict about it.

So Congress could wait. So could I. I chose the English reading room in Frankfurt to wait, where I could read all of the English papers, find my name and my pension to be. Days passed. In late May in an English newspaper I found a majority on the Senate Committee on Pensions decided I didn't need one, tabling the bill *indefinitely.* This was not the half of what I read. There was lack of precedent and *insufficient* need. I was wealthy. I had $60,000, had *appropriated public property* for my *personal use,* was living royally, and *there were darker facts about me* that the committee *had yet to consider.*

I read it and I fainted, passed right out, and hit my head on the table on my way down.

I went to the mountains for refuge, to the Marienbad, Bohemia spa for the month of June. I took long walks through the woods, and at night, in my third floor *garret,* I wrote more letters to get my pension.

By July, it was clear Taddie and I were to be trapped in a German - French war. We had to leave for England.

Sumner was still fighting for my pension, and those arguing against it sank to new lows in assassinating my character. Richard Yates of Illinois, not *Georgia,* not *South Carolina,* but the Senator from *Illinois* said the following before the Senate: "There are recollections and memories, sad and silent and deep, that I will not recall publicly, which induce me to vote against this bill . . . a woman should be true to her husband . . . I shall not go into details . . . her family all through the war sympathized with the Rebellion."

True to my husband? Sympathy for the rebellion?

Fenton of New York said I had been indiscreet, and had lost respect for it; Trumbull asked what my character had to do with the bill, and Senator Henry Wilson wanted to get on with the Army bill.

Twenty-four hours before the close of the session my pension bill was to be voted on. The same old thing was put forth - I didn't need the money - and don't forget the old clothes' scandal - and the silver spoons and the White House settees smuggled out under my hoops - and then Senator Simon Cameron of Pennsylvania rose to be recognized. He was. He said the gossips had tried to make a bad reputation for me *and my husband* - "They could not destroy him, but they did . . . destroy the social position of his wife. I do not want to talk, and I say, let us vote."

On July 14 I was voted my lifetime annual pension of $3,000 - 28 for, 20 against, 24 not voting, and Grant signed it the same day.

James Orne telegraphed me the good news in Innsbruck, Austria, where Taddie and I were vacationing. On July 16 I wired James Orne my appreciation, "The kindness of yourself & your family, will always be deeply engraved on our hearts . . ."

In the beginning of September we sailed to England. On the seventh I wrote my letter of thanks to Charles Sumner, ". . . my feelings of deep gratitude in return of your unparalleled efforts in my behalf. . . you are noble and true . . . Words are inadequate to express my thanks, for all of your goodness to me . . . With many apologies for this hastily written scrawl, and with assurance that your untiring devotion to the cause of the 'fatherless & widow' will always be prayfully remembered by me."

I was able to hire a tutor for Taddie, who studied seven and a half hours a day, six days a week, and I was able to hire a servant for myself. After visits to York, months in the Shakespeare country in Leamington, and a short trip back to Frankfurt, Taddie and I took rooms in 9, Woburn Place, Russell Square. There, I wrote letter after letter, to dear friends and to my dearest daughter in law. I wanted to see the dear sweet face of my little namesake, and Taddie was wild to see his brother and his little niece. I had thought of sending Taddie to Robert's for Christmas of that 1870, but the danger of winter gales at sea stopped me from doing it. *I could not give up Taddie, too.* To Robert's dear Mary I wrote in November, "To trust my beautiful darling *good* boy to elements, at this season of the year, makes my heart faint within me . . . You know you will always be FIRST LOVE of daughters- in- law. I often tell Tad I can scarcely flatter myself he will marry to suit me quite as well as dear Bob has done."

Robert had become *Bob,* as his father later called him, and I decided with his tenderness to his wife and precious baby, he was not completely Todd.

There were people who saw me in England then, and they recorded what they saw. I am passing it on to you, for I have gone down in history as always a raving lunatic. Ask about me. This is the first thing you will hear - SHE WAS CRAZY. SHE DIED IN AN INSANE ASYLUM. General Badeau, our Consul General in London, was quoted about me in the *New York World.* He saw *very* much of me in England, as I visited his ill wife many, many times. He wrote that he found me "bright, sympathetic, cordial, sensible, intelligent. . . No trace of eccentricity appeared in her conduct or manner. She was simply a bright, wholesome, attractive woman. I could not for the life of me recognize the Mrs. Lincoln of the newspapers with the Mrs. Lincoln I saw."

Sally had heard I had gone deranged, and she wrote to Charles Sumner, November 27, 1870, "I have watched her closely - by day and by night - for weeks - and fail to discover any evidence of aberration of mind in her." Benjamin Moran, of the American legation in London, wrote in his journal, September 4, 1870, that he had met me and was, "agreeably surprised to find her an unpretending woman of excellent manners, much intelligence and a very lady like appearance." I had "an expressive face" a "very decided Southern accent," and - "After seeing her, I am prepared to believe that all of the attacks upon her in the newspapers were sheer scandals and falsehoods." And, I heard, Mr. Moran had never in his life talked himself into liking too many people!

A friend of Mrs. shipman who knew me said I was " by nature light hearted, never light headed." Another wrote, "No woman ever sustained the dignity of widowhood with more appropriate behavior. I wore black the rest of my life "as an external emblem of her incurable grief."

I had my usual winter bad cough and the pains up and down my spine. My physician told me to get out of the bitter English winter and go to Italy, and so I did. I enrolled Taddie at Brixton, outside of London, went south to Italy, leaving in early February, 1871, visiting Milan, Lake Como, Genoa, Florence and Venice. From Florence I wrote to Bob's Mary on my husband's birthday,

1871. Florence was beautiful - "We came through the charming Tryrol, via Milan and Lake Como, had a day's sail on the latter the beauties of which are *indescribable.*" If anything could lift my spirits, aside from my children, it was seeing beautiful mountains and *historical* places. Every minute I was there, I thought how *he* would have loved to be there, too. Every minute I was within beauty, within a place so filled and so haunted by history, I looked for even a fleeting *tall shadow* - but there was none.

When I returned to England, Taddie and I were so homesick to see *Little Mamie*, Bob and his dear wife, that I said, "Taddie, let's go home!"

He smiled, the tender sweet smile of his father, and he said, "You and *Tad* will go home."

The voyage across the Atlantic was terrible, bitterly cold and storm filled, and *Tad* caught a dreadful cold. Our ship docked on May the eleventh, and we left for Chicago on May 15. Tad still had his cold, *but how high our spirits were!* We talked of renting in Chicago, as close to Bob as we could, and maybe *Tad* would study law. He was tall, dark, very, *very* good looking; his manners were impeccable. He was so mature, so adult, and he was only eighteen. He was so clearly - highly intelligent - he was *in all ways* like his father.

"After I study law, I can clerk for Bob," he said happily.

I had my pension and the interest from my bonds, which were increasing in value all of the time, as were those of Tad and Bob. On that train ride, with our America flashing by our window, I said, "Tad, our life will be *good.*"

"It is so marvelous to hear you say that."

"And I feel your father - so near to us! For the first time - he is so clearly *here!*"

"Papa - day," he said, affectionately. "Papa-day," he repeated, as if his father were riding with us, looking out, too, at the land he had served so well, *America, the land of my life, my liberty and my love.*

Bob had purchased a charming home on Wabash Avenue, and our reunion with him was joyous beyond words. He had a very, *very* successful law practice, was investing money and increasing it and could give his lovely wife and darling child a comfortable future. My two sons revealed their love for each other; Bob was so proud of *Tad*, and *Tad* was so proud of Bob.

Word came that Mary's mother was gravely ill, and she had to go at once to Washington to be with her. Suddenly, Tad's chest cold got worse, and he had to go to bed, but he and Bob still visited and recalled old times, and talked of their *law* future together, how as a family, we would never be away from each other again.

I wrote my usual letters. To Rhoda White, on May 21 - "I found my son

- his wife - & child rejoicing over our arrival -" I had my "head throbbing with pain," which was not unusual, and wished I had the money to purchase a home for Tad and me. Which was not unusual, either. If the pension *had just gone five years back* - if it had been $5,000 instead of three - to my cousin, Eliza Steele, I wrote on May 23, "My son is confined to bed with a severe cold and in consequence we will not remove to the Clifton House until Saturday-" Bob, "all that is noble and good," did not want us to leave, but I would not impose on his family any more than necessary. I recalled the blessings of my life "so enriched by the most loving and devoted of husbands which makes the present all the more sorrowful to bear." I wanted her to visit, for she would surely remain in town a little longer. To Rhoda White I wrote the same day, "My youngest son, is confined to his bed today, with a severe cold. I hope, by great care, that he will soon recover." I hoped we would all be in Chicago, our family and Bob's family *always* together. I was not in the least worried about *Tad's* cold, for he had them so often.

He improved, and we were able to move to the good old Clifton House, Room 21, that had sheltered us so many times since my husband's murder. The old timers there were drawn as usual to Tad. Mr. Jenkins, the keeper of the hotel, remembered how *everybody* loved him, how he was so good- natured and gentle-mannered - and had grown so *very pleasant looking.*

By the end of May Tad had great difficulty in breathing, and had to sleep sitting up in a chair. The doctors said he had dropsy of the chest, and when he was quietly sleeping, on June 8, I wrote to Rhoda White about him. "My dear boy, has been *very, very* dangerously ill - attended by two excellent physicians who have just left me, with the assurance he is better. May we *ever* be sufficiently grateful, should his precious life be spared. Dr. Davis, a very eminent lung physician, says, that thus far, his lungs are not at all diseased, although water has been formed on part of his left lung, which is gradually decreasing. His youth and vigilant care, with the mercy of God, may ward off future trouble. With the last few years so filled with sorrow, this fresh anguish bows me to the earth. I have been sitting up constantly for the last ten nights, that I am unable to write you at length today."

I did not write another letter until Thursday, July 27, and it was to Eliza Slataper. "In my great, great agony of mind, I write you. I pray you, by all that is merciful to come to this place - if but for a few days - I feel that I *must* see you." Robert was out of town for two weeks, his own strength gone, his wife was still with her ill mother, and I was staying at Robert's house. " . . . each day I am entirely alone, in my *fearful sorrow. Come, come to me.*"

My Taddie, *my troublesome little sunshine,* as I called him when he was a boy, my *sunshine* as I called him when he was grown - was gone. I didn't know I had any heart left for him to take away with him. Judge Davis had visited on Saturday, July 8, and I could tell by his face, and even by Tad's, they both *knew*. And yet, Tad, as he insisted I still call him, was more concerned with me, with my anguish, and he kept telling me he would be well, and not leave me. One night he got out of his chair to show me he *was* better, that he *could* stand, and he fainted.

Now they said he had pleurisy, and had had it for months. But he rallied. On July 11 he rallied and Bob and I saw the look of distress leave his thin face, his eyes, and never once, *never once,* during the six weeks of suffering had my Taddie complained. Bob was to write that never had he seen so much suffering and such "marvelous fortitude." He brightened when Bob handed him a photo of his niece. But on July 14 we all knew Taddie was dying, and he all but apologized for it. Bob was with us until eleven that night, and when Taddie seemed to be resting, he went home for some sleep. I was alone with Taddie and two nurses, and I ached to hold that dear face and cover it with kisses, use a mother's *power* to *heal* a dying son, and as midnight slowly passed, and the hours after it, Taddie began to struggle to breathe, and I knew that no matter what I willed, no matter what I could bear or not bear, my beloved little sunshine was slipping away.

He slumped forward and stopped breathing at seven thirty, July 15, 1871.

His father had died at seven twenty two.

There was a funeral for Taddie at Robert's home on Wabash Avenue on Sunday afternoon, and the services were simple, his old Bible class attending, and I do not remember it at all. They said Robert was on one side of me, and the minister on the other, as I sat "dazed" and "numb" on the sofa. I do not remember my Taddie dead. I do not remember seeing my Taddie dead, for Taddie dead I could not bear, could not, could not, and I began to turn toward a quiet and desperate - fear - horror that Bobby would slip away, too - that my little Marmie would die - *that they all would be gone.* A shadowed world without any hope of a sunrise enclosed my frail body that had enough strength for me to hurt and hurt and enough strength to keep me a suffering prisoner within it.

Bob accompanied Taddie's body to Springfield, where high on Aristocracy hill, the family attended services for Taddie, his casket on the same spot in the elegant Edward's front parlor, right in front of the marble fireplace, where I had stood as a bride of the best man who ever walked the face of the earth.

Chapter Thirty

Taddie's part of the estate was now $37,000 dollars, and by law, three fourths of it was mine. I wrote to Judge Davis about that on November 9, 1871. "I feel that I would be carrying out the wishes of my beloved son Taddie, when I suggest that an equal division be made by the bonds in your possession. Dividing them equally between Bob & myself . . . I should prefer only the half . . . My beloved boy was the idol of my heart & became my inseparable companion . . . without his presence, the world is complete darkness -"

I wrote to my sister, Elizabeth Todd Grimsley Brown, on March 20, and April 12, of 1872. "One by one I have consigned to their resting place, my idolized ones, & now, in *this* world, there is nothing left me, but the deepest anguish."

When Eddy was carried off by that beautiful angel, I had my husband and soon was pregnant again, and when the angel took away my "sobersides" Willie, I had my husband and Taddie, and when his father was taken so cruelly from us both, I had my Taddie. Now - what use was I? *I have to refute the lies of Billy Herndon - do you think my husband lived only from 1861 to 1865? Who was the man behind the monuments - the marble - the penny and the five-dollar bill?*

Bob was spent, exhausted, in ill health from Taddie's death. He had had such high hopes for him. He had found Taddie to be so self- reliant, so mature for his years. Bob was changing his law firm in 1871, and I lived in Chicago, but took excursions, long ones, and I began to buy again. I bought things that I did not need. I bought things for a house when I had no house, for both of them were rented. I wouldn't live with Bob. I would not impose on his precious family and had to remain independent.

Bob hired a sort of nurse maid-companion for me, Mrs. Richard Fitzgerald, the mother of actor- to- be- Eddie Foy, and she put up with me, though barely, and Bob took his family to Europe in the summer and fall of 1872. When they were gone, Ward Hill Lamon, who had fallen on hard times, decided to publish a book about my husband and make some money - after all, he *had* been around him - and as he was a charming lazy man, he paid noxious Billy for his noxious notes on my husband, me, and our lives, and then he hired a ghost writer, Chauncey F. Black, who did not like my husband *in the slightest*, to write it. That book, the life of my husband, came out in late 1872, and created a calumny of vicious gossip about my husband and our life together. This was not just one of Billy's vicious lectures. It all was *in print*, between a *book cover*, lying there like truth and reality, and it had in it all of Billy's sick perversions. Of course the ever-faithful Ann was back, and the wedding between my husband and me he did not show up for, and how we married each other, *finally*, to get revenge and send each other right into lives of misery, *and my husband was a bastard*, Tom and Nancy never having bothered to get married - I quote: "there exists no evidence but that of mutual acknowledgement and cohabitation."

This was why I still lived? To see printed these damnable lies and distortions?

It was more than I could stand, for of course the vampyre press picked it all up and wore it like nose rings, and I ran away to Canada. On December 12, 1873, noxious Billy did another lecture on his inside access to my husband's soul, and said he was not a Christian, that, I, myself had *told him this*, and my husband's legitimacy *still had not been proven* to his satisfaction. Of the marriage between Tom and Nancy he said, "I aver there is no such record." Billy, the noxious little man, shabby, dirty, bird nests in his beard, drunk more than ever, living in poverty in the outskirts of town, law practice failed, lived to suck away my life blood by attacking the glory of the man I worshipped.

I *had* to tell the truth to the people. I had to show Billy *a dirty dog liar* and that all of the books based upon his lies, lied as well.

Bob was furious with Billy's lies and would not fight the viper in print, *but I did*. I said I had *never* told this man my husband was an atheist - to quote *me* to attack my husband? He was twisting what I did say, and that was my husband had not *formally joined a church, but no man revered God more.*

Billy then published an article to the world calling me a liar and I called him one, and it was obvious that I hated him and he hated me. *That* makes me *very* proud yet.

The *good* thing that happened in 1873 was that on August 14, I had a grandson named for my husband.

In October of 1874 the old dispute over my husband's tomb being in Oak Ridge emerged again, and Billy was now calling me a witch, liar and a lunatic - I had *always* had this thing he termed "spasmodic madness."

I have owned that I *did* have spells of irrationality, and grief brought them on. Now, I grew more terrified of demons that would come into my life again and take away Bob. I did see assassins around him, *for I should have seen the one that killed my husband.* The nights were long and dark. Within them my terror but grew. I had lost them all save for Bob. I had said that I thought people high in my husband's government had plotted his murder. I was not safe either, for I suspected Johnson as being in on my husband's murder, and I wondered about Stanton - he had total control of the conspirator trial - and why had Booth jumped on the stage *to be so visible?* How had he so easily escaped into Maryland? No one was to cross that bridge - didn't a soldier say that Stanton gave a code word for one to cross it, and Booth gave that word? *Was* it Booth killed at the Garret farm? Why had Stanton killed the telegraph news out of Washington right after my husband's murder? Was Johnson really supposed to have been killed, or was there a story for it to *look like it?*

Darkness closed in on me. I felt frozen on a small beam of shrinking light. Assassins were stalking me so I could not talk about my doubts as to my husband's murder. Why wasn't Grant with us that night? Eckert? Why did Parker go unpunished for leaving his post? Why were the papers for the trial of the conspirators kept closed for a hundred years? Why did John Surratt get off so easily?

I kept candles burning all night.

The only thing I had now for security was my money. Would that be taken away, too? Would I have to live on the third floor in a bare unheated windowless room again? What would I do - impoverished one more? Would Congress sneer, the vampyre press sneer, Billy gloat because I was poor again and begging?

Dear Friends, I have this beautiful shawl to sell - our carriage is gone - but Taddie will keep his pony and Bob his horse - his father's last gift - I will see to it – I must see to it!

I want a home for us so much!

Bob worried that I was rational on all things but the management of my money. He said that since my husband's death. I would not give him my money to manage. I would not live with him in his fine house. I insisted that I could care for myself.

By March of 1875 I decided for my security I had to wear a money pocket. In it I kept my bonds that were now worth $57,000. No bank could steal it. No bank could lose it. No one could conspire with the bank to keep it from me. And when I needed it, *I had it!*

I sought spa relief for my hurting spine - my head was cooperating with it, sending balls of fire out of my eyes to rush down my back, to make me want to constantly scream with *agony.* But that was nothing - I thought over and over - n*ow it has come! Bob is going to die! A vision has shown me that*

Bob is going to die!

I was in Florida for spas, and I had had a clear dream of Bob dying, as my husband had had a clear vision of his coming back to Springfield dead - and he did - just as he had dreamed of himself in the White House coffin - so, on March 12, I sent a wire to Chicago to Bob's physician, "My belief is my son is ill; telegraph. I start to Chicago tomorrow."

The doctor found Bob, I think at his office, and Bob was well, and said he had not been ill for years. He wired me and told me to remain in Florida. I wired him back, "My dearly beloved son - Rouse yourself and live for your mother; you are all I have; from this hour all I have is yours. I pray every night that you be spared to your mother."

On the fifteenth I was in Chicago and checked in at the Grand Pacific Hotel. Bob came to my room and begged me to stay at his house, but I refused. I would never interfere with his little family. He then took a room adjoining mine.

My candles dipped and swayed as if there was a breeze from the window, when the window was closed. A coldness permeated the air about me, and it had the energy of living things, *evil* living things, and they wanted Bob dead and they wanted me dead – for then who would question my husband's murder – who would point out the dreadful slandering of my husband by the dirty dog drunk?

The candles flickered their way down to liquid wax. It was the pit of the night when the day is done and no other one has come, or will come save through deeper and deeper darkness.

My heart hammered with terror. Something *dreadful* was brewing. Something dreadful was about to happen to my last child. I tapped on his door. *"Bob, you will be murdered!* Someone will come tonight *to murder you!"*

"Mother - they will not."

"And someone is trying to poison me, and then Billy's lies will be *history!"*

"Mother -"

"When I am dead I cannot defend myself or your father against drunken Billy - son, I think I am being poisoned, right now!"

"Mother - no one is trying to kill us."

"They are - not just with words -"

"Mother, you are being totally irrational -"

"They will take my money and see me out in the streets! Then they can scoff at poor vain – *thing!"*

"Mother - there is no - *they!"*

"The vampyre press is the *they!* That lying Lamon book about your father is the *they!* This is in print and will be accepted as truth when it is lie! That - Bob - is the *they!*"

Bob paid people at the hotel to look after me; he paid a woman to stay with me at nights, and by April 1, it was obvious to Bob I had had a mental breakdown and was mired deeper and deeper in its middle. On that day Bob saw me get into an elevator, not fully clothed, and in humiliation he took me by the arm to lead me back to my room. "Now *you* are against me!" I sobbed, and for some reason, I *knew* he was. "I fight Billy and you say nothing - nothing!"

"He is not worth a word."

I went out on more panic shopping sprees. The more I felt time awry, the more watches I had to have, and Bob hired Pinkerton detectives to follow me, and when I told him about my money pocket with my whole fortune in it, color left his face. "You can be robbed - killed - and more likely, you will lose it all, and *really* have nothing!"

"I have been carrying it around for two months and no one has tried to take it from me -"

"Two months? *Two months?*" He got even whiter.

On May 19, 1875, I was in my hotel room having eaten my lunch there. I heard a knock at my door, and there was my dear friend, and my husband's dear lawyer friend, Leonard Swett. He was tall, not as tall as my husband, and they used to joke a little about that. They had ridden together on the judicial circuit, with the judge being Davis - "How very, very happy I am, dear friend, to see you!" I said, wishing I had on a better dress. "Are you visiting Chicago?"

He looked *miserable,* as if he were about to lead a cavalry charge right off of a cliff. "I have some bad news for you," he said, "and I think you should sit down."

I had to. My legs had turned to water. "Someone murdered Bob," I said. "Now - they are *all* gone."

"No. It is not that."

"What else can be bad?"

"Your friends think you have had too much pain to bear - that you have had too much trouble - that you have had to pass through too much - and you have suffered from it so much - to now have a mental disease."

"You mean to say - I am crazy, then, do you?"

"Yes. I regret to say - that is what your friends all think."

Anger flooded through me - *What friends?* "I am much obliged to you, but I am abundantly able to take care of myself, and don't need any aid from any such *friends*. Where is my son Bob? I want him to come here -"

"He is waiting for you in court."

"In court? In court? What do you mean - in *court*?"

"The Cook County Court -"

"That will decree me *insane*?"

"Yes."

"Who says I am insane? What *friends* say I am *mad*?"

"Judge Davis, and your cousin John Todd Stuart -"

"Not John Todd Stuart - my favorite cousin, *all of my life*-"

"And Robert."

"Bob - *my son*? My - own - son?" I began to tremble and could not stop myself. I didn't tremble. I shook. *"My only son left to me is saying I am insane?"*

"He wants you safe. He wants you where you cannot be hurt."

"Where I cannot be *hurt*," I repeated sarcastically. "He does not want me *hurt*."

"I do not want to throw the responsibility of this on others. I say so, too."

"That I am insane. How would you know?"

"It is by the irrational things you do." He pulled letters from his pocket, and read the names of doctors who said I was insane.

"I have not even seen those physicians; they do not come to see me; they know nothing about me, so what does that mean?"

"Robert has filed an affidavit in the county court that you are believed to be insane, and a writ has been issued for your arrest and that you be taken to court."

"No wonder you asked me to sit down," I said, getting out of the chair. "No wonder! Betrayed, *shamelessly* betrayed, by my own son! And you - the friend of my beloved husband all of these years, and my friend, I thought - you will take me and lock me up in an asylum, will you?"

I threw up my hands and tears of anguish ran down my face. "If I could die now! Dear God, if you could let me go home to our house, and have them all meet me at the gate - once again - oh, dear God, let this miserable, suffering little body give up its *real* being!"

"You will have to leave with me. The hearing is at two."

"I do not *have* to do anything! How dare you! I am no criminal! I have never harmed anyone in my whole life!"

"You cannot avoid this. If you do not go with me, there are sheriffs waiting downstairs to take you into court."

"Handcuffed? The widow of *the President of the United States* - handcuffed?"

" I don't know. But we have to leave right now."

"I certainly will not leave in this dress. You must leave me alone so I can change into a nice dress, and choose the bonnet for it."

"I cannot leave you alone to change your dress."

"I beg your pardon? Why *not*?"

"They said you might jump out of the window."

"*They* said - my son? Or did my *friends* from Illinois already write this - to the jury? I *am* to have a jury?"

"Yes. There is always a jury in cases like this. Now we have to leave."

"Not until I have changed into a decent dress before I am put *away.*"

I changed my dress in my closet. There was plenty of room, as I had shrunk to less than one hundred pounds. When I was properly dressed he said, "Will you take my arm?"

I said, "No thank you. I can walk yet."

Inside of the courtroom, I cringed back. It was filled with all men. "You have to go inside," said Mr. Swett. Robert rushed to greet me, and sat by my side, and my so-called counsel, Isaac Arnold, another *friend*, sat on my other side. "Let us make this as painless as possible," he said, and I graciously replied, "Oh, yes, we *must* do that."

Those are the last words I said during the three-hour recitation of how mad I was. How quietly I sat. How *lady like* with such *gentile* composure. A reporter wrote I was "modest and gentle looking, and acted throughout like a *perfect lady.*"

Robert got to the stand, and his eyes were red with weeping. I looked at him, and I thought of Bobby, my precious little Bobby, who sampled the lye before I could get it into the soap, who chopped the little wood while his father chopped the big wood - Bobby - gone with Bob, now, and only Robert the Todd left. He was telling how irrational I was, how I thought he was going to be murdered, and how I tapped on his door at night to say assassins were after us both. He broke down and wept, and this was so strange for the proper *always* Robert the Todd, I felt a pang of sympathy, for no son cries that a mother does not rush to comfort.

I saw the members of the jury wiping their eyes.

He was asked if he thought it safe for me to be unrestrained. "She has long been a source of much anxiety to me," he replied. "She has always been to me exceedingly kind, but she has been of unsound mind since the death of my father. She has been completely irresponsible for the last ten years.

She will not heed my advice. She is completely unmanageable. She makes purchases for no reason. She has trunks filled with dresses and valuables of which she makes no use. (What I could not sell) She wears no jewelry and always dresses in deep black."

The jury returned a verdict of insanity, in the first degree. Robert came up to me and took my hand, with very great tenderness. "Oh," I said to him. "That my son would do this to me!"

He turned his face away. "Do you know what you have done?" I asked.

He did not reply, and with his face still turned from me, he was wiping his eyes. "You have marred me for all of history," I said. "You have declared your mother, and the *wife of your father*, a lunatic. And now, forevermore, that noxious little liar, Billy Herndon, will be believed, and no one will know whoever I was, but that mad woman assigned to an insane asylum by her only surviving son!"

Mr. Swett came up to me and asked for my securities. "You are not going to rob me," I said. "That is all that is left to me now - those securities."

"Don't make me get an order for the sheriff to take them away from you," he said. "Now, why don't you give them to Robert?"

"To Robert? To - *Robert*? No. Never. He will never have another thing of mine. *Never*."

"What about handing them to your lawyer, Mr. Arnold."

"My lawyer? *My lawyer?* I have no lawyer, but my lawyer son has a lawyer, hasn't he?"

"We will have to take those bonds by force," said Mr. Swett, but sadly.

"Do you *really* want to do that?" I asked.

"Why not?"

"They are in my underwear."

Mr. Swett and Mr. Arnold accompanied my bonds and me to my room, and on page 506, of the Lunatic Record, my name was entered. It did say that though insane, I had not shown any homicidal or *suicidal* tendencies.

Little did they know. Robert the Todd had signed me away, *mainly*, to get my money, to keep me hidden from embarrassing him by my grief, by my inability to handle it *rationally*, but I would like to know who is rational about losing three sons, along with their father, all closer to me than my own heart, and have the son that's left - lock you up.

Chapter Thirty-one

We left the courtroom, Mr. Swett and Mr. Arnold, and I, through some kind of tunnel. In my room, I was asked to give them my bonds. Mr. Swett wrote down what I said, as I was weeping. "You are not satisfied with locking me up in an insane asylum, but now you are going to rob me of all I have on earth; my husband is dead, and my children are dead, and these bonds I have for the necessities in my old age, and now you are going to rob me of them."

I must admit that when I did hand over my security, the $56,000 in government bonds my husband had purchased in 1865, the gentlemen who took them, and would take them to Robert the Todd, looked very sorry for me. And Mr. Swett wrote, "From the beginning to the end of this ordeal, which was painful beyond parallel, she conducted herself like a lady in every regard."

"Now leave me alone to sleep," I said. "I want to be rested before my trip to the insane asylum."

They left me, and I went out to the nearby drug stores and asked for camphor and laudanum. "My shoulder is causing me great pain," I said. But clerk after clerk would not give me *both* the camphor and the laudanum, until finally, after much pleading, one said I could have the prescription. I paid for it and took it back to my room. I drank the bottle down, all of it, enough to kill me, and lay down on my bed to die.

I didn't, for the druggist had just given me *one* of the drugs, and it was enough to make me violently ill, and Robert the Todd was sent for and stayed with me until I left Chicago for the sanitarium of Bellevue Place in Batavia, Illinois. I was put under the care of a Doctor Patterson, and my estate was put under the care of Robert the Todd.

I should make it clear that I was not put into any cell or chained to any walls. I had a large airy room, ate with the Patterson family and took frequent drives with them out into the country. I took long walks by myself, and if I met children doing the same, did not scare them up the nearest tree. Sally Orne checked with Robert the Todd about my *confinement,* and he pointed out that I lived with the Patterson family in a private part of their house "and her associates are the members of his family only. With them she walks and drives wherever she likes and takes her meals with them or in her own room as she chooses, and she tells me she likes them all very much. ... Indeed my consolation in this sad affair is in thinking she herself is happier in every way, in her freedom from care and excitement, than she has been in ten years. So far as I can tell she does not realize her situation at all. ... I can tell you nothing as to he probability of her restoration. It must be the work of sometime if it occurs..." He had done his duty as he saw it.

He has done his duty? I didn't know my situation? What was I, an unformed *first* cell of the primordial sea? Now, *confined,* was happy as a lark? Well, I didn't know if I was one, or a chicken in the barnyard - AS TO THE PROBABILITY OF KNOWING THE DIFFERENCE - IF it occurs?

In a pig's eye!

Robert the Todd dutifully visited me once a week. I received him *very* courteously, and that is why he thought I did not know my *situation.* But how busy my mind was. How busy my pen was. I arranged a visit from two dear friends, Judge James Bradwell and his wife, Myra, who was the first female lawyer in Illinois. They could see that I was no lunatic, and they said my confinement was an outrage. They made plenty of noise about it too, rescuing me from one of the bitterest episodes of my life. And Lizzie and Ninian Edwards joined in! In September, after a little less than four months at Bellevue Place, I was allowed to go and live with the Edwards in Springfield, high on aristocracy hill. Still, however, under judgment of *insanity.*

There I was again, where I had bloomed as a young woman, sought by so many eligible men, where the Sangamon had rushed by so clearly and so sweetly into a future shining with the daydreams of the young. And not so far away, stood our beloved little brown cottage, at Eighth and Jackson, with its crooked gate, its apple tree in the back yard, and I am sure Evil Eva was still in residence. Another business was in Joshua Speed's store, and another jeweler near my husband's old law office sold wedding rings to other young men who had fallen in love.

I made no attempt to see any old friends, if there were, indeed, any of them left in town. "Lizzie, they all now think me mad. And if I met them and said that the moon that comes out at night was really made of cheese, they would politely nod, politely smile, and say, 'Mary, of course!'"

So I remained quietly within the Edward's mansion, and it was obvious that the Edwards hated the stigma on my name, for it was also a stigma on theirs. I heard that I had another grandchild born on November 6, 1875, and she was named Jessie Harlan.

In that great house I never went into the elegant company front parlor, where I had been married, and where Taddie had *lain in state,* as they called it. After nine months, Ninian Edwards petitioned the Chicago court for another sanity hearing for me, and Robert the Todd put up no objection. My new trail was on June 15, 1876, and it took only minutes, unlike the three-hour trial to put me away. Robert the Todd did not appear, and my lawyer was Leonard Swett, and he and I were friends once more. I was declared "restored to reason," and capable of managing my own affairs. Lizzie had come to Chicago with me, and on the train ride back to Springfield I told her over and over my appreciation for what she had done to help me. And I told her how I loved her grandson, our dearest precious Lewis, eighteen, who was, to me, so much like Taddie. "He is like my own son now," I said.

"You have Robert -"

"No. I had Robert, but I never had Robert."

And four days after I was declared a person again, on June 19, 1876, I wrote Robert the Todd a letter. It was a very nasty letter, a letter full of hurt and rage, and out of *no* pride *whatsoever,* I enclose the full thing.

"Do not fail to send me without the least delay, all of my paintings, Moses in the bulrushes included - also the fruit picture, which hung in your dining room - my silver set with large silver waiter presented me by New York friends, my silver *tete-a-tete* set also other articles your wife appropriated (she really did no such thing) & which are *well known* to you, must be sent, without a day's delay. Two lawyers and myself, have just been together and their list coincides with my own & will be published in a few days. Trust not to the belief that Mrs. Edwards' tongue, has not been *rancorous* against you all winter & she has maintained to the very last, that you dared not venture into her house & our presence. Send my laces, my diamonds, my jewelry - My unmade silks, white lace dress-double lace shawl-one black lace deep flounce, white lace sets 1/2 yd in width & eleven yards in length. I am now in constant receipt of letters, from my friends denouncing you in the bitterest terms, six letters from prominent *respectable* Chicago people such as you do not associate with. No John Forsythe' & such scamps, including Scammon. As to Mr. Harlan - you are not worthy to wipe the dust from his feet. Two prominent clergymen have written me, since I saw you - and mention in their letters, that they think it advisable to offer up prayers for you in Heaven. In reference to Chicago you have the enemies, & I chance to have friends there. Send me all I have written for, you have played your game of robbery long enough. Only yesterday, I received two telegrams from prominent eastern lawyers. You have injured yourself, not me, by your wicked conduct."

I certainly did not sign off - *mother.*

Actually, as I look back on it now, Robert did not steal one thing. He did not steal one penny. He was a good husband and a good father, and an honorable honest man always. He was a private man, a painfully, *painfully* private man, and that is why he burned my love letters to my husband and my husband's love letters to me. They were too private, he thought, to be shared. He was appointed Secretary of War by President Garfield, and was standing by his side at the Washington railway station when Charles Guiteau shot the President. Twenty years later he was among those near President McKinley at the Pan- American Exposition when Leon Czolgoz fatally shot McKinley. "I think I had better avoid standing by any President in the future," he said grimly. How many times he was to visit the Ford theater, that fatal spot where my husband was shot, and he did mourn all of his life - *if I had just gone with them that night as asked, might I not have seen the door was unguarded - Booth enter to do so much more evil than taking a human life?*

Robert remained Secretary of War until March of 1885, and then he returned to his lucrative law practice in Chicago. In 1887 he signed the deed to our home a Eighth and Jackson over to the people of Illinois on the condition the house be kept in good repair and open to the public. That year he and his family moved to the elite Lake Shore Drive, and from 1889 to 1893, Robert served as our ambassador to England. There, he and his wife dined with Queen Victoria. She wrote in her journal at Windsor Castle that Robert was "pleasant and sensible." Friends with Andrew Carnegie, friends with the rich and the famous, high in society in America and abroad, he *did* have a quiet pride about it. And then he learned, really learned, what his father and I had gone through with the loss of Eddy, and Willie - the doctors saying, *he will get well;* the doctors saying, at last, *there is no hope at all.* My husband's name-sake was nicknamed Jack, and he was brilliant and had the sweet temper and the magnetism of his grandfather. Robert had such high hopes for him. He must go to Harvard, of course. He was sixteen the summer of 1889, and Robert sent him to France to study in preparation for Harvard. Robert knew very well how difficult the entrance exams to Harvard were, from his own experience. In November, Jack developed what was called a carbuncle under his arm - *nothing to worry about,* and on the 6th it was removed. The incision did not heal. By the 26 Jack had blood poisoning, but for Christmas he was better; he was eating more and was very cheerful. By January 12 of 1890, Robert and his wife wanted Jack moved to London, and an English physician accompanied him and his parents to Robert's residence at 2 Cromwell House. Now the worry was over. He was getting well; *all* of the attending doctors said so. On February 21 there was a "pleuritic effusion" crowding the lungs, and just as Taddie had done, Jack went through an agony of trying to breathe. On March 5, he died. Robert wrote to John Nicolay ". . . our boy's life was very precious to us as his character & ability became year by year more assured, I had good reason for setting no limit in our hopes for him. Now there is nothing left but a memory, the loss is very hard to bear."

In 1893 Robert returned from England and that year was awarded by Harvard an honorary degree of Doctor of Law. In 1897 he was made President of the Pullman Company, and was a real captain of industry, one of America's best-known financiers and business leaders. He was a millionaire many times over. In 1902 he bought hundreds of acres of mountain and valley land near Manchester, Vermont, and built his English gentleman mansion he named *Hildene*. His family would go there for the springs and summers to escape Chicago heat. He had other retreats, but all of his homes were retreats, for he had only a few private friends allowed in them.

Billy's lying book on my husband had been published in 1889, when Robert was in Europe, and Robert wrote of its hatefulness, "The malice arose, I am quite sure, from the fact that my father could not see his way, in view of Herndon's personal character, to give him some lucrative employment during the War of the Rebellion."

Robert was asked to speak at Galesburg on October 7, 1896, the thirty-eighth anniversary of my husband's debate there with Stephen Douglas. "My father called the struggle one between right and wrong," he said. "In spite of the great odds against him, he battled on, sustained by conscience and supported by the idea that when the fogs cleared away the people would be found on the side of right . . . In our country there are no ruling classes. The right to direct public affairs according to his might and influence and conscience belongs to the humblest as well as the greatest. The elections represent the judgments of individual voters . . . the power of the people, by their judgments expressed through the ballot box, to shape their own destinies, sometimes makes one tremble. But it is times of danger, critical moments, that bring into action the high moral quality of the citizenship of America. The people are always true. The people are always right, and I have an abiding faith they will remain so."

On the hundred-year anniversary of my husband's birth in 1909, Robert returned to our home at Eighth and Jackson. I know the memories that flooded over him, and I know, when he asked to be left alone in his old room, he knew the *greatness* of his father - at *last*, he knew.

In May of 1909 Robert was to attend the unveiling of his father's statue done by Adolph Weinman at Hodgenville, Kentucky. Robert's health was poor, and his special car stopped at Louisville for his aunt Emilie Todd Helm, now also well into her seventies, and they talked of old times as the train bore them to my husband's birthplace. At Hodgenville Robert rode behind a marching band that stopped in the public square. Robert took his place on a platform by the flag draped statue of his father. A friend from his childhood Springfield days came to him, and little children brought him nosegays and he took them with deep appreciation. It was hot, very, very hot, and Robert did not like heat any more than I did. Emilie pulled the cord that released the flags and there, before Robert, was the statue of his father, so life like, sitting in a quiet pose as he had seen him do so many times, that Robert was overcome with emotion. He stayed on the platform until the key speech and the ceremonies were over, but he could not go to out to the farm where his father was born. He had to be rushed to the train near collapse, with his left side numb. On the train ride home he said, with tears in his eyes, "I wanted to drink out of the spring there. I wanted to walk over that farm and drink out of the spring. I'll come back next year and do it."

He never did.

Robert. Bob. Bobby - what a mystery he was to me and still is. My three other sons I knew so well. It was hard for him to be known mainly as the son of his father. It was impossible for him to match his father, but how many could, or have? And my breakdown was intolerable for him, but Robert was not so much in our family as he was to the Todd wealth. My "derangement," as he called it, forbade any of my letters, that he had not destroyed, to be printed, even by his cousin Lizzie Grimsley. That "derangement" made him ashamed of me, and that never changed. Robert did not have his father's ability to accept a human frailty, as Taddie could also do, *unconditionally*.

There are no descendents today of Robert and Mary Harlan. His daughter, Mary, married Charles Isham and she had one son, 1892-1973, who left no descendents. Jessie eloped with Warren Beckwith, a man Robert and his wife did not approve of at all, and finally she did not either, for they were divorced. They had two children, Mary Beckwith, 1893-1975, and Robert Todd Beckwith, 1904-1985, and neither of them left any children.

In 1911 Robert was made Chairman of the Board of Directors for the Pullman Company. In 1912 he and his wife moved from Chicago to a three storied colonial brick mansion in Georgetown, Washington. The address of the elegant home was 3014 N street.

In 1920 Robert gave his father's papers to the Library of Congress on the condition that they were not to be opened until twenty- one years after his death.

I hated to see my letters burned, so many of my husband's letters to me burned. Robert did mark the humble graves of Tom and Nancy. He did venerate his father late in his own life. He was wealthy, powerful and *aloof*, because he was shy. He could not enjoy shaking hands as his father did; he could not fit in with the most humble man as his father could. Those who knew him in his tight knit circle of friends and family loved him.

Because of ill health Robert quit the Pullman Company in 1922. In the fall of 1923 Lloyd George came to America and saw that he met Robert. He told him that he placed no man in history higher than his father.

Robert died in his sleep of a stroke on July 26, 1926, six days short of his eighty-third birthday.

When the work on the Washington memorial to my husband had begun, Robert was very proud. He watched every step of the construction, and when it was completed, he gazed through the temple portals into that familiar kindly face, and tears rushed down his own. He was there at the dedication, and many a wintry night he would return alone to his father's memorial, and look up into the cold stone made luminous by the memory of what his father was, a man who took the essence of himself, the purity of his being, and laid it, as he had told Mrs. Bixby she had done, upon the altar of freedom.

Chapter Thirty-two

I did not choose to remain in Springfield where everyone thought I thought the moon was made of yellow cheese. In the fall of 1876 I went to Europe, away from the American vampyre press. I did not write to Robert. My letters were to my *dear Lewis* who was more and more like Taddie. I wrote him first from Le Havre, France, and then from Pau, France, a health resort in the Pyrenees. I took mineral baths for my back pain, my chills, my neuralgic headaches, my colds and colds and colds. If my health was poor, my mind was keen, and my letters prove it. *In truth, there is not one thing I ever wrote to prove that I was insane.* I kept minute care of all of my finances in Illinois through a friend of my husband, Jacob Bunn. I acknowledged every mortgage, pension and interest check sent to me. When my quarterly pension certificates came, I had them witnessed and returned with no delay. I accounted for every single penny I drew. I was the one who advised on investments. And I still pinched the pennies. To be honest, my desire to receive money, to spend, *and* to hoard, lasted for almost forty years. But my letters regarding my finances prove I was very much aware of the safest bonds, the best interest, and *how to manage my money.* And this was the charge that had put me away - not being able to manage my money.

By 1877 the interest on my $60,000 bonds was $1,800 annually - in gold. I was helping out my sister Frances Wallace, writing to dear Lewis and sister Lizzy Edwards, and sent gifts to my granddaughter Marmie. I still thought, and wrote it in a letter to Lewis, June 22, 1879, that Robert had cruelly and *unmercifully* wronged me. During my four years abroad I visited Paris, Vichy, Avignon and Marseilles, and went to the beautiful seaside resorts of Biarritz and St. Jean de Luz. I traveled into Italy as far as Rome and Naples. Whenever I saw beauty I shared it with my husband, my *real* sons, as if they were still with me. *As if?* They *were.* I did not see them again, my Eddy, Willie and brother Alec. Why, oh why, couldn't I have this joy again? Why, oh why couldn't my husband break through my veil of grief and let me see he still *was!*

In 1879 news came about the high and mighty snob Kate Chase Sprague. Roscoe Conkling was paying attention to her he was not supposed to, and Kate's husband, ex-Senator Sprague, attacked Conkling with a gun and the Spragues were divorced. Kate, surprisingly, was to die in poverty.

In 1879 I was hanging a picture over my mantel, and I fell from my stepladder and injured my back. Now *each movement* was agony, and I had thought my body could not be any more troublesome. The following June, I stumbled down some stairs of the Hotel *de la Paix,* and hurt my back again. I knew I was soon going to drop this torturing little shell of mine, for surely, I would not have to tolerate its pain one more year.

I wrote to *My dear Lewis* on October 7, 1880, from Bordeaux, France. "I have concluded to return by the *Amerique,* which sails for New York, from Havre, October 16. I cannot trust myself, any longer away from you."

I estimated the voyage would take nine days and arranged and paid for Lewis meeting the ship. The voyage was not the stormy one Taddie and I had taken together in 1871, and on this ship I thought, *at last,* I am being carried *home.* I pictured myself in that ship my beloved had dreamed himself into, that ship that moved so swiftly through mystery and mists toward a luminous shore. He had said I would *become the light,* but he never had explained what he meant.

Light. I thought of his poem he had written long, long go in February of 1846, *My Childhood Home I See Again.* It had played light upon light and, within it, all the time - was death. *Were life and death both - always surrounded by light?* I had carefully read that poem. I had memorized that poem, and now tried to remember it.

> My childhood-home I see again,
>   And gladden with its view;
> And still as mem'ries crowd my brain,
>   There's sadness in it too.
>
> O memory! Thou mid-way world
>   Twixt earth and Paradise,
> Where things decayed, and loved ones lost
>   In dreamy shadows rise.
>
> And freed from all that's gross or vile,
>   *Seem hallowed, pure and bright,*
> *Like scenes in some enchanted isle,*
>   *All bathed in liquid light.*

And then the words left me. I was walking on the outer deck, and the words seemed forever lost, as if when I could not remember to go on, past the *light* lines, there was nothing. There were bugle tones that fade away - as twilight chases the day - memory hallows all we've known - but know no more. Childhood is gone, the children of that time fled - or dead - and sadly, so sadly -

> *I hear the lone survivors tell*
>   How naught but death could save,
> Till every sound appears a knell,
>   And every spot a grave.

> I range the fields with pensive tread,
>   And pace the hollow rooms;
> *And feel (companions of the dead)*
>   *I'm living in the tombs.*

Then the death of the mind, of *reason,* and there were his mother's angels again -

> *Seemed sorr'wing angels round*
> Their swelling tears in dewdrops fell,
>   *Upon the list'ning ground.*

The boy is gone, with the poet walks away -

> The very spot where grew the bread
>   That formed my bones, I see.
> How strange, old field, on thee to tread,
>   *And feel I'm a part of thee!*

That was the triumph of the poet. That was the triumph of the man. He had *merged* so far beyond himself - to be a part of the All - human sorrow on his broad shoulders - human tears falling to be heard within the chambers of a caring heart.

Now, smelling the salt air of the sea, looking down on its restless, ceaseless movement, I felt that every man and every woman are a part of an invisible living light, a tide unseen, a tide of beginning and ending in a circle of immortality. When the ending is its own beginning - that was the sacred circle of the All - and thus was my love, and his love, and I reached out in that cold salt air as if I could touch that beloved face again, see those eyes filled with such love for me again, the tender lips awaiting one more kiss.

I felt sudden exaltation, as if I were not a grieving mother and widow trapped in a failing hurting little body, but as if I had slipped into this unseen tide and had merged within the glory of love itself, the glory that had flung the stars into a night sky to give us light and life.

We move within divine majesty. As the reality beyond any I had known before gave me peace, gave me strength, gave *me* a totality far beyond myself, I thought - we are loved to return to love, and if we know this, we can cast the glory of what we are into the deepest dark, and transform it as God did, when he created the first star to create the first dawn.

How my husband had met the savage dark. He saw justice as divine, and injustice as an error of eternal night. That is why he saw himself going to a shore of light. When he would put down the burdens he had born so magnificently, he saw surcease in light. Is this what he meant when he said *I would become the light* - that I would absorb my terror of lightning, and become instead – of its energy?

Exultation remained, and so sure I was that he was with me again, I held out my hand for him to take it within his own. But my hand reached nothing, touched nothing but cold, cold sea air, and the waves that were swelling around me, so shadowed now and darkening more under a lowing sky, were just that. Water that was mighty and water that was cold, and water that swallowed away men and their ships and men away from their ships. It was not benign. This was no sea of light and love, and the idea that there was such a tide vanished with the sun now gone from the sky above me. My sudden exultation was as brief as the sea foam around me, whipped away to become nothing in the wind.

I was in the real world, totally and miserably, shrunken and aching.

My youth was dancing before my eyes, and I looked into my own as they were then, and I gave a flirtatious little curtsy to that time and was proud that my figure was said to be so fine, my skin so perfect, my hair bronzed with lights, my eyes so blue and so long lashed. All of those silly little vanities bowed at me one last time and twirled away into another waltz, and I grieved after them. I did. For after the waltz he was presented to me – and he is gone. He said love is eternal and had that put on this ring and he is gone.

Rosemary Benet wrote a poem about Nancy and her son. If she came back as a ghost, she would ask of the son she so loved – so very poor – did he grow tall? Did he learn to read? Did he get on? Do you know his name? What has he done?

Jules Silberger gave a reply. What has he *done?* Nancy, he lives in the heart of everyone.

Words can sing. Statues live – maybe as if they are alive. But the tide around me then was a lethal tide, the high waves taking from me the sky, even the little light the waning day afforded. Tears streaked my face and flashed cold and not warm, and stayed on my face, cold and not warm. We live and we love to lose. A flower of a sweet and cherished time - so carefully pressed into a family bible - turns to dust along with those who had held and revered that bible, their names now forgotten, carved on many a tombstone in some quiet far off country cemetery, where another couple passes happily by, making plans for a bright future - and sees them not - for the moss, so alive, so green, has quite hidden the names away.

I put my outstretched hand into my coat pocket. *Father, is this all there is? Father, were you wrong – no shore of light - no magic tide of light- no end - that is no more than the beginning?*

Shuddering, I walked back into shelter, warmth among people, and those people, those phantoms moving all about me, with husbands and children and plans - what to choose for dinner, what to wear for dinner, what to do when *L'Amerique* reaches shore - whom to meet - whom to greet - whom to know - where to go - east, west, north, or south?

I was near a stair well and we hit a sudden swell, and I would have been hurled down the stairs and surely killed, but a very handsome *large* woman grabbed me and prevented this. I thanked her. She looked at me kindly, but she also looked surprised. "Madame, do you *not* know who I am?"

"No," I said.

"I am an actress, a very *famous* actress."

"I never go to the theater any more," I said. "Now, I know of no actresses."

"I am Sarah Bernhardt."

Evidently, a *great* Sarah Bernhardt. "I wanted you to know who I am," she said.

"Madame," I said, stiffening. "Do you know *who I am?*"

"No, I do not," she replied honestly.

"Well," I said. "I am Mrs. Abraham Lincoln."

She wrote later that I was a *tiny* woman dressed all in black with "a dreamy gentle voice," and a "sad resigned face," and when I told her *my* name, she said she had never heard anyone's name given with such loving pride.

When the *L'Amerique* docked, wild cheering crowds greeted the great Sarah Bernhardt. She and her entourage were the first to leave the ship, and the crowds at the gate were so immense, her carriage had difficulty getting through. Dear Lewis, so much like Taddie, was there to meet me, and we quietly watched the clamoring crowd. A police officer touched me on the shoulder and impatiently told me to stand back.

From New York, we went directly to Springfield, I to my old room at the Edwards' mansion. I stayed mostly within it, and my presence was a strain on Lizzie. She thought I was not as ill as I was, that I kept my room with the shades drawn because I was moping, but light hurt my eyes even more. I did still wear my money belt around my waist, and, I joked, grimly, "I had better keep it there in case Robert should pay me a visit."

He did, in May of 1881. He brought along eleven-year old Marmie, and the news he had just been appointed Secretary of War by President Garfield. We visited, but we never accepted each other, at least, the way it had once been for me. Robert also believed I was not as ill as I *acted*. He wrote to Sally Orne about me, "She is undoubtedly far from well & has not been out of her room for more than six months & she thinks she is very ill. My own judgment is that some of her trouble is imaginary."

Hardly. I was going blind. My back was a torture chamber making the old migraines seem a walk at the beach. In the fall of 1881 I went to New York to be treated by a prominent orthopedic surgeon, Dr. Lewis Sayre, at Miller's Hotel on West Twenty-Sixth Street. Here were Turkish, Electric and Roman Baths. By this time I had to be carried. And by this time, Congress was considering *giving me more money*. Why? Very clearly, *why*. In September President Garfield was assassinated, and he left his widow with five children. She was to get, without the slurring and the venom of the vampyre press, $5,000 a year. If she were to get this, then *my husband's* widow should get less? So, now, I was to also to get $5,000 a year, and I was to receive another $15,000, one thousand dollars for each year since my husband's death. This was the bill offered, and I waited for hell and brimstone to fall on my head over it, to hear again about the stolen White House silver spoons, my marrying some count from somewhere - but the bill passed, after only eighteen days of debate, and I had not been listed among America's most wanted criminals, either.

The hotel was expensive and the electric baths $2.50 each, and they were not doing me any good. On March 21, 1882, from Grand Central Hotel, New York, I wrote *Dear Lewis* my last letter.

Could he meet my train at Springfield?

And so I came back to my old room in the great house from which *he* had taken me away as a bride, on that glorious stormy night of November 4, 1842. I thought of our house at Eighth and Jackson, how our sons would be born there, and how they would lead their father home, *maybe*, even in time for a warm meal from Evil Eva. Or how lightning would flash and the thunder roll out across the prairie, and he would come right home to me, to shield me from my terror of lightning. Or, some Saturday night, he would put on his giant apron and make toffee for the children and their friends, and for it Evil Eva would purr and coo.

I lay in my bed with the shades drawn, and I could hear children shouting and laughing outside of my darkened room. I did not know they pointed up to my window and said, *A crazy lady is up there, so don't get too close to that house.*

In July paralysis began to creep over my body, and I waited for him to take me toward that shore of light he had so clearly seen. Day after day passed, and my beloved did not appear to me. *Father, is the end no more than the beginning?*

"What?" asked Lizzie, a trifle impatiently as if I were *putting on* a death scene.

> *They wreathed her head with thorns when living,*
> *With nettles though dead.*

Marion Mills Miller

She wrote that about me. Or was to do it.

"Father - this tide toward light - *is the end the beginning?* "Why doesn't he answer me? Lizzie, why can't I see him?" I asked in panic.

"Molly, you are blind."

"What does that have to do with it?" I asked angrily.

July 16, 1882 - that was the date. I had asked the date, and that is what I was told. I was sixty-four. "Why have you deserted me?" I wept to my husband.

"God is with you," someone said, a male or a female.

And then came words I loved so much, words of *light.*

I will never do what is wrong to gain what is right.

I would like it said of me that I took a thistle and planted a flower, where I thought a flower would grow.

This is my land, land of my life, my liberty and my love.

I know no North, no South, no East, no West, but only the Union that holds them all in their sacred circle. It is not the idea that all states are equal, nor all citizens are equal, but all men are created equal.

What is the real defense of America? Our armies, our ships, our frowning battlements? No. These can all be turned against our liberties. Our reliance is the love of liberty God has planted in our hearts - the prize that is the heritage of all men, in all lands, everywhere . . . Remember, put chains of bondage on others and you prepare your own limbs to wear them.

There is no middle ground between right and wrong. It is like being neither a living man nor a dead man.

My dear Little Grace Bidell -

In your hands, my dissatisfied fellow countrymen, and not in mine, is the momentous issue of civil war.

We are not enemies, but friends. We must not be enemies. Though passion may have strained, it must not break the bonds of our affection. The mystic cords of memory, stretching from every battle - field, and patriot grave, to every living heart and hearthstone, all over this broad land, will yet swell the chorus of the Union, when again touched, as surely they will be, by the better angels of our nature.

The assault and the reduction of Fort Sumter was, in no sense, a matter of defense-

Four score and seven years ago, our fathers brought forth on this continent, a new nation, conceived in Liberty, and dedicated to the proposition that all men are created equal. Now we are engaged in a great civil war, testing whether that nation, or any nation, so conceived and so dedicated, can long endure -

I have been shown in the files of the War Department a statement of the Adjutant General of Massachusetts, that you are the mother of five sons who have died gloriously on the field of battle. I feel how weak and fruitless must be any words of mine which should -

With malice toward none; with charity for all; with firmness in the right, as God gives us to see the right, let us strive on to finish the work we are in; to bind up the nation's wounds; to care for him who shall have born the battle, and for his widow, and his orphan –

And I said, my heaven is where you are.

I began to walk toward light, beautiful, beautiful light- and I heard my favorite waltz and I was walking into Lizzie's ballroom! The elegant *coterie* was all there, and I was young and dressed in soft lilac. *I did not hurt!* Oh, I was *alive* again! What did I want to do with it - this *long* beautiful life? I knew, and I must have known from its beginning, and Lizzie's ballroom grew even more luminous - and I was centered in the beautiful music- and I knew that every *beautiful* thing man creates *to share* is the sound of those angels his mother heard singing so close to the earth.

I looked for him; with all of my soul I looked for him, and there he was – so tall, so dearly beloved. His eyes, his beautiful eyes, bore the lights of love for me that always made my heart sing. "Miss Todd," he said. "I would like to dance with you the worst way."

We were back at the beginning.

He took my hand in his; we did *not* stay for the funeral.

My name was Mary, but my family and my husband called me Molly. I have told you of my life because I just wanted you to know that I *was* worthy of being Mrs. Abraham Lincoln.

THE END

Epilogue

I am going to let Billy speak for Billy, on November 1, 1888, by quoting from his book, his *so-called* life of my husband. In the *Author's Preface* he says the whole truth concerning my husband should be known – he is going to tell about him "truthfully and courageously- nothing colored or suppressed – nothing false either written or suggested, so you can feel the presence of then living man." But - he is going to tell some facts for the first time that some persons will doubtless object to." (the objections of all who knew my husband and me were vitriolic to say the least.) And he is going to be "avoiding as much as possible any expression of opinion and leaving the reader to his own conclusions," but mind you, it is Billy and Billy alone who has "become the personal depository of the larger part of the most valuable *Lincolniana* in existence." But he quotes an *un-named* friend of my husband who declares, "there is a skeleton in every house," and "Don't let anything deter you from digging to the bottom; yet don't forget if Lincoln had some faults Washington had more…" And so Billy is going to dig for *all* the facts, and he tells us "-we must to take him as he was." Billy is going to tell all the facts by "which posterity is to learn what manner of man he was." He brings in the posterity thing again – "This preliminary statement is made so that posterity, in so far as posterity may be interested in the subject, may know that the vital matter of this narrative has been deduced directly from the consciousness, reminiscences and collected data of WILLIAM H. HERNDON." Abraham Lincoln, says Billy, rose "from a stagnant putrid pool," and Billy is out to make it more so. He goes into the fact that Nancy Hanks was illegitimate. He said in his lectures that my husband was also, also an infidel, an atheist who did not accept the Bible as the word of God or Jesus his son. To prove this garbage he quoted me! In Chapter 6, on page 105, Billy steams ahead into his Ann Rutledge story, and I am going to let him speak for himself - "Now we approach in timely order the grand passion of his life – a romance of much reality, the memory of which threw a melancholy shade over the remainder of his days. For the first time our hero falls in love. The courtship with Ann Rutledge and her untimely death form the saddest page in Mr. Lincoln's history. I am aware that most of his biographers have taken issue with me on this phase of Mr. Lincoln's life." (With good cause!) Then he goes on to say he knew Ann and her family well. "The score or more witnesses whom I one time or another interviewed on this delicate subject, and from my own knowledge and the information thus obtained, I therefore repeat, that the memory of Ann Rutledge was the saddest, saddest chapter of Mr. Lincoln's life." He describes Ann as an angel "worthy of Lincoln's love," and a beauty – she had a fine complexion, violet long lashed eyes, auburn hair, was five foot two inches and weighed one hundred and twenty pounds. By some chance he described me- for her fiancé said Ann was blonde. Now here Billy has an already-engaged Ann- and to Mr. Lincoln's best friend, John McNamar. What to do? John has to go back to New York to help his family. John does not write as he should to Ann, so "Ann begins to lose faith – her heart sick with love deferred." Lincoln fills in for friend John as he has, at last, found another melancholy soul to equal his own, Ann grieving for no letters and all, so he follows Ann into quilting bees where in a crowd of women he whispers love sweets into her ear. But let Billy tell it –"He whispered in her ear the old, old story. Her heart throbbed and her soul was thrilled with joy as old as the world itself. Her fingers momentarily lost their skills. In her ecstasy she made such irregular and uneven stitches that the older and more sedate women noted it and the owner of the quilt, until a few years ago still retaining it as a precious souvenir, pointed out her memorable stitches to such persons who visited her." This attachment that ruined quilt stitches grew and grew - by page 111, into an "intense and mutual passion." It lit up the whole town of New Salem and so the whole town "encouraged his suit." And Mr. Lincoln swore "nothing in God's footstool would keep them apart." (*God's footstool?*) But on August 25, 1835, Ann tragically died. She had been allowed no visitors at the end but Mr. Lincoln. When she left him he went crazy, wandering around in the local forests and had to be put under a suicide watch for weeks. Tears endless were shed on "his yellow and shriveled cheeks." When he recovered, he began to court Mary Owens, and you read his own account of that courtship. Billy has it come after Ann's death, but it had started in 1833. In Chapter Nine *I arrive* to make Mr. Lincoln's life hell. Why did he court and marry me, anyway? Let Billy tell you on page 163. "Conscious, therefore, of his humble rank in the social scale, how natural that he should seek by marriage into an influential family to establish strong connections and at the same time foster his political fortunes. This might seem an audacious thing to insinuate, but on no other basis can we reconcile the strange course of his courtship and the tempestuous chapters of his married life." Facts "long chained down" are rising in Billy's story now. "When all is at least known, the world will divide its censure (not to me) but between Lincoln and his wife." He tells about a dance with me. He told me, he says, I danced so gracefully, like a serpent, and that I did not like being compared to a snake. He calls me proud, handsome and vivacious, having a strong passionate nature and a quick temper. I had a quick intellect, was a good conversationalist in English and French, ordinarily affable and charming but when offended - all the good things "disappeared beneath a wave of stinging satire or sarcastic bitterness and her entire better nature was submerged." I was the belle of the ball because I - *she* - "kept back all the unattractive elements of her unfortunate organization." I had to hide that, you see, because I was telling around that I was going to marry a president. Alas! Mr. Lincoln had again fallen in love - Billy owns up to it, and we get engaged. But I fall for Mr. Douglas and he courts me while I am engaged to Mr. Lincoln. (!!!!) Well, a lady, named Harriet Chapman told Billy – on November 8, _1887_, that I loved Douglas and "but for her promise to Lincoln she would have accepted him." (p.167) This whole problem made me ill and Dr. Wallace told Douglas to stop his pursuit. Mr. Lincoln hears of my betrayal and wants to break the engagement and writes me a letter doing it. But Joshua Speed tells him to break it off in person, and I cry when he does and so he doesn't, and drawls to Billy, "Well, if I'm in it again, so be it. It's done and I shall abide by it." (p.169) So we are to have a big lavish wedding at the Edwards' mansion on January 1, 1841, and I am in white gown and veil, flowers in my hair and one hour passes, and then two hours AND THERE IS NO GROOM. (No marriage license taken out by Mr. Lincoln either) Well - I am REALLY angry and so plot my revenge. Mr. Lincoln is so shattered by his narrow escape he has to be under suicide watch again – no razors around etc. and then time passes and "he permitted the memory of his engagement to Miss Todd to trouble him no longer. Their paths had diverged, the pain of separation was over, and the whole thing was a history of the past." (p. 178) Now - why *did* we marry? *Billy has a web woven around us* - by page 179, "much to the surprise of both." And he asks - WAS IT LOVE? No. Here is what caused us to marry: "The tact of a woman and the diplomacy of society had accomplished what love had long since despaired of ever doing or seeing done." And so on November 4, 1842, "as pale and trembling as if being driven to slaughter Abraham Lincoln was at last married to Miss Todd. ...One great trial of his life was now over, and another still greater one was yet to come. To me it has always seemed plain that Mr. Lincoln married Mary Todd to save his honor, and in doing that he sacrificed his domestic peace. ...He knew he did not love her but he had promised to marry her...the hideous thought came conflict between honor and domestic peace. He chose the former, and with it years of self torture, sacrificial pangs and the loss forever of a happy home." (p. 181-182) Now - why did I marry *him?* Billy knows! On page 182 he tells you: "With Miss Todd a different motive, but one equally as unfortunate, prompted her adherence to the union. ... in him she saw a position in society, prominence in the world, and the grandest social distinction. By that means her ambition would be satisfied. Until that fatal New Year's Day in1841 she may have loved him, but his action on that occasion forfeited her affection. He had crushed her proud, womanly spirit. She felt degraded in the eyes of the world. Love fled at the approach of revenge. ... She led her husband a wild and merry dance." Billy just <u>had</u> to let the world know the truth about us –"The world will have the truth as long as the name –of Lincoln is remembered by mankind." In 1840, when my husband and I had our treasured year of courtship, Billy has my husband proposing marriage to Mrs. William Butler's sister – when she was sixteen and he thirty-one! Billy loves to denigrate my husband – his *yellow* and *withered* cheeks for the Ann Rutledge tears, for instance, his *ungainly* form, his *hollow* chest, his stoop shoulders his high *squeaky* voice, the fact that he did not love nature or appreciate it like Billy – his mind - *heedless of beauty*, his laughing so hard at his own jokes, *a lazy man with no knowledge of literature,* (p.258) who never read a book through - just scanned them – "I never knew him to read a law book of any kind." "I doubt if he ever read a single elementary law book through in his life." (p. 271) He did not care about dress, kept important records in his hat, including his bank- book and letters. And he had on his desk a bundle of papers tied up with a string and under it a note, which read, "When you can't find it anywhere else, look in this." And the lazy dig again –"He was naturally indisposed to undertake anything that savored of exertion." (p.257) "Lincoln was not a good conversationalist nor a good listener." (p.269) When Judge David Davis gave such a fine eulogy for my husband, as it *was* a eulogy, "he could not admit of as many limitations and modification as if spoken under other circumstances." Billy says the judge told him that my husband had "no managing faculty nor organizing power, hence a child could conform to the simple and technical rules, the means and the modes of getting to justice better than he. ... "I," says Billy, "easily realized that Lincoln was strikingly deficient in the technical rules of the law."(p. 271) In spite of his *stoop* shoulders, *hollow* chest, *high piping* voice, *yellow withered* cheeks and being so *lazy* and so *incompetent,* my husband had a little engine of ambition that knew no rest. (p.304) And it got us a home - and Billy takes you right into it! In Chapter Fourteen we go "through the doorway into his home." (Which he never once entered) "Lincoln," he says, "had none of the tender ways that please a woman." He had "no positive act of his own to make her happy." (p. 342) In this home I repent my marriage, done anyway for revenge, as my husband really dislikes fashionable society and I want to exercise my rights of *supremacy* over it. "Both she and the man whose hand she had accepted acted along the lines of human conduct and both reaped the bitter harvest of conjugal infelicity." Now as my husband and I are both dead, Billy says he can tell it as it *was* and the world seems ready to hear his *facts*. This miserable marriage is *important* to know - important in *history* -why? Because I made his home life so hellish he had to go outside and get into it! My temper fits caused him to be President! He could not bear to be with me so he went out and mingled, became well-known and popular, and an *unnamed* close friend is quoted, "If, on the other hand, he had married some less ambitious but more domestic woman, some honest farmer's quiet daughter (Ann Rutledge?) – one who would have looked up and worshipped him because he uplifted her, -the result might have been different. Yet I fear he would have been buried in the pleasures of a loving home, and the country would never have had Abraham Lincoln for its President." (p. 350) On page 343 he declares *me* to be decidedly *pro-slavery!* So, as I scurry around our home foaming revenge for that January 1,1841 dumping, abusing my servants and declaring l won't be where slavery isn't, does Billy hear this from my husband? No, he never heard my husband say anything negative about me, nor did *any* of my husband's friends either. "BUT," says Billy, "*I could always realize when he was in distress <u>without being told</u>.*" (Emphasis mine) How? "If, on arriving at the office I found him in, I knew instantly that a breeze had sprung up over the domestic sea, and that the waters were troubled." (p.348) This seems to be especially true to Billy if he says good morning to my husband and he replies with a grunt. Well, while the *entire world* knew my bad temper and disposition, Billy is sure that it was really (just) a *cerebral disease*. And Billy never gives Ann a rest. My husband tells Billy his heart is buried in Ann's grave. And as he leaves Springfield for Washington D.C., he tells an old pioneer of New Salem, who tells Billy, of his love still for Ann Rutledge! And all of this from a man Billy even says "was the most secretive-reticent-shut-mouthed man who ever existed." Here is what the *Chicago Journal* said of Billy's book: "It is one of the most infamous books ever written and printed in the garb of a historical work of a great and illustrious man. ...It reproduces shameless gossip and hearsay not authenticated by proof...the obscenity of the work is surprising and shocking... Its salacious narrative and implications, and its elaborate calumnies not only of Lincoln himself but of his mother, and in regard to morals generally of his mother's side of the family, are simply outrageous." Regarding Ann Rutledge and Mary Owens, it "with his final marriage to Mary Todd, is indelicate, in every way bad taste, is insulting to the memory of the dead and calculated to mortify and lacerate the hearts of the living...We declare that this book is so bad it could hardly have been worse."

There you have it. Billy says in his book that my husband never "poured out his soul to any mortal creature at any time and on no subject." Again -"He was the most secretive – reticent-shut mouthed man that ever existed." So, says Billy, he had to fill in –"you had to <u>guess</u> at the man" and "this process would lead you correctly *if you knew human nature and its laws.*"

I say again that Billy was a liar. His lying book is labeled history and my book fiction. I can document all of mine except how my husband and I first met - go figure.

Bibliography

Angle, Paul. The Lincoln Reader. New Brunswick, New Jersey: Rutgers University Press, 1947.

Basler, Roy, and The Abraham Lincoln Association. The Collected Works of Abraham Lincoln, Volumes 1 - 8. New Brunswick, New Jersey: Rutgers University Press, 1953.

Bishop, Jim. The Day Lincoln Was Shot. New York: Harper and Brothers, 1955.

Davis, William C. Lincoln's Men. New York: Simon and Schuster, 2000.

Donald, David Herbert. Lincoln. New York: Simon and Schuster, 1995.

Eisenschimil, Otto. New York: Why was Lincoln Murdered? Grosset & Dunlap, 1937.

Hawley, J.R. & Co. The Assassination and History of the Conspiracy. New York and Cincinnati, 1865. Republished by Hobbs, Dorman & Company Inc., New York, 1965.

Helm, Katherine The True Story of Mary Lincoln by her Niece. New York and London: Harper and Brothers, 1928.

Herndon, William. The Life of Lincoln. New York and Cleveland: World Publishing Company, 1930.

Mellon, James. The Face of Lincoln. New York: Viking Press, 1979.

Oates, Stephen B. Abraham Lincoln, the Man Behind the Myths. New York: Harper and Rowe, 1984.

Randall, James. The Civil War and Reconstruction. New York: D.C. Heath & Co., 1937.

Randall, Ruth Painter. Mary Lincoln, Biography of a   Marriage. Boston: Little Brown & Co., 1953.

------------------------. Lincoln's Sons. Boston: Little Brown & Co., 1955.

------------------------. The Courtship of Mr. Lincoln. Boston: Little Brown & Co., 1957.

Sandburg, Carl. Abraham Lincoln, the Prairie Years, Volumes 1 &11. New York: Harcourt Brace & Co., 1939.

------------------------. Abraham Lincoln, the War Years, Volumes 1-4. New York: Harcourt Brace & Co., 1939.

Stern, Van Doren. Life and Writings of Abraham Lincoln. New York: Random House, 1940.

Stoddard, William 0. Abraham Lincoln, The True Story of a Great Life. New York: Fords, Howard, & Hulbert, 1884.

Turner, Justin G. & Linda Levitt. Mary Todd Lincoln, Her Life and Letters. New York: Alfred Knopf, 1972.

Windham, Thelma, Joseph Hanks/Nancy Hanks Genealogy. http: flusers. erols. Com/Condrada.